FAIRYTALE OF NEW YORK

Miranda Dickinson has always had a head full of stories.
From an early age she dreamed of writing a book that
would make the heady heights of Kingswinford Library.
Following a Performance Art degree, she began to write
in earnest when a friend gave her The World's Slowest
PC. She is also a singer-songwriter. *Fairytale of New York*
is her first novel. To find out more about Miranda visit
www.miranda-dickinson.com

MIRANDA DICKINSON

Fairytale Of New York

AVON

AVON

A division of HarperCollins*Publishers*
77–85 Fulham Palace Road,
London W6 8JB

www.harpercollins.co.uk

A Paperback Original 2009

11

ISBN-13: 978-1-84756-165-7

Typeset in Minion by Palimpsest Book Production Limited,
Grangemouth, Stirlingshire

Printed and bound in Great Britain by
Clays Ltd, St Ives plc

Mixed Sources

Product group from well-managed
forests and other controlled sources
www.fsc.org   Cert no. SW-COC-1806
© 1996 Forest Stewardship Council

FSC

FSC is a non-profit international organisation established
to promote the responsible management of the world's forests.
Products carrying the FSC label are independently certified
to assure consumers that they come from forests that are managed
to meet the social, economic and ecological needs
of present and future generations.

Find out more about HarperCollins and the environment at
www.harpercollins.co.uk/green

I've read so many authors' thank-you's and they always seem to miss the most important people – the ones that pick up their book from the shelves. So I'd like to thank *you* first. And let you know that, when you chose my book, you officially made my day. I hope my book officially makes yours in return!

Thanks to the wonderful, über-talented community on Authonomy.com, who supported my book when it was *Coffee at Kowalski's*. I have made so many firm friends on the site and love being part of such an awesome bunch of people. Thanks especially to Simon Forward and Philip Gilliver, who championed my book in the Forums, Matt 'Sesty' Dick and Kim 'Inky' Curran – all incredible authors in their own right and great friends to boot. Thanks also to the lovely Laura, Clive and the Authonomy team.

Huge thanks to the amazing team at Avon, who have not only helped this complete newbie to understand the scary world of publishing but who have also given me the encouragement and space to create something I hope everyone will be proud of: Maxine Hitchcock, for her faith in me and excellent advice; the truly gorgeous Sammia Rafique, my editor, for going above and beyond in everything from editorial advice to sharing a love of chick-flicks (I *told* you you'd love *While*

You Were Sleeping); also thanks to Keshini Naidoo and Yvonne Holland.

Finally, thanks to my fantastic family and friends, who have encouraged and inspired me more than any of them realise; Mum, Dad, Bev, Ro, Freya and Gran; the wonderful Whites and Davies'; the truly awesome former Edenhurst/Peppermints massive; my brilliant family at Calvary Church, Kingswinford; Helen (best mate extraordinaire); Linsey, for bugging me till she got the next chapter; Danielle for proof-reading and being a great chum; and my lovely Bob, who is my best friend and Prince Charming rolled into one. For everything, all honour to the Master Storyteller, who knows me better than anyone else.

Dreams *can* come true – you're holding one in your hands right now.

For Linsey –
because she wanted to know what happened next.

Chapter One

This city is not mine by birthright: I was born over three thousand miles away in a sleepy town in the heart of England. But ever since the day I set foot on its sidewalks, I have felt caught up in the biggest, most welcoming embrace by every street, store and tree-lined avenue. I don't know if a city can make a heart decision, but if it's possible then New York *chose* to make me belong. And even though some of my most difficult and painful days have taken place here, somehow this city has always softened the blows – just like a good friend who sits you down with a cup of tea and tells you to be patient because things will turn out OK in the end. And you know they will. Eventually.

My friend Celia tells me that I'm a 'Frustrating but Adorable Optimist in the Face of Overwhelming Evidence to the Contrary'. If you think this looks like a dramatic newspaper headline then you'd be on the right track: Celia writes a column for the *New York Times* and she's lived here all her life. She was one of the first true friends I made in the city and she watches out for me like a slightly neurotic older sister. She won't mind that description of her – come to think of it, that's probably one of hers anyway.

Celia's apartment is on the second floor in an elegant

Upper West Side brownstone residence just off Riverside Drive on West 91st Street, and every Saturday morning we meet there to put the world to rights over coffee. Sitting at her maple table by the large picture window, I can see out to the street below. 'Sit for long enough in New York and you'll see everyone in the city walk by,' Mr Kowalski always used to say. He was the original owner of my florist's shop, before he retired to his beloved Warsaw with his daughter Lenka, where he lived until his death, just over five years ago. Mr Kowalski was another of the first true friends I made in my adopted country.

'Rosie, you have *no* idea how blessed you are to have History in England,' Celia declared one Saturday morning as she appeared from the kitchen with the coffee and a basket of warm muffins. As usual, we had entered a conversation a little way in from the start and continued as though we'd been there from the beginning. I couldn't help but grin at her as she flopped down into the chair beside me.

'Ah, *history* . . .' I replied in a learned tone.

'I mean, you Brits just don't appreciate the *awesome privilege* of having kings and queens going back *centuries*. I can't say that my ancestors were walking in New York in the tenth century. I can't say that my family is born-and-bred American. I mean, heaven only knows where my family came from. I'm probably four-sixteenths Ukrainian with a touch of Outer Mongolian thrown in somewhere along the line.'

I was about to say that there is actually no such thing as a true English person either, and remark that my family probably came from Moravia or somewhere originally, but I could see this was a serious topic of concern for Celia. So I stayed quiet and poured the coffee instead.

'Why are you so hung up about it, mate?' I asked.

Celia's troubled countenance softened and she reached for a muffin.

'It's my column for the *Times* next week. I'm thinking about the importance of history for humans to find their place in the world. The more I consider it, the more I realise it's a non-starter. Most of us don't know our own history here – save for what we learn at school. We're a hotchpotch of immigrants, convicts and dreamers, all clamouring for some damn utopia that doesn't exist. We want to belong, yet we don't know *what* we want to belong *to.*'

Somehow, I suspected those sentences would appear in her column soon. This is a regular phenomenon; in fact, I think our Saturday morning chats must be the best documented in history. If, in a thousand years' time, historians want to know what things twenty-first-century friends were discussing, all they will have to do is to examine the archives of Celia's column at the *New York Times* (which will, by then, be thought-transmitting to its readership, I suppose).

'You are such a *writer,*' I smiled. 'Every word beautifully crafted . . .'

'Honey, *everything* is copy. My father always said that.' She picked up a teaspoon and frowned at her reflection. 'And *I* am starting to look like my *mother.*'

I couldn't help but smile at her. 'You are *not.*'

It has to be said, Celia is a good-looking lady, immaculately turned out at all times and with one of those complexions that most women would walk over burning coals (or inject odd bits of animal into their skin) to achieve. To look at her, you could never guess her age; despite her strenuous denials of the fact, she can easily pass for an early thirtysomething, when in reality she's nearer the middle of her forties than she would ever admit. She has a style that seems to exude from deep within her – a quality my mum would call 'effortless'. Even that morning, when her only appointment was in her own apartment for coffee with me, her jeans and blue linen shirt looked a million times more elegant than they would have done on anyone else.

'*So*, my Authors' Meet next Tuesday night . . .' she said, discarding the subject and brandishing the next with a warp-speed that would impress even Captain Jean-Luc Picard of the Starship *Enterprise*, 'I thought Café Bijou in TriBeCa would be ideal. It's new but worth a risk, so I'm told.'

'Sounds promising,' I said, watching sunlit steam rise as I broke open a warm muffin, letting the pieces fall onto my plate. 'Who's coming?'

'Henrik Gund is a definite, and I'm awaiting replies from Mimi Sutton and Angelika Marshall, though of course I'm kinda confident they'll find it hard to resist. In fact, most of New York's finest will be there. It has the potential to be amazing . . . of course there are still a few worries to iron out . . .' Celia paused, turned squarely to face me and smiled one of those immaculately painted, high-maintenance Jewish smiles of hers that, I have learned, always precede a Celia Reighton Big Favour.

Somewhere, way in the back of my brain, a familiar little voice began screaming, *Don't do it! Don't do it . . . !*

But it was too late. I had already conceded to the inevitability of surrender. With acting that would have had Spielberg arm-wrestling Scorsese for my services, I replied as if I hadn't a notion of what was coming, 'That's wonderful, Celia. It sounds like everything is going to plan, then.'

'Well . . . *almost* everything, Rosie,' Celia replied slowly.

So, it starts, announced the irritated voice in my head. The smile was widening with every grovelling word Celia spoke.

'It's a little delicate, but I have to tell you ... seeing as we're such good friends ... it's just that I've been let down by Philippe –' (for your information: incredibly pretentious and over-priced 'Floral Artiste') – 'you know how whim-driven these people can be – And I really need some stylish table pieces.'

'Oh, that's dreadful, mate,' I sympathised, mirroring her agonised tone.

You are SO *on your own* ... The little voice in my head let out an exasperated sigh, packed its suitcase and caught the first Greyhound for Vegas.

'It is *so* dreadful you wouldn't *believe*.' Desperation was setting in. 'Honey, you *know* I only use Philippe because my agent is seeing his brother. His creations often verge on the vulgar, in my opinion. Did I mention how I just adored what you did for Jessica Robards' wedding last fall?' Celia's increasing grip on her coffee mug was threatening to crush it completely and her smile was fast becoming a cheery grimace.

It was time to put my friend out of her agony.

'How many pieces do you need and what flowers did you have in mind?'

'Oh, *darling*, would you?' Celia flung her arms around me, lifting me several inches from my chair and letting out a squeal of delight.

'Yes, OK, I give in! You can have my great expertise at extremely short notice and, no doubt, at a sizeable discount. Now, let me go before you kill me!'

I was duly released and she fell back into her chair, giggling like a delighted schoolgirl.

'Ooh, you're so wonderful, Rosie! I knew you wouldn't let me down! Well, let's see ... I need ten – no, make it twelve – with gardenias – no, roses ... Or maybe both? I'll leave it to you to decide – after all, *you're* the designer. But I'm picturing them hand-tied, of course, with plenty of that straw stuff.'

'Raffia?' I offered.

Celia didn't hear. She was already in full artistic flow, gesturing flamboyantly with each new idea that she stumbled across. 'Well, *absolutely*, honey, that too! And baskets – ooh, yes . . . little woven rustic ones like they have in England.'

'Ah, you mean *historical* ones . . .'

Celia stopped abruptly and chastised me with a mock frown. 'You see, that's what I was saying, sweetie. You British have *so* much history that you can afford to throw it away in jest. Pity the poor American here . . .'

Once again, the conversation shifted, as New York hurried by on the street below.

Work began on Celia's displays the following Monday. The order from Patrick's Flower Warehouse was due at 7 a.m. so Marnie, my assistant and Ed, my co-designer, agreed to meet me at the store at 6.45 a.m., on the strict understanding that I would shout them breakfast in return for their loyal service. Once all the boxes were safely inside we locked the store, pulled down the shutters and walked across the street to claim our reward.

There is something ultimately satisifying about walking into a coffee house first thing in the morning. You are invited in by the cosy sofas; then, once over the threshold, wonderfully evocative scents of fresh coffee and warm pastries surround you and draw you in further. Even though the world outside scurries past, inside there is a feeling of unhurried indulgence – a chance to sit a while and enjoy the moment.

Or, in our case this morning, wake up and smell the coffee.

'So, remind us again why we're selflessly crucifying ourselves today?' Ed yawned, his humour much sharper than the rest of his body at this hour.

'It's a favour. For Celia,' I said.

Marnie groaned into her cappuccino.

'Ah, *Celia*,' said Ed, raising an eyebrow. 'Now tell me, would this be the same Celia who got us making forty Christmas garlands for the *Times* party with only one week's notice? Or the Celia who "simply had to have daffodils" in November?'

I pretended to hide behind my mug.

'Or the Celia who booked our biggest rival for her Valentine Ball but "let us" provide all the gift roses because we were cheaper?' Marnie added.

'OK, OK, guilty as charged!' I protested.

Ed and Marnie exchanged knowing glances, and then faced me with uniform seriousness

'See, I have this theory about the cause of the worrying symptoms our patient here is displaying,' Ed began.

'Why, Dr Steinmann, what could it be?' asked Marnie with a squeaky Southern-belle accent she could only have picked up from watching too many episodes of *Days of Our Lives*.

Ed consulted his paper napkin with practised flair and turned to face her. 'The problem here is very simple, Nurse Andersson. Our patient is a classic sufferer of *Malaise Anglais*.'

Marnie placed a hand to her heart. 'Oh, Doctor, are you *sure*?'

'What exactly are you trying to say?' I giggled.

'You're way too *British*, Rosie,' Ed declared with a smile. 'You're missing the gene that enables you to say No . . .'

'. . . It won't allow you to learn from each and every mistake,' said Marnie, clearly enjoying this assault on my character, 'and it unfortunately manifests itself in repeated attacks.'

'Of course, it's the friends of the sufferer that I feel sorry for,' continued Ed, with merciless vigour. 'Because, you see, *they* are the ones who ultimately face the hard work of providing support to the patient.'

'But, it needs to be said, there can be benefits for them too,' I said.

'Such as?' asked Ed, his blue eyes sparkling.

'Such as, the privilege of enjoying breakfasts at the patient's expense.'

Marnie smiled and Ed reached across to squeeze my hand.

'Absolutely. And it *is* a privilege. We simply mock because we care, Rosie. When are you going to understand that some people are always out for themselves?'

I let out a sigh. We must have had this conversation a thousand times, but I'm never successful in getting Marnie and Ed to see the situation from my point of view. Undaunted, I began Attempt Number 1001.

'I know it seems like Celia's always taking advantage, but she really *is* a good friend. She's been there for me every time I've needed her. I just want to repay her kindness, that's all.'

Ed's expression softened a little and he shook his head. 'Rosie Duncan, we love you dearly. And if it makes you happy, we'll gladly spend the many, *many* hours required in order for you to repay your friend.'

'Well, thank you,' I said, draining the last of my latte.

'Seriously, though, you work too much, Rosie. You need to live a little too.' Marnie's voice was full of concern. An alarm bell began to jangle in the back of my mind: I knew where this was going. We were approaching forbidden territory. I braced myself and, sure enough: 'You *so* need a man—' she breathed. My heart sank and I immediately cut her off.

'I don't, thank you. So, the schedule for today—'

Marnie wasn't about to be put off so easily. 'No, I mean it, Rosie! You're such a lovely person – if you'd just let a guy get close enough to you, I'm sure you'd be happy . . .'

Feeling cornered, I gave a too-forced laugh and attempted to lighten the atmosphere. 'Ah-ah, no – that is a non-negotiable subject and, I need to warn you, will result in a breach of the conditions of your contract if you choose to discuss it further.'

Ed threw his hands up in surrender. 'OK, OK, boss, we get it. We hereby pledge to pursue it no longer.'

'Finally, they understand!' I looked heavenwards, hands outstretched in gratitude. I could hardly believe it – had I really averted the inevitable lecture?

Nope.

'. . . Suffice to say, that Marnie and I are committed to bugging you on a regular basis about this—' Ed was stopped mid-sentence, by Marnie, or rather by Marnie's hand as it clamped firmly across his mouth.

'Quiet, Steinmann, I need this job!' she laughed.

After a brief struggle, she let him go and they both collapsed back, smirking like a pair of naughty schoolkids. Despite my recent discomfort, I had to smile at the pair of them. Ed likes to pretend he's the serious, surrogate older brother in this terrible twosome, yet often he's the worse culprit. They are forever swapping jokes, winding each other up or just acting like a couple of big kids – and I love them for it. It makes me feel I'm part of something positive and gives a real, beating heart to Kowalski's. Most importantly, I know that, behind the humour, they are fiercely protective of each other – and of me.

Ed's eyes twinkled and he flashed a wide grin at me.

'Suitably chastened, m'lady,' he said, giving a little bow as we got up to return to the store. But in the doorway he grabbed my sleeve and pulled me to him. 'However, this topic won't go away, Rosie Duncan. It's definitely one To Be Continued.'

Chapter Two

At the age of twelve and a half I decided I wasn't going to be a florist.

I made this Important Life Decision whilst helping my mum to create buttonholes for a wedding at five o'clock one Saturday morning. The bride's mother had called our home an hour before in a blind panic, after realising she hadn't ordered enough for the groom's family. I think this was the same day that I made my next Important Life Decision – I was never, ever, *ever* going to get married. Never. People just seemed to lose all common sense when they were tying the knot.

Mum said that she could separate the soon-to-be-married ladies who visited her shop into four categories: Neurotic, Laid-Back (but usually accompanied by neurotic mothers), Bossy ('I-know-exactly-what-I-want so you'd-better-do-what-I-say-or- else'), and Nice and Uncomplicated. It seemed to me that the last category was sadly lacking in members. As I grew older and was given a Saturday job in Mum's shop, I saw three fist-fights, countless heated arguments and one engagement broken, all over the matter of flowers. Totally crazy. What never ceased to amaze me, however, was the way Mum calmly and gently responded to each rude, obnoxious, or just plain psychotic customer, managing to bring them to a satisfactory decision every time.

With a name like mine, the floristry connection was almost impossible to get away from. Mum called me Rose after my grandmother, but it's also part of her name – Rosemary. My brother, James, often jokes that he should have been called Daisy to make the floristry theme complete. Nevertheless, as soon as I could, I got as far away from floristry as possible. I studied media and communications at university, got a good degree and moved south to work for a London advertising agency. It was a great job and I loved it. I loved the excitement. I revelled in the deadlines, the intense periods of high creativity and the fulfilment of seeing my finished campaigns on giant billboards across the city. Mum was incredibly proud of me and put a display of my adverts in one corner of her shop, just behind the stargazer lilies. 'The stars are the limit for my little dreamer,' she used to tell her customers. But every now and then she would remind me that, in her opinion, my design ability came from my gift for floristry. 'You're a natural designer,' she would say, 'and nothing will ever give you a thrill like creating something with living things.' I would laugh at this, but Mum's calm and knowing smile always left a little discomforting question mark at the back of my mind.

Then, just when I thought my life was complete, I found there was something missing. And one of my Important Life Decisions was put to the ultimate test. I fell in love.

That one, singular happening in my life changed everything. It led me to leave England and a family and career I loved, to move to America and chase my dream.

When my dream died, my other Important Life Decision was reversed and floristry became my saving grace. I rediscovered the joy of creating something with living things; twisting, moulding and combining scents and colours, forms and foliage into something new, something worthwhile. I found that catching the fleeting beauty of flowers seemed to awaken something hidden deep within me: a need to celebrate *life* – however brief – after my own life had been exposed to so much death. As I placed my creations in the hands of my customers, I found my work marking their lives too – celebrations, commemorations, condolences – and the thrill it gave me to be part of their stories far surpassed anything I'd felt during my previous job. Just like Mum had told me. And now I can't imagine ever doing anything else.

Celia arrived at noon on the day of her big event to inspect the progress of her order. I was proud to report that we were almost done – only two more arrangements to complete. She skipped around the workroom like a delirious three-year-old, squealing with delight at the 'quaintness' of the baskets, the 'gorgeous English scent' of the roses and the quality of craftsmanship 'that Philippe himself could never equal'. After several minutes of gushing and promises of many future orders to come, she was gone again, racing off to her next interview.

Ed wiped his brow and flopped down onto a chair.

'Rosie, that woman is a human whirlwind. How on earth do you keep up with her?'

I giggled. 'Sometimes, I ask myself the same question. But her heart's in the right place, you know.'

'Sure, but where's the rest of her?'

Marnie and I finished the final arrangements and stood back to view the wonderful spectacle that is a completed order. 'Perfect!' I said. 'We're done.'

Ed frowned. 'Wait – we've got to have the Kowalski Ceremony before you can say that.' He picked up an old, rusty pair of half-moon spectacles from a shelf, placed them on the end of his nose and adopted a slow, gentle Polish accent. 'So, I think maybe we are *done* now, everybody? Good! Let's clear up and *deliver!*'

I smiled at him. Some days I miss Mr Kowalski so much my heart aches.

'Can I go for my lunch break?' asked Marnie, hopefully.

'No problem,' I said, checking my watch. 'Take an hour, mate. You've worked so hard the last two days. Enjoy yourself.'

But before I'd finished speaking, Marnie had grabbed her bag and coat and was out of the door, shouting her thanks over her shoulder as she went.

Ed raised an amused eyebrow. 'Now there's another whirl-wind in training,' he said. 'Must be the guy she met last week in drama class.'

I smiled as I began to collect the scrap foliage and raffia from the worktables. 'Ah. Another chapter of Marnie's life begins.'

'Poor Marnie. Her love life reads like a plot of a daytime soap,' Ed agreed, and began to carry completed arrangements to the cold store. 'I was attempting to explain this to my mother the other day. Let me see if I remembered the highlights: there was the med student – he lasted four months, till he announced he wanted to become a gynaecologist . . .'

'Always a passion-killer, that one.'

'Then came the Italian stallion, who said he was on an exchange programme from romantic Sicily, when really he was from romantic Queens.'

'Hmm, and he only told her that small detail of his life *after* she'd spent most of her money showing him the sights of New York for three weeks.'

'And, of course, who could forget the guy she fell head over heels with, who turned out to be her long-lost half-brother?'

We both grimaced at that one. Ed shook his head and picked up the last two arrangements. 'Now, you make the coffee and I'll finish up here.'

My coffee machine is just about the best thing ever. It's one work requirement that I've retained from my old days at the advertising agency – I need my coffee in order to be creative. Customers have told me that the comforting scent of coffee mingling with the flowers makes them feel at home when they enter the shop. It seems to encourage them to spend time making their decisions. Nowadays, it's strictly decaf after 2 p.m. – not least because we all need our sleep at night, but also because Marnie under the influence of too much caffeine is downright *scary*, and I don't want to frighten the customers away. My coffee machine doesn't look or work like it used to, but its battered appearance and the strange noises it emits are all part of its endearing character. Marnie thinks it should be retired, but Ed agrees with me that it makes the best cup of coffee around, and that makes two votes to one. Motion carried. So Old Faithful (as he is affectionately known) remains an important member of my staff.

When the coffee was ready, after much huffing, puffing and weird clunking from Old F, Ed joined me behind the counter for lunch. Ed always eats the most enormous pastrami sandwiches at lunchtime. He buys them each morning from Schaeffer's Deli, a few blocks down from his apartment in the East Village, on his way to work. I asked him once how he manages to eat so much without becoming the size of a small planet, and he informed me that he has an 'excellent metabolism'. I reckon it's more to do with the fact that he runs five

15

miles every day, goes to the gym regularly and seems to spend most of his free time running after (or being chased by) the beautiful women of New York.

After several minutes of happy munching, Ed gave the meat monstrosity a time out and shot me one of his serious looks.

'So what about *your* dating history, Rosie?'

Uh-oh. This was one road trip I knew all too well:

YOU ARE NOW ENTERING UNCOMFORTABLE
Population: Just Me

I tried a detour. 'Not much to tell, really.'

Of course, this wasn't likely to put him off. In hindsight, it was probably the worst thing I could have said: there is nothing Ed Steinmann likes more than a challenge. I might just as well have slapped him in the face with a gauntlet.

'Oh, come on, Rosie, there must have been guys you left back in old Blighty?'

'Umm . . .'

'Buzzzz! Hesitation!' Only Ed could turn an embarrassing conversation into a quiz show. 'Travelled across the Pond leaving a string of broken hearts behind you, eh?'

I swallowed hard. 'Something like that.'

'And then there was . . . where was it you came here from? DC? Chicago?'

'Boston.'

'Ah, Boston. So – any broken hearts there?'

'I – *no*, OK? Can we change the subject, please?'

Ed held up his half-eaten sandwich in surrender. 'Hey, I'm just making conversation. You've been here, what, six years and we've never seen you dating.'

I let out a long sigh. 'I don't have time to date.'

Ed took another bite and munched thoughtfully. 'That's because you spend half your life chasing the whims of that mad journalist friend of yours.'

'Ed, that's unfair. Celia's a good friend.'

'So how come she's never set you up on a date then?'

'*Ed!*'

'I'm just making an observation. I mean, there must be countless eligible hacks at the *Times*.'

I folded my arms in a vain attempt to feel less vulnerable. 'Since when was my love life such an area of fascination for you?'

'It's not just me, it's Marnie too. Actually, mainly Marnie, to be honest. She worries about you.'

Knowing that my staff were discussing my personal life was more than a little disconcerting. It wasn't that I minded them caring for me – that's something that I'd always found about my team and it was great to know we all looked out for one another. It was more that I didn't want to discuss my love life with *anyone*, especially not my past in London or Boston. Believe me, I had my reasons.

'Well, she shouldn't worry. I'm fine. Besides, between the two of you I think we have the eligible contingent of Manhattan pretty much covered, don't you?'

He nodded. 'Good point. So, ask me about *my* love life then, seeing as *you* don't have time for one.' Ed has this amazing capacity for making you smile when you really should be hitting him *hard*. It is completely disarming but devastatingly effective.

'Fine. Who's the lucky lady tonight, pray tell?'

Ed looked like the cat that got the cream, sapphire blue eyes twinkling. 'Lawyer.'

'Oh, nice.'

17

'Yep, she is.'

'Name?'

'Mona. I think she's Italian.'

'Let me guess: second name Lisa, can't really tell what she's thinking, bit of an oil painting?'

Ed was unmoved by my humour. 'Maybe you should call 911, Rosie. My sides are in the process of splitting. No, she's representing my cousin Klaus.'

'What's he up for?'

Ed rested his sandwich on the counter and wiped his hands with a paper napkin. 'How come you instantly assume my family are all crooks?'

I looked sheepish. 'Sorry.' It was nice to be in control of the conversation at last.

'Hmm. Well, don't do it again, Duncan. No, he's being sued by a former patient who claims Klaus hypnotised him during one session, causing him to make a series of disastrous business decisions, which led to the collapse of his company.'

'Is your cousin a hypnotherapist?'

'No – that's the crazy thing. He's a psychiatrist. *All* my family are psychiatrists, for pity's sake, apart from me.'

'Is this client likely to win?'

'No way. The guy's clearly a nut, but hey, this is New York: sneeze in the wrong place and someone's going to sue your ass from here to eternity. Mona reckons the judge will take one look at him and throw the case out. But, while we're waiting for that to happen, I owe it to my cousin to ensure that his lovely lawyer is as fully briefed as possible.'

'Knowing you, it's probably more a *lack* of briefs you're interested in?'

'Hey, so she just couldn't resist me. What can I tell ya?'

'Yeah, yeah, whatever,' I laughed, taking our mugs to Old F for a refill.

'See, Rosie? Look at all the fun you're missing out on.'

'Lawyers aren't my type and I don't know any psychiatrists.'

'Then try a policeman, or a photographer – or a taxi driver, even. Heck, *anyone* would be worth a shot, if only to get you "out there" again! How about we get Marnie to recommend one of her exes?'

Bringing the filled mugs back, I gave one to Ed and sat down. 'I don't think so, thank you very much. Somehow I don't think any of them will be my type. Now drop it and eat that cow in bread you've got there.'

'Don't try diversionary tactics. You know they won't work on me. Just be prepared for us to keep bugging you about it, OK?'

I ignored a sinking feeling and attempted a breezy smile. 'I wouldn't expect anything less.'

'Uh-huh,' Ed agreed, resuming his one-man onslaught on the mountain of meat.

I watched him for a while. Ed is one of those people you instantly like. I love his quick wit and cheekiness, despite being on the receiving end of it more often than I'd like. Ed can deliver a one-liner faster than a speeding bullet and that always makes me smile. Maybe it's this mischievous quality in him that the good ladies of Manhattan find so irresistible. I have to admit, when Steinmann puts his mind to something, it's difficult to say no to him. Mind you, if I believe Ed and Marnie's theory about me, I seem to have this problem with everybody on account of my *Malaise Anglais*, so perhaps that doesn't count. Even when he's tired or hungover, the charm is never far away; in fact, it is often particularly endearing when he's looking more dishevelled than usual.

19

Ed's style is what he calls 'relaxed', but what my mum would term 'scruffy'. His dark brown hair never really looks tamed no matter what he does with it, but this suits his style down to the ground. He does make an effort occasionally and never looks unprofessionally untidy, but most of the time he has the kind of appearance that makes guys want to hang out with him and women want to take care of him. Today he was wearing a slightly crumpled charcoal shirt over a white T-shirt with faded black jeans. When I asked him why he'd chosen this sombre colour scheme, he remarked that he thought it would be good for counteracting the Marnie Effect, a phenomenon unique to Kowalski's: my young assistant looks as if she has been bombarded by a spectrum of colours – from her hair (this week, vivid orange), to her clashing T-shirt, skirt, tights and bright yellow Doc Marten boots. As for me, I like to think I'm a foil to both of them. I like to look smart for work, although comfort is a major consideration. One thing Marnie and I have in common is our love of vintage clothes – and in New York we're blessed with countless boutiques selling retro clothing and one-off pieces. Living in New York I've noticed my style has become more relaxed – much like I have.

Since the day I first met Ed, we've been really close. And even though to the casual observer it can appear that we mock each other constantly, I do actually care what he thinks of me. While events in my life have made me much more wary of letting people close, having Ed and Marnie there to worry about me is strangely comforting. We're an odd concoction of personalities, backgrounds and dress styles, but it seems to work. Welcome to Kowalski's – where the staff are as varied as the flowers!

* * *

At four thirty, I packed Celia's arrangements into the delivery van and headed off to Café Bijou. Marnie and Ed had agreed to man the store for the rest of the day so that I could go, after it became clear that Celia was fast losing the plot. Her anxiety attacks had begun at two o'clock with a frantic phone call, and I found myself promising faithfully that I'd meet her at the venue at five fifteen. Marnie and Ed's expressions said it all and, once I got into my van, I noticed Ed had drawn up a doctor's prescription and stapled it to the order sheet.

PRESCRIPTION FOR MS ROSIE DUNCAN FOR THE TREATMENT
OF CONFIRMED CONDITION *MALAISE ANGLAIS*.
THE FOLLOWING SENTENCE TO BE ADMINISTERED LIBERALLY
AND ORALLY BY THE PATIENT, WHENEVER NECESSARY:
'NO, I COULDN'T POSSIBLY. SORRY.'

When I arrived at the restaurant, Celia was already there, clipboard in hand, nervous energy in full flow. I immediately felt sorry for the poor maître d', who was in danger of being totally overwhelmed by her tirade of questions. When he saw me, his face brightened and he rushed over, leaving a frustrated Celia standing mid-sentence, fuming gently.

'Oh, Madame, permit me to 'elp you wiz zese flowers. I will take zem to ze room *pour vous*,' he gushed.

'*Merci beaucoup, Monsieur.*'

I approached Celia as he fled.

'That man is so *exasperating*!' she exclaimed, tossing her clipboard onto the polished bar. 'I have so much to organise and it's five twenty already. Does Claude have *any idea* of just how much is left to do?'

I smiled and gave her a hug. 'Now sit down, Celia. Take a deep breath. Count to two thousand . . .'

Celia looked up at me like a chastened child. 'You sound like my mother,' she said miserably.

'Things are going to be just great,' I reassured her, sounding quite a lot like mine. 'You have plenty of time. Take a moment to come and see the arrangements. The roses smell beautiful and we've added some lavender to calm any nerves that might be fraying.'

Celia's furrowed brow smoothed out as she followed me into the main restaurant area, where Claude was taking his frustration out on one of his staff.

'Wouldya look at da state of da napkins, Joey?' he shouted, his French accent sounding decidedly more like the Godfather now. I suppressed a giggle as he spun round and quickly rediscovered his Gallic roots. 'Ah, Madame Reighton, I trust za room is satisfactory *pour vous*?'

Celia took a deep breath. '*C'est trés bon, Claude, merci.*'

Claude smiled briefly and hurried off into the kitchen. I squeezed Celia's arm. 'Well done.' For the first time since I'd arrived I witnessed the slightest glimpse of a smile appearing on her flushed face.

'I don't know what I'd do without you, Rosie!'

Café Bijou was very new indeed – you could still smell faint traces of fresh paint in the entrance lobby. But it was comfortable and welcoming, approached from the sidewalk via some impressive stone steps that rose elegantly from the tree-lined street. The interior was warm and understated, decked out in dark wood tables and chairs with aubergine velvet seats, subdued lighting, and walls painted in shades of brown, caramel and cream. Each table was covered in crisp white linen, and polished oak floorboards creaked satisfyingly beneath my feet. Though I say it myself, the floral arrangements worked incredibly well in this setting – cream and palest pink rosebuds, offset by dark green foliage and small bunches of dried lavender, packed tightly into dark wicker baskets and finished with generous amounts of pale yellow-gold raffia, which trailed out onto the tablecloths.

When all the tables were finished and place cards had been distributed, Celia stood back to view the scene. She let out a sigh. 'You were right, Rosie,' she said, flinging a relieved arm round my shoulders. 'Everything is just fine.'

Now I know that, to many people, Celia appears completely impossible. She even tested my mum's famously steady countenance when they first met. But I've known her long enough to realise that beneath the crazy exterior beats a heart of pure gold. Celia is *very* New York – she isn't happy unless there's some aspect of the world she's putting to rights. The rents are *astronomical*, restaurant and hotel prices are *ridiculous* and have you *seen* the state of the parks these days? Not to mention the fact that New York *simply has not been the same* since Giuliani finished as mayor (even though she moaned constantly about him while he was in office . . .). Her column is much loved by New Yorkers for its wry perspective on city life. She writes like they talk – a mixture of intellect, snobbery and good, old-fashioned complaint, seasoned with inimitable humour and completed with sly observation. It's largely due to Celia that I have grown to understand and love the idiosyncrasies of this city, its unique take on life.

Let me tell you how we met: Celia befriended me at a party I went to, not long after I decided to move from Boston to New York. She was in town visiting her recently relocated mother, and a mutual friend suggested she come along to the event as a celebrity guest. Most of the guests at the party were Harvard graduates who met up once a year for an informal reunion. My friend Ben was one of these illustrious alumni.

23

I met him at university and shared a house with him and five others in the not-so-posh bit of York. After graduation he decided to complete a Master's degree at Harvard and subsequently stayed in Boston to work. I lodged with him there for nearly six months until I left for New York. He introduced me to Celia and we liked each other straight away. She invited me to stay with her and her partner Jerry until I found an apartment of my own.

It's always easier to go to a new city when you know someone, and Celia proved to be a good person to know. She found my apartment for me and, after she'd learned I knew about floristry, persuaded me to meet her life-long family friend, Mr Kowalski. He was looking for someone to take on his business when he retired and Celia was certain I was the right person to do it.

I remember the very first time I walked into the shop – it felt like I was coming home. The little bell on the door that tinkled when we came in was identical to the one at Mum's shop. The flowers in neat little galvanised steel buckets were arranged in a rainbow of colours – great swathes of reds, yellows, blues and purples from left to right. And there was that unmistakable smell, which you can't really describe but recognise whenever you walk into a florist's shop.

Mr Kowalski told me to call him Franz, but somehow 'Mr Kowalski' seemed more appropriate for a man of his great experience and wisdom. He had, like me, grown up around flowers – his family had lived and worked in New York's Flower District from the time his parents arrived from Poland in the early 1920s. Although born in New York – the youngest child of six – he retained a strong Polish accent. He taught me so much when I worked with him during the year before he retired. Celia was overjoyed that she had been right in her judgement, and made sure all her friends came to our shop for their flowers.

Celia may give the impression of being completely self-absorbed, but deep down I know she worries about how people see her. It's this secret, slightly self-conscious person hidden so well inside the brash, confident exterior that I love and respect so much.

It has been said that a true friend is one who is willing to share the pains and joys of your life in equal measure: well, I can honestly say that Celia has always looked out for me, always championed my cause. She has cried with me when things have gone wrong – she is one of the few people who knows all the details of why I came to the States – and she has been an amazing source of strength to me at my lowest ebbs. She has celebrated with me when good things have happened too, like the time Kowalski's won a top industry award the first year I was in charge. And when Celia puts her mind to celebrate, she does it with every last drop of her energy.

Celia's events are the Golden Fleece in the Upper West Side. She is one of the few people in the country who can gather a stellar group of America's finest in one room at less than a year's notice. Her knack for creating interesting groups of guests is unsurpassed. And she always invites me. Which is the best bit, really. And while I suspect her main motive for including me in the guest list is to introduce me to eligible men, I love her for it. It is always a pleasure to meet the fascinating, creative people at Celia's parties and I have made many firm friends that way in the past.

Celia's guests began arriving just after eight, and within an hour Café Bijou was filled with the happy hum of conversation. Many of the writers present had not seen one another for some time, kept busy by national tours for their latest works or the ever-fruitful lecturing circuit. Small groups of friends gathered, excitedly inspecting the gift bags that Celia had given to each guest – neat little linen carriers filled with selections of the latest books from the authors present. As I navigated the room, checking my creations as I went, drifts of conversation washed over me.

'. . . It seems to me that Bernann's critique of Gershwin's contribution to the American musical identity simply focuses on one solitary point . . .' '. . . And you should have *seen* the hotels my agent found for me in Quebec . . .' '. . . But I cannot abide the style of modern English favoured by Ivy League departments right now . . .' '. . . Call me Neanderthal if you wish, but I have yet to find a credible philosopher to match the ancient greats in twenty-first-century America. I know, I know, I'm hard to please . . .'

One conversation caught my attention particularly. A group of three women and two men were standing by one of the tables, inspecting the basket arrangement closely.

'No, I think you'll find it *is* French Lavender,' said one woman, positioning her reading glasses on the end of her nose and peering at the flowers.

'Well, what's the difference between French and English?' asked the younger of the two men.

'Easy, I know that one,' said the other, with a wide, happy grin. The group looked at him, expectantly, waiting for the answer. 'One comes from France and the other comes from England!' This was received with good-natured groans and the investigation resumed.

'If I may join the debate,' I ventured, entering their conversation, 'the difference can be seen in the flower heads. French lavender has a much bigger head, with two or three large petals, while English lavender has a smaller head with tight, compact flowers. The lavender in question is English lavender and we import it especially from a farm on the Isle of Wight.'

The group appeared pleased and the lady with the reading glasses extended her hand.

'Thank you for your knowledgeable contribution. I'm Mimi Sutton.'

I returned her warm handshake. 'Rosie Duncan. I'm Celia's friend and also her florist.'

This information was met with murmurs of approval and congratulations from the others in the group, whom Mimi proceeded to introduce to me. Anya Marsalis, a tall, angular woman with striking black hair and huge green eyes was first. She was new to the literary circuit, having recently retired as an international model and published her first book – a travelogue of her time in Milan, Paris and Rome. Next was Brent Jacobs, the man with the wide grin, who had worked for twenty years as a criminal psychologist and now wrote very successful thrillers. His stomach was almost as broad as his smile and his thinning grey-blond hair curled up around his ears. The third woman, diminutive in both stature and personality, was Jane Masterson-Philips, a fortysomething history specialist whose biographies on great Americans had won her much critical acclaim. Her whole appearance seemed to be pulled back and neatly pinned in place, just like her tight chignon.

The final member of the group caught my attention the most. He was younger than the rest – my guess was about thirty-two or so – with a laid-back casual air and clothes to match. I was instantly reminded of a phrase Mum often uses to describe my brother, James – 'he's always so comfortable in his own skin'. Aware I was staring, I checked myself and looked at Mimi. But before she could introduce him, he stepped forward. He effortlessly swung one hand out of his trouser pocket to meet mine in a single movement.

'Hi,' he smiled, his voice soft and low, 'I'm Nathaniel Amie. Call me Nate.'

'Nathaniel works for Gray & Connelle Publishing,' Mimi informed me. 'He's a professional pessimist and the protagonist of many a nightmare for us in the literary fraternity.' This description seemed far removed from the apparently warm and easy-going person I had just been introduced to.

Anya guessed my reaction and explained, 'Nathaniel is the one who decides whether or not our precious works reach print. Thankfully for all of us, he has taken big risks to make sure we're published.'

'And we love him dearly,' Jane added, her cheeks reddening as Nate winked playfully and brought an arm round her for a quick squeeze.

'I love you all too,' he replied, then shook a finger at Jane. 'But you still have to make those changes we discussed today before I'll let it through.'

'See what I mean?' Mimi confided. 'Absolute nightmare.'

'I see you've met my *wonderful* friend,' sang Celia, breezing in. 'Mimi, you simply *must* let her create the floral decor for your upcoming Winter Ball. She is a *genius!*'

I winced as I caught Nate's amused expression. 'Genius?' he mouthed, his dark chocolate eyes twinkling with fun. I tried to smile and looked at my empty glass to avoid his stare.

'Well, *sure* . . .' Mimi said as she consulted her pocketbook and produced a business card. 'Any recommendation from Celia Reighton is well worth following up. Give me a call next week, Rosie, and we'll discuss.'

'Thank you.' I replied, taking her card. Celia was beaming so brightly she could have lit up Times Square all by herself.

'Do you have a store?' asked Brent, taking a small black leather notebook from his jacket pocket and brandishing a pencil. 'It's my wife's birthday at the end of the month and I'd love something special for her.'

'No problem,' I replied, handing him a business card, pleased with these new opportunities. 'I'm on the corner of West 68th and Columbus. The store's called Kowalski's. Come in and we'll design something original for you.'

'. . . And you're guaranteed something special. Rosie's designs are to *die* for,' Celia emphasised with a manic grin and a flamboyant gesture reminiscent of one of those over-zealous salesmen on cheap TV commercials. 'Now I won't allow you to hog my florist a moment longer. I'm whisking her away!' And, grabbing my hand, she was good to her word.

As we left the group and they returned to their conversation, I was aware that Nate Amie didn't move to join them. Celia was already introducing me to someone else, but I could see Nate looking at me across the room. He raised his glass to me and smiled, then turned back to his friends.

Much later, when the food had been enjoyed, the speeches made and the conversations done, Celia was still beaming.

'An incredibly successful evening all round, I think,' she proclaimed.

'Absolutely,' I agreed, taking the last arrangement from the table and handing it to her. 'To the hostess for her latest overwhelming triumph.'

Celia clamped an impassioned hand over her heart. 'A Kowalski's creation, for me? I'm so honoured!'

I smiled and shook my head. 'My strange old American friend.'

'Hey – less of the old. Though I'm beginning to feel it.' She pulled a face and rubbed her neck. 'I'm thinking my entertaining days are numbered.'

'You? Give up your famous parties? Never!' I retorted, pleased to see her face brighten in reply. 'It was another amazing gathering of people. Once again you've orchestrated orders for my business and allowed me to meet some fascinating individuals. As I said, a triumph!'

We finished clearing up, packed my van and then I drove Celia back uptown to her apartment. Though it was late, the lights along Broadway burned brightly as ever as we made our way slowly up through Manhattan to Columbus Circle and on into the Upper West Side.

There is something uniquely magical about driving through New York late at night. It's almost as if you should hold your breath in reverence as you pass through the neighbourhoods, each with its own trademark architecture and atmosphere. All-night diners are packed with customers hunched over their never-ending coffees, whilst brightly lit store windows reveal their treasures even when their doors are locked. The ubiquitous yellow taxis are everywhere, winding in and out of the traffic as if travelling on air. Sometimes it can feel as if the whole city has been put into slow-motion mode; its perennial activity transformed into a deftly choreographed ballet – a symphony of movement, sound, light and scent. No matter how many times I drive through the City That Never Sleeps, I never cease to be amazed by its majestic beauty and proud self-assuredness. Just like the people who walk its streets, work in its resplendent buildings and call it home, New York *knows* that it is special and unashamedly declares it to the world.

We arrived on West 91st Street and parked by the steps to Celia's apartment block. As she was about to leave, she turned back. 'Thank you, Rosie. Thank you for putting up with my panics. Thank you for always being there for me. I don't say it often enough, but you are a true friend. See you Saturday?'

I smiled. 'Sure. Good night, Celia.'

'Good night. I'll call you!'

As I began the drive back home, I couldn't help but smile. It had been a surprisingly good evening all round.

Chapter Three

Mimi Sutton called the day after Celia's event to invite me to meet her at her offices in SoHo the following day. I arrived a little early, design books in hand, and was shown by an assistant to a waiting area in the atrium of the ultra-modern building. In typical artsy minimalist style, the whole area was filled with clean lines with shiny metal and glass. Cobalt spotlights, discreetly hidden everywhere – behind frosted glass screens, in the middle of lush green foliage and inside tall steel and glass pillars – bathed the area in a soothing glow. This was a perfect complement to the white marble floor, which produced a rhythmic percussion as people crisscrossed its wide expanse.

I love arriving somewhere early to get a feel for the place. In this city you never know what to expect when you walk through the door of a building. You can experience classic styling, baroque opulence, bohemian chic or even puritan austerity as you move down a single street. It's nothing short of inspirational. Maybe it's my designer instinct, but I have days when everything inspires me. Even the scary kitsch stuff that most people with any remote sense of taste would be appalled at. I love trying to interpret the styles I see with my

33

flowers – it's a constant challenge I like to set myself to keep my designs fresh and different.

Mimi Sutton is a highly successful writer-turned – literary agent. She made her name writing blockbuster novels, most of which have, in turn, become blockbuster movies. She is constantly courted by Hollywood's movers and shakers. The film rights for her most recent book had been sold three months before she began work on it, and a gaggle of screenwriters (if that is the correct collective term) had accompanied her for most of the writing period. When I asked Celia why on earth Mimi wanted to be an agent for other people when she had achieved so much success of her own, Celia smiled.

'It's all about power, Rosie. And power in Manhattan is something Mimi simply cannot do without.'

About fifteen minutes after I had arrived, the elevator doors opened to reveal a familiar face, though I couldn't remember the name or the exact place I knew him from. Thankfully for me, the person fast approaching didn't have the same problem.

'Ms Duncan!' he exclaimed loudly as he strode briskly across the atrium to where I was. Reaching me, he took my hand between both of his and gave a wide smile. 'I guess you don't remember me? Brent Jacobs – from the Authors' Meet? Good to see you again. You here to see Mimi?'

'Yes I am.'

He smiled. 'Excellent. Hey, don't forget you said you'd help me with flowers for my wife. Would the last Thursday of the month be convenient?'

I checked my diary. 'Yes, no problem. About eleven?'

'Wonderful. Good to see you, Rosie.' He shook my hand quickly and strode away. I was about to sit down again when the assistant behind the pale green glass reception desk called to me. 'Ms Sutton will see you now, Ms Duncan.'

34

I took the glass elevator up eleven floors to Mimi's office. Another efficient, black Armani-suited assistant took me through two huge pale wood doors into a sumptuous office. Mimi sat at her desk at the far end, the dramatic backdrop of New York skyscrapers adding to her presence. She rose immediately and swept towards me.

'Well?' she questioned, waving a hand to indicate her surroundings. 'What do you think?'

'Very impressive,' I affirmed. She led me to three enormous cream leather sofas situated round a frosted glass coffee table on the other side of her office. It was easy to be completely overawed by the sheer luxury of these surroundings, and I was grateful that Celia had phoned with a pep talk earlier that morning so that I was well prepared to meet this character who, I was reliably informed, 'doesn't do small'. And Celia, for once, wasn't exaggerating.

'Sit, sit!' Mimi beckoned, draping herself magnificently over one sofa, three strings of pearls undulating around her throat as she spoke. 'Now, let me see your designs.' I offered my books, which she eagerly accepted. 'I'm *so* glad we met, Rosie,' she continued, without looking up as she flicked through the pages of photographs. 'You know, you caused quite a stir at the Meet the other night.'

'I did?'

'Sure, honey. The conversation was all about you when you left us. Like, how come you've been right under our noses all this time and we've never seen you? These designs are *good* . . . You know, Philippe is *so* last year. I *love* what you've done here.' She held up a page with big mounted displays that I did a few years back for an architects' ball. 'This is what I want for the Grand Winter Ball. It's just before Christmas and we intend to make it *the* social event of the season. So the décor needs to be the best, naturally. I would need, maybe, thirty of these large displays, plus garlands to cover the grand staircase in the ballroom. Could Kowalski's handle it?'

I was expecting a large order from this larger-than-life lady, but this took me by surprise. It was huge. I did some mental calculations, and then nodded. 'I'm sure we can. I'll put together some initial sketches with my co-designer and get them back to you with an estimate for your approval, if that's OK?'

Mimi snapped the book shut. 'Fantastic, Rosie. I'll have my planners call you and we'll go from there.' We stood up. 'It's been a pleasure,' she said, smiling broadly but escorting me swiftly to the door. 'I'll see you soon. Goodbye.'

Going down in the glass elevator, I let out a huge sigh as the enormity of the task ahead finally sunk in. I knew that, after the initial shock and protestations, Marnie and Ed would relish the opportunity to work on that scale. But quite how I was going to broach the subject with them, I had no idea.

I was lost in these thoughts as the elevator reached the ground floor and I stepped out. Straight into someone coming the other way. Losing my balance completely, I fell. My books flew out of my hands, opening mid-air before crashing to the ground, sending photographs and business cards sliding, skidding and scuttering across the atrium floor. I landed on the chic polished marble in a decidedly unchic position, surrounded by my belongings, which lay scattered in all directions.

You know how, when something embarrassing happens to you, it's like someone hits the Pause button and the world seems to stop and stare? Well, this was one of those moments. All the frantically hurrying people found a good reason to postpone their journeys and a hundred spotlights homed in on me as their eyes surveyed my misfortune. *Why had I chosen today to wear a shorter than usual skirt and no tights?* Dazed from the ugly tumble, yet alert enough to realise I was in grave danger of revealing my choice of underwear to all assembled, I struggled to my knees in a vain attempt to rescue any remaining scraps of my dignity, scrabbling for my belongings as I did so. Stumbling eventually to my feet, I cursed my flushing cheeks and made a woeful attempt at a smile in the direction of the flash mob gathered around me. Only when I was fully upright did I realise that the someone I had collided with was still there. Laughing. *Very* loudly.

He stood, bent double, chest convulsing wildly, with one hand wiping tears from his eyes while the other reached out to help me. His laughter seemed to bounce off every hard surface, filling the space with great booming guffaws. I hugged my books to my chest, still aware of all the unwanted attention from the atrium's beautiful people.

'I'm . . . so . . . sorry,' the man gasped. 'I shouldn't laugh, but . . . but that was *just hilarious.*'

'Well, thank you.' I could swear I heard a stifled Armani-clad giggle from the green glass reception desk. *Great*, said the little voice in my head, *nice one, Duncan*. The someone was still laughing. The beautiful people were still laughing. But I *wasn't*. Realising my embarrassment, the someone regained his composure and straightened up. I was just about to give him a piece of my mind when our eyes met and, instantly, his expression changed from amusement to sincere shock as he recognised me – and I recognised him.

'Rosie Duncan? Heck, I'm so, so sorry. Are you OK?' he stammered, his voice suddenly full of genuine concern that defused my anger.

'I'm fine – um – Nathaniel?'

There was more than a hint of relief in his smile. 'Yes.

Uh, Nate. Call me Nate – please. Are you sure you're OK?' He bent down and quickly collected the remaining detritus of my fall, carefully handing them back to me. His warm hand rested on mine for a second. 'Are you sure you're OK?'

'I'm fine – really. Ego a bit dented, that's all,' I replied, smiling weakly.

'Good – great . . .' His voice trailed off and his brow furrowed as he struggled for something else to say. He ran a hand through his closely cropped chestnut-brown hair and then a warm, one-sided grin broke across his face. 'Uh . . . well, it was good to – um – *bump into* you again!'

It was a bad joke, but I still found myself laughing. 'Yeah – you too.' We exchanged polite smiles and an uneasy pause. It was obvious this conversation was fast running out of road, so I said goodbye and walked away. I was nearly at the glass entrance doors when I heard Nate call after me.

'Rosie! Where's your store?'

'At the corner of West 68th and Columbus,' I called back. 'Kowalski's.'

Nate bent down to pick up something else from the floor and waved it in the air. 'Hey, don't worry, it's OK – I've found your card!'

I could feel the hot rush of embarrassment return. As the floor ignored my urgent telepathic request for it to open up and swallow me, I smiled, hastily turned and made a speedy exit.

'*How* many?'

Arms folded, Ed and Marnie stood, like a matching pair of incredulous-looking bookends. This was not going well.

'Just think of it this way, guys. You're forever saying we don't get enough exposure for Kowalski's – well, this will get us noticed by *really* important people. Press people, publishers, celebrities. We can take on extra staff for this job. Corey Mitchell at the Molloy College in Bethpage has offered to lend us some of his floristry students any time we want. You guys can really go to town on the whole design process. Come on, I'm confident we can do this.'

Marnie took a deep breath and looked at Ed. They then had one of their weird unspoken conversations. They do this all the time. I hear no words, but somehow a decision is made. Eventually Ed nodded at Marnie then looked at me.

'OK, OK, let's do it.'

I whooped and clapped my hands. 'Thank you so much. It's going to be so exciting! Time for Kowalski's to take over New York!'

Marnie and Ed shot me one of their 'humour her, she's insane' glances and Marnie took her position behind the counter while Ed followed me into the workroom at the back of the shop.

One thing Ed loves to do is psychoanalyse people. He says it's because he comes from a long line of psychiatrists and it's an inescapable part of his genetic makeup. Ed's father has never forgiven him for abandoning what has been the family profession for the past three generations. When Ed began his apprenticeship at Kowalski's he had to regularly defend his decision – and, in turn, his sexuality – to his father, who considered men who worked with flowers to be gay by definition. Even when Ed moved from Kowalski's to work at Charters, one of Manhattan's most respected florists, Mr Steinmann refused to be impressed. I wonder sometimes if this is why Ed dates so much – still publicly asserting his heterosexuality to prove his father wrong.

He never told his father he was unhappy at Charters, even

though most of his five years spent working there were impossibly miserable as, time and again, he was denied the opportunity to progress in the company. In fact, the only person he confided in was Mr Kowalski, who had remained a friend throughout, which was why Ed ended up accepting the position of my co-designer. Mr Kowalski not only offered the fatherly advice denied Ed by his own father, but was also instrumental in affirming Ed's work and worth. Yet another reason why we all love and miss Mr K so much.

'So,' Ed said, resuming work on a hand-tied bouquet of roses, asters and Asiatic lilies, surrounded by deep green banana leaves, 'Mimi Sutton – what kind of vibe did you get about her?'

'Quite businesslike. Difficult to tell that much about her, really.'

'Rosie, turn off the optimism gene for one second and tell me what you *honestly* thought. I won't tell. Scout's honour.'

I thought for a moment. 'OK, the vibe was – *strange*.' I confessed. 'It feels like something's missing there.'

Ed looked up from his hand-tying. 'How do you mean?'

'I dunno . . . I mean, she's very polite, very friendly, but I can't tell how genuine she is. It's like all the fire and individuality that she must have had before she got successful has gone somehow. I'm not sure what's left in their place.'

'Uh-huh,' said Ed, nodding. 'Heart replaced by a dollar sign. Soul replaced by a resumé. She sold out.'

Ed is always able to condense an entire conversation into a three-line conclusion. I keep telling him he should be writing tag lines for Hollywood movies. He'd make a fortune.

'Shame,' he said, picking up a pale peach rose and spinning the stem between his fingers absent-mindedly, 'I've always liked her books. Just goes to show that the person you think you know from their writing is only the person they *want* you to see. And what about the other guy – Brent, was it?'

I smiled immediately. 'Yes, Brent Jacobs. He's fab. I like him. You'd like him.'

'Always a good sign. Why?'

'Because he used to be a criminal psychologist.'

Ed laughed. 'Uh-oh. Better not let us meet then. I may have been a case study in his former career. I've a checkered past, you know.'

'Oh, I forgot. Ed Steinmann, criminal mastermind. Must be why you fit in so well here.'

'Hmm, because I'm not the only one with an intriguing hidden history.' The comment sliced through the humour like a knife through butter. 'I'm still here if you want to talk, Rosie.'

'Well, I don't.' Instantly I saw hurt narrow his eyes. 'I'm sorry. I shouldn't have said that . . . I'm fine, Ed, really. But thanks for caring.'

His expression instantly changed and his eyes twinkled.

'Someday I'm going to write a book about you: *Rosie Duncan – One of the Great Unsolved Mysteries of the Modern Age*. A surefire hit!'

People often tell me they sense about the team at Kowalski's a closeness they don't see in other shops. Sometimes customers ask if we're related – and you should see the look of horror on Ed and Marnie's faces – as we are every inch the typical family: fighting occasionally, bickering sometimes, but always there for each other. And we have Mr Kowalski in common.

One thing Mr K said again and again was that we were a family. 'You are children to me. And like a good father, I worry for you. We are a family at Kowalski's – it is the heart of everything we do.'

I've tried to keep the same feeling at Kowalski's since it became my business. And, odd though it sounds, I sense him here still – five years after his death – that broad, crinkly smile lighting up his lovely old face as he watches the 'Kowalski's kids' with pride.

'What are you doing Thursday evening next?' Marnie asked later that afternoon, poking her head round the workroom door. Ed and I looked up from the red, white and gold-themed table centrepieces we were working on for Mr and Mrs Hymark's Ruby Wedding party. Mrs Hymark worked for Mr K as a Saturday girl in her teens and has trusted Kowalski's with her floral orders for every occasion since – from her own wedding to the birth of her children and grandchildren, birthdays, anniversaries and funerals.

Ed, obviously unwilling to commit, deferred to me. 'Uh, Rosie?'

'Don't look at me, Steinmann, I don't manage your diary. I'm free, Marnie.'

'Yeah, whatever. Although I *was* planning a quiet one . . .'

I smiled firmly. 'Ed and I are *both* free, Marnie.'

Marnie gave a little whoop and clapped her hands. 'Great!'

Ed groaned the groan of dread-filled experience. 'What have we just agreed to?'

'The opening night of my community theatre play, of course!'

A look of panic washed across his face. 'Oh – wait – I just remembered, I have a . . . a . . . *thing* next Thursday.'

Marnie's face instantly fell. 'What thing? Oh, Ed, can you reschedule? It's really important that you guys come. It's the *world premiere*, you know.'

Ed opened his mouth to protest but I got there first. 'We wouldn't miss it for the world, Marnie.'

* * *

A week later, Ed and I stood in the small queue outside Hudson River Players' tiny studio theatre. To call it a theatre was lavishing high praise indeed: in truth, it was an old dock warehouse that had been converted ten years ago into a theatre space for the local neighbourhood. Nevertheless, for all the effort and care the drama group's members had gone to for the 'world premiere' of their new play, it might as well have been Radio City Music Hall or Madison Square Garden.

'Welcome,' boomed a stony-faced, wiry-framed man clad entirely in black, who was handing out programmes like they were death warrants.

'That's debatable,' muttered Ed as we passed into the shadowy heart of the black-curtained warehouse space.

'Would you stop complaining?' I hissed under my breath as we found our seats – or rather, wooden bench.

'So, remind me again why we're willingly inflicting this torture on ourselves tonight?' Ed remarked, looking round at the other, equally unenthusiastic members of the audience.

'We're here for Marnie,' I replied, trying to look interested in the Xeroxed programme but seeing only spelling mistakes – such as 'dirrectors' and 'tragik'. 'We promised.'

'But it's *community theatre*,' he protested. 'It's like death, only much, much slower! I mean, come on, Rosie – look around you: *nobody* wants to be here. This place is worse than Edgar Allen Poe on twenty-four hour repeat. Oh, wait, no – I think I've just seen him leaving because *it's too depressing.*'

'Be quiet and enjoy the experience. It's Marnie's play. Part of Kowalski's family, remember?'

Ed's shoulders dropped in defeat. 'Sure, I get it.'

The play, it has to be said, was everything bad you've ever heard about experimental theatre – and then some. When we'd asked Marnie what it was about, she had solemnly informed us that *Armageddon: The Miniseries* was an 'existential politico-comedy with tragic overtones' – which did nothing to enlighten us or prepare us for the experience. All seven actors were dressed in black and appeared to be playing about thirty parts each. 'We use the Brechtian device of *gestus* to completely remove the audience from any perceived reality of the play, choosing instead to represent rather than impersonate,' intoned the programme notes. 'We have also challenged the concept of a single director, opting for a group-conscious approach in its stead.'

A player ran onstage carrying a pig's head in one hand and what appeared to be two pounds of tripe in the other.

'This is the play that they make you watch when you're eternally damned,' whispered Ed, 'over and over and over . . . Ow! That was my ankle!'

'*Shhhhh*, Marnie's coming on.'

Marnie walked slowly to the centre of the stage with an expression like stone and a red ribbon tied around her left wrist. 'Enough!' she shouted, hands aloft like a Druid priest. 'Time is not what we think it is!' I could see her counting to three slowly and then she exited as solemnly as she had entered.

'Two lines? I just sat through three hours of the worst play in the known universe for *two lines*?' Ed moaned as we sat in the all-night diner across the street afterwards.

'I know, but Marnie was so thrilled we came. And look, I bought you your favourite chocolate cheesecake to say thank you,' I replied, pointing at the slab of dessert in front of him so big he could barely see over the top of it.

Ed's blue stare zoomed in on me. 'Don't think the "family" excuse is going to work on me every time, Duncan. Tonight I felt generous, that's all.'

I smiled. 'Fine. You just keep telling yourself that, if it makes you feel better.'

Ed muttered something obscene into his cheesecake.

There's always a lot of banter when Ed and I are together, mainly because we have so much in common. We share similar tastes in movies and music; we both consider huge steaming hot dogs and ice-cold papaya shake from Gray's Papaya on West 72nd Street the finest guilty pleasure on a Sunday afternoon; and we both enjoy psycho-analysing everyone we meet in a manner that would impress even the cast of *Dawson's Creek*. Most of all, we share a passion for New York: Ed because he's lived here all his life and me because, well, I fell in love with the city the moment I got off the train at Grand Central Station and walked into the frenetic bustle of the world-famous concourse with its stunning star-strewn ceiling. Before I came here I didn't really believe people who said New York felt like a place where dreams are made, yet that is completely what I felt on that first day; like *anything* was possible in this city – even the most implausible hope or wildest aspiration.

It was Ed who encouraged me to explore New York and Ed who volunteered to escort me on my journey of discovery. So, most Sundays for the past five years or thereabouts, Ed and I have met on the subway and headed off to a new destination: strolling down Bleecker Street with its boho-chic boutiques; browsing superheroes old and new at Forbidden Planet, the comic shop on Broadway; watching the sun set across the city from the observation deck of the Empire State and Chrysler Buildings ('You have to see both views to understand the race to be the tallest,' Ed says); eating oysters in the vaulted brick bar nestled deep beneath Grand Central; sneaking into private Gramercy Park once after being slipped a coveted key by an old school friend of Ed's who works at the Gramercy Hotel (seriously, the people Ed knows in this city you wouldn't believe); and hour upon hour of long, laughter-filled conversations in various coffee houses, diners and restaurants across Manhattan. It's true what they say about this city: it's a million different experiences in one place. Even now, six years since I arrived, I don't think I've even scratched the surface of the delights New York has to offer.

The day after Marnie's play was an unusually quiet one for Kowalski's. Usually we don't stop on a Friday from the minute we lift the shutters to the moment we turn the Open sign to Closed. We took the opportunity to do some long-overdue housekeeping around the store – the kind of jobs you always intend to get round to doing yet invariably end up putting off. We gave the light wood floor a good clean, dusted the shelves behind the counter, restocked the flower buckets and tidied up the workroom. Even Mr K's old half-moon spectacles received a much-needed polish and sat resplendent on the shelf afterwards, sparkling almost as much as Mr K's eyes used to.

By three o'clock it was obvious that the good people of the Upper West Side didn't want flowers today, so I was about to suggest we close up early when Ed asked, 'Are you guys OK to finish up here without me? I mean, it's quiet and I'd like to leave early tonight.'

I smiled. 'It's probably worth closing now anyway. I think we've all worked hard enough today.'

Marnie looked at me and shrugged. 'That is so typical. I was hoping you might need me to stay later tonight. My crazy landlord's fixing my shower and I really don't want to be there while he's working.'

'Ah, still trying to match-make you and his son, huh?' Ed grinned.

Marnie pulled a face. 'Is he *ever*.' She hunched her shoulders and adopted a gruff, Italian-American accent. '"You such a nice lady, Ms Andersson, you could do a lot worse than my Vinnie, you know. He's gonna inherit the building when I retire. He got prospects – a lady like you needs a guy with prospects . . ." Yeah, and a lady like me also needs *cleanliness* – and fresh breath. All Vinnie has to offer me is too much butt-crack over his jeans and halitosis like you wouldn't believe.'

Ed and I giggled – not least because of the hilarious sight of Marnie, colourfully attired as always, stomping around like Don Corleone in pigtails.

'Hey, I have an idea,' I said, giving her a wink. 'Seeing as our esteemed colleague is deserting us, how about you and I head over to SoHo for something to eat?'

Marnie's eyes lit up. 'Ooh, Rosie, that would be amazing! I could show you that store I was telling you about – the vintage one?'

After a day at Kowalski's the thought of a spot of retail therapy followed by a great meal was more than a little tempting. 'You're on.'

Ed shook his head. 'What is it about the word "shopping" that makes women go nuts?'

'It's a girl thing, Steinmann. You're not invited,' Marnie grinned.

'So, how come you're skiving off early?' I asked him.

Ed lifted his chin and attempted to look aloof, the success of this severely compromised by the mischief dancing in his blue eyes. 'Can't tell you. It's a *boy* thing, Duncan.'

'So what's her name?'

Sly humour began to pull up one corner of his mouth. 'Carly, if you must know.'

'Hang on, isn't this the *same* Carly you saw last Saturday night?'

Ed looked decidedly sheepish. 'It might be.'

Marnie's eyes widened. 'Wait – you saw Carly on Wednesday as well, didn't you?'

A scarlet blush slowly creeping up Ed's neck was giving the game away. 'It's . . . possible . . .'

I whistled. '*Three* dates with the same girl?'

Ed rubbed the back of his neck self-consciously. 'Four, actually.'

Marnie let out a squeak and flung her arms around Ed's waist. 'It's *serious*! Oh, *Eddie*, I'm so pleased for you!'

Ed wrestled himself free of her limpet-like embrace. 'It is *not* serious. She happens to have tickets to a show tonight that I quite like the idea of seeing.'

'Is he talking about the show or Carly?' I smirked at Marnie.

'You *like* her . . .' Marnie said, singsong style, poking a finger in his ribs.

'Stop it.'

'Four dates with the same girl? That's practically an *engagement*,' I laughed. 'Should we buy our hats now? I can recommend a *great* florist for the ceremony.'

Ed let out a groan and grabbed his jacket from behind the workroom door. 'Whatever. You two have a great time tonight doing your girl stuff, OK?'

He left, shaking his head, as Marnie began singing a gutsy rendition of Mendelssohn's 'Wedding March'.

It was only when Marnie and I were browsing Victoria's Vintage in SoHo later that afternoon, that I realised how much I needed a 'girly' evening. Work had been pretty intense at Kowalski's lately, with an unexpected rush of small orders that all seemed to be needed on the same days and I had become so wrapped up in the sheer volume of day-to-day stuff at the store that I had neglected my own free time.

'Isn't this fun?' Marnie said, appearing from behind a crowded clothes-rail with a vivid sixties tie-dyed T-shirt.

'It's bright,' I smiled.

'I don't mean *this*,' Marnie frowned, waving the garment dismissively, 'although it *is* rather fabulous. I mean us hanging out.'

'Yes, it's great. Just what I needed. So are you buying that?'

Marnie checked the price tag and her face fell. 'I would be if I didn't have to pay my rent this month,' she replied, hanging the T-shirt back on the rail and stroking it wistfully. 'Shall we go and get something to eat?'

I nodded. 'There's a Biba blouse I liked over there I think I'm going to buy. I'll meet you outside, OK?'

Five minutes later we had crossed the street to Ellen's, a small cosy restaurant much beloved by the local art fraternity. More a laid-back, all-hours coffee shop than a high-class eaterie, Ellen's was a lazy hum of activity; its expansive, well-worn couches littered with chatting, colourfully-attired customers making the interior look as if a shabby rainbow had exploded and strewn its fragments haphazardly across the room. It was no wonder this was one of Marnie's favourite haunts – there weren't many places in New York where she could 'blend in', but Ellen's was a notable exception. Surreal and abstract paintings on huge canvases adorned the bare brick walls and a jazz trio nodded sleepily in one corner. We found a table with mismatched dark wood chairs by the window and sat down.

'I love it here,' said Marnie as we perused the hand-drawn menu. 'My art class used to come here all the time last semester.'

'I like it,' I smiled. 'I wonder how Ed's getting on.'

Marnie surveyed me quizzically. 'Now why in the world would you say that?'

Something about her expression unnerved me a little. 'No reason. I was just wondering, that's all.'

Marnie leaned forward and lowered her voice, as if the other customers may suddenly take an unwelcome interest in her next comment. 'Do you like him, Rosie?'

'Of course I like him, mate. He's one of my best friends.'

Marnie gave my hand a playful tap. 'I don't mean it like that. You *know* what I mean.'

'Don't be silly. I was just wondering how he was going to cope with so many dates with the same woman. You have to admit, it would be a first for him.'

Marnie nodded. 'That guy has almost more dates than *me*. I don't know where he meets them all.'

'Wherever he goes, apparently. He even got a date when he called an emergency plumber last year.'

'He dated the plumber?'

'No, the plumber's sister, who was along for the ride.'

'I don't know why he spends so long chasing women he's no intention of settling down with,' Marnie said, turning the menu card over.

'He likes the chase, I think.'

'Hmm. I reckon you and he should get together.'

'Excuse me?'

'Seriously, Rosie, I mean it! Think about it: you spend loads of time together already, you like the same places in New York, you're both crazy about old movies and eating out—'

'Stop right there, please. You're scaring me.'

'Oh, come on, you mean to tell me that you don't find Ed in the least bit attractive?'

'Well, I . . .'

'*Exactly!* He's *gorgeous*, Rosie! That guy could charm pollen from a bee. I tell you, if I wasn't his friend and he didn't bug the hell out of me like some annoying older brother, I *would*—'

'Marnie!'

'OK, right, so when he comes into the store the morning after a rough night, and he's all ruffled and unshaven, you haven't *once* considered . . . ?'

Just as this conversation was veering wildly towards the point of no return, a waiter appeared by our table to spare my blushes.

'Hi, ladies, welcome to Ellen's. Our special tonight is Pancetta Mac Cheese and . . . *wow* – uh – hi, Marnie.'

Marnie looked slightly flushed but pleased. 'Hey, Todd.'

Todd's eyes appeared transfixed by the vision in orange and purple sitting before him. 'It's really good to see you.'

'You too. Oh, this is my boss, Rosie.'

Todd wrenched his gaze away from Marnie long enough to shake my hand. 'The florist, right? Hey.'

'Nice to meet you,' I replied, noting the chemistry between them.

'So – we'll have the specials, please, if that's OK with you, Rosie?'

I nodded. 'I'll go with your recommendation.'

'Great,' Todd replied, scribbling the order on his pad. Tearing off a strip, he placed it carefully in front of Marnie. 'Call me,' he smiled shyly before disappearing into the dimly lit depths of the restaurant.

'Well, *he* was nice,' I said, full of curiosity.

Marnie shrugged and played with a napkin. 'He's OK, I guess. We dated a little last year.'

'Looks like he's keen to see you again,' I smiled, indicating the strip of paper laid lovingly on the table. 'He's a nice-looking guy too.'

'Too restrained for me,' Marnie replied coolly. I couldn't help but think this probably could apply to most of Manhattan's single male population when compared to Marnie's vivid personality and appearance. She beamed cheekily. 'Not as fine as Ed though, hey?'

Although I would never dream of admitting it to Marnie, I had to privately concede that Ed did have an alarming skill for looking great when most men would just have looked rough. Of course, I could understand how he managed to find so many women eager to go out with him; it was that legendary Steinmann twinkle that rescued him from so many otherwise tricky situations with devastating effect. Even when we have had the biggest rows at Kowalski's, I've never managed to stay angry at him for long. Which is frustrating in the extreme, but then, that's Ed: like that brown leather jacket of his – a little beaten up by life but so warm and engaging that you forgive the lack of polish immediately. I suppose all those women found themselves torn between admiring the Steinmann twinkle and wanting to take care of him. Unfortunately for them, Ed's idea of a perfect woman seemed to be, 'spend time with me when it's fun and then don't bother calling'. Not that he was ever cruel: from the little he told us of his dates it appeared that most of the ladies shared his ethos.

Halfway through our Pancetta Mac Cheese, I couldn't wait any longer to hand Marnie the turquoise Victoria's Vintage bag I'd been masquerading as my mythical Biba blouse. Flinging aside the vivid magenta tissue paper, Marnie let out a squeak that momentarily made the whole clientele of Ellen's stop and look at us.

'It's the one I was looking at! Oh, Rosie, you *shouldn't* have!'

I smiled. 'You deserve it.'

What many people who see Marnie today don't realise about her is that her confidence was hard-won. A painfully shy child, her formative years were spent hiding from the other kids in her New Jersey neighbourhood who had noticed early on that both she and her family were different. They taunted her for the colourful handmade clothes her artist mother lovingly dressed her in; for her smiling, bearded art teacher father, whose style remained firmly locked in the sixties; and for the orange VW camper van parked outside their home, standing out like an alien spacecraft amid the sea of sedans that lined the street. While her parents always encouraged her to assert her individuality, it took an incident at Marnie's 'Sweet Sixteen' school prom to change how she viewed herself.

Without a date for the night, she had joined the ranks of the singletons sitting around the periphery of the dancefloor, watching and waiting for someone to notice them. To the surprise of everyone, one of the most popular guys in her year left his date to walk over to 'no date land' and ask Marnie if she wanted to dance. Struggling to combat her embarrassment, Marnie shyly accepted and walked with him to the centre of the floor, all eyes following her. As she was about to take his hand, however, a cruel smile broke across her partner's face as he flipped her skirt over her head and yelled, 'Freak on the dancefloor!' to the utter delight of those watching.

It was then that Marnie experienced what she describes as 'my epiphany'. In the centre of the hall, battling the urge to run away, all the years of pent-up frustration and hurt finally found a vent and, like a multicoloured volcano, Marnie erupted.

Popular Guy didn't stand a chance as Marnie's left fist slammed into his jaw, laying him out cold in the middle of the high school gym, encircled by sparkles from the revolving mirror-ball overhead.

'I'd rather be different than a jerk like you!' she yelled, as the 'no date land' inhabitants broke into spontaneous applause. The event brought about a deep change in Marnie – not least for the rest of that evening, where boys who had never acknowledged her existence before suddenly stood in line to dance with her. From that moment to this, Marnie's love life has always been well populated, if limited in terms of success. Nevertheless, the confident, kooky young woman who bounces into Kowalski's every morning is a breath of fresh air and I wouldn't be without her for the world.

If Marnie and I had entertained any ideas that Ed might finally have found a longer-term prospect in Carly, we were to be quickly proved wrong. By Monday, he had already agreed to see three other ladies and Carly's name was never mentioned again. When Marnie pressed him for more information a week later, all she got in return was a disinterested shrug and a mumbled excuse about them 'wanting different things' – which, translated, meant she was probably keener than he. In an odd way, knowing that the Great Steinmann Dating Express was still on its non-committed tracks was strangely comforting. It confirmed that Kowalski's was still the same: Ed was still dating, Marnie was as colourful as ever, Celia continued to fly in and out and the shop was as much as a neighbourhood hub as it had always been. It felt *safe* – and nobody knows the value of that feeling like I do.

Little did I know then that seemingly innocuous events just around the corner were going to change *everything*.

Chapter Four

There is nothing quite like returning home after a long day. Don't get me wrong: I love my shop. But I get a kick from turning the key in the lock to reveal the welcoming sight of my apartment. It has this unique smell – wood polish, old coffee and lavender. It signifies just one thing to me: I'm home.

The first thing I do is crank Old F's sister, Hissy (after the noise it makes and the fits it occasionally throws in the process) into action. Slightly younger than my workmate, but equally as unprepossessing, my home coffee maker gurgles happily into life and infuses the whole place with its fragrance. Then, mug in hand, I check my answer machine.

This particular late summer's day there were three – the first two were from Mum, reminding me about my brother's birthday and informing me that James would be in the States on business next week. It's possible to have a conversation with Mum's answer machine messages because she leaves gaps where you would normally say 'Mmm', 'I see', or, 'Oh dear' in a phone call.

'It would be lovely if James could visit you, but he says he'll be tied up in Washington the whole time . . .'

'That's a shame . . .'

'It's a shame, I know.'

'Hmm . . .'

'I'd like to say he'll call you, but you know what he's like, dear.'

'Yes, so wrapped up in his own universe that no one else matters . . .'

'He's so wrapped up in his work commitments that he never has time to do the things he wants. Anyhow, darling, I must go . . .'

'I expect this call's expensive . . .'

'It's *so* expensive to call you at this time of night.'

I smiled. 'Love-you-miss-you-bye!'

'Love-you-miss-you-bye!' The message ended. I shook my head and smiled before taking a long sip of coffee. For the tiniest second, I wished myself home with Mum in England again.

The last message was from Celia. There are normally several messages from Celia, their length, volume and coherence depending on how near a total breakdown she is at the time.

'Rosie, it's me. It's six forty-five. Where *are* you? Call me *the second* you get this.'

'OK, OK, wait one second while I get changed,' I muttered, walking into my bedroom.

True to form, Celia wasn't listening. No sooner had I kicked off my shoes, the phone rang.

'All right, *fine*, seeing as you insist, I'll talk to you first then,' I sighed.

'Rosie – thank goodness, honey. I was thinking something *awful* must have happened to you.'

I smiled despite myself. 'I caught a bus to the deli and then walked home. It's actually light this time of day in August, you know. What could possibly have happened to me?'

'*Anything*, Rosie! My colleague has been working on a piece about how many single young women meet supposedly wonderful young men in bars after work, only to have their apartments *ransacked* once they've slept with them . . .'

'Celia, listen to yourself! I'm fine. I haven't slept with any supposedly wonderful young men today and everything in my apartment is just as I left it this morning.'

'Well, I only worry because I care about you,' Celia said, with more than a hint of offence in her tone.

'I know – and I really appreciate it. Now, what can I do for you?'

'I need you to come by the office tomorrow, if you can.'

'Why?' I asked carefully, picturing Ed and Marnie's stern faces.

'I want to feature you in our "West Siders" column. So many guests who met you at the Authors' Meet have been asking about you.'

I frowned. This was the second time I'd heard that today and it seemed weird. All I'd done was have one conversation about lavender and take part in a lot of polite smalltalk. 'Mimi Sutton said the same thing when I rang her today, Celia. Just who has been asking about me?'

'*Everyone,* sweetie! Angelika, Henrik, Jane, Brent – in fact I spoke with Brent this evening and he said he'd seen you briefly at Mimi's office. He's *very* taken with you, y'know. He said you're like an English Sandra Bullock.'

'I look nothing like Sandra Bullock,' I commented.

'Oh, you *do*, Rosie! *Everyone* says it! Mimi said it at the party and I've heard that Ed from your store say it too.'

'Ed said it?' I repeated, making a mental note to challenge him on that tomorrow. 'Well, I have dark hair and dark eyes, but there the similarity ends,' I replied, 'I mean, if Sandra Bullock put on a stone then maybe we'd be more alike.'

Celia was obviously getting tired of this subject. 'Well, what-ever, Rosie, you're officially a *hit*! Just like I said you would be. Look, my editor asked me today to find interesting, upcoming West Side individuals for the new column and I thought what a great opportunity it would be to get the word out on you! Come by at one tomorrow and we'll discuss it all. Love you, must go.'

And with that, she was gone and blessed peace was restored.

Slowly, I put the receiver down and reached for my diary, as my mind clicked into hyperdrive. Why had there been so much interest in me from the party? I couldn't understand it. The question remained at the forefront of my mind as I grilled chicken and made a large salad. As I ate my evening meal, my eye kept returning to the open diary page for tomorrow. While I found myself quite excited at the prospect, an undeniable underlying note of caution sounded too.

Publicity can, I have discovered, work one of two ways. Either it can be incredibly successful, or it can backfire on you Big Time. Like the time my mum paid to place an advert in the local paper, informing readers that, 'Eadern Blooms are taking 50% off prices for the first week of May', yet somewhere between Mum faxing the details and the newspaper being printed, Eadern Blooms had become 'Eadern Bloomers' and for a week she was inundated with irate OAPs demanding cut-price underwear. Or, like the time my brother, James, was in the paper for one of his early business ventures. He was pictured with a girlfriend, who, the interview stated, had been going steady with him for three years and was looking forward to becoming Mrs James Duncan in the not-too-distant future. Problem was, four girls who he was *also* seeing at the time read that article too. They turned up at our house *en masse* and all hell broke loose. Still, James had always said he wanted

58

to travel in an ambulance with its siren blaring and lights flashing . . .

With this in mind, I decided that I would go to see Celia as planned, and politely but firmly refuse her offer. We were doing fine at Kowalski's: the neighbourhood business was as good as ever and now, with Mimi Sutton's commission for the Grand Winter Ball, things were looking decidedly healthy on the event front. The publicity we could gain from me being in the 'West Siders' column might only serve to swamp us with work we were unprepared for – and the last thing I wanted was to run before we could walk. Right now the balance between day-to-day sales and special events was just about right. I wasn't about to sell out and ruin what, in my opinion, set Kowalski's apart from other, larger florists in New York. Decision made, I went to bed content and fell asleep almost straight away.

That night, my dreams were incredibly vivid. Images flashed through my mind at supersonic speed – Ed smiling, Mimi Sutton in her magnificent office, Brent's wide grin, bumping into Nate Amie and Mum's phone message about James. Then, suddenly, I could feel a man's heartbeat, the warmth of his arms around me, his breath in my hair. It was wonderful. I felt . . . *safe*. I raised my head from his chest to look in his eyes . . . At first, I couldn't make out his features. Then, I recognised him. The feeling of safety dissolved, replaced with a vice-grip of nausea. Suddenly, the scene changed. I was now standing in a garden, facing a group of familiar faces. They were smiling at me. I heard myself speak – voice full of emotion, fighting back tears: *'I'm sorry. I'm so sorry . . .'*

I woke with a start. Shafts of moonlight pooled in through the bedroom window. Breathing hard, face wet with tears and perspiration, I sat bolt upright and looked around to regain my bearings. Reaching across to the bedside table, I snapped the light on. A warm golden glow bathed the features of my room – the antique whitewashed chair by my bed with its flea-market-find patchwork quilt throw, the painting of Bridgnorth that Mum had brought on her last visit, the dark wood chest of drawers Celia had donated when I first moved here – familiar décor soothing my burning eyes. I wiped my brow and forced myself to breathe deeply. Slowly, the hammering of my heart eased. But the nausea sat defiant in my stomach.

'Get a grip, girl,' I chastised myself. 'It's just a dream. It's gone now – it isn't real.'

Well, it isn't real now, said a voice inside my head. *But it was once.*

Chapter Five

'Rosie, no! You *have* to do this!' Ed insisted, banging down his coffee mug on the counter to emphasise his point. 'It's the best potential publicity we've had in years. The entire readership of the *New York Times* – think how many potential customers we could reach.'

My amazing, fail-safe plan for getting out of Celia's 'West Siders' column was obviously going well . . . I thought I'd picked the perfect moment when Ed came into work early the following morning. Marnie wasn't due in for another hour so I figured I could talk Ed round and avoid too many disagreements. Simple – or so, I thought. I'd made him a coffee as usual and then mentioned, so casually that the comment could have carried a Gap label, what I was planning to do. I was already reconciled to the fact that I'd probably face the standard Steinmann Rant but I was certain that even he, eventually, would have to agree with my point of view.

He didn't, of course. This wasn't what I wanted. Not this morning, still unnerved by the dream from last night. I dropped my head behind the battle lines and dug in for a long fight. Taking a deep breath, I began my defence.

'I just don't see why anyone would want to read about me, Ed. About Kowalski's – yes, fine – but not about me.'

Ed's expression changed from incomprehension to incredulous. 'What?' he said, looking at me like I'd just told him the Statue of Liberty had been painted pink. 'How do you figure that, Rosie?'

I struggled to find a reply. 'I . . . I . . . just think there are other, more deserving people than me, that's all . . .'

Ed shook his head. 'Exactly *how* more deserving? What are you afraid of?'

I punched my hands onto my hips, my anger rising 'Nothing. I just—'

But I didn't get the chance to finish. Ed had rearmed and was sounding dangerously like Mum. 'Rosie, you've made this store a success. So much so that you've single-handedly scored our biggest commission to date with Mimi Sutton. And don't give me that "we can't cope with any more big orders" crap. We don't stop being who we are just because our arrangements are a little bigger. I've already told you, Marnie and I are more than happy to branch out. I think maybe it's time, don't you? So I don't know why on earth you think people wouldn't be interested to read about you . . .' His voice trailed off as understanding dawned across his features. His voice was low and conspiratorial when he spoke next. 'Ah. Yeah, I see now. I get it.'

'What is *that* supposed to mean?'

'This isn't about you being embarrassed. Or about Kowalski's growing too big too soon. This is about you facing the danger of having to open up, for once. You're scared,' he taunted, jabbing his finger at me.

'I am *not* scared—'

'Yes, Rosie, you are. You've read this kind of interview before: name, age and favourite colour isn't enough for journalists these days. Maybe they'll be content to cover the basics about you. But then again, maybe they won't. And *that's* what scares you the most.'

'Ed, I can't believe you're making such an issue out of this—'

'And I can't believe you think I'd fall for your "I'm too humble to court fame" line. I know you too well, Rosie.'

'Well, obviously you don't know me as well as you think. Because if you did you'd understand why I don't want to do the interview.'

Ed's eyes widened and his cheeks flushed as he squared up to me. 'OK, so *tell me* why.'

Halfway between tears and righteous indignation, I struggled to reply. I hate it when Ed and I fight. He always knows how to get right under my skin and it's so annoying that he's better at the whole shebang than I am.

'I . . . I don't know. I just don't want to do it. So stop bugging me and leave it now, OK?' I looked away.

Ed threw his hands up. 'Ha! *Exactly* what I thought! You have no good reason. Except maybe one.'

'Would you just leave it? And since when does my supposed reluctance to share every single detail of my life with everyone have anything to do with you?'

'Because it stops you doing so much.'

'Like what? Like spending my entire life on a never-ending rollercoaster of one-off dates? A million identical conversations, the only difference being the new face on the other side of the table? Oh, yeah, I'm really missing out on that one.'

Ed let out a groan of frustration. 'What I choose to do on my own dates is up to me, don't you think?'

'Absolutely. I just feel sorry for the girls who date you, that's all.'

'Well at least I have a ready supply of willing volunteers to

63

be let down by me,' he returned, looking hot under the collar. 'I don't hear any of them complaining.'

'Maybe that's because you never stick around long enough to find out the truth. You're a *tart*, Ed Steinmann. A single-date, commitment-phobic tart!'

'Well, at least I'm not hiding away pretending I'm happy,' he shot back. 'At least I have a life outside this store. And sure, it may not be the kind of life you'd choose, Miss Highly Principled Florist, but I get by.'

I snorted and looked away. 'Whatever.'

Ed shook his head. 'I don't get you, Rosie. I'm sorry, I just don't. You obviously have stuff you don't want to share with other people – I mean, heck, who doesn't have things hidden in their past they'd rather keep concealed? But you don't even open up to your closest friends. Marnie and I still don't know why you came to New York. It's like there's a whole side of you we know nothing about.'

'You don't need to know,' I replied, pushing the rising fear away at the mention of the subject. 'I am not my past. I don't look back. So just accept me for who I am or don't bother at all.'

Ed crossed his arms. 'Do the interview, Rosie.'

'No. I don't want to.'

Ed's stare narrowed. 'Fine. You don't want to tell the story? Maybe I'll just do it for you, right now.' He strode over to the door and flung it open. 'Ladies and gentlemen of Manhattan, may I present, for your consideration, the great Rosie Duncan, who thrives on each and every challenge her business throws at her, but is *so damn scared* of sharing her heart with anyone . . .'

'You idiot!' I grabbed his arm and dragged him inside, slamming the door shut. Wounded, but certainly not down yet,

I found a renewed impetus to fight and promptly returned fire. 'You're unbelievable, Ed! And this diagnosis of my life from the great Ed Steinmann, amateur psychiatrist, who feels licensed to comment on everyone else's life but never shares his own! The man who must be *so damn perfect* because he's apparently the only person in the whole world with no cares at all?'

My last comment hung in the air like gun smoke. We stopped firing and stared at each other, our breathing quick and short, our minds whirring. But remorse was beginning to kick in.

Ed looked away and took a long, deep breath. 'You have no idea what my cares are, Rosie.' Gone was the anger, replaced instead with a steady, measured defiance.

'And you don't know mine,' I returned. My voice sounded weak and shaky.

Tears stung my eyes. We were like two gunslingers one minute after high noon, waiting for someone to realise we'd been mortally wounded. For a moment, I was determined not to give in. Until Ed spoke.

'Well. Thank you for your honesty. At last I know where I stand.' Real fear hit me as his words sunk in. Someone had to back down. I took a step towards him, scanning his expression in the hope I might catch a flicker of redemption there.

'Ed, I'm sorry. You didn't deserve that. I'm just . . . I shouldn't have said that. I didn't mean it . . . I'm sorry . . . Can we be friends . . . please?'

I could see the tension gripping his broad shoulders as they rose and fell quickly with his breath. Head lowered, staring at the floor, his mussed-up dark hair was almost obscuring the blue eyes that had burned into mine moments before. I waited for his response, fearful of what it might be. It seemed an eternity before he slowly raised his eyes to meet mine. He studied me like he couldn't believe I could hurt him so much.

My pulse quickened, scared I could have blown our friendship for the sake of a few cheap shots. The store was silent except for the slow, rhythmic tick of the clock behind the counter. The world outside seemed to be holding its breath. Watching. Waiting.

Finally, Ed sighed and came close. His hug was warm and forgiving, the scent of his woody cologne mingling with the fresh cotton of his shirt, soft against my cheek. Relief washed over me as I held him tight. 'I'm sorry, Rosie . . .' he breathed, stroking my head. 'I didn't mean it either. It's OK, it's OK now . . .'

Then my tears came, gently at first but rapidly increasing in intensity, until soon I was sobbing hard against Ed's shoulder. For a long time the only sounds were my tears and the insistent beat of his heart. Then he spoke in a soft whisper right by my ear.

'It's time you started to live a little, OK? That's all I'm saying. You have people who care about you and this amazing city to play in. You can trust us with anything, you know?'

Slowly, my tears began to ebb. I pulled my head up and we locked gazes.

'You just have to trust me on this, Ed. I know you care about me and I know I can tell you anything. It's just that the reason I came to New York is something I'm still trying to work out. I can't tell you about it yet. But I promise you, as soon as I'm ready, you'll be the first to know. Is that OK?'

Ed shook his head, the faintest glimmer of a smile appearing. 'You are very lucky to have me as a friend. I'll hold you to that promise, you know, Duncan.'

I smiled back, relieved to be moving away from the subject I dreaded more than anything. 'Absolutely.'

*   *   *

Nobody ever tells you when you're little how hard life can be when you grow up. They don't explain that friendships stop being simple, choices stop being easy and the joys of childhood stop altogether. They just ask you what you want to be when you're older. Whatever the minefield of life could hold in store for you, it seems the answer to this single question is all you need to be armed with. Which is all very well if you happen to have picked something sensible for your future career – like being a doctor or a brain surgeon – but not if, like me, you say you'd like to be Tinkerbell. They smile and pat you on the head . . . but you guess from this reaction that they will be relating your career aspiration at their grown-ups' dinner parties for years to come. And the world of the Grown-Up becomes an irresistibly romantic utopia: one that you would do anything to visit. Well, *almost* anything.

Now that I have reached that illustrious pinnacle, I often find myself wanting so badly to be five years old again. Choices were simpler (orange or blackcurrant squash?) and I knew what I wanted (always blackcurrant). I remember thinking that being a lollipop lady like Mrs Pearson, our next-door neighbour, was really cool (if you couldn't achieve your fairy ambitions, that is). In fact, I spent a whole summer when I was five making my brother pretend to be a car so I could step out in front of him with my homemade paper-plate-and-stick lollipop. When you're a kid, your whole ethos about what makes a good friend can be turned upside down by the offer of a Fruit Salad chew from a 10p mix. Friendships were simple – I'll be your friend if *today* you're not speaking to *her*, but not if you're her friend tomorrow. Come to think of it, though, that's not altogether unlike the way some so-called grown-ups behave right now. Maybe there are a lot of people who are really just big kids in suits. *Especially* in a city like New York.

As I was soon to discover.

At twelve thirty I left the shop and hailed a yellow taxicab to travel to the offices of the *New York Times*. My morning had been incredibly hard. Coming so close to revealing my past to Ed had unnerved me, but sitting in the back of the cab now, I couldn't shake the niggling doubt that I might not get another chance. I shifted my position, still feeling uncomfortable.

'You OK, lady?' asked the smiling oriental taxi driver, looking at me in his rear-view mirror. I managed a smile. 'I'm fine, thanks. How are you?'

This is not always a wise question to ask in New York. You are usually treated to a delightful combination of complaints and strongly worded opinions about anything and everything from the price of rents and the state of the US domestic situation to the possible parentage of the driver in front. Usually, I don't ask. But my mind was attempting to process too many thoughts and needed distracting for a while.

Thankfully today, Ken, my friendly driver, only wanted to talk about his new baby girl. He reached behind the sunshield, pulled out a photo and passed it over his shoulder to me. A smiley lady was pictured holding a tiny, equally smiley baby.

'What's her name?' I asked.

Ken smiled. 'Sunshine. Sunshine Wang. We call her Sunny for short. She'll be five weeks tomorrow. My wife is so proud. She always wanted to be a mother. You know she left a good job on Wall Street to look after Sunny? I'm working double shifts so she can be a stay-home mom.'

'That must be difficult for you,' I sympathised, handing the precious photo back.

'Nah, it's OK, lady.' he replied, taking it from me and carefully replacing it. 'I just spend every day showing New York my little blessing girl.'

I smiled and sank back into the cab seat to watch New York pass by. Buildings, people and traffic merged into a colour-filled blur as I let my aching mind drift a little in the soothing anonymity of the yellow taxi carrying me through the city I love. I was tired; wearier than I had felt in a long time. But there was something else, too: something new. Deep inside me I sensed a change, subtler than the switch from late summer to early autumn, heralding a new season of sorts. The dream last night had brought so many well-concealed memories bubbling back up to the surface and a large part of me felt completely ill-equipped to deal with them. Just as I was six years ago . . . Only this time, there seemed to be even more at stake.

Hiding a secret takes more than simply not revealing it to others. It involves *every* part of you: conscious thoughts, physical actions, untold emotions; and still, even when each is covered and supposedly well-guarded, your work isn't done. In every situation you enter, the ever-present mental checklist remains: conversation topics you should avoid, light-hearted comments that might give more away than you plan, and, most of all, people you shouldn't get too close to, for fear of the secret slipping out.

Whilst I hated to admit it, Ed had absolutely hit the nail on the head earlier:

It's like there's a whole side of you we know nothing about.

There was a good reason why I guarded my secret: I had no intention of letting anyone get close enough to me to find out why I came to America and why I eventually sought sanctuary surrounded by Mr K's peaceful blooms. Only one other person in New York knew what I hid: Celia. And even she didn't know it all.

The cab made a sharp right turn, as if to mirror my train of thought. *But it's been six years*, my conscience ventured shyly, well aware of the magnitude of this suggestion. *Perhaps the dream last night meant it was time to let go of the past?* I caught my breath as the bold assertion glimmered before my eyes like the sunlight glinting along the roof of a taxi speeding alongside mine. How long *should* you hold on to something like this? What would be the worst that could happen if someone else knew? Were Ed and Marnie likely to allow the revelation of my past to affect how they saw me now? My heart rate began to increase and heat began claiming my face as a dim image of the possible scenario played out like a flicker-book film in my mind.

As the cab slowed to approach the home of the *New York Times*, I quickly bundled the debate to the darkest recesses of my mind and forced my thoughts to snap back to the present as I rummaged in my handbag for my purse.

Celia was waiting by the building's grand entrance. I could see her checking her watch irritably and looking accusingly up the street as my cab pulled up. Once out on the sidewalk, I turned to Ken and handed him a few more notes than he'd asked for. On seeing his puzzled expression I explained: 'Something extra for your little blessing girl.' Exit one immensely proud and smiley father.

Celia grabbed my arm impatiently and whisked me inside the building. Before I knew it, we were already in the elevator and up to the fifteenth floor. When Celia is on a mission, you end up moving *fast*.

'I can tell you've had a bad morning, sweetie,' she said, as the chrome doors opened to reveal her office, 'but we'll talk about it later, OK?'

I agreed, not taking the slightest offence. Celia cares deeply about her friends and will get to chat about their important stuff *eventually*, once whatever is driving her at that moment is resolved. I don't mind. I especially didn't mind today. I was in no hurry whatsoever to repeat the whole discomforting soul-searching thing. It felt like my soul had, this particular morning, been scrutinised way too much already.

'Now, about the interview – I'm so thrilled about it! I've got our new features reporter, Josh Mercer, to do it for us,' Celia informed me once we were sitting in her office. 'I thought his take on you would be fresher and more immediate than mine. We'll need a photo too, but Josh can do that when he visits. I suggested he come to Kowalski's to talk to you – is that OK?'

Hands raised in surrender, I had to smile. 'Fine.'

'Wonderful! So, he'll come by Tuesday next week? That way we can be ready for the weekend edition.'

There was no point trying to argue with her. 'Sounds great,' I smiled, hoping I sounded somewhere near convincing.

But Celia was already well into her next task, tapping accusingly on her keyboard and looking decidedly vexed. 'How *annoying* can technology *be*? Oh, where *is* it? I had it on screen just a second ago and now it's not there . . . ah, *here* we are . . .' She stopped, looked over at me and gave a sheepish smile. 'Wait, I'm sorry, Rosie. I haven't even said hi to you.'

I grinned back and gave a little wave. 'Hi, Celia.'

'Hi, Rosie. Sorry.'

'It's OK.'

A new page loaded on her screen and the Celia Reighton Express was off again. 'Now, where was I? Ah, mmm . . . *this*.' She pointed to the screen. 'I wanted you to see this, Rosie. You said you didn't know why people have been asking about you since the Authors' Meet? Well, *this* will show you how big a stir you've caused.' She motioned for me to come to her side of the desk. On screen was an email from Mimi Sutton:

To: celia.r@nyt.com
From: madamemimi@suttoncorps.com
Re: Your wonderful English Rose
Darling Celia,
I just got another call from your florist – who is adorable – she definitely has something new with her designs. I'm impressed already. In fact, I emailed my entire address book today with the news about her store. So now anyone who wants to be anyone in this town will choose her. Though I say it myself, it's another trend New York can thank me for. Rosie Duncan is now, officially, the Next Big Thing. As for Nathaniel Amie . . . well, expect an order from him VERY SOON, if our conversation today was anything to go by – dare I suggest he might be about to finally make an honest woman of Caitlin? We can but hope . . . Don't forget – drinks at Viva Gramercy next Thursday at 6 p.m.
Much love, Mimi x

'How about that?' asked Celia, triumphantly. 'You've only won over one of the most influential women in Manhattan!' I wasn't quite sure what to say. Before I could formulate a reply, Celia continued, 'But the *best* of it is the call I got today.'
'Who from?'
Celia paused for effect. 'Philippe. He is *fuming*, Rosie!'
Uh-oh. Not good.

'What did he say?' I asked slowly, not wanting the answer.

'He's had calls from some of his biggest clients informing him they no longer require his services.'

Incredibly not good. I pulled a face. 'Let me guess – all these people feature in Mimi's address book?'

'Corr-ect!' Celia sang as I groaned and dropped my head into my hands.

'Great,' I yelped. 'Just great. Have you any idea how much trouble this could cause Kowalski's?'

Celia's smile faded slightly. 'How do you mean, honey?'

'Think about it! I don't want to make an enemy of Philippe Devereau. Pretentious and vastly over-priced he may be, but he's also the market leader in New York. His business is *huge*. He is not going to take kindly to a little boutique business like Kowalski's stealing his best customers.'

Celia gave me a hug. 'You're not stealing them,' she smiled. 'You're being *given* them! You worry far too much, Rosie. It's business – and all's fair in it.'

I desperately hoped she was right.

Chapter Six

The next morning was fine and bright. Small wispy white clouds were draped theatrically across the sky and made an impressive spectacle as I pulled back my curtains to let the day in. The silver maple tree planted in the street outside my window was just beginning to adorn itself in its gorgeous yellow-gold hues for the autumn. There was a decided chill in the air as I opened the front door and walked down the brownstone steps onto my street.

It's only a short walk from my apartment to Celia's but it's an essential part of my Saturdays. My Saturdays are as close to sacred as they can be and I guard them jealously. Well, I do now. This was not always the case. When I first took the helm at Kowalski's I felt I had to be there every single minute the shop was open. I developed a disaster-movie mentality to my business; as if the moment I wasn't there things would start blowing up, or a meteor would burst through the atmosphere on a collision course with the shop, or aliens would invade – or *all* of the above – and I would return to find the place gutted with my staff staring blankly at me, asking, 'Where *were* you when we needed you?'

After about a year I got so tired and so stressed out that all my creativity drained and we started to lose customers because my designs became lacklustre. It was then that Ed took me to one side and politely but firmly suggested that I needed time away from the business – for everyone's sake.

'You need some down time, girl,' he told me, in no uncertain terms. 'Marnie and I are more than capable of running the store without you for one whole day. You say you love this city so much? Well, give yourself the time to enjoy it. If you don't, you'll never survive here.' As ever, he was right. So I set aside my Saturdays for seeing Celia and other friends, while Sundays were designated for reading, researching new styles and ideas and generally just spending time exploring my wonderful city, mostly under the wise (if slightly food-obsessed) guidance of Ed.

Talking of food, on my way to Celia's I always make a one-block detour south to visit M&H Bakers, my neighbourhood bakery, to pick up some warm pastries, bagels or muffins for our chats. I love the New York combination of good food and good conversation. I'm not sure why, but somehow it's a whole lot easier to solve life's problems when you're in the middle of demolishing a warm bagel smothered in cream cheese with smoked salmon, or a slice of blueberry pie. Even Ed, who vociferously dislikes the Upper West Side, is impressed by this place.

Frank, the small round guy behind the bakery counter, shouted out as I walked in, 'Good mornin' to ya, Ms Duncan!'

'Hi, Frank. How are you today?'

He waved his hand from side to side. 'Oh, so-so. You know.'

'Uh-huh,' I replied with a nod. No matter how brightly the sun is shining, how many customers he has or generally how good his life is, Frank will *always* find something to despair over. In that sense, he is every inch a New Yorker. 'So,' I asked with a smile, 'what's the special today, then? Anything good?'

Frank placed a hand across his heart and feigned offence.

'Do I have anything good? *Do I have anything good?* I am shocked you gotta ask me! OK, lady, how's this . . .' He reached behind him and lifted a basket onto the counter. 'Check *these* babies out.' I surveyed the basket full of large, golden brown bagels. The smell was amazing – like warm spiced apple pie.

'Wow. Apple, sugar and cinnamon, right? I'll take six, please.'

Frank let out a whoop and clapped his hands. 'She got it!' He spun round and called loudly into the back of the store. 'Hey, Luigi, she got it right again!'

A short, incredibly hairy arm appeared round the door that led to the kitchen, and waved. A thick breathy Italian-American voice called back, 'Dat's great, Frankie!'

Frank turned back and filled a brown paper bag with bagels. 'You're *too* good, Rosie,' he smiled, shaking his head. 'Too good. But we'll get you one day soon.'

In all the years I've come to this place, I've never actually *seen* Luigi. Well, only the incredibly hairy arm and the disembodied voice. Why is he always out back? What if they *have* to keep him there? What if the sight of all of him is simply too traumatic for the average bakery customer? I have this theory about Luigi. Picture the scene: a young couple in Italy go to see the priest in their small village, late at night. In the priest's small, dimly lit kitchen they present their one and only child to him. Horror paints the priest's face and he has to look away. Even in the meagre candlelight the child is hideous. The mother sobs and turns to her husband. In desperation, the father begs the priest: is there anything, *anything*, you can do for our son? His life will be miserable – people will judge him by his appearance, not what he can do . . . The old priest's face is filled with compassion for the plight of this child. He thinks for a while. There is one thing, he replies.

77

If we can teach him a trade – one that brings pleasure to others – he may have a chance of respect . . . The parents place their son in the care of the local monastery, and he learns to be a pastry chef . . . Many years later, after the young man finishes his apprenticeship, he emigrates to America to seek his fortune and finds work – here – at M&H Bakers, and the wise old priest's plan appears to have been successful. But prejudice runs deep – even in the Land of the Free – and while his delectable creations bring undeniable pleasure to Upper West Side residents, his physical appearance leaves him condemned to always, *always* stay out back . . .

'Your imagination is crazy,' laughed Celia, emerging from the kitchen as I recounted my theory, 'but your taste in pastries is *impeccable!*'

I gave a little bow. 'Well, thank you.'

Celia sat down. 'So tell me. What happened to you yesterday? You looked white as a ghost when I saw you.'

I winced as still-fresh images took centre stage in my mind. 'Um, I had a bit of a difficult conversation.'

Celia frowned. 'Oh?'

'With Ed.'

'Oh . . . why difficult?'

'We had an argument about—' I stopped and checked what I was saying. 'You know, it was so petty I can't even remember what it was about.' I looked at Celia, hoping she wouldn't press me. Luckily for me, she was far too concerned with details of what happened next. 'Anyway, it got ugly, I apologised, we made up, and then . . . um . . .'

Celia leaned forward, coffee mug almost spilling with antici-pation. 'And then . . . ?'

'. . . Then I nearly ended up telling him everything. About why I came to America. About what happened.'

Celia gasped, her face a picture of surprise. 'But you didn't?'

I shook my head. 'I couldn't. What's worse was it made me look like I don't trust him enough.'

Celia let out a cry. 'Oh, sweetheart, it doesn't look that way at all.'

'You don't think?'

'Not one bit. But I take it you're not sure you made the right decision?' She was right. I wasn't. Celia reached across the table and clamped a hand over mine. 'You are perfectly at liberty to tell anyone whatever you choose to – or not. Nobody has the right to demand that kind of information from you, honey, you understand?'

I nodded. 'Ed said I'm scared to let people close. And he's right, I am.' I took a long sip of coffee and looked out to the street below. 'I don't know, maybe I should open up more. Maybe it's time. There's just this feeling I have that I'm not ready yet. But then, do you ever reach a point where you know you're ready, or does it just happen?'

Celia straightened up and smiled, squeezing my hand. 'From my experience, you'll discover you're ready when you're in the middle of telling someone.'

'I hope you're right,' I replied, taking another sip of coffee. 'I'm just not sure if I missed my cue there, you know?'

'Rosie, you'll do this in your own time, believe me. I mean, look at when you told me: we'd barely known each other longer than a couple of weeks and out it came, right in the middle of my kitchen, when I was making chicken soup for Jerry.'

I had to smile. My impromptu revelation to Celia had surprised me even more than it had her. 'How New York was I with that? It was almost worthy of its own series on HBO.'

Celia grinned. 'As I recall, our outfits were nowhere near as fabulous enough for that!'

I cast my gaze around the rich creams and dark blues of Celia's living room, noting the antique painting of a jar of lilies, which we often joke about, seeing as she cannot stand the real article. 'The fact is, I think deep down I'm scared of becoming my past. I don't want to become synonymous with what happened to me, you know? I'm scared of being given a label that people use instead of my name – like they do on those reality talk shows: "Monica, 34, Idaho, Desperate for a Baby . . . Jim, 27, Tennessee, Clinically Depressed . . ." I'm frightened of the inextricable link that would be made between my past and who I am now.'

Celia saw my struggle and smiled.

'Rosie, you are a beautiful person all round. You have so many people who love you and accept you for who you are. What happened to you in Boston was *not your fault*, remember? You couldn't possibly have known it was going to happen and you were *not* responsible for the mess that drove you here. Look at you now: you have a successful business, you're in a city you adore more than any sane individual should, and, most importantly, you are a *good person*. The people who matter won't think any differently of you if you trust them with your secret.'

I smiled a little. 'You think so?'

'I know so. Hey, I'm the reporter here. So trust my journalistic instincts, OK?'

'OK.'

'And talking of journalism, I'm sure you'll get a good piece in the Saturday edition. My editor thinks your story is going to be perfect.'

'Really?'

Celia nodded. 'Absolutely. Josh Mercer's not just a great reporter, you know, he also happens to be the finest photographer we've had in years too. Only the best for Kowalski's! You'll be in very safe hands with him. So stop worrying already.'

'Thanks, Celia. Not just for that, for everything.'

She smiled with satisfaction. 'You're most certainly welcome. Oh . . . oh!' she exclaimed, as her thoughts violently altered course. 'I meant to tell you yesterday, but I guess I forgot. How could I forget? It's so *interesting*.' She waved her hands in the air, struggling to catch her breath in the sudden rush of excitement that now had her in its grip.

I giggled. 'Celia, take a breath – calm down – what is it?'

She paused for dramatic effect, then gestured as though presenting a precious gift to me. '*Nathaniel Amie*,' she announced triumphantly, her expression lit by fires of expectation.

My reaction failed to play its part. 'The publisher guy? From the party?' Celia was nodding impatiently. I pretended I was still in the dark. 'What about him?' I asked breezily, appearing unconcerned, but secretly enjoying this new game.

Close to spontaneous combustion now, Celia's eyes were in danger of leaving their sockets. She let out an incredulous cry. 'Oohh, Rosie Duncan, you are *impossible*! You might at least *try* to look interested.'

I could hold my serious face no longer. 'Sorry, Celia. I am interested, honest.'

Celia pulled a good-natured grimace. 'Well, act like it already.'

I clasped my hands together. '*Please* tell me about Nathaniel Amie, Celia, I *beg* you!'

She clapped her hands with delight. 'OK, OK. How about *this*. When you left yesterday I had to go see him about my book – did I tell you I'm writing a book?'

'Only a few thousand times.'

She didn't rise to the bait. 'Well, anyway I am. So, I had to

81

go see him about publishing my work with Gray & Connelle. And he asked me – about *you*!'

'Really?' I said carefully, suddenly interested for real.

'Mm-hm,' she affirmed and then accused me with a wagging finger. 'You didn't tell me you saw him at Mimi's place.'

'I did – er – *bump* into him, yes.' I smiled, hoping Celia didn't know all the details.

She did. 'He told me. He said he walked straight into you and sent you flying.'

'Great,' I groaned, slapping my hand over my eyes.

'No, sweetie, he was concerned he'd hurt you. Really. He said you shot out of the building faster than Britney from rehab. He was worried he'd offended you.'

I groaned again. 'I was *so* embarrassed, Celia. It was *not* the best way to make an impression.'

Celia tried unsuccessfully to stifle her amusement. 'Well, you made an impression on Nate, apparently.'

Outside the sun broke free from the clouds that had been steadily building all morning, and bright rays flooded into the room.

'I did? What did he say?'

'He asked me about you. How old you are. Where in England you're from. How long you've lived in New York. What brought you here in the first place.' She saw my expression. 'Don't worry. I didn't tell him. I just said you were offered a job in Boston, Ben invited you to stay with him so you could take it up and then later you decided to switch career and move here. Acceptable?'

I couldn't hide the relief in my voice. 'Yes – most acceptable – thank you.'

'You're welcome. As I was saying, he wanted details. He said he might just have to come see you at the store. He has *very* expensive tastes when it comes to flowers. He orders *a lot*, you know . . .'

'He does? You're such a journalist, Celia.' I moaned. 'OK, OK, yes, I want to know *why* he orders so many flowers.'

'Well, you know he's been dating Mimi's daughter Caitlin?'

Suddenly, the reference I remembered seeing in Mimi's email made sense. So the Caitlin in question was Caitlin Sutton. No wonder Mimi wanted a wedding so badly.

'No, I didn't know. Is she nice?'

'Hmm – *nice* is not the particular adjective I'd choose.' Celia frowned, her eyes twinkling. 'Try manipulative, self-centred or, in fact . . .'

'. . . Just like her mother?' I ventured.

'Ha! You got it. But gorgeous, though.'

'Ah. I see. The old adage: "You can forgive a woman anything so long as she looks great"?'

Celia's eyes lit up. '*Definitely* . . .' She stopped and changed her mind. 'Well, no, actually. I guess Nate just figures it makes good sense to be with her. She's rich, she's influential and, well, it undeniably adds to his profile to have her on his arm at parties.'

That was odd. From the little I knew of him, Nate didn't seem to be the type of guy who looked for 'trophy' girlfriends.

'How come she wasn't at the Authors' Meet, then?'

Celia grimaced. 'She *hates* books. And writers. *Especially* writers. She's a businesswoman – things have to be cut and dried, black and white. Artistic people confuse her. She thinks creativity is something people with no intelligence resort to in order to find work.'

'Bet she loves you, then.'

'About as much as my mother loves waiting. And I guess you can imagine what she'd make of you. But she has one weakness – flowers. Lots of them. Nate orders her several bouquets a week . . .'

'Oh, well, that's sort of romantic.'

'. . . At her *specific* request,' Celia finished. 'But she only has them in her office. She likes her colleagues on Wall Street to think she is adored. People who visit her home always comment on the flowers in every room, yet I have it on good authority that the house staff are instructed to remove them as soon as visitors leave. Now, I don't know if this is true, but I heard she gave Nate a list of bouquets she expected to receive on Valentines Day – the bill ran to over $2,000! She even specified the *exact* words to be written on each accompanying card.'

'Right . . .' I said, amused. 'Romance and spontaneity not her strong points, then?'

Celia rose and collected our mugs to take to the kitchen for refilling. 'It's more like a necessary evil for her.'

'And for him?' The question was meant to be inside my head, but instead it inexplicably found a handy escape route out through my mouth. There was a pause. I could hear bird-song outside and coffee being poured in the kitchen. And I swear I could hear Celia *smiling*.

She returned and sat down. She handed my mug back, wincing slightly as the heat from its contents scorched her fingers. 'Now *why* would you want to know that, Rosie?' she asked slyly.

I blew on my coffee to avoid eye contact. 'No reason, no reason at all.'

When I got back to my apartment later that afternoon, there was a message from Ed. 'Rosie, if you get this before 5 p.m, call me at Kowalski's. Things are happening, girl. *Big* things.'

I didn't wait to call back. Instead I caught a cab and got there as fast as I could.

Marnie met me at the door, her beaming smile almost as bright as her yellow braids. 'Rosie, it's *so* exciting!' she chirped, grabbing my hand. 'Come and see!'

She pulled me over to the counter and showed me a pile of order forms, each completed in her swirly handwriting. Ed looked up and was about to approach us when the phone rang. He held up a hand and grabbed the receiver. 'Yep, this *is* Rosie Duncan's store,' he said down the phone, grinning at me and giving a thumbs up. 'How can I help?'

'It's been like this *all day*,' Marnie explained excitedly. 'It's crazy! We got in and all was quiet, then at nine o'clock everything went nuts. People calling and coming in – all asking after you. We even had *Martha Stewart's* PA call earlier! They all want to order. We've filled the order book almost right up till Christmas and we've got three weddings booked for June next year.'

Ed finished the call and came over, brandishing another order form with delight. 'Jon O'Donner,' he proclaimed. '*Only* the CEO of the biggest acquisitions company in New York. We got the order for his daughter's wedding next fall. It's worth serious money, Rosie.'

While I have to say I was excited, I was also a little anxious, knowing most of the new clients were probably Philippe's ex-customers.

'Mimi Sutton's recommended us to her entire circle,' I explained. 'They're leaving Philippe in droves because they're scared of offending her.'

Ed's smile disappeared as he saw the concern in my eyes. 'Ah. Not good, then. Still,' his smile returned, refuelled by hope, 'we have always been more than a match for him artistically. Kowalski's is due some recognition, don't you think?'

I had to agree. Of course it was OK. It was an open market, after all. Philippe Devereau had no more right to all of it than we did. And Kowalski's could handle the new business, no problem. We'd need to take on extra staff, but that would be fine. We might need another delivery van. But that would be OK, too. I smiled at Marnie and Ed and allowed myself to feel the tiniest shiver of excitement. 'I think we've finally arrived in New York!' I replied, as Ed let out a whoop and we grabbed each other in a big group hug.

I decided to stay at the store, breaking my sacred Saturday vow. There was no way I could leave all this excitement. I took over the phone duty and watched in amazement as order after order came in. Now, I've always known Kowalski's had the potential to do well – I've always been the one telling everyone else that when things have been decidedly to the contrary – but this level of sudden success took even me by surprise. Putting aside my concerns about Philippe, I resolved simply to enjoy the moment, aware that it couldn't last at this pace indefinitely.

Just before we were due to close for the night, Ed caught my hand and led me into the workroom at the back of the store. He shut the door and turned to face me.

'Rosie. About yesterday . . .'

I took a step back. 'Ed, I . . .'

I was stopped in my tracks as Ed's fingers gently touched my lips.

'That row shouldn't have happened yesterday. I guess we both said things we didn't mean, right? For my part, I'm sorry.' He registered the relief in me. His eyes softened. 'I just thought you might be worrying.'

I smiled back. 'Thanks, Ed. I'm sorry too.'

'Then it never happened, huh?'

'What never happened?'

For a moment, we faced each other with mirrored grins. Then he clapped his hands, making me jump.

'Now, what is the owner of the most happening floristry business in this town doing indulging in idle chat? We have *work* to do!' He laughed, flung open the door and marched off onto the shop floor.

Watching him leave, I leaned against the tall worktable and revelled in the peace returning to my mind. It was good to welcome back a certain sense of normality, even in the light of today's extraordinary trading. I felt exhausted from the marathon of emotions I had been running. Now finally, it seemed, I was nearing the home straight. Allowing myself the tiniest ounce of smug satisfaction, I walked slowly through the flower stands to rejoin my assistants. Hope filled every part of me, opening dusty dark windows to let the sunlight inside. For the first time in a long time, it felt like I was turning a corner in my history. My life, like my shop, was blooming again. Things were going to be wonderful from now on.

I was wrong, of course.

Chapter Seven

I have always counted optimism as one of my best features. I think it's always been a part of me; there isn't a time I can recall ever really being without it. That doesn't mean to say I don't lose sight of it when things get tough. Believe me, it's been challenged enough over the last few years – not least with the events directly preceding my arrival in New York. But despite everything, it remains, sometimes obscured by worry, sometimes shining brightly for all to see – a constant in an ever-changing world. Mum says she's always relied on that quality in me. Come to think of it, James – for all his self-obsession – has often said it too. Being able to see a bright side has always proved to be my saving grace.

'If you have hope, you are better than a millionaire,' Mr Kowalski used to say, 'because you can give it away every day and it will never run out. You, Rosie, have a large account of hope. So use it to give to the people you meet that have none.'

Mr K lived as he spoke. And, for a man who had endured terrible poverty, prejudice and hardship, this was no mean feat. He always said that God – 'my papa in heaven' – was the one who helped him. Mr K wasn't religious like you'd expect a man of his generation to be. His faith was who he was. To coin a phrase, he walked the talk.

'Rosie, Papa is the only friend who has never judged me, let me down or beaten me up. He loves me. End of story. It don't matter what I do, what mistakes I make, he loves me whatever. That's all the riches I need, *ukochana*, and they're free every day.'

Somehow, I always felt life was calmer – brighter, even – when Mr K was around. Just before he left to return to Poland, he handed me a small, hand-painted glass plaque. It bore the words, 'Nothing is Impossible with God'. Someone gave it to him when he was really young, he explained, and it helped him remember that he wasn't alone.

'Take it, Rosie,' he'd said. 'Let it remind you, too. Papa's watching.'

Today, it hangs at the back of the counter in pride of place, and when I see it, I sense a little bit of the calm he brought returning.

It caught my eye again on Monday, as I was refilling metal buckets at the front of the shop with gorgeous lavender hydrangea and sweet-scented freesias. In sharp contrast to the previous Saturday, the shop was blissfully quiet, though it was still early – only 9 a.m. I smiled sadly as thoughts of Mr Kowalski came to mind. It's always a bittersweet experience to remember him. I still can't quite believe he isn't here any more. I expect him to call any minute, or for his friendly old face to appear in the shop doorway. Somehow the world seems just emptier without him in it.

Lost in my thoughts, I didn't see the silver limousine pull up outside. It was only when the front door opened so fast that the bell nearly came off its fixings that I noticed the tall, perma-tanned, Versace-clad man striding in. Behind him scurried two nervous-looking assistants, both impeccably dressed, both holding notebooks and both attentive to the man's every move.

He possessed an immense presence that seemed somehow to fill the entire store and command the undivided attention of everyone.

'Rosie Duncan.' It was meant as a question, but appeared more like a statement of disdain.

'Mr Devereau. Welcome to my shop. How are you?' I responded, my heart racing. I had put him out of my mind over the weekend and had almost forgotten the fact that Kowalski's had apparently emptied his order book overnight.

'Cut the sweet talk,' Philippe snapped. 'You know why I'm here.'

'To admire our designs?' suggested Ed, suddenly appearing from the workroom and standing protectively at my side.

Philippe glared at him. 'Don't mock me, Mr Steinmann. I want to know what the hell you . . .' he frantically searched for the word, '. . . *tiny, insignificant* people think you are doing here.'

'We're selling flowers, Philippe. What are *you* doing here?' I calmly replied. Far from diffusing the situation, this served only to inflame Philippe's anger.

'How *dare* you? How *dare* you presume to even pretend to know more than me? Because it *is* pretence, Ms Duncan, merely pretence. You cannot hope to aspire to even a *fraction* of my business expertise and artistry—'

Coolly, I cut across him. 'But it would appear your customers don't agree, Mr Devereau.' Light the blue touchpaper. Stand well back . . .

Boom! Philippe went stratospheric like an expensive bleach-blond rocket. 'So it would appear. Now, I don't know *what* you have said to entice them from my company – in the most underhanded and unprofessional way, I may add – but rest assured, Ms Duncan, they *will* be back. Soon. You are merely a passing phase, a fad. You can't possibly fulfil my clients' demands. I am the only one able to do that. I fulfil demands you can't possibly imagine.'

Oh, I can, I thought. I've heard the rumours. But I didn't say it. Philippe's anger was far too entertaining right now.

'*My* emporium is a palace compared to this . . . this *hovel*,' he spat. 'Talent-starved traditionalists like yourselves can only dream of owning a business like mine!'

I had dared to venture into the sacred halls of Devereau Design just once: what I saw made me glad to own a shop like Kowalski's. Far from being a welcoming sanctuary of form, colour and scent, Philippe's store was little more than a showroom: no flowers were available for passing trade and a large security man on the door was seemingly employed with the solitary task of dissuading any would-be browsers from setting foot over its hallowed threshold. Walls, ceilings, display surrounds and even the doors were uniform white; the counter, with its black granite top, resembled a hotel reception desk more than a service area; flowers were regimented into stiff, contrived displays – unearthly lit in identical white display boxes by tiny green, blue and magenta spotlights, frozen and unnatural like chilling exhibits in some kind of futuristic freak show. A few staff members paraded around in harshly tailored black suits, wearing matching disinterested expressions, each sporting communication headsets and carrying black clipboards. It was as if the flowers in the stark white boxes were prisoners on display. Worse still, the whole space was devoid of scent – it was like walking into Starbucks without smelling coffee. Completely wrong. It makes me shudder even thinking about it now – the lack of life in the place was almost sinister and completely alien to what a florist store should be like.

'I sincerely hope that Kowalski's never looks like your

emporium,' I returned. 'We believe in allowing the flowers to be themselves – something you and your team will never understand.'

'Kowalski's is *nothing*, and your questionable talent for floral art is so limited that I fear your business will shortly collapse. In fact, I intend to see that it does.'

'Threaten her again and I'll personally throw you out,' Ed growled, stepping to within an inch of Philippe's face. I caught his arm and pulled him gently back to my side, where he stood glowering at our unwelcome guest.

'For your information, Mr Devereau,' I said, white-hot anger seething beneath my cool, steady voice, 'I have not *stolen* your customers. They were recommended to try Kowalski's by another of your clients – Mimi Sutton. I believe you know her? If they have *chosen* to leave you, it is entirely their choice and nothing to do with me. You do not have the monopoly on floristry in this city, Mr Devereau, and neither do I.'

'That may be true, Ms Duncan, however I will not tolerate Kowalski's pathetic attempts at stealing my *considerable* share. I pity you, not only for your over-inflated idea of your worth in this city, but also for your abominable designs. I intend to drive your business into the *dust* . . .'

Ed leapt forward and flung the door wide open. 'OK, buddy, you've said enough. *Out!*'

'But I . . .'

I moved to Ed's side. 'We'd like you to leave. Immediately, please.'

Philippe's mouth opened, but nothing came out. His sapphire eyes flashed, his face flushed bright red and he let out an exasperated cry. Spinning round, he strode magnificently out, the two assistants scurrying in his wake. The door slammed and the shop was quiet. Ed and I exchanged glances.

'*Not* a happy bunny,' I grimaced.

'Hmm,' agreed Ed, thoughtfully. 'I'm afraid Kowalski's has just made a very dangerous enemy.'

'Good morning!' Marnie arrived, stopping abruptly in the doorway when she saw our worried expressions. 'What? What happened?'

'Philippe Devereau just called by to wish us well,' Ed smiled nonchalantly.

Marnie's eyes lit up. 'Philippe? He's *so gorgeous*. What did he want?'

Ed picked up a pile of order forms and moved towards the workroom. 'Oh, you know, he was in the neighbourhood so he thought he'd say hi.' He turned back at the door and gave a wide-eyed grin. 'Oh, yeah, and he mentioned he was gonna drive Kowalski's into the ground as soon as possible.' He disappeared into the back room.

Marnie's smile fell and she rushed over to hug me, her blue curls bouncing as she did so. 'Oh, Rosie, that's *awful*,' she wailed. 'What are we going to do?'

I didn't know. But this was not, I resolved, the time for doom and gloom.

'We're perfectly OK,' I said, hoping my voice matched my optimistic statement. 'We'll be *fine*. What does Philippe have to offer that we don't?'

Marnie looked despondent. 'He's been Floral Artiste of the Year for the past ten years. His business is worth multimillions. He scouts the world for the best designers and gets them. Ooh, and he has the biggest range of tropicals and exotics to order—'

I interrupted her. Philippe was looking too invincible. 'Yes, I know, *OK*, but he doesn't spend time with his customers. Or provide free delivery. Or . . .' I was struggling already, '. . . or . . .'

'Offer them coffee?' Marnie suggested, a little less hopefully than she'd intended.

I snapped my fingers. '*Or* offer them coffee. Exactly! But *we* do. We have,' I continued, walking over to my beloved coffee machine and patting its cracked lid, 'the ultimate advantage right here.'

'Old F?' asked Marnie, still unconvinced. 'Old Faithful is our secret weapon?'

'Absolutely. Philippe Devereau *may* be able to head-hunt the world's finest for his business, but he'll never be able to make a decent cup of coffee for his clients, will he?'

Ed appeared in the workroom doorway. 'Maybe we should give Old F a raise,' he suggested, 'or promote him to CEO.'

I smiled confidently. 'So, if we all stay positive and make sure Philippe doesn't try to head-hunt our coffee machine, Kowalski's will survive this!'

Ed and Marnie made a brave attempt at a helpful cheer, but their expressions spoke otherwise.

After the excitement of Monday, Tuesday arrived with little fanfare – so much so that I almost didn't remember Celia had arranged my dreaded *New York Times* interview for later that day. In fact, when the young, ginger-haired reporter entered my shop, I initially mistook him for a student seeking part-time work. It was only when he produced his card that I saw who he was.

'Josh Mercer, *New York Times*? Celia arranged an interview today?'

'Yes, of course, I-I'm sorry,' I stammered, extending my hand for him to shake. 'I'm Rosie Duncan and this is my co-designer, Ed Steinmann.'

Ed and Josh shook hands. 'You guys grab the sofa and I'll

make some coffee,' Ed offered, much to Josh's delight. It turned out that he'd spent the morning interviewing warring parties involved in a dispute over a controversial neighbourhood regeneration project in the East Village.

'So, great news story but not so great if you're expecting a decent cup of coffee,' he explained, flopping down on the old leather sofa and rummaging through his canvas satchel for his notebook. 'Disgruntled people aren't predisposed to good hospitality, I'm afraid.'

'Well, you won't find disgruntled locals here,' I joked as Ed arrived with two mugs of coffee. 'Just friends, flowers and a great cup of medium roast.'

'I love the vibe in your store,' Josh smiled, sipping his coffee and looking around as if he was mentally photographing every angle, feature and detail. 'I mean, Kowalski's is so different from the other Upper West Side florists – like Devereau Design. This isn't a boutique – it's . . . more personal, I guess. How do you keep it that way?'

'We have a long tradition of serving the neighbourhood,' I replied – and right on cue the silver bell over the door tinkled cheerily as a lady in her eighties entered, laden with shopping bags. Ed rushed over to her, gathering the bags from her as she feigned protest.

'I'm fine, Edward. Quit fussing so!'

'Now, Mrs Schuster, what kind of gentleman would I be if I didn't assist you?' Ed smiled, offering his arm, which she accepted, her hand the colour of rose-tinted tissue paper daintily placed on his sleeve as he escorted her to a small white wicker chair by the counter.

'You're just like my late husband, God rest his soul,' she smiled. 'Upright and uptight – that was Henry. And I've told you before, young man, you *must* call me Delores.'

Josh was watching Delores Schuster with intense interest, his ballpoint pen hovering thoughtfully over his notepad as his reporter's eyes drank in every detail.

'She's a regular?'

'Oh yes. Mrs Schuster's been coming to Kowalski's since her family got their apartment on West 71st Street, over forty years ago. She was one of Mr Kowalski's first customers and she's been coming here ever since.'

'Do you find it difficult to balance the day-to-day side of the business with the growing number of large-scale commissions you're now taking on?'

It was a good question, but one I hadn't really considered before. We don't have to make a special effort to keep both the day-to-day and the event stuff running. It is just what we do – and something I love my business for. Yes, sometimes we are so busy I can't even tell you what day of the week it is and, equally, in our quieter times, there are sometimes days on end where you can count the customers venturing into the shop on the fingers of one hand. But that's the nature of the business: you can only work with what you have available at the time. The unpredictability would scare many, but I enjoy it.

'Despite my shop now increasingly catering for larger events, we've never lost the neighbourhood business – and that's what I love,' I explained. 'One minute you're sitting with a prospective bride discussing thousand-dollar arrangements; the next you're chatting with someone like Betty Myers, who's been a Kowalski's customer for over twenty years, and is a former waitress in Buck's diner just round the block from my house, designing a $25 gift basket for her niece. It's all part of the mix.'

'Unlike places like Devereau Design,' Josh repeated, raising a telling eyebrow.

I couldn't resist a smile. Philippe is the kind of florist that my mother despises. 'All fuss and bluster,' she'd proclaim with trademark disdain. 'Nonsense and showmanship are no substitutes for real talent. Swanning about in their designer suits and stapling banana leaves together like it's the height of skill – charging a King's ransom for greenery, I ask you! *Any* idiot can do that!'

'Devereau Design caters for a very different market from Kowalski's,' I smiled, deciding to be diplomatic. 'Their customers expect something a little—'

'Who is this young man?' Delores suddenly appeared beside me, making Josh jump.

'This is Josh Mercer, from the *New York Times*. Josh, let me introduce you to Mrs Delores Schuster, one of Kowalski's most distinguished customers.'

Josh shot to his feet, respectfully offering his hand to Delores. 'It's a pleasure to meet you, Mrs—'

'Call me Delores, please,' she answered, her cheeks flushing slightly. 'You're here to interview Rosie?'

'I am indeed.'

'Oh well, in *that* case,' Delores began, bustling in between us and lowering herself shakily onto the sofa, gripping our arms for support as she did so, 'let me tell you all about Kowalski's and why it's the greatest florist's in the whole of New York.'

For the next thirty-five minutes, Delores regaled Josh with long, rambling accounts of her many visits to the store, each one accompanied by generous helpings of Schuster family trivia along the way.

'. . . So *then* there was the time my late husband, Henry – may God rest his soul – forgot his aunt Bertha's Golden Wedding Anniversary. Well, *you would not believe* the commotion in the family. I tell you, it was like the day they elected Nixon and my grandmother swore she wouldn't leave the house again while he was in the White House. Aunt Bertha was the kind of woman you *don't* forget, take my word for it, young man – she had a holler that would scare a werewolf – and she comes storming into our apartment, face all red like a tomato, and skirts flapping like laundry in a tornado, and she yells, "Fifty years of marriage to the same dumb putz and all I wanted to make my sorry life happy was for my one and only nephew to remember!" But my Henry was fast at thinking, if nothing else. He took her hand and he walked her all the way to Kowalski's – *three whole blocks* he walked her – and he walked straight up to Mr Kowalski and he said, "Franz, would you please tell my beloved aunt Bertha about the surprise arrangement we're planning for her Golden Wedding Anniversary, which she thinks I forgot?" And – would you believe it – Mr Kowalski stands there, bold as buttons, and calmly describes the most beautiful basket of flowers you ever heard of. Well, Aunt Bertha was not a woman to be lost for words – I mean, even when her husband, Charlie, proposed to her he had to endure a ten-minute lecture on her expectations of marriage, you know – but two minutes of listening to Mr Kowalski and she was a changed woman. And *then* – to finish it all – Mr Kowalski explains that the reason for the unfortunate delay is that the flower warehouse was all out of pink lilac, which he knew was her favourite flower – which it *was* – but there's no way he could've known that because, right up until my Henry marched in there, he hadn't even known Aunt Bertha existed at all! So that's why we come to Kowalski's – even though Mr Kowalski is long gone, probably laughing about the whole Aunt Bertha scenario with my Henry right now. Young Rosie here is a woman after his heart; he

99

taught her well, you know. Have you got all that down in your book now, Joshua?'

Josh nodded dumbly, his eyes glazing over.

'You'll forgive me if I don't pose for a photograph,' Delores said, nodding at the camera in Josh's lap. 'I'm not one for publicity, you see. Well, I can't stay here chatting all day. I got things to do, people to see. Edward! Help me up, please!'

Ed stifled his mirth as he assisted Delores back to the counter.

'Like I said, Kowalski's is first and foremost a neighbourhood florist,' I smiled, shaking my head at Josh's amused expression.

He checked his list of questions. 'So, how did an English rose like yourself come to be blooming in New York?'

Somehow, I knew this phrase would end up in the article – being friends with Celia has prepared me well for the ways of journalists.

'I moved here from Boston just over six years ago, worked for a while with Mr Kowalski and then took over the business when he retired,' I replied, hoping that this would be enough information. Of course, it wasn't.

'And were you a florist in Boston?'

'No.'

'Oh? What was your previous profession?'

My heart began to thud as my defences prickled. 'I was creative director for a small advertising firm.'

'Which one?'

'It doesn't exist any more.'

I could tell Josh could sense my discomfort. He looked up from his pad. 'All the same, it would be good to have some background . . .'

'My mother is a florist, so I learned the trade from watching her and helping out in her shop when I was young. Then after university I chose to enter advertising and – wound up here, eventually.'

'Forgive me, but I'm curious: why leave your country behind to come to the States?'

'Well, look around you: New York is fabulous. What girl wouldn't want to live here? The shops, the restaurants . . .' I answered breezily, trying without success to deflect his train of thought.

'I see. But *England* – it's so . . . so . . . infinitely more interesting than here, don't you think?'

'Well, I—'

'I mean, all that history and literature and amazing country-side; to be able to walk daily in the steps of Shakespeare, Byron and Keats; to visit the great places of learning like Oxford and Cambridge; to revel in the generations of royalty and stand in the birthplace of the Industrial Revolution – surely there was enough to keep you there?'

Josh's monologue on the greatness of my home country took me aback and I – like Aunt Bertha, many years before – found myself lost for words.

A crimson flush spread over his pale cheeks and he ran a hand self-consciously through his mop of copper-coloured curls. 'Wow. I am *so* sorry, Ms Duncan. I kinda got carried away there. I adore your country, as you may have gathered.'

Relieved that the interview had strayed from my past, I smiled. 'Not a problem. Yes, I love all of that about England. Although Stone Langley – the small town where I grew up – is nothing like the regal England you'd expect. But New York stole my heart and this is where I want to be, more than anything.'

After the interview was concluded and Josh had taken all the photographs that he needed, I saw him to the door.

Ed, now a gentleman-at-ease following the departure of Delores Schuster, watched me with intensity. 'Good interview?'

'I think it went OK.'

'Like I said it would.'

'*Yes*, like you said it would, O Wise and Noble One.' I gave a small bow.

'Good,' Ed replied with a self-satisfied air. 'So how come he grilled you about ending up here then? Checking you had your Green Card?'

'He seems to be a bit of a serious Anglophile. Couldn't understand why I wanted to live here.'

'Hmm – rainy middle England, where the beer is warm and the summers are wet, versus glorious New York with Mrs Delores Schuster and her not-so-potted family histories? Tough call,' he grinned. 'Go figure.'

A few hours later, as Marnie and I were replacing the large displays in the window, the workroom door swung open and Ed entered, battered brown leather jacket slung over one arm.

'So long, sad single people,' he breezed over his shoulder as he strode through the store.

Marnie and I exchanged glances.

'Where are you going?' asked Marnie.

'I have a date. A *hot* one.'

'But it's a Tuesday night. Who goes out for a date on a Tuesday night?'

'*I* do,' Ed replied, supremely pleased with himself. 'I admit, a Tuesday date is a first for me in quite some time, but – to quote the lovely young thing in whose delicious company I will be spending this unusual night – "I just can't wait till Friday." So who am I to keep the lady waiting, eh?'

I winked at Marnie. 'She's due in court on Friday for a heinous crime.'

Marnie's eyes lit up. 'Or her parole officer visits on a Friday.'

'Or maybe she's fleeing the country on Friday after a bank heist she's doing on the Thursday . . .'

'. . . Which she's *planning* on Wednesday . . .'

'. . . So it *has* to be Tuesday night!'

Ed stared at the pair of us, shaking his head slowly. 'Well, thank you for your support, ladies.'

'Aw, Ed, ignore us and just go and have a lovely time.'

'Thanks, Rosie.'

'. . . with the crazy jailbird master criminal!' Marnie squeaked, sending us both into hysterical giggles once again.

Ed groaned and opened the door. 'Fine. Laugh all you want, but *I* will be loved up and happy tonight,' he turned in the doorway to deliver his parting shot, 'unlike *you* guys.'

Ouch.

I had to laugh. Ed claimed not to be seeking relationships, preferring the delights of general non-commitment dating instead.

'I'm young, I'm in no rush to meet The One – whatever that means – or settle down, or have kids. I just like to date. So sue me.'

Meeting people was something Ed was incredibly adept at. His cousin's lawyer a few weeks back was *nothing* compared to some of his dates. It was almost as if everywhere he went he would fall across eligible women: 'I was out last week and I stopped for a paper and right next to the newsstand was *this woman* . . . I swear, I was just walking down Amsterdam Avenue when this beautiful girl stops me and asks me for a date . . . I took my dry-cleaning to Mrs Ling's and got chatting to this *babe* . . .' I never met any of the ladies in question (or should that be 'questionable ladies'?), but that was probably because most of Ed's dates lasted only a few weeks, so far too short a time to introduce them to the Kowalski's family.

Next morning, the Ed who walked into the store was very different from the Ed who had walked out of it the night before.

'So, how did the date with Tuesday girl go?' I asked eventually, after Ed's uncommon, unshaven and decidedly dishevelled silence had reigned supreme for nearly half an hour.

Ed stripped the leaves from a long-stemmed red rose in one swift motion, adding it to the bouquet forming in his left hand. 'Fine.'

'Right . . .'

I surveyed him carefully as he moved along the flower buckets, choosing, sizing and stripping leaves off the selected blooms as he went. Turning the untied bunch in his hand to check the arrangement, he then dropped his head and slunk back to the counter. 'Oh, who am I kidding? It was a disaster.'

'Really?'

'There's no need to look so smug about it.'

'I'm not. Honestly.'

'I mean at least I *date*, right? Not like you.'

I let that one go. 'Absolutely. So what about last night?'

He grabbed a length of raffia from behind the counter and wound it irritably around the gathered stems. 'Hmm. Well, it wasn't a total disaster, I guess. Sarah was perfectly nice and decent, attractive, good company, you know? But . . .'

'But what?'

He tied off the bouquet, picked up a pair of scissors, moved to the bin on the other side of the counter and trimmed the stems with one cut. 'I dunno, Rosie. I just didn't feel it was worth pursuing. Crazy, huh?'

'No – no, I don't think it is.'

'Well, *I* think it is. What's wrong with me? I date all the time, a whole selection of perfectly acceptable women. But none of them, you know, *fits*.'

'Fits what? Your ideal? Your lifestyle? Your apartment?'

'Hilarious. You missed your calling when you chose to be a florist. There's a stand-up mic somewhere with your name on it. No, I mean they don't fit *me*.'

'Ah, right. Well, I think you'll find *that's* the point of dating.'

'Which of course *you'd* know so much about,' Ed added, quick as a flash. I kicked myself for not seeing that one coming.

'The difference is that I don't feel I need another person to make me feel complete,' I shot back.

'Do you *really* believe that, Rosie?' He threw the bouquet to me and I caught it as he passed and disappeared into the workroom, shaking his head. His last comment hung accusingly in the air above my head – a question I wasn't willing to answer.

Not yet.

Celia met me on Wednesday night at Bistro Découverte at the edge of Riverside Park, not far from her apartment. It's one of my favourite places. In the summer, it's a great place to eat al fresco, your table lit by the rows of tiny white lights across the front deck and the sounds of Café de Paris music drifting lazily in the air. Celia and I come here often. It's quieter than the other bistros in the area, and many tourists don't even know it exists. The usual clientele consists of writers, artists and the occasional journalist or celebrity actor, and the hum of conversation is low, welcoming and homely. Tonight, however, the hint of autumn chill drove us indoors. As we began to eat our main course, sharp splats of rain peppered the window and the little lights outside were tossing about in the breeze.

Celia shivered. 'I can't believe it's nearing fall already,' she moaned. 'Where has summer gone? Before we know it, it'll be Thanksgiving, then Christmas. Did I tell you I got a call from Jerry today?'

The question was so deftly inserted into her conversation that I almost missed it. 'Jerry? He *called* you?'

Celia gave a fatalistic shrug and took a mouthful of wine-poached salmon. 'Eleven months he's been gone and then today I get a call.'

Celia and Jerry have been partners for well over fourteen years and were, it seemed, blissfully unaffected by each other for all of that time. She went on her assignments, he went on his business trips. They spent three weeks together every summer at their beach house in Martha's Vineyard, and New Year with his family in Wisconsin. They were a typical high-achieving New York couple. Until eleven months ago. Jerry announced he was 'off to find himself', packed a suitcase and disappeared. His company didn't know where he was. His friends didn't know where he was. Even his mother didn't know where he was: which was incredibly worrying, as Jerry's mother is the domestic equivalent of the FBI. Her powers of investigation are unsurpassed and could prove invaluable to the State one day, should it ever need to know exactly, in minute detail, about an individual (eating habits, connections, rumours, bowel movements and so on). I'm convinced she has a vast, underground network of spies, who regularly feed back to her at apparently innocent locations. Come to think of it, she hosts an awful lot of dinner parties and is forever on the phone, so maybe 'Yes, Rabbi, you're invited to dinner Wednesday at eight', *actually* means 'Thank you, Agent 482, your information has been received and you will be rewarded well.'

It was unclear whether Jerry's disappearance was a life-changing, traumatic experience for Celia or just an annoyance. She rarely even mentioned his name and I knew she had been on more than one date recently. Even now, as I faced her across the table, I couldn't detect any kind of emotion in her measured expression. Except, perhaps, resignation.

'So how did he seem? What did he say?' I asked.

Celia shrugged again and looked over my shoulder. 'That he's sorry. That he's in Palm Springs and the golf is good. That he wants me to forgive him.'

'But he's not coming home?' I asked, trying to judge her countenance, which flickered slightly.

She nodded.

'Oh, Celia . . .'

She held up a hand and looked me square in the eyes. 'It's fine, Rosie. Honestly, I'm fine. He can go – no, he's welcome to go. I'm amazed we lasted as long as we did. We never married – what can I say? Such is life. There isn't anyone else, though. And I don't think I'd care if there was. Besides,' she added, her wry smile making a welcome comeback, 'I hear *toy boys* are all the rage for women over forty now. So maybe I'll get me one of those. *Maybe* I'll give Nate Amie a call . . .' her eyes twinkled naughtily, '. . . unless you have any objections, that is?'

It was obvious that the Jerry topic was now closed, so I played along, glaring at her. 'I don't object at all. But Caitlin Sutton might have something to say about it.'

'Aha!' Celia's face was a picture of triumph. I had obviously fallen for her bait. 'Not if what I heard today is anything like the truth.'

I leaned forward, curious to hear more. 'So, tell me, then. What did you hear?'

Celia looked shocked. 'Rosie Duncan, I do believe you are enquiring about a *man*!'

I protested. 'Only out of sheer curiosity and the need for a bit of juicy gossip.'

'Like I believe *that* . . . Well, I was talking to Brent Jacobs this morning, and he told me – ooh, and make sure you don't forget he's—'

'Coming to my shop tomorrow morning, yes, I know. What about Nate?'

'Patience, Rosie! I'm coming to that,' Celia stated, delighting in my suspense. 'He told me he was at a theatre premiere at the Lincoln Center yesterday and he saw Mimi, Nate and Caitlin. Right in the middle of the performance, Caitlin stormed out. And Nate didn't follow her. Then Mimi received a call at the after-show party and had a *blazing row* with Nate, in front of everyone. He called his driver and left, and Mimi was heard to say that he had not heard the last from her on the subject. She was in such a foul mood that she totally ruined the party and most people left as soon as she did.'

I was still interested. 'And . . . ?'

Celia sat back. 'That was it.'

Disappointment is always a difficult thing to hide. 'Oh . . . What was Brent's take on things?'

Celia took a sip of Pinot Gris. 'He was as much in the dark as everyone else. But his theory is that Caitlin and Mimi have been pressing for marriage and Nate won't play ball.'

'So, does this mean he won't be ordering those large and frequent bouquets from me, after all, then?' I moaned with a smile.

'Well, Brent reckons he'll—' she was interrupted by the waiter, who informed her she had a phone call. 'Excuse me one second, Rosie. I'll be right back.'

I refilled my glass and sat back in my chair to look out at the driving rain and wildly swinging fairy lights. Why I found this information interesting, I couldn't exactly pinpoint. After all, I didn't really know Nate Amie. Only that he had a laugh that could fill an atrium and knew nothing about lavender. Yet somehow I found myself intrigued that his name had cropped up in conversation so often this past week.

Celia returned about five minutes later, shaking her head. 'Can you *believe* that?' she asked. 'I leave them alone for five minutes and all hell breaks out.' She saw my mystified face and took a breath. 'Sorry, honey. I've got my sister's twins over for a few days. Didn't I tell you? Well, I have. They're on vacation from Washington State and wanted to see New York. It appears they decided to throw a party while I was out and have played music so loud that my good neighbours called 911. I need to go sort it out. I'm sorry, sweetie. Call you tomorrow?' She grabbed her bag, kissed me and hurried away to her engagement with New York's finest.

The waiter approached. 'Will madam be ordering dessert?' he asked.

'No, no, thank you. I'll settle up, if I may.'

'Sure. No problem.' He disappeared again. I finished my wine and took a last look out at the windswept Hudson. For the briefest of seconds, my mind flashed up an image of a lopsided grin and a soft, low voice. Surprised, I checked myself and rose to leave.

As I stepped outside into the icy rain, I wrapped my coat tightly round my body and began the short walk home. The wind whipped at my hair and New York seemed to be asking me the same questions that already filled my mind, despite my desire to avoid the subject.

It was an unusual relief to click the key into the front door of my block and jog the three flights up to my apartment. Once inside, I closed the door and leaned against the frame, breathing in the familiar scent and willing my heart to slow down. I was removing my coat when the intercom beeped. I jumped.

'Hello?'

'Hi, sis. Aren't you going to let your big bruv in?' chirped a familiar voice.

'James!' I squealed. 'Come on up!'

I pressed the door release button and within a minute my brother walked in. It's funny that I'm always shocked at how tall he is whenever I see him. He looked tired, but thrilled that he had surprised me by arriving with no warning. He dropped his heavy leather bag on the floor, scooped me up and spun me round.

'Rosie! It's so great to see you,' he yelled. 'Are you surprised?'

'Too right I'm surprised!' He plonked me down and I hugged him again. 'I can't believe you're here! Mum said you'd be too busy to visit.'

James grinned, nut-brown eyes sparkling with mischief. 'I *swore* Mum to secrecy. I wanted to surprise you. Can I stay?'

'Sure, no problem. I'll have to make up the couch for you. Is that OK?'

'Perfect,' James said, dropping into the nearest chair. 'I'm so tired I'll sleep anywhere. I'm not proud, y'know.'

'Good job my couch is an incredibly comfy sofa bed, then,' I replied, going into the kitchen to put the kettle on. 'Tea?'

'How about Yorkshire Tea?' James asked, appearing by my side and brandishing a box. 'I've got you some Marmite too. And Dairy Milk.'

I let out another squeal. I don't miss many things from home, but these gifts are like the Holy Grail for me. 'Thank you so much!' I yelped, ripping open the tea box and dropping two bags into the pot. I poured the boiling water and savoured the long-missed aroma as the tea began to infuse. '*Heaven*,' I breathed.

'How long are you staying?' I asked, once the tea was made and we had sunk down into the sofa with our mugs of steaming nectar.

James looked offended. 'You want me to leave already?' he laughed. 'I'm kidding, Rosie. I can only stay till Saturday morning, I'm afraid. Then I need to be back at the DC office for four days, before I fly home again. Look, are you sure it's OK to stay with you? I could book into the Four Seasons, if not.'

'Why on earth would you want to stay at one of the best New York hotels when you can rough it here with me?' I asked.

James smiled. 'I'd much rather be with my darling little sis than in a swanky place like that. *You* provide decent breakfasts. And your prices are unbeatable.'

'Undoubtedly,' I laughed. 'Now, can I interest you in room service, sir?'

A quizzical expression spread across his face. 'What's on the menu?'

'Well, we have a rather special tub of cookie-dough ice cream – it's a house speciality. Might I interest sir in a small helping?'

'Absolutely. But make it a large one, please, I'm starving!' James cried, clutching his stomach in mock agony. As I struggled to release myself from the sumptuous embrace of my sofa, my brother grabbed my hand and genuine affection filled his eyes. 'It's so good to be here, Rosie. Thank you.'

As a younger sister I have learned to be wary when my brother is being sentimental. These fleeting glimpses of affection usually occur when James is in trouble and needs me to bail him out. Later, once he was settled on my couch and I was in bed, I found myself wondering if this was to be another of those occasions. Quickly, my optimism gene sprang into action and I decided that this might actually be a time when my gut reaction was wrong. Self-centred though he may be, surely even James was capable of conveying real, heartfelt emotion sometimes.

Wasn't he?

Chapter Eight

'What are you doing this evening?' James asked, next morning, as we sat eating breakfast.

I thought for a moment. 'Nothing. Why?'

He tapped the side of his nose. 'I'd just like to do something nice for my darling little sister, that's all.'

He's in trouble, I told you, said a little voice in my brain.

I ignored it and smiled at him. 'What sort of nice, exactly?'

James winked. 'Rosie, you're always so suspicious. Just make sure you've got something posh to wear, OK, because I've got reservations at somewhere rather special tonight. And *I'm* paying.'

I frowned. 'If you've already made reservations, why did you bother asking me if I was free tonight?'

James surrendered. 'Curses, rumbled again . . . OK, OK, I checked your diary while you were making the tea last night and I called the restaurant when you went to get the ice cream.'

'OK.' The explanation would suffice. For now.

ARE YOU LISTENING TO ME? demanded my conscience, stamping its foot. *He is in big, big trouble and you're going to get involved in it. Again. You don't need this!* I let out a breath and mentally pushed the voice into a corner.

113

'Is everything OK?' asked James, seeing my expression.

I smiled. 'Everything's fine.'

Marnie was waiting for me as I arrived to open up the shop. She sat slumped against the windowledge looking like she'd lost a million dollars and found a nickel. Even considering her rollercoaster of a love life, it was extremely unusual to see her like this.

'Hi, Marnie. How are you?'

She stood up as the shutter lifted and we walked inside. 'I'm good.'

'You're obviously not,' I said, switching on the lights and taking off my coat. Marnie followed me into the workroom and hung her coat up next to mine. 'Want to talk about it?'

Her eyes blinked quickly as tears welled up. 'Please. But I don't know if you can help.'

I smiled. 'Let me try. How about you sit down and I'll fire up Old F? And,' I added, reaching into my bag and producing a warm M&H Bakers bag, 'I took the liberty of getting some of Luigi's double choc-chip cookies this morning, so you can help me with their disposal.'

Marnie's eyes lit up and she threw her arms round me. 'Thanks, Rosie. You're a good friend.'

Once Old F had noisily produced a jug of rich, smoky coffee, I joined Marnie on the well-worn brown leather sofa by the window. This is another long-serving fixture at Kowalski's and, I now realised as I sat down, yet another secret weapon in our struggle against Philippe. When customers are deliberating designs it is so much more civilised to seat them in a comfy corner, surround them with flowers and let them enjoy the fruits of Old F's hard labour. Ed and I rescued the sofa from a closing-down coffee house not long after I took over from

114

Mr K, and I still have fond memories of Ed risking life and limb to stop the traffic on West 68th Street as I tried to push it across the road. Marnie certainly seemed to be responding to its comfort as I sat down next to her.

'OK, Rosie. Here's the deal,' she began, nibbling a cookie. 'I've met this guy at my community theatre. His name is Mack, he's from Brooklyn but now he lives in East Village and he's twenty-two years older than me. He lectures English at Columbus University and he's one of the Hudson River Players' directors. He's *so amazing*, Rosie. You know, it's like everything he says is worthy of recognition? I'm totally in awe of him.'

'So what's the problem?' I asked.

Marnie sighed and looked into her coffee. 'He doesn't even notice me. I overheard him saying to one of the others that he's just come out of a long, lonely marriage and he's got his eye on someone in the class. I kinda hoped it would be me, you know?'

'How do you know it isn't?' I asked.

'That's just it. I *don't* know,' Marnie wailed. 'I haven't slept for a whole week. I can't get him out of my mind. How do I approach him? What do I say?'

'I'm not sure you're asking the right person,' I smiled. 'After all, I'm not the world's greatest authority on relationships . . .' I looked at Marnie. She wore a smile, but it was weak and transparent. It was time for a different tack. 'Um, OK . . . Why don't you invite him out for a drink after class? Say you'd like to get to know him a little better. Or . . . tell him about your work here and invite him over to see your latest project? Just try to be his friend for a while and see what happens.'

Marnie looked up at me. 'But what if he's repulsed by the sight of me?'

I patted her hand. 'Not possible, mate. You're gorgeous.

Concentrate on becoming his friend. Look at it this way: if he likes you, you'll have opened the door for something to begin; if he doesn't, well, then you'll have gained a friend you already respect. You win either way. OK?'

'OK,' Marnie said, still uncertain but brightening slowly. She hugged me again. 'Thanks, Rosie, I'll try.'

The bell on the front door chimed as Ed arrived. 'Ugh!' he exclaimed, covering his eyes with his copy of the *New York Observer*. 'Female bonding alert! Get me out of here . . . I need air . . .' The paper was whipped away, revealing an eager smile. 'No, wait – tell me *all* the juicy details.'

Marnie and I stood up. 'None to tell,' Marnie said, walking past him aloofly.

'Great,' Ed moaned. 'As usual I'm discriminated against purely because I have no womb.'

'Ooh, Ed with a womb – now there's a scary thought . . .' I began.

'Hey, I'd be great with a womb,' Ed protested, following me over to the counter. 'I pride myself on being fashionably in touch with my feminine side. Despite the fact that it's obvious to anyone I'm an undeniably awesome hunk of manhood.'

'Oh, yeah?' Marnie laughed. 'Name your feminine attributes then.'

'I understand flowers,' he replied proudly. 'I eat chocolate when I'm depressed. I'm not averse to a good bit of gossip every once in a while. So spill the details, sisters!'

Marnie and I exchanged looks. 'Should we be worried?' I asked.

Marnie giggled. 'Does he have a weekend name?'

Ed looked mystified. 'A weekend name?'

'Oh, you know – "At weekends my name is Janice."'

The look on Ed's face was worthy of exhibition at the

Guggenheim. 'The only name I answer to at weekends is Mr Highly Desirable,' he answered haughtily, as Marnie and I collapsed in hysterical laughter. 'Oh, yeah, go ahead. Laugh. But I'll have you know I turned down two – that's *two* – offers of dinner for tonight from a couple of very lovely ladies who are impatient to date me. Because tonight, my friends, I am going to a Broadway show with a certain lady by the name of *Yelena Ivanova*.'

His careful emphasis was wasted on Marnie and me. Our blank expressions revealed that we had absolutely no idea who this was.

He groaned. 'Yelena Ivanova – *you know* – "The Face of Jean St Pierre"?'

'The model?' Marnie asked incredulously. 'How did that happen?'

Ed smiled. 'She's going out with my best friend, Steve, who's a photographer for several big fashion houses. He got called away to a shoot in Hawaii but he was supposed to be taking Yelena to see Kevin Spacey's latest play on Broadway tonight. So there was a spare ticket. So I offered to step in.'

I grinned. 'Ah, Ed Steinmann, Kowalski's resident chivalrous knight in shining armour.'

Ed shot me a sly smile. 'That's *Sir* Ed Steinmann to you, peasant! Although, maybe not so chivalrous. See, I heard Yelena's on the verge of breaking up with Steve so I'm hoping to catch her on the rebound.'

'What?' Marnie exclaimed. 'Ed, you're *awful*!'

'I know,' he said happily, disappearing into the workroom, 'but that's why you love me.'

The morning continued with more calls and customers than on a usual Thursday. Kowalski's was obviously still benefiting from the Mimi Sutton Effect.

At eleven the door opened and Brent Jacobs strolled in. His extra-wide smile appeared as soon as he saw me.

'Rosie! Hi! Hope I'm not too late?'

'No,' I reassured him, 'you're right on time. Welcome to Kowalski's.'

'Do I smell coffee?' Brent beamed, his eyes wide and innocent as a child attempting to win sweets with charm.

'You most certainly do. Milk and sugar?'

'Black with two, thanks.' A sudden sheepish look temporarily usurped the grin. 'You don't mind, do you?'

'Not at all.' I smiled, handing him a hand-painted blue and white mug bearing the store's name.

'Cute mugs. You do these yourself?'

I laughed. 'No, my friend Lucy has a ceramics store in West Village and she made them for me.'

We sat down on the sofa and I presented my design books for Brent to view. After much discussion, he decided on a large hand-tied bouquet of yellow and cream roses, lilies and gladioli, accompanied by dark green foliage, eucalyptus and rosemary sprigs. Yellow was, I discovered, his wife's favourite colour and the hue of her bridesmaid's dresses on their wedding day. Rosemary was her middle name and the name Brent called her when nobody else was listening. On their honeymoon they had visited his relatives in Australia and had been taken to see koalas munching eucalyptus in a local nature reserve . . . I filled out the order form and arranged delivery for the following morning at ten thirty.

'Have you spoken to Celia recently?' Brent asked.

'Yes, I saw her last night,' I replied, not looking up from the counter.

'Did you hear about Jerry?'

I stopped writing and looked at him. 'Yes – how did you . . . ?'

'I heard. Word gets around. My wife works for his old company. How did Celia seem to you last night?'

I decided to be noncommittal. 'Like her usual self, I guess. Maybe a bit quieter.'

Brent's concern remained etched across his face. 'Hmm. I care about her, Rosie. And I don't think she's coping as well as she shouts out to the world.'

My discomfort was increasing. 'Brent, maybe you should talk about this with Celia, not me. I'm not sure how much of her situation she wants others to know.'

Brent smiled his reassurance. 'Listen, kid, Celia and I go back a long, long way. You needn't worry. If you speak to her again before I do, just tell her that Old Bee Jay is still there for her, OK? She'll know what I mean.'

Still in the dark, I smiled. 'Fine, I'll do that.' I handed Brent his copy of the order.

'Thanks. So, did you hear what I saw at the Lincoln Center, Tuesday night?'

My interest level jumped up a few thousand notches. 'Celia told me. Have you heard any more?'

'Ah, we're always ready for gossip here,' quipped Ed as he walked past with an armful of roses. 'Who's the object of rumour today?'

Brent grinned. 'A certain young man who was *very impressed* with Ms Duncan a couple of weeks back at Celia's soiree.'

Ed raised a quizzical eyebrow. 'Oh? You didn't tell me about *that*, Rosie.'

My heart had begun a bid for an Olympic sprint record and I tried to change the subject. 'Ed, have you phoned Patrick's with our order for the weekend yet?'

'Did it earlier.'

'Good . . . um . . . then isn't there something you should be getting on with *out back*?'

Ed leaned against the counter, obviously revelling in my discomfort. 'You know, as a matter of fact I'm just taking a break. So I have a moment to listen to any extremely interesting information Mr Jacobs cares to share. *So*, this young man . . . ?'

Brent could see my embarrassment rising and honourably declined to conspire against me. Gossip thus denied for the second time that morning, Ed groaned and returned to his work.

As he was leaving, Brent inclined towards me and whispered, 'Rosie, right now I'm working on further details. But let's just say Nate isn't as in love as *certain journalists* would have you believe.'

He said his goodbyes and left the store.

Brent's last comment buzzed around my head all through lunchtime and well into the afternoon. Which was annoying and intriguing in equal parts.

At two o'clock Marnie left early for her art class and I joined Ed in the workroom to begin an order due to be delivered at close of business. Any illusions I may have had of Ed forgetting about Brent's comment dissipated like steam from Manhattan drains when I saw the tell-tale sparkle in his eyes. Mr Steinmann was determined to have his fun and nobody would stop him.

'Nice guy, that Brent.'

I drew up one of the wooden stools around the workbench and started stripping leaves from a carnation stem. 'Yes, he is. I told you that you'd like him.'

'Great guy. Very observant.' He pulled a length of ribbon from a spool on the bench and began looping it skilfully into a bow. 'Especially when it comes to certain guests at Celia's events.' He lifted his gaze and winked at me.

I shook my head, adding vivid orange lilies to the cream carnations and greenery held in my left hand. Much as I didn't want to rise to the bait, I had to concede that the subject was unavoidable. 'So, ask me.'

His eyes returned nonchalantly to the Cellophane he was arranging around the large bouquet before him. 'Ask you what?'

I let out a long groan. 'About the guy? He's nobody, Ed, really. Celia's been stirring again, that's all.'

'I see. Sure, OK . . . So, this Mr Nobody . . . is he a *special* Nobody?'

'What? No! He's just a guy I met at the Authors' Meet the other week. He seems perfectly nice, I suppose. I've only spoken to him twice, so I don't know any more.'

'Twice, huh?' If Ed's eyebrow got any higher, NASA could send an astronaut up with it.

At that moment, however, someone came into the store. Relief spread from my head to my toes. *Saved by the bell. Thank you, God.* I breezed past Ed on my way to the shop floor. 'Sorry, Ed, there's a customer – I'd better go . . .'

Ed growled in defeat as I left.

'Good afternoon, welcome to Kowalski's,' I chirped happily.

The new customer was inspecting one of our large displays by the door. When he heard me, he spun round. 'Hi.'

I froze. 'Hi,' I responded weakly.

Nate Amie grinned as he approached me. 'Your store is cool,' he said, offering his hand.

I regained my composure and accepted his greeting. 'Thanks. I like it.'

'So do your customers, it would seem.' Nate smiled, his deep brown eyes circumnavigating my shop and then finally returning to me. 'I heard you're rapidly gaining favour with the great and the good of New York.'

'Yes. Thanks to Mimi Sutton, it seems . . .' I checked his expression, but it didn't alter. 'Although I think it's going to bring me more problems than benefits. I'd prefer people to recommend me on my own merits, rather than being a token of someone else's—' I stopped, shocked at myself. 'I'm sorry – I shouldn't have said that.'

Nate's amusement was evident as a smile danced across his face. 'No, no, I agree with you. It's no fun being a pawn in someone else's power game. Believe me, I know.'

Hmm, interesting . . . But while the temptation to press him further on this comment was immense, I fought it valiantly and changed the subject. 'So, how come you decided to sample the great delights of Kowalski's today?'

'I was in the neighbourhood and . . . Oh, wow, you have coffee too?' He moved to the counter and laughed when he saw Old F. 'I see the culprit, but I don't believe it. Tell me, how can a smell so good come from something so battered?'

'Don't mock Old Faithful till you've tried his coffee,' I defended, walking behind the counter and patting the machine protectively. 'Appearances can be deceptive, Mr Amie. Don't be fooled. You are looking at one of the great, undiscovered talents of New York City.'

Nate turned to look straight in my eyes and I caught my breath. 'Oh, really? I'm always waiting for my perceptions to be disproved. So, surprise me . . .' Seeing my expression, he added, 'If that's an offer, I'd love a coffee.'

As I prepared Old F for another vociferous onslaught on fine espresso blend, I checked myself. For absolutely no reason whatsoever, my hands were shaking. *Get a grip, girl*, the little voice in my mind scolded me. *This is not – repeat, NOT – a big deal. He's simply come to see the shop, like any other customer. You are in control, repeat with me now, you are in control.* I am in control, I repeated with silent internal obedience. Really, I am ... I poured three mugs of coffee and put two on the counter. Picking up the other, I looked up at Nate.

'Here's your coffee. Feel free to look round ... I'll just take this to my co-designer.'

'No need,' Ed said, appearing beside me and nearly getting a hot caffeine shower in the process. 'He's here. Hi, I'm Ed Steinmann, Rosie's co-designer.'

Nate smiled and they shook hands. 'Nate Amie – I'm an admirer of Rosie's work.'

'That so?' Ed turned to me with an innocent smile, thinly veiling the mischief within. 'Good, well, I must carry on her great work, so if you'll excuse me ...' As he passed me, he whispered, 'Mr Nobody, huh? *Ni-i-i-ice* ...' I resisted the urge to trip him over, resorting instead to a forced smile in his direction.

Nate sampled his coffee and let out a low growl of satisfaction. 'Now that is *great* coffee.'

I patted Old F lovingly. 'You see, I told you.'

'Indeed you did.'

There was a pause. We exchanged smiles and sipped our officially certified Excellent Coffee. Now, at this moment I suppose I should have been thinking of the next highly efficient and consummately In Control thing to say. But I wasn't. I was too busy noticing the way Nate's right eyebrow lifted at a complimentary angle to his lop-sided grin. And how the shadow of his brow darkened his eyes, increasing the intensity of their gaze ...

'So ... I decided to come visit because I need to make an order,' Nate stated suddenly. 'It could be a regular order,' he added.

123

'That's fine,' I replied, my control returning.

'It's just that I don't know what to . . . uh . . . I guess I need some advice, Rosie,' he frowned. He put his mug down on the counter and twisted it slowly from side to side. 'Here's the thing: I've ordered I don't know how many of these bouquets before, but they're all the same. I want to send something different now. I . . . I *need* something different.'

I nodded. 'Ah, I see you're experiencing what we in the business call The What Do You Get For The Woman Who Has Everything dilemma?' I smiled calmly, mentally awarding myself several brownie points. *Thank you, Celia* . . . It's amazing how one titbit of background info about Nate's love life had transformed me now from Regular Florist to Official Font of All Knowledge.

His eyes widened slightly. 'Yes – how did you know?'

'I just guessed,' I replied, hoping my air of wisdom didn't belie the truth. 'Well, I suppose it all comes down to what you want to say to the lady in question.'

Nate shook his head, confused. 'Sorry, you lost me. What I want to *say*?'

I took a breath. It's always difficult attempting to explain how I work. Right from the first time I ever designed a floral arrangement, I found I instinctively knew what I wanted to say. 'Say it with flowers' is an old cliché, I know, but it's essentially what I do in my work. My designs aren't solely based on colours, species or scents, although these are obviously important components. Instead, each one has a meaning, an emotion to convey, with a deeper significance than just a nice thought. Mr Kowalski used to say there are many reasons why people choose to send flowers – celebration, commemoration, declaration, apology, regret . . .

'But you got to look beyond the reason and convey the Big

Story. It's not the What but the Why. Why is this man saying sorry? Is he apologising for a mistake he made, or for the man he finds he has become? You gotta be detective, doctor and counsellor when you create something, believing that what you create will have the power to change somebody's life. Design with your eyes, your wisdom and your heart.'

People have said that I design as if I intimately know the person who is going to receive the flowers. I can't explain it any better than Mr K put it, really – I design with my eyes, my wisdom and my heart.

Nate's eyes focused on a point a million miles away. Thoughts I wasn't party to washed over his face and his voice was quiet when he spoke. 'I . . . I guess I need to think about what *my* story is, then. I need to think . . . I'd like to come back and hear more, Rosie. And talk about it. Would *you* talk about it with me? Look, I have some time free tomorrow – about the same time. Can I make an appointment for coffee then?'

This was utterly unexpected, but inexplicably welcome. 'Of course,' I replied softly. 'No problem at all, Nate.'

Once Nate had left the shop, Ed appeared from the back room like an inquisitive meerkat from its burrow. 'Hmm. So that'll be *three* times you've spoken, to date. And would I be correct to assume he's just booked a fourth?'

I ignored him and flipped the Open sign to Closed.

'Aw, come on, Rosie, you gotta tell me now. I just shook hands with your secret guy. We're practically family.'

'I'm going to cash up,' I replied coolly, going to open the till. But Ed never gives up. Not without a fight, anyhow. He reached over, pushed the till drawer shut, stole the key and sprinted to the other side of the room, holding his trophy aloft.

'Don't be an idiot, Ed. Give it back please.'

He held out his hands, a wicked expression lighting up his azure-blue eyes. 'So come and get it, already.'

'Fine.' Annoyed, I walked over to him and attempted to retrieve the key. But it was no use. As my fingers touched the palm of his hand, Ed lifted it high above his head, laughing as I fell forward and ended up face to face with The Grateful Dead on his faded vintage T-shirt.

'Well, *hello* there,' he grinned down at me as I rested awkwardly against the warmth of his chest, ruffling my hair with his free hand before stepping away, the key still frustratingly out of reach. It's one of the things I hate about being five feet four inches tall; it means irritatingly tall people like six-foot-two-inch Ed always have the upper hand on me. Literally, in this case.

After much jumping about and other failed tactics like pleading, demanding and tickling (which, I must confess, made the fight far more amusing than annoying because Ed has a giggle like the Mayor of Munchkinland), I resorted to the vertically challenged person's ultimate move. Mustering every scrap of strength possible, I stamped on his foot. Surprised and shocked by pain, he doubled over and I skilfully caught the key as it fell from his hand. Works every time.

'Too easy,' I mocked. 'Never underestimate a shortie, tall guy.' Flushed with victory, I swaggered back to the counter and resumed my task.

'That's *so* not fair!' Ed wailed, clutching his wounded limb.

'Sorry. Are you OK?'

'Oh, sure, I'm fine,' he shrugged.

I let him sweat it out for a while. But once I'd finished cashing up, it was time to put him out of his misery. Grabbing his hand, I led him to the sofa and we sat down.

'OK, mister. You want details? I'll give you details.'

Ed did his best to feign disinterest, but his eyes were far too twinkly for someone who didn't want to know what I was about to divulge. 'Well, in the light of the callous injury you've just inflicted on me, I reckon that's the least you can do,' he sniffed.

In truth, there wasn't an awful lot I could tell him. I wasn't sure why Nate had chosen to visit today. After all, I still didn't know a great deal about the man. But I could see there was a lot more to him than first impressions suggested. And I found that . . . well, *intriguing*. Ed smiled as I tried to explain this. The only way I could represent my gut feeling was by comparing Nate to an iceberg. Which, inadvertently, revealed my secret theory about Ed, when I added: 'He's just like you.'

'You think I'm an iceberg?' he repeated, more than a little taken aback.

'Yes. In a good way, though.'

Ed ran his hand through his dark brown hair and shot me a quizzical look. 'What's *good* about an iceberg?'

I have to admit I was stumped for an explanation, but I made a valiant attempt anyway. 'Well, you're a good iceberg – meaning there's a lot more to discover about you than first meets the eye. You know, as opposed to a bad iceberg, as in bad news for the *Titanic*. You get what I'm saying?'

Ed's expression remained unchanged. 'I'm an *iceberg* . . .' he muttered, as though considering an awful diagnosis and finding a deeper implication that I hadn't meant.

I put my head on one side and peered at him, my hand lightly resting on his knee. 'Trust me, it's a good thing. I find you . . . intriguing.'

He laughed despite himself. 'You sound like Celia Johnson in *Brief Encounter*.' He adopted a clipped, old English film actor accent. 'Do you find me *terribly, terribly* intriguing, darling?'

'You are such an idiot sometimes,' I smiled.

'Hey, but this is only one-tenth of me,' he replied. 'Imagine how bad the other nine-tenths could be.'

I squeezed his leg and let my eyes rove around my shop, so still and quiet now the Closed sign was turned. Outside New York continued to pulse with life, the rush-hour traffic along Columbus Avenue crawling at a snail's pace; a colourful procession of frustration past our window. 'Glad I'm not stuck in that today.'

'The subway is a great invention,' Ed agreed. 'So Nate, huh? Reckon we'll be seeing a lot more of him, then?'

I took a breath and looked him straight in the eye. 'You know, I think we might.'

So there we sat: my hand still on Ed's knee and his hand stretched across the back of the sofa, his wrist making the lightest contact with my shoulder. He smiled but his eyes were strangely serious as they bored into mine. Taxi horns blared in the traffic jam along Columbus and the clock behind the counter marked the passing seconds with its long, measured ticks. Just when the scrutiny was beginning to feel uneasy, he spoke. And it wasn't what I was expecting to hear.

'I'll make the delivery tonight, Rosie.'

'Oh.' Disorientated by this sudden mood-shift, I stuttered, 'Y-yes, great – if you don't mind?' I tried to gauge the emotion in his eyes. 'You *don't* mind, do you?'

'No problem.' He turned and walked briskly to the back room, then reappeared carrying the pair of bouquets.

'You have the paperwork?' he asked, looking straight at me. His smile was bright as ever but somehow the tone was wrong.

I reached behind the counter and handed him the order sheet. He thanked me and I followed him to the door, switching off the lights as we stepped outside into the noisy buzz of the city. As he went to leave, I grabbed his sleeve. 'Ed, are you . . . is everything good here?'

Ed leaned forward and gently kissed my cheek. 'We're good, Rosie. Stop worrying. I'll see you tomorrow.' He smiled, turned and began to walk away quickly.

Remembering something, I called after him. 'Ed!'

He spun round. 'Yeah?'

'Have a great time with Yelena tonight.'

Without answering he raised a hand, saluted briefly and resumed his journey.

I watched him until he disappeared round the corner of the next block. A ball of anxiety rolled to the bottom of my stomach. I pulled the shutter down, locked it and slowly set off on my journey home.

New York was as loud, hurried and colourful as usual, but as I passed familiar blocks and crossed familiar streets it seemed to fade into the background somehow. Questions flitted around my ears like the insistent butterflies inside me. Nate, Ed, Marnie's love life, Mimi and Caitlin Sutton, and that *thing* about 'certain journalists' that Brent had mentioned – all appeared like jigsaw pieces before me that didn't quite fit.

I was two blocks away from my street when I heard a familiar shout.

'*There* you are, sis!' James appeared at my side, face flushed and happy. 'Mind if I walk back home with you?' He held up a brown paper grocery bag. 'I've stocked up from Dean & DeLuca.'

'Then you're more than welcome to come home with me,' I laughed, suddenly glad of the company.

Chapter Nine

I remember watching the six o'clock news one time with Mum when I was about eight. When I was growing up there were several things we always did together: watching the news was one of them. Mum disliked the 'game-show host' journalists on ITV, preferring instead the serious-faced, crisply spoken newsreaders of 'the good old BBC'.

But one occasion sticks in my memory because a very out-of-the-ordinary news event was headlining. Some British hostages were finally released from Beirut. I remember Mum telling me that the three bearded, excruciatingly thin and tired-looking men had been missing for five years. We saw one of them speaking at a press conference. He was smiling – telling the world how he and his fellow hostages had thought this day would never arrive. I remember commenting on how happy he looked to be free.

'His *face* may be happy, but his eyes aren't,' Mum had replied. 'Always look at the eyes, Rosie. They'll tell you the real story.' Her own eyes were filled with tears – and I remember her going up to the screen and covering the bottom half of the ex-hostage's face. Sure enough, his eyes showed pain, anguish and fear. When Mum removed her hands, the smile returned but the eyes remained dead.

I learned to look for those signs in people's eyes and consequently witnessed awful truths in others as I grew up. I saw it in Mum's eyes when she heard about Dad. I saw it in Ben's eyes just before I left Boston. Worst of all, I saw it in my own eyes almost every day since New York adopted me. Sometimes I wish Mum hadn't told me about the eyes thing. Sometimes the truth is better hidden away inside.

Ed's eyes had scared me that day. There was a whole other story going on in those eyes. And I couldn't read it completely. Their piercing blue was usually warm and mischievous, impatiently awaiting any chance to sparkle. But that afternoon his eyes had been cool, questioning – guarded, even. I hadn't seen that before and it unnerved me. He had said things were OK. His smile and friendly kiss said things were OK. So I should have believed him – I *did* believe him – yet that stubborn question mark remained. He had said he was OK, but his eyes maintained their silence.

On the walk home, I noticed something odd in my brother's eyes too. Though James chatted happily about his day and joked about the people he'd met, I couldn't shake the feeling that there was something he wasn't telling me. It had been steadily building since he'd arrived and he had done nothing to dispel my suspicions.

It was still on my mind two hours later, when James and I ventured out again to Blue: One, the current restaurant of choice in New York. I was stunned that James could even get a drink in this place, let alone reserve a table. Celia could normally get a reservation anywhere, but even *she* had to wait a month for one here. The restaurant sat beneath one of the top hotels just off Broadway and its clientele included theatre stars, television celebrities, directors and lawyers. It was said that Blue: One had a waiting list four pages long for bar and waiting staff, due mainly to the fact that jobbing actors regarded it as *the* place to be noticed by the People Who Mattered.

James and I were shown to a table towards the back of the restaurant. Blue was undisputedly the theme here. The walls were painted dark navy and illuminated by aquamarine up-lights, whilst tiny blue lights dotted like cobalt stars around the main halogen spots in the turquoise ceiling, adding to the intimate ambience of the venue. Efficient waiters scurried about in white shirts and navy-blue trousers, carrying blue linen cloths over one arm. A large aquarium was set into two of its walls, filled with a plethora of tiny, multihued fish, which appeared to be moving with the same momentum as the staff.

The waiter brought us each a mojito and we ordered our meals. James took a sip of his drink and looked at me. 'Right, Rosie, what's up?'

'Sorry?'

'Don't give me that. You've been quiet all evening.'

I smiled at him. 'I'm fine, James, really. I had a busy day. That's all.'

'Phew! I thought you had a major problem and I'd have to work at you all night to get at it. What a relief!' James has never been the World's Most Tenacious Bloke. Which is one thing I like immensely about my brother: I know he's too lazy to pry too far. Satisfied with my answer, he continued, 'So, I had fun today . . .'

'You did?'

'Uh-huh. I did some cheesy sightseeing first thing – you know, Empire State, Statue of Liberty, Macy's – and then I caught up with an old friend from Oxford.'

'Who?'

'Do you remember Hugh Jefferson-Jones?'

I did. My friends and I called him *Huge* Jefferson-Jones, on account of his considerable height, build and the devastating impression he left on our young minds the moment we saw him. We weren't alone in calling him this: so too (allegedly) did a considerable contingent of his fellow female students and at least two of his female lecturers, although for an entirely different reason . . . Huge used to come to our house and stay for weekends so he could go rock climbing and sailing with James. I was about sixteen at the time and all my friends fancied him like mad. Huge was the ultimate charmer, one of life's naturally gorgeous people. And he knew it – even at nineteen years old. Standing tall at six foot four, he dwarfed my brother (much to James's annoyance) and had a body like I'd only ever seen in action movies. He was a star of the rowing team, a leading light in the drama society, a general all-round hero. Hailing from a millionaire's family, he spoke the Queen's English with a deep, velvet-smooth voice, which made my tummy flutter. I had a *massive* crush on him but, seeing as my vow to never, ever get married was still intact at that point, I resolved to be happy just looking.

'How is he?' I asked.

James smiled. 'Still Huge. Still popular with the ladies. And still a good old toff, to boot. He's working at the British Consulate-General and has to go to the UN regularly.'

I grinned at the thought of Huge charming the ladies of the world as part of his job. 'I bet he's a whiz at diplomacy. He always had a way with words.'

'Hmm, amongst other things,' laughed James, ice cubes clinking as he took another sip of his drink. 'He asked after you, by the way.'

'Did he? What did he say?'

'He said, "How's that adorable chubby little sister of yours?"' James laughed, enjoying my mortified expression. 'He couldn't believe you were living here now. So I told him to get the *New York Times* on Saturday and see how much you've changed. I gave him your card, said you weren't a patch on Devereau Design, but that he should support his fellow ex-pat Brits.'

'Thanks, James.'

'You're welcome.' Sarcasm is always lost on my big brother. 'Yeah, so we had some lunch and he showed me round the consulate building. He's just split from his second wife you know.'

'*Second?* I didn't know he was married at all.'

'Of course he was – where have you been, Rosie? You must know that, surely? Oh, well, he met his first wife just after uni, but they lasted only eighteen months. Then he moved to the consulate after his divorce and hooked up with an intern at City Hall. They lasted six years. Sad really. She left him a few months ago for one of his colleagues.'

'Who'd get married, hey?' I commented. And it was weird, but I'm certain I saw James flinch. I said nothing, but watched with interest as he changed the subject quicker than Celia on a good day.

'Ah, splendid. Here's our food at last. Don't know about you, but I'm starving . . .'

When we got back to the apartment there was a message from Celia so I called her while James made a pot of tea.

'Rosie, *darling*, I've seen the proofs for your piece on Saturday. It's *wonderful* – you're gonna be so *thrilled*, honey! I'm due to meet Henrik at The Aviary on 66th tomorrow for lunch, so can I come see you first? I want to get all the details on your meeting with Brent. *And* Nate Amie.' I could hear her smile right down the phone.

'How on earth did you find out about that?' I asked incredulously.

Celia giggled. 'I'm a *journalist*, honey, it's what I do. And I'm afraid I can't reveal my sources. That would be highly unethical . . .' She paused, waiting for my reaction.

I played hard to get. 'Absolutely. Quite right. You stick to your principles, mate.'

Bingo! Celia exploded with pent-up frustration. 'Rosie Duncan, you are infuriating! OK, OK, I'll tell you who it was . . . but only because you're my closest friend and I love you dearly. Nate called me this evening and told me he'd been to see you. And he mentioned the word "remarkable" in the same sentence as your name!'

I made a mental guess at what that could be. 'Rosie Duncan's store was *remarkable*' – that would be OK. 'The coffee from Rosie Duncan's percolator is *remarkable*' – that would be good too. But what if it was something like, 'It's *remarkable* how weird Rosie Duncan is'? Hmm.

'Well, I can tell you all about his visit when you come to the shop tomorrow,' I said. 'I'm sure you've got lots to tell me too.'

'Absolutely,' she affirmed, '*especially* considering the fact I also saw Mimi Sutton tonight.'

'Ah, the plot thickens.'

James arrived with two mugs of tea. 'Is that your wacky friend? Say hi from me.'

I smiled. 'James says hi.'

Celia's tone changed. 'James? Your *brother* James? He's *there*?'

'Yes times three. He surprised me yesterday.'

'But I thought he was in Washington . . .' Celia sounded distracted, thoughtful.

'Yes, he was. He's just staying with me till Saturday morning, then he's going back. Are you OK, Celia?'

There was a brief pause. I could hear her breathing. 'I'm

fine, Rosie. Yes, just fine . . . Well, gotta go. The kids go back tomorrow, *thank heaven*, so we're getting pizza tonight and they've rented some gosh-awful movie. I may not survive the night . . . I'll see you tomorrow morning, honey. Bye.'

James saw my puzzled expression as I put the receiver down. 'And how *is* the inimitable Ms Reighton?'

'She's fine, I think.' Truth be told, I wasn't sure. 'She seemed a little surprised you were here.'

James flopped down beside me. 'There isn't a great deal of love lost between me and Celia, Rosie, you know that. The last time I saw her we had a blazing row – don't you remember?'

I did. I'd just as soon as forget it, though. It was one of those Really Bad Ideas you have in all good faith, only to repent at leisure. *Wouldn't it be a great idea to invite Celia to have dinner with my brother?* I'd thought, in my naïve innocence. It was about a year after I'd settled in the city and I'd finally completed refurbishing my apartment – including my prized 1920s dining-room table that I'd found at the Boston Flea, a wonderful flea market that Ed and I visit regularly, with the most eclectic collection of vintage furniture, lamps and clothing. (I go for the vintage stuff, Ed goes for the waffles.) So, thought I, who better to invite to my housewarming than my brother, my best friend and her partner?

Now, a self-confessed optimist I may be, but I defy even Pollyanna to find something in that evening's events to Be Glad about. As I recall, Jerry kicked off the argument by remarking that *everybody* agreed that Oxford and Cambridge were far inferior to Harvard or Yale – to which James responded with an attack on American 'all-mouth-no-substance' intellect. Celia attempted to change the subject by talking about her latest gathering of New York writers but James was on a roll and proceeded to reduce every author after Steinbeck as 'mere pretenders and band-wagon jumpers'. By the time I served dessert, the debate had run its course and my guests had resorted to defiant silence. And coffee was accompanied by averted eyes, served with generous helpings of underlying rage. I still harboured hopes that, one day, Celia and James would get on. But it appeared that, for now, those hopes must remain safely stashed in the file marked Highly Unlikely.

James was dismissive as ever about Celia's reaction, but I was aware of a jumpiness about him. It was carelessly hidden – like the dodgy magazines he used to stash under his bed as a teenager – with just enough showing to reveal their existence, but not enough to tell you exactly what they were.

Once I knew his guard had dropped, I broached the subject, handing him a pack of Oreos to soften the impact of my question. 'So – what's the story, Jim?'

'How do you mean?' he replied innocently.

'The visit – the meal tonight – Celia's reaction . . . what's going on?'

James's smile remained bright as ever, but I saw him shift uneasily.

'Nothing . . .' His voice was strained. He cleared his throat. 'Nothing, sis. I just needed to get away from DC for a while and . . . and I missed *you*, believe it or not.'

'I know Mum thinks you can do no wrong, but I worry about you. I mean, let's face it: trouble has a habit of finding you, doesn't it?' Careful to maintain direct eye contact, I continued: 'When I mentioned marriage earlier you flinched. What was that all about?'

James cleared his throat again. 'Ha! Rosie, that's a guy thing. I'm only thirty-four; that's way too young to settle down. Believe me, I'm enjoying playing the field too much right now.' Was he sweating? 'Plus, I thought it was a weird thing for you

138

to say . . . *considering*.' That one hurt. I looked away. His smile dropped and he reached across and took my hand. 'Really, I'm fine, sis. Let's just have a good time together and enjoy these few days . . . You know if I need help I'll always ask you first, yeah?'

I smiled and gave him a hug. Even now, all grown up, my arms were barely able to go the whole way round him. His broad shoulders seemed to relax and he held me for a long time. 'Thanks for caring, little sis,' he mumbled.

Later that night in my room, I thought I heard a noise. I put down the battered copy of E. F. Benson's *Mapp & Lucia* that I was reading (a present from Marnie from her favourite old bookstore) and climbed out of bed. Tiptoeing to the door, I noticed the living-room light still on and as I got closer I was aware of James's hushed voice. I opened the door slightly and peered through the gap. James was on the couch-bed, propped up on one shoulder, hunched over his mobile phone. He was whispering with hoarse insistence and, although a glimpse of his face was denied me from my vantage point, his aggravation was obvious.

'. . . Never mind what I said . . . I want *out*, understand? . . . Whatever you have to do, get it done. I . . . I can't do this anymore . . . I *just can't*, OK? . . . Yeah, yeah, whatever . . . Look, I'll be back Saturday . . . Yeah, we'll talk then . . . Uh, I . . . Yeah, you too. G'night.' He snapped his phone off and flopped back onto the bed, his hands over his eyes.

Silently, I closed my door.

Chapter Ten

The sunlight of Friday morning broke through my window a lot earlier than I would have preferred. I had been restless all night and felt drained and heavy-limbed as I reluctantly vacated my bed. One glance in the bathroom mirror revealed the full, uncensored horror that was Rosie Duncan on approximately three hours and twenty-six minutes' sleep. 'Well, they say true beauty lies within,' I said to my reflection, which remained unconvinced. I swear I heard the mirror breathe a sigh of relief and request counselling when I walked away.

James was fast asleep when I passed his makeshift bed to get to the kitchen. He is the only person I know who never loses sleep over anything. Ever. And, believe me, he has had plenty to worry about over the years. I should know: I've bailed him out of countless crazy situations that would have caused serious sleep deficiency for most people. At Oxford they called him 'Straight-Eight Duncan', meaning that he always got at least eight hours' sleep every night – even during end-of-year exams and finals.

I finished my breakfast and made him a cup of tea as I got ready to leave. Kneeling down by the side of the bed, I gently touched his shoulder to wake him. He stirred, eyes struggling first to open and then focus, all warm and disoriented like a small child. 'Hmm?'

'Morning, sleepy,' I whispered, smiling at the almost endearing sight of my semi-awake sibling.

A lazy smile spread across his sleep-crumpled face. 'Mmmhh . . . morning, Rosie.'

I reached out and ruffled his messed-up ginger hair. 'Sleep good?'

'Yeah, great – as ever. You off now?' His nut-brown eyes studied my face in a slow, side-to-side sweep.

'I am. But I'll be back about seven, so think of something you want to do tonight, OK?' As I rose to leave, James's expression changed and he reached out to grasp my hand. 'Rosie, about what you said last night . . . there *is* something going on.'

I felt a twist in my stomach. 'James, you don't have to talk about it if you don't want . . .'

His eyes widened, the grip on my hand tightening. 'That's the point, Rosie. I *want* to tell you, but . . . but it's not possible right now. Give me some time and I promise I'll explain everything, OK?'

Resisting the urge to press him further, I released his grip with my other hand, pushing the mug of tea into it instead. 'I'll hold you to that,' I smiled, but out in the hallway, I had to lean against the wall for a moment to quieten my insistent heart rate as a familiar sensation of impending trouble wrenched at my gut. *What had he managed to get himself mixed up in this time?*

Nobody was waiting at Kowalski's when I arrived. No Marnie, no Ed. Which was a surprise, to say the least. I opened up alone and waited for the order from Patrick's to arrive. At seven thirty the large green and white delivery truck pulled up and Zac jumped out. He's a lovely guy: athletic, blond and strikingly good-looking, but gentler than a kitten. He is completely in love with Marnie, although she has so far thwarted his every attempt at securing a date with uncharacteristic indifference – especially as she has confided in me (on more than one occasion) that she thinks he is cute.

Zac joined Patrick's the same week I started with Mr Kowalski, so we have a shared history. Like me, he left a high-flying City career to work with flowers. Unlike me, however, his decision was due to a near nervous breakdown he had suffered at the age of twenty-four, when the pressure of being a Dow Jones trader finally took its toll.

'Zaccai is another example of the miracle Papa does when He uses His flowers to heal,' I remember Mr K commenting.

And it was true: flowers did appear to make Zac happy. His smile was as regular a sight as his green and white company shirt, or the short pencil stub he kept permanently lodged behind his left ear. Ed often speculated on why it was that the pencil stub never got any shorter in all the years we'd known him: maybe *all* company pencils were that short, or maybe he spent his weekends whittling his pencils down to the correct length . . .

'Mornin', Rosie!' Zac shouted as he swung open the back doors of the truck and jumped up inside.

'Hi, Zac,' I called back, stepping off the sidewalk onto the road. He consulted his order sheets and began pulling out the long boxes to make a stack.

'OK . . . we got roses, we got button pom-poms, Bells of Ireland, lisianthus, Char Hu . . . uh, did ya want some extra greens today, 'cos Jackson's ordered too much?'

'Um . . .' I consulted my list.

'Hey, Rosie, you'd be doing me a *big* favour. I won't charge ya a bean, OK?' Zac's smile was a winner every time.

'OK, yeah, great. Thanks, mate.'

He hopped down and slid the pile of boxes to the edge of the truck. 'Ha – "mate". That's so cool. I love it when you say that . . . it's so *British*, so *quaint!*'

We made two trips to get all of the order into the work-room, then I signed the chit. Zac looked round the store, frowning. 'No Marnie this mornin'?'

'I don't know where she is.'

For a moment his perma-smile receded. 'Oh.' Then it quickly returned. 'Tell her Zac the Fit Guy says hi, OK?' He set the little bell swinging as he opened the door and turned in the doorway. 'She thinks I don't know she calls me that. But I do. See ya, *mate!*' He waved at the window before slamming shut the back doors of his truck and jumping into the driver's seat.

As he drove away, Ed walked past the window and waved weakly before entering the shop. He winced when the bell chimed happily. 'Can't you make that damn thing any quieter?'

I smiled. 'Zac and I managed just fine without you this morning, Ed. So *thanks* for being here like you said you would be.'

Ed clamped a hand over his dark-circled eyes. 'Uhhh . . . I'm sorry, Rosie. I completely forgot . . . I had a rough night.' As he approached me, it was plain that this assessment was a strong contender for Massive Understatement of the Year.

I reached behind the counter. 'Strong, black, two sugars.'

Ed grasped the mug like a vessel from the Fountain of Eternal Youth. 'You are a wonderful woman,' he breathed.

'Yeah, yeah, whatever. Just drink up.'

But I couldn't shake the knot of irritation wrapped tightly around my gut. It was unlike Ed to get in a state like this – and for him to forget the weekly Patrick's delivery was just ridiculous. And where on earth was Marnie? This was the last thing I needed today. The situation with my brother had thrown my peace of mind off kilter this morning and was claiming enough of my thoughts already without me having to deal with strange behaviour from my staff as well.

Caffeine administered, Ed and I unpacked the order and separated the blooms, ready for display or arrangement. The day's tasks then began in earnest, with Ed in the workroom and me minding the shop while I made a start on the ever-present pile of paperwork. And then, all of a sudden, it was 9 a.m.

Ed appeared at my side, looking decidedly less like an extra from *Revenge of the Living Dead* now. He cleared his throat and began the necessary grovelling process, as is customary on occasions such as this. 'About this morning, Rosie . . . I should explain—'

'No need.' I smiled serenely, before spoiling the illusion of Saintly Benevolent Employer by digging for gossip. 'What I'm more interested in is how you got on last night with The Beautiful Face of Jean St Pierre.'

Ed groaned. 'Yeah, yeah, beautiful Yelena. She *was* beautiful . . .' He trailed off and he clamped one hand to his forehead as his eyes screwed up in a vain attempt to dull his hangover. 'My brain is exploding in here . . .'

I reached behind the counter and threw a box of Advil at him. '*So?*' I pressed.

Ed let out a breath and glared through the pain at me. 'So, Miss Marple, she was beautiful and charming, as expected . . .'

'Right . . .'

'. . . And so, *so* committed to my best friend like you wouldn't believe.'

I winced in sympathy. 'Ah.'

Ed rubbed a hand across his stubble-covered chin. 'Hmm.

145

I took her to the show, then to dinner at Orso. It cost the earth but, hey, I thought, it's worth it, right? I mean, she isn't married; in fact she's only been with Steve since July. *Two months*? Who gets serious with someone in two months?'

'Well, maybe some people do . . .' I ventured, suddenly feeling defensive.

'Yeah, sure, like *no one else I know* does . . . So I took her home, whereupon she graciously left me in the cab and I ended up at Frank's drinking Jack D's till 2 a.m. So some hot date that turned out to be. Welcome to the story of my life.' He dropped his aching brow into his hands once more and let out a long, low groan.

It was time for a Rosie Duncan Rescue Attempt™. This method has been successfully employed on more than a few occasions when Ed has needed cheering up.

'Hey, don't worry,' I smiled encouragingly. 'I'm sure Yelena had a really good time last night. And so what if she didn't want anything else? I mean, you're a great guy, Ed. You're funny, you look great – this morning aside of course – and . . . well, most importantly, you're a brilliant friend . . .' I patted his shoulder. 'So one lady in this city didn't fall for you? Big deal! There are plenty of others who will.'

Ed lifted his head and suddenly things went horribly wrong. Instead of the warm placated smile I was expecting, I found myself facing arctic-blue eyes frozen by cold fury. 'And that is your answer for everything, isn't it? Optimism: it's going to save the day, right? Yeah, yeah, that's right. Sure it will. Why can't you just be like every other damn person on this planet and admit that sometimes life sucks? Well, I have news for you, my friend. You can't save the world with a smile or a pat on the back. There are millions of people who are lonely and you and I are part of the statistic. I mean, what good has your world-famous optimism ever done *you*, Rosie?'

Stunned by the intensity of his words, I found myself floundering. 'What – where on earth did that all come from? I was only trying to help . . .'

Ed shook his head. 'Then practise what you preach.'

'Sorry?'

'Get yourself out there; get in the game. You said it yourself: there are plenty of people in this city who will want to date you.'

I backed away from him and crossed my arms. 'I was talking about *you*.'

'Well, I'm talking about *you* now.'

'Well . . . *don't*.'

'Why are you being so defensive, Rosie?'

Hot tears made my eyes sting. 'Because you're attacking me and I've done nothing to deserve it.'

Ed threw his hands in the air. 'Exactly! You've done *nothing*. All you do is watch other people living their lives, like it's the only way you'll ever get to experience things. You spend your whole time at Kowalski's trying to understand what our customers' stories are. But what's *your* story?'

'*Stop* this . . . I—'

'Let me ask you one question, Rosie: what would Mr K think if he were here, huh? All he ever talked about was the importance of living life to the full. He *wanted* you to move on from whatever you were running away from when you came here. He never stopped worrying about you. Hell, even the last phone conversation I had with him he was asking me to keep an eye on you. Would he be impressed that, six years on, you're no further forward than you were when he met you? I don't think so. He had great faith in your ability to live, Rosie – was that

147

justified? Or should his hope for your future just have died with him in that Polish flower meadow?'

His words dropped like red-hot rivets in my stomach. Mentioning Mr K like that – when I missed him so much and really needed his advice right now – was almost too much to bear. I was burned, but unwilling to launch into another row.

My voice was scarily cool and calm when it came out. 'Well, thanks for that. So have you heard from Marnie at all? She should have been here by now.'

Ed struggled to pack his anger away as he answered. 'Uh – I'm sorry, yes, I did. She left a message on my voicemail – I only got it when I was in the cab on my way here. She's got flu. Doctor reckons she'll be out of action for a week. Forgive me, I should have said—'

'Yes, you should. Right. More work for us, then. Let's get on.'

'Yeah . . .' He let out a sigh and sent his thawing blue gaze my way again. 'Look, Rosie, I—'

I headed to the back of the store. 'If you could mind things here, that would be good. I'm going to make a start on Brent Jacobs' order now. I need it ready to deliver by ten-fifteen.'

'Yeah, cool, whatever. I'll check the orders for next week while I'm in here.' He sounded hurt. The door opened to reveal a new customer, who nodded in our direction and began to browse the flowers. I walked quickly into the workroom, shut the door sharply and started working quickly, tears falling freely onto the stems of the bright yellow roses I was stripping. I needed the distraction, desperate to remove the image now firmly ensconced at the forefront of my mind: Mr Kowalski, alone and dying amidst the wildflowers, his last earthly emotion an intense sadness at my inability to learn how to live.

*   *   *

I didn't like to think about how Mr K died. He suffered a heart attack whilst walking in the flower meadows near his home. The doctors said it took him so quickly that he wouldn't have known anything about it, but still the thought of him dying alone has haunted me ever since.

As I worked on the bouquet for Brent's wife, I was aware of the tension in my body-slowly ebbing at last. Flowers are the best therapy, Mum says. You can never be angry for too long when you're with them. And I guess she's right. There's something about being surrounded with their scent and colour that soothes you. It sounds very New Age to say that, but it's not what I mean. It's just impossible not to be moved by the simple beauty of natural things. When I'm stressed or over-worked, I make myself remember Mr K in the middle of all the rush and somehow I always find myself slowing down.

Every now and again in life you meet someone who can truly be described as inspirational. I don't mean rich, or famous, or even out of the ordinary. I mean someone who makes you feel a better person, just by standing alongside you.

Mr K was inspirational. He seemed to be constantly surrounded by peace. He *knew* who he was supposed to be. I don't know many people like that. I know an awful lot of people who are searching for that, though, and I'm one of them. Mr K had the ability to find tranquillity in the middle of the busiest times. One time we had a huge order to complete for a bridal show and I became so stressed that everything I attempted failed. Mr K didn't shout, didn't judge. He just walked up alongside me and put his arm round my shoulders.

'Rosie, take some time. Find some peace now. Listen to Papa.'

I didn't understand. I asked him *how* I could listen. A broad smile lit up his wrinkled features.

'*Ukochana*, listen to the flowers. They don't say "Hurry", they don't fret or complain. Their colour says "Peace".'

I didn't really understand; I still don't. But I did start to take time out in the middle of my work – to enjoy what I was doing for its own sake. And it works.

Sometimes I miss Mr Kowalski so much it makes my soul ache.

There are people you know all your life who never really make a difference to who you are; others arrive for a short time and change everything. Mr K was definitely one of the latter. He influenced so many people in his own, unassuming way. I actually saw it happen: from the customers that he talked with, to the hours he spent listening to Marnie when she first started at the store – most of which consisted of her pouring her heart out to him while Mr K took it all in – and the way he still encouraged the best out of his former apprentice Ed, always urging him to push his creativity, whilst remaining fiercely proud of everything he did. Not to mention the way he helped me, of course.

Right from the very first day I walked into the store that I would one day call my own, Mr K saw something in me that everyone else had missed. My confidence was at rock bottom; in many ways I'd lost sight of what I was capable of, but Mr K saw it as plain as day. Unlike Ed, or Marnie, or even Celia to begin with, Mr Kowalski never asked why I had come to New York. I suspect he had his theories, but he just accepted me for the person I was.

Mr K was so much more than a father figure to us all. He was confidant, teacher, friend, even devil's advocate at times. And I needed all of that. My own father had never been around enough to bother about how my life was going and, when he eventually abandoned his family, he stopped

150

bothering about me at all. In fact, the last contact we had was when he wrote to inform me that he was emigrating and didn't want to stay in touch. Meanwhile, Mum always had a million and one things to worry about, what with a business to run single-handedly, and my brother's seemingly genetic capability for causing trouble to contend with – not to mention the pressure of keeping it all together when Dad left.

I think Mr K's faith influenced a lot of what he did, although I would always contend with him that it was also because of the type of person he was. I remember him smiling at me, his sharp old eyes seeing more than he'd ever let on.

'Ah, Rosie. Always questioning, always sure of your own belief. It's good to be an enquirer, but sometimes you have to accept things that are greater than your comprehension. I am what I am because of who Papa is; that I try to make the world a better place is due to my love for Him. You cannot separate the two.'

After all his years of hard work and sacrifice for his family, Mr K had only a year in Warsaw to enjoy his retirement before he died. To me it seemed like such a meagre recompense for a lifetime of work, but his daughter, Lenka, wrote to me after his death to say that he'd never been happier than she saw him during that short time spent in his beloved homeland. Lenka sent me a small leather-bound journal that Mr K had filled with pressed wildflowers – something he did every day during his retirement. I have it on my bedside table and look at it often, reading Mr K's notes in his elaborate handwriting around the beautifully preserved blooms makes me feel close to him again somehow.

I bound the bouquet now and stepped back. Pulling a chair up, I sat down and checked my watch. It was nine forty-five.

I rubbed my eyes as lack of sleep began to creep up on me. I didn't hear the door open.

'You look beat,' Ed said from the doorway. He might not have held a white flag, but I knew a ceasefire had been signalled.

'I am. I didn't sleep well. James is here for a few days and I think I'm conscious of him being there when I'm asleep.'

He held out a mug. 'Old F sent you this.' There was the merest hint of a smile. 'May I bring it in?'

'Of course.' I rose to meet him. 'Thanks.'

'I'll take Mr Jacobs' order, if you like. I could – uh – do with heading home for a shower.'

'Sure. Take all the time you need.'

Ed nodded and made to leave. He stopped in the open doorway and, without turning, spoke over his shoulder. 'You know you're my true friend?'

My wounds still stung from what he'd said earlier, but I smiled. 'Yes, I know,' I replied.

'I have *news*, Rosie!' Celia sang as she flew into the shop and swooped to land on the sofa by the window. She was brandishing a beat-up newspaper, which turned out to be a copy of the *New York Post*. 'Look, look, look!' she pointed excitedly as I sat beside her.

'Where did you get this paper, Celia?' I asked as I surveyed the torn, coffee-stained page, which, by this point, was being held about three inches from my face.

'Somebody left it on the subway train. But that's not important. Look here!'

'Hey, great! Bloomingdale's sale starts Tuesday!' I exclaimed in mock delight.

Celia whisked the paper away and gave me a stern look. 'Rosie Duncan, you do *not* deserve me.'

'But you're stuck with me anyway, aren't you? OK, OK, I promise to be nice.' She brought the paper back and I had to suppress my amusement when I saw exactly what had elicited her attention. 'You mean you're reading "Gloria Weinberg's Word on the Streets" column now?'

Celia pulled a face. 'You know I can't abide the woman, Rosie. She dares to describe her gossip-mongering as journalism. She is an insult to the written word. But this one thing caught my eye ...'

Underneath a suitably glitzy photo of Ms Weinberg was the heading 'NY – Oh My!' and the piece below read:

BIG news of a BIG day in the City ... I have it on a VERY reliable authority that the ladies of New York are soon to lose yet another eligible bachelor (*sob*!). Word on the street is that rising star of the publishing fraternity Nate Amie has proposed marriage (at last!) to stunningly beautiful girlfriend Caitlin Sutton. The buzz goes that he poured his heart out to her at her family's deluxe Long Island residence. My source confirmed that the Sutton family are overjoyed and expect the happy couple to wed in a lavish, star-studded ceremony early next spring. Whilst we single ladies mourn the loss of another adorable young man, we have to send our hearty congrats to the beautiful couple and wish them every success for what is sure to be a very prosperous future.

'So, no prizes for guessing who the reliable source was, then,' Celia grinned.

'Who?'

'Mimi Sutton, of course!' Celia studied my expression and took my hand. 'Rosie, honey, are you OK?'

'I'm fine. It's just he didn't say anything about it yesterday when he—'

'Well, he wouldn't, would he?' Celia retorted. 'Because it's not true! I met Mimi last night and it was all she could talk about. She said "wheels were in motion" to *make* Nate's decision *for* him. This was obviously what she meant.' She stopped. 'You could at least try to see the funny side of this, Rosie. Nate is too laid-back for his own good. He'll be Mr Caitlin Sutton before he's even realised what's happening. Or, at least, that's what Mimi's counting on.'

'Brent said something about Nate and the press yesterday,' I began, as a dim recollection formed in my mind, 'but I can't remember what it was. He was very concerned about you, though,' I changed the subject almost as speedily as Celia usually does. I saw her eyes flicker and continued, 'He says Old Bee Jay is there for you.'

Celia's expression softened and she wriggled a little in her seat. 'He is so *sweet*. He shouldn't worry about me. I'll call him later. But, Rosie, about your brother . . .'

Out-manoeuvred once again. I took a deep breath.

'He sends his love, Celia.' I saw her expression and stopped joking. 'He mentioned some trouble he's in. To be honest, I don't want to know.'

Celia squeezed my hand. 'Frankly, Rosie, it's best you don't.'

There was something about her tone that sent the little voice in my head muttering worriedly. I decided not to press Celia for any more; in any case, I got the impression that she had no intention of enlightening me further.

'Gracious – look at the time, honey! I gotta go. I'll call you tonight. Will you be coming by tomorrow?'

'Yes, of course. Any preference on cakes?'

Celia was already halfway to the door. 'No – no, I'll trust

your impeccable taste as always!' She grabbed me for a huge hug and paused for the briefest of moments. 'Be careful, Rosie. Don't get involved. You *mustn't* get involved, OK?' And with that, she hurried out.

Ed was gone a long time. When he finally reappeared he had company.

'. . . Well, I never knew you were a Mets man. Look, I got tickets for the game next week – we oughta go.'

'Sure thing, buddy – count me in . . . Ah, hi, Rosie. Look who I found on the sidewalk,' Ed grinned. 'Did you know Nate's a Mets fan? And I thought I was the only sane individual left in this sea of Yankees.'

Nate smiled. 'Hi, Rosie.'

'Hi.'

'Coffee?' Ed walked behind me to get to Old F. As he passed he squeezed my arm and said, 'Mr Jacobs' wife was blown away by the bouquet, Rosie.'

'Great.' I tried to look busy and in control. Which was difficult as inside I was annoyingly flustered and shaky again. Why was that?

Ed made the coffee, followed by his excuses, before disappearing into the workroom. For a moment Kowalski's was uncomfortably silent. Nate smiled again. I smiled back. I took a deep breath and moved over to the sofa. 'So – flowers for the woman who has everything . . . any more thoughts?'

Nate looked both relieved and frustrated as he joined me. 'Uh, yeah . . . I'm still trying to get my head round what you said yesterday . . . about my story, I mean.'

I took a long sip of coffee and braced myself for the answer that would inevitably follow my next question. 'And?'

His brow furrowed and he appeared to be locked in a battle

with his thoughts. After some time, he turned to face me. 'Rosie, I don't know. That's just it. I don't know.'

'Ah . . . Nate, look – don't lay too much store by what I said. I mean, yes, it's important for me to know what a customer is trying to say, but often they have no idea themselves. They just want to send a bunch of flowers. End of story. It's my job to try and see beyond that.'

Nate's dark eyes narrowed. 'So what do you see in *this* customer, Ms Duncan?'

'Er . . .'

Why is it that when you are presented with a genuine opportunity to say something truly profound, your mind goes blank? Here I was, faced with a gift of a question from this person who had all of a sudden appeared in my life and made everything – well – *weird*, and now I found myself unable to immortalise my position as Fount of All Things Wise. *Come on, Rosie!* chided the little voice.

'I don't know you, Nate,' I began. 'I don't know how you feel about this lady. I'm presuming it *is* for a lady?'

Nate's eyes were very still. 'It is for a lady, yes . . .'

'Well, I'm not sure what to say.'

The dark eyes remained intent on mine. 'Please say what you think, Rosie.'

'Um . . . it's just that looking at you . . . well, you just don't strike me as a man in love. Not truly, passionately, completely in love.' I hesitated. Was that too much?

'Go on,' Nate insisted.

'Or, at least, you don't look like I imagine a man in love to look like. Not that I really know, of course . . . What I mean is I don't . . . um . . .' Mayday, mayday, mad Englishwoman in mortal danger of swallowing own foot! I chose a different

156

approach. 'I haven't seen that many people who really look like they're in love. My maternal grandparents did – even in their late eighties they walked everywhere hand in hand and would frequently finish one another's sentences. Sometimes it was like they only had one mind between them. But they were definitely in the minority.' I made a mental list of people in my life: Mum and Dad, Celia and Jerry, James, Ed, Marnie . . . I could honestly say that I had never seen *any* of them truly in love with someone. 'This may be wrong, but I reckon if you love someone you shouldn't need a whole day to determine how you feel about them. You should just . . . *know*, I guess. That sounds really harsh, doesn't it?'

Nate smiled but his eyes were far away. 'No . . . you're right. I *should* know. But I don't. I – just don't. People think I'm crazy; I mean, Caitlin's beautiful, obviously. But I can't shake the feeling that it's not all it could be, you know?'

After another silence, the lop-sided grin made a fleeting reappearance. 'So, what about you, Rosie Duncan?'

The question was a bolt from the blue. 'Pardon?'

Nate let out a laugh at my befuddled expression. 'Ha, sorry, did I floor you there?'

I swear he could hear my heart beating. 'I – I thought we were talking about *your story*.' Aha, nice move, there – the patented Duncan Dodge™ – perfect for avoiding awkward questions. Sometimes it even works . . . But not today.

The dark eyes twinkled. 'Yes, we were. But *your story* seems so much more interesting.'

'Well, I'm not the one ordering flowers.' A masterstroke.

My opponent held his hands up and laughed out loud, a sound that seemed to warm every corner of the store. '*Touché*! I surrender! So we'll talk about me and me alone, then. If that's the rule of our conversations I hereby agree to abide by them from now on. But I'll remain intrigued: how do you know so much about what a man in love looks like?'

We were entering forbidden territory and I felt my defences building, but something about Nate's countenance prevented me from changing the subject. An inexplicable calm overcame me and the weirdest thing happened: I found myself wanting to trust this relative stranger. And that *never* happens. My words faltered as I ventured out onto uncertain terrain. 'Well . . . I don't know, really . . . I thought I did once, but . . .'

'Go on.' His voice was gentle and low – almost a whisper. I wasn't sure I should continue. I mean, I didn't really know him. But something about the softness of his expression made me continue.

'But I was wrong. And it won't happen again.'

Surprised by this, he sat back, looking perplexed. 'That sounds incredibly final, Rosie. I figured you as the ultimate romantic.'

'I work with flowers. It's an occupational hazard,' I smiled, the old vulnerabilities beginning to show as I found myself hiding behind humour to avoid honesty. 'I see romance every day. For other people. And it's great – for them. I'm more than happy to watch other people's dreams come true, because . . .'

'It's safer?' Nate finished, with perception that was far too sharp for comfort.

I didn't answer. I couldn't. Not if I wanted to remain In Control.

'That's a great shame,' he remarked quietly. 'So . . . the officially designated subject of Me and My Love Life it is then. I guess you read about my engagement?'

His honesty startled me. 'Celia told me. I don't usually read the gossip columns, of course. Congratulations, then. I suppose that answers the question of what your story is.'

Nate looked away. 'It isn't true, Rosie. That is to say, it *shouldn't* be true. I still can't figure out how I ended up engaged. See, I never expect things to go well but they have a habit of happening to me anyway.' His eyes returned to me. 'Know what I mean?'

I had to smile. 'No, I'm afraid I don't. I expect the best – always – and it never seems to happen for me. Maybe we should swap lives for a bit and then we'd both be happy.'

A huge grin lit Nate's features. 'I like you, Rosie. Can we be friends?'

Taken aback, I laughed. 'We are friends.'

Nate shook his head and waved his hand. 'No, you don't understand. I mean I'd like to get to know you – well. Look, Rosie, here's the deal. It's obvious I need some of your romantic optimism in order to enjoy my love life and . . . well . . . I guess you could use a healthy dose of pessimism to keep your heart safe. I'll order flowers if you'll listen to my muddle of thoughts and we'll ask Old Faithful to provide the coffee. OK?'

It was the most improbable and idiotic suggestion I think I've ever heard in my life so far. But I liked it.

'OK, Mr Amie, you have a deal.'

'So, what did Nate say about Caitlin?' Celia was in grave danger of bouncing off her seat with anticipation.

'Nothing,' I replied truthfully, knowing this would never satisfy the active volcano sitting opposite me at the large maple table in her apartment. True to expectations, the Saturday tranquillity of the apartment was shattered as Mount Celia erupted.

'He *can't* just say *nothing*!' she spluttered. 'He must have said more?' I shook my head and braced myself for her reaction. 'Nate Amie is *so* infuriating! How can he *not know* whether he's engaged or not? What is he thinking? He can't possibly be in love with Caitlin Sutton! Doesn't he know she can never make him happy?'

I reached into the M&H Bakers bag and pulled out another of Luigi's near-legendary double-choc-chip cookies. 'I don't think he expects her to make him happy,' I said, taking a bite and thinking back to the conversation yesterday. 'I think that's the point: he doesn't ever expect good stuff to happen. But it just *does* for him. So maybe he thinks he'll be pleasantly surprised after all.'

Celia scratched her head. 'Seneca,' she pronounced solemnly. 'Who?'

My nutty friend shook her head in pity at her ignoramus English companion. 'Do you know nothing about Classics with all your generic history? Seneca was a Roman philosopher who actively practised pessimism, so nothing ever came as a surprise to him when bad things happened. His theory was that, this way, good things would always be a fortuitous occurrence because they were never expected. A classical genius he may've been, but that man has a *lot* to answer for.'

'Celia, being your friend is a constant education. I am in awe.'

She shot me a look and jumped up as another thought sent her hurtling onto a new topic. 'Well, you won't have seen this yet, but *here we are.*' She produced a crisp copy of the *New York Times*, quickly flicked through till she found the article and read out the headline triumphantly. '"A Real English Rose Thrives in the Heart of Manhattan" – how about that?'

The photo was good, even though I'm decidedly unphotogenic, and Josh's article was excellent. It focused on Kowalski's more than me, which was a relief, and enthused about the wonderful atmosphere in the shop.

'An atmosphere that a certain confused, Seneca-revering

publisher seems to find particularly welcoming,' Celia remarked, with all the subtlety of a sledgehammer. 'So he'll be making regular visits then?'

I smiled. 'That's what he said.'

'And you don't mind?'

I shrugged. 'Not at all. It's fine by me.'

Celia took a bite of cookie and nonchalantly returned to the paper. 'Oh *good* . . .'

Chapter Eleven

Nate's visits were most definitely regular – increasingly so as autumn took Manhattan in its colourful hold. He began to visit my shop most weeks – usually on a Thursday afternoon when he could sneak out of his office – and our friendship seemed to grow with each new conversation. I couldn't help it: I liked him, from the easy way he seemed to breeze through life, to his delight at meeting some of my customers, and the utter regard he had for my profession. He liked nothing better than watching me and my team at work, mug of Old F's finest decaf in hand, and I found myself looking forward to his visits as the days and weeks passed. This was the start of what promised to be a beautiful friendship: the optimist and the (admittedly happy) pessimist, drinking coffee and surrounded by flowers on the corner of West 68th and Columbus.

Just after lunchtime one Thursday in the middle of October, the small silver bell above Kowalski's front door heralded the unexpected arrival of Nate. After nearly two months of his visits, I was becoming more accustomed to his arrival, its effect on my pulse rate marginally less devastating than it had been in the beginning.

'This is a surprise,' I said, wrapping paper around an enormous bunch of assorted blooms and foliage for Mrs Katzinger, who arranges the flowers in the local Episcopalian church, two blocks south of Kowalski's. 'I thought the world of publishing waits for no one?'

'It doesn't,' Nate grinned, his cocoa-brown eyes sparkling like a cheeky schoolboy's, 'that's why you have to have escape routes planned. Today, just so you know, you are a retired history professor I'm trying to sign up. You have a fascinating manuscript on late eighteenth-century industrialists that I'd love to get my hands on.'

I ignored his *double entendre* and attempted to maintain my jovial air. This was not lost on Mrs Katzinger, however, who raised an eyebrow with the merest hint of sly humour.

'Well, Mr High-Powered Publisher, I'll do my best to decline your generous offer,' I smiled back at him, our banter sending a shiver of joy right down my spine. 'After all, a professor of my calibre can't be *bought*, you know. But I'm glad you could pencil me into your schedule. Right, is that everything, Mrs Katzinger?'

'I think so,' she replied, her face reddening as a million and one things raced through her mind. Mrs Katzinger is one of those people who are always busy, always flustered and always on the way to several other places at the same time. Marnie reckons she probably even finds sleeping an exhausting pursuit. To that end, she is pure New York – something I wasn't quite prepared for when I first arrived here. Whereas in England people are just busy, in New York they are *manic*. Even getting a take-away coffee is a time-consuming activity in their crazy day. Ed jokes that even the homeless guys in the church-run shelter near his apartment have packed-out schedules: he once helped out at the soup kitchen there (when he was trying to date a girl from the congregation) and he said everyone in the line was complaining about how much precious time they were wasting standing there.

Mrs Katzinger handed me her money, shaking her head. 'Thank you for this, Rosie. You have no idea how busy I am, what with the church flowers and the coffee morning next Thursday. You would not *believe* how long it's taking me to find a good deal on cupcakes.'

'Have you tried M&H on 88th?' I suggested.

Mrs Katzinger's face lit up. 'You know, I haven't. That's another stop on my journey then!' She scooped the bundle of flowers into her matronly arms and bustled out of the door, the silver bell jangling a noisy farewell as she hurried away.

'You are a *fountain* of knowledge,' Nate observed. 'Much more than your average florist, eh?'

'Absolutely. It's all part of the service Kowalski's offers to the neighbourhood. Therapist, City guide, advisor, life coach – and sanctuary for escaped editors, of course,' I grinned.

Nate's eyes flashed. 'And an irresistible one at that.'

Blushing, I decided an urgent change of subject was in order. 'Coffee?'

'Love one, thanks.' His gaze remained disconcertingly fixed on me as I powered up Old F, who provided the necessary afternoon decaf after a little gentle coaxing. Then we sat down on the sofa.

'I was talking about the store being irresistible, by the way, not me,' he said, and instantly I felt stupid for thinking he meant *I* was irresistible. As he spread his tailored jacket over the arm of the sofa and stretched out his long legs, I found myself admiring again his effortless style. Moss-green V-neck sweater and pristine white T-shirt underneath, smart yet casual nut-brown trousers and polished expensive brogues – Nate was every inch the man about town. 'I love this place, Rosie. I feel like I can relax here, you know? Be "me" – whoever that is.'

165

'Glad to be of service to you – well, my shop is, at least.'

Nate shook his head. 'It isn't just the store. It's *you*. Let's face it: Kowalski's is you. But I'd like to hazard a guess that if I met you anywhere else, it would still feel like I didn't have to pretend with you. My life—' he broke off, as if unsure of how to phrase the sentence. 'Uh . . . so much of what people see when they look at me is what other people have prescribed, you know?'

I didn't. 'Not really, sorry.'

'At Gray & Connelle I'm the boy-wonder: the editor who signed three *New York Times* Bestsellers during his first month at the company and quickly rose to the top. To my parents I'm the blue-eyed boy – difficult, I know, as my irises don't quite fit the bill – but I'm incapable of doing wrong, as far as they're concerned. To Caitlin, I'm – well, I don't exactly know what I am to her, apart from a constant source of disappointment and frustration, it would seem. And as for Mimi – it's like she's already storyboarded my existence for her real-life family blockbuster. The only person who accepts me for who I am – who asks nothing more of me other than that I just show up for coffee once in awhile – is *you*. Don't give me that look, Rosie; I mean it. Ever since I started coming here, things have been falling into place, you know? I've had so much all my life; I've never wanted for anything. But it's all been just – *stuff*. You see the real Nate, I think; perhaps more than any other living soul. And I want to discover who *he* is. I like the version of me that I see in your eyes. That's why I had to see you today.'

I was flattered by what he said, but still I struggled with the picture Nate painted of me. I'm *not* wise: in many ways events of my life have attested to this fact. I guess I'm just interested in people, in their stories and personalities.

It never ceases to amaze me the number of stories I hear in my day-to-day dealings with the good people of my neighbourhood. There are at least a hundred different people I could tell you about who visit my shop, from occasional customers to people we see week in, week out. Some of them, like Mrs Katzinger and Mrs Schuster, were Kowalski's customers long before I was here. Like Gloria O'Keefe, for instance, who told me her grandmother bought flowers from Kowalski's right from when she was a little girl, and Mrs O'Keefe is now a grandmother herself, buying flowers for her own granddaughter's birthday. But there are also a lot of people who have appeared since I took over the business.

Take Billy Whitman, for example. He started coming to my shop at the end of last year. He is hopelessly in love with the girl whose desk is across the office floor from his. The highlight of his day is when she crosses the office to the water-cooler by his desk because she always smiles at him. That daily smile has become the reason he can't wait to get to work in the morning and, even though this is the only contact he has with her each day, it is enough to have completely stolen his heart. Billy sends roses from Kowalski's every first Monday of the month to the girl across the office – always red and always a dozen, with a card that says, 'From your office admirer'. To date, he hasn't yet had the courage to add his name to the card, even though Ed, Marnie and I have all urged him to do so. Consequently, Miss Emily Kelly thinks the roses are from one of the managers and is slowly dating her way through middle management in a bid to discover the sender of her monthly bouquet, while Billy contents himself with the daily smile and tries to muster the nerve to reveal his secret identity to her.

It's stories like these that make my job so enjoyable: tiny

snapshots of other people's lives that catch my interest, like driving down a street at night and peeking into lit windows.

But not all the glimpses are good ones. For every hopeful, fascinating story, there are darker, sadder ones. Like the man who came into the store not so long ago. He caused such consternation that the mere mention of 'BlackBerry Guy' – as he has become known – is enough to send Ed and Marnie into animated diatribes about how ungrateful some people are.

It had been raining solidly for a whole week and business had been sporadic, to say the least, with only the bravest of customers daring to brave the New York pelt. By Friday afternoon it was so quiet that I made the decision to close early and we were just starting to shut up shop when BlackBerry Guy came in. Dressed impeccably in a smartly cut dark suit and trench coat, he was engrossed in a call on said BlackBerry and didn't even acknowledge Ed, who had walked across to greet him. It took Ed physically standing four inches from BlackBerry Guy's face for him finally to register his existence.

The first thing that annoyed Ed was that BlackBerry Guy didn't end the call. He merely mumbled, 'Hold on, would ya? I just gotta sort something,' into the device and put his hand over it. 'Flowers, yeah?'

I could see Ed swallowing the comment he would have liked to have made before he politely asked, 'Any particular type?'

BlackBerry Guy cast a cursory glance at the impressive selection of blooms in our galvanised buckets. 'Whatever,' he said with a disinterested swipe of his hand. 'Just make them expensive, yeah? Money's not an object here, OK?' Before Ed could speak again, BlackBerry Guy had returned to his call. 'Murray, you still there? Yeah, just getting a peace offering for Susie, making sure she doesn't sue my ass for every nickel. What? Oh yeah, she found out about that bit of skirt I picked up in

Philadelphia. Threatening to divorce me. *Again*. What? Damage limitation, yeah.' His laugh was dirty and disgusting – and the *second* thing that annoyed Ed, who cleared his throat loudly and waved at BlackBerry Guy to wrench his attention from the blasted device. 'Oh wait, the shop guy's bugging me,' he said to the caller, placing his hand over the receiver once more and glaring at Ed. 'What?'

Ed smiled with gritted teeth. 'Sorry to bother you, *sir*, but I need to know what kind of arrangement you require and if you need it to take now or wish for us to deliver it?'

BlackBerry Guy let out an irritated sigh and resumed his call. 'Yeah, Murray? I gotta go. Seems you gotta endure the third degree to get a damn bunch of flowers round here. Ha, I know! Later.' He had ended the call and raised both hands. 'Good for you?'

'Much better, *thanks*,' Ed replied, the sarcasm in his tone evident to everyone else except the man stood before him.

By the time BlackBerry Guy had finally left Kowalski's – after having answered three further calls and sent numerous emails – *everyone* was wound up. For a man who had betrayed his wife, he'd showed little remorse – in fact, he'd only stopped joking about it when he saw the disgusted looks on our faces. He'd spent over a hundred dollars on an apology that was more about saving him from an expensive divorce than it was about saying sorry. It's sad, but it's life, and just another part of the rich mosaic of individual stories that make this city what it is.

'Do you ever wonder if you could end up like BlackBerry Guy?' Ed asked one Sunday morning, as we sat on burgundy-red cushions in the window seat of Caffe Marco on Lafayette Street in NoLita, eating *bomboloni* – tiny Italian breakfast doughnuts filled with chocolate, custard and jam (a particular favourite of Ed's). We come here quite a lot on our weekend expeditions. Ed is fascinated by the décor in the café: it's typically over the top, from the huge crystal chandeliers and ornately carved white-painted wooden chairs to the neat, regimented lines of pastries standing to attention in glass and steel display cabinets beneath the polished white marble service counter. The coffee's pretty good too – rich and dark with the kind of kick that can wake up even reluctant-riser Ed on a Sunday morning.

'I don't think either of us could be so callous,' I replied, taking a sip of smoky espresso and enjoying the instant buzz.

'Nevertheless, I worry about it sometimes, you know? That I'll one day get so wrapped up in my own life that I'll stop thinking about other people. I guess it's something you don't notice about yourself until it's too late.'

'You want to watch that Caffe Marco espresso,' I smiled. 'It looks like it could be melting you, Mr Iceberg.'

'Mock all you want, Rosie, but any one of our customers could be us one day. What was it Mr K used to say? "Everyone's story is one step away from yours."' He shuddered. 'Remind me never to buy a BlackBerry, OK?'

'I really don't think the device determined the man there, Ed.'

'I know, but when you see everyone else's lives, the comparison with your own is inevitable, don't you think?' He popped another doughnut into his mouth and I could almost see his brain whirring as he munched away. 'I mean, look at Billy Whitman: I bet he never thought that one day he would fall so hopelessly in love with somebody that he'd end up spending hundreds of dollars because he didn't have the nerve to tell her his feelings.'

There are many things I'm *not* certain of in my life, but I can honestly say that Billy Whitman's situation was one I was pretty convinced wasn't likely to happen to me. 'Billy will tell Emily how he feels one day,' I said with conviction. 'These things just take time. And no, I don't worry that will happen to me.'

A strange look passed across the ice-blue Steinmann stare. 'Still, it's a scary thought, huh?'

A pretty young waitress appeared by our table, instantly summoning Ed's attention.

'Hi, I'm Lydia,' she smiled.

'Hi Lydia.' Ed's cheeky expression made me groan and avert my gaze.

She blushed and shifted position self-consciously. 'Can I get you guys anything else?'

'Rosie? More coffee?'

I politely declined, not that he was listening.

Lydia turned to Ed. 'And for you, sir?'

'Well, I'm fine for coffee, but I wouldn't say no to your number.'

Watching Ed the Serial Dater at work is truly a sight to behold. Lydia didn't stand a chance against the Steinmann charm. I've seen it so many times and yet it never fails to fascinate me. He can make any woman feel like she's the only other person in the room, just with his attentive smile.

'Well, when you ask so nicely . . .' Lydia scribbled her number on a napkin and handed it to him. Ed, his eyes never leaving hers, accepted it and placed it with great care into his shirt pocket.

'Call me anytime after seven,' she beamed.

'I'll do that,' he replied. 'Thank you.'

He watched her skip away and looked back at me. 'What?'

I laughed. 'You are impossible, Ed! I can't take you anywhere.'

He took a triumphant sip of coffee. 'I'm just in the game, Rosie, that's all.'

'Who do we have here?' a familiar voice interrupted. My heart sank and I looked up to see Philippe Devereau standing by our table, expensively attired arms folded angrily and perma-tan flushed. 'The talentless Rosie Duncan and her scruffy guard dog, I presume?'

My hard stare at Ed prevented him from saying something he might come to regret.

'Philippe, what a pleasure. Day off, is it?'

Philippe snorted. '*Some* of us in this business are able to function outside of our stores, Ms Duncan. Unlike lesser concerns such as Kowalski's.'

I raised my coffee cup. 'Proud to be a neighbourhood florist, Philippe. May it ever be thus.'

He slammed a fist down on our table, making the white crockery, silver coffee pot and cutlery jump. People around us had stopped eating and were staring over at the orange-hued, black-suited angry man by our table.

'Give it up, Ms Duncan! Know your market: the unremarkable masses who think Asiatic lilies are exotic. Leave my customers alone.'

I stared straight at him, keeping my voice low and cool. 'On the contrary, Mr Devereau, my customers *are* remarkable and understand far more about flowers than you ever will. They appreciate natural beauty – something I think you lost sight of years ago.' The nervous-looking assistant who had just scampered to Philippe's side gasped. But I wasn't finished. 'And as for your customers, as I said before, I have no intention of pursuing them. But *they* seem intent on pursuing *me*. Now, if you don't mind, this happens to be my day off and I'd like to finish my breakfast in peace.'

172

'I don't believe you!' Philippe snarled. 'To think that I, Manhattan's premier floral artiste, should have to endure such treatment from a two-bit florist with ideas above her place! Who the hell do you think you are?'

Ed jumped to his feet before I could stop him. 'Who is she? I'll tell you who she is, you phony jerk. She is the kind of innovative, passionate designer that this City needs. Rosie understands form and beauty in a way you never will. We both do. Mark my words, Mr Devereau, our designs are going to set this whole damn place on fire and leave you wondering what the hell happened. Now why don't you just shimmy your little orange ass back to that flower freak show you call an emporium and leave us the hell alone?' He calmly resumed his seat. 'Amazing the losers they let in here on a Sunday, huh?'

I smiled at Ed, genuinely touched by his chivalrous defence of me. 'I couldn't agree more.'

Philippe and his minion made a noisy exit from the café.

Flowers are very subjective – not everyone likes the same. I dread to think what Philippe's idea of a perfect bloom is. Celia can't stand the scent of stargazer lilies, for example. In fact, she is famously picky when it comes to flowers: hyacinths, jasmine and viburnum all elicit her most violent disapproval. That's why what I do as a florist is more like analysis than simply pure aesthetics. Flowers, as Mr K used to tell us, are like people: each one of us has our own special blend of characteristics just as flowers have different colours, shapes, scents and so on.

Celia once asked me what flowers everyone at Kowalski's would be. I didn't even have to think about it. Ed, for example, would be something like an ornamental thistle or a protea – strikingly attractive yet complex and guarded beneath.

Marnie is absolutely a gerbera girl – bright, kooky and original. Mr K was always like a chrysanthemum, rotund, solid and jolly, multilayered yet somehow completely familiar and approachable. Celia is an easy one: she'd be a gladioli – bold and showy, an acquired taste for some yet irresistible for others. And as for me . . . well, I suppose my name gives it away: I'm a rose through and through – full of life on the outside, yet incredibly well defended underneath the colour. Those thorns are there for a reason; they have become necessary to help me face the future.

If I was to add Nate to the list, I guess he would be a daisy: laid-back and happy, unashamedly displaying his colours to the world regardless of what they think, but – like the thick foliage beneath the bloom – concealing a more complex character behind the impressive display.

For now, I was content to enjoy the friendly colours on Nate's surface, but I was already aware that his hidden complexities would become more apparent. The more time I spent with him, the more I was aware of a whole other story going on underneath it all. Whether he would admit to that remained to be seen.

Celia, as ever, remained intensely interested in my and Nate's burgeoning friendship, keen to analyse each new development. Most of her incessant interrogations took place over food, either at her apartment or at one of the many restaurants and cafés she frequents across the city.

'Don't you just *adore* brunch?' Celia grinned, buttering a slice of toasted brioche one Saturday morning. 'Whoever thought of this splendid tradition should be cannonised immediately.'

'Maybe there's a statue of them somewhere,' I smiled. 'Or a pancake named in their honour.'

'Well, there should be,' Celia nodded, brushing crumbs off the blue checkered tablecloth. 'I might just write about that next week.'

Brunch is an institution in New York, especially at the weekends and particularly in my neighbourhood. Celia introduced me to its delights shortly after I arrived in the city – and you would be amazed at the number of venues catering for 'brunchers' here. Today we were enjoying eggs, pancakes, brioche and crispy bacon with never-ending cups of strong, chocolate coffee at Annie's, a small yet perfectly formed eatery three blocks east of Celia's apartment. It resides in the basement of an old brownstone building and legend has it that the premises were formerly an illegal drinking den that enjoyed considerable success – and notoriety – during Prohibition in the 1920s. Annie's had been one of Jerry's favourite haunts and he spent many happy weekends courting Celia there. While she never admits it, Celia maintains a few things in her life that she and Jerry used to do together. I think it's comforting for her, in an odd way. She still has his Mets baseball on her desk in her apartment, for example, and still buys smoked salmon from Schumann's deli – even though she constantly complains about the prices and is forever asserting her intention to shop elsewhere.

At best, Annie's can hold about twenty diners at a time: today the place was packed and a relaxed queue was forming on the steep steps leading up to sidewalk level above.

'I think we got here at the right time,' I said. 'They're queuing already and it's only ten thirty.'

'My mother always says it's important to head for the restaurant with the queue,' Celia smiled. 'She doesn't trust places that people aren't flocking to. But then, she hates waiting. I've lost count of the number of times we pass restaurant after restaurant with empty tables just so she can wait in line some-where else – and then have to endure her constant complaining about how long she's having to wait. It's a no-win situation. But, that's my mother. Never happier than when she *isn't* happy.'

'But you still love her, eh?'

Celia smoothed out the red checked napkin on her lap. 'Of course I do. It's just not always as simple as I'd like it to be. See, you have to understand that we've never had an easy rela-tionship. Not like I see you have with your mother. Mom always wants better for me, you know: better career, better wealth, better relationships – which is good for me, don't get me wrong; but the end result is that she's never satisfied with who I am or where I'm at. I always get the feeling she's disappointed in me somehow. So,' she brightened and I sensed the subject was being hastily discarded in favour of another, 'how's life for you? I heard you and Nate went to the Noguchi Museum on Long Island last week?'

'Yes, we did. We had a great time – the art is so amazing.'

'That's different for you guys, isn't it? Meeting *outside* of your store?'

I smiled. 'Nate said he wanted to see if our conversations would work outdoors. As it turned out, we proved his theory.'

'So, did he say any more about the Caitlin situation *outdoors*?'

It was a good question, yet here's the odd thing about last Saturday: we talked for four hours solidly and yet even now I couldn't actually tell you what we discussed. I hadn't been to Long Island before and Nate knows one of the curators of the museum, so he suggested we visit. The Noguchi is awesome – especially given the approach we made to it walking over the Roosevelt Bridge which, Nate reliably informed me, was the way the great master sculptor walked to work every morning. It was impossible not to be stirred by Isamu Noguchi's stun-

176

ningly simple sculptures in marble, alabaster, terracotta, slate and glass, amongst other mediums – and I noticed that everyone walking round seemed to be feeling it too, as a sense of reverent calm pervaded each room we entered.

The only snippet of our conversation I remember clearly is when we were strolling round the Noguchi's tranquil sculpture garden, bathed in warm autumnal sunlight. Nate suddenly went quiet.

'This place is wonderful,' I ventured, trying to make conversation.

Nate paused to look at a stone sculpture with water cascading over its surface, his face reflected and distorted by the undulating flow. 'It's peaceful,' he said, his voice sounding far away. 'You can get rid of all the stuff in your head here, you know?'

'Stuff like what?'

He sighed and I sensed the weight of his concerns bearing down on his broad shoulders. 'Just *stuff*. I dunno, Rosie – sometimes I wish life could be as simple as this garden. No clutter, everything in its place, just peaceful and ordered.'

'Sounds lovely. But it would drive you mad.'

He turned to look at me. 'Why?'

I patted his arm. 'Because you're a native New Yorker: you thrive on chaos and unpredictability. If everything was simple and organised in your life you'd be craving excitement in no time.'

Nate's trademark grin made a welcome reappearance. 'You know me so well.'

'So *what* did he say then? Did he mention Mimi or Caitlin? Or *anybody*?' Celia was staring at me like an impatient child waiting to meet Santa.

'No, that was it, and then he changed the subject,' I said, pushing my fork into the poached egg on my plate and watching the rich yellow yolk dribble over my pancakes. 'But I got the impression that things are more or less carved in stone for the two of them. I mean, he protests a lot, but at the end of the day he's still with her.'

A couple seated at the table beside us began to giggle and held hands across the blue plaid tablecloth. Celia and I watched them for a while.

'Do you ever get the feeling that everyone's moving on except you?' I asked, accidentally out loud.

Celia let out a long sigh. 'All the time, Rosie. All the time.'

Chapter Twelve

I'm always amazed at how quickly the nights draw in during autumn and the days rush headlong into winter. It's one of my favourite times of the year – especially walking in Central Park when all the trees are exhibiting their colours. It's something I loved about Boston and I thought I wouldn't see it when I moved to New York but, to my delight, New York 'does' autumn so well. It seems to get more magical and sparkly with every week that passes through September and October into November and Thanksgiving.

OK, time to be honest here: I really didn't get the concept of Thanksgiving when I first came to America. It seemed like such an odd, archaic excuse for a big meal and, when I asked people about it, nobody could quite explain it in a way that made sense to me. But then I met Celia and experienced a Reighton Thanksgiving, which is, like so many other things Celia does, truly a sight to behold. Featuring three basic ingredients: food that would make Fortnum & Mason quiver; a guest list that Jay Leno would kill for; plus the unique hostess that *is* Celia in all her glory – the combined result is pure New York magic. It was only when I was sat by the bulging Thanksgiving table at her home that I finally understood its significance for my American friends. It's something instilled into them from birth: the need to be thankful. And the festival has seemingly taken on a much deeper significance for people today, in light of the highly materialistic lifestyle everyone here is bombarded with every day. It's part of who they are as a nation and adds to that strange mix of modern consumerism and a strong sense of morals from a bygone era that is wrapped around the psyches of people who live here – where it's every person for themselves when it comes to getting ahead in life, but impoliteness is still frowned upon. Thanksgiving reminds people where they came from. And now I wouldn't miss it for the world.

'Celia's invited me to Thanksgiving at her place,' Nate grinned as we sat drinking coffee and watching the good people of New York battling against the icy prevailing wind on the street outside. 'I hear it's an awesome event.'

I rested my chin on the edge of my mug and inhaled the rich dark aroma as I raised my eyes heavenwards. 'Hmm, it sure is. Celia is not known for doing anything small when it comes to celebrations.'

'She said there'd be plenty of food.'

I took a sip of coffee. 'She's not joking! I hear the State of New York has been warned to brace itself for a food shortage after her order's been met.' I paused, debating whether or not to ask the question. 'Are you coming then?'

Nate's eyes drifted to the street outside. 'I don't know yet. I'll know after the weekend.'

Cue awkward moment. 'Ah . . . I guess Caitlin will want you to join her family?'

His expression was hard as stone and the reply was incredibly matter-of-fact. 'No.'

'Oh, right.' I was granted a temporary reprieve from a diffi-cult silence as two taxi drivers screeched to a halt right outside and began an obscenity-screaming match. I had to giggle. 'I love New York – it's such a *friendly* city.'

'Only you could find romance in a street brawl.'

Placing my hands Buddha-style on my knees I intoned, 'Nate-Student must learn from Optimism Master. Rosie Duncan say: man without optimism in New York is like Old F's coffee without good company.'

I think by now Nate had figured I was in fact completely insane. 'And what, O Great One, is that supposed to mean?'

I shrugged. 'I have no idea. But it sounded good.'

He laughed. 'So I'm good company?'

I checked my watch. 'Yes, thank you, but I'd better do some work,' I replied happily.

The door opened and an old man entered.

'Hello, Rosie! The wind blew me in this direction and I wondered why. And then I remembered that today is the second Thursday in the month so I should be here.'

I shook the age-crumpled hand of Mr Eli Lukich. 'I have your order ready. It's right here as usual.'

Eli followed me to the counter. 'You are such a good girl. I was saying to my dear Alyona only this morning what a good girl you are. You remind me of my mother, Valentina Nikolaiova, God rest her soul, when we were in the Old Country. She always remembered special days. You know, she never had a calendar? She just *knew*. So the house in Losk had flowers for birthdays, holy days and saints' days.'

I handed Eli a small bouquet of yellow roses. His hooded blue eyes scrunched up as he breathed in the scent. 'Beautiful. Beautiful, Rosie. Like my mother used to love . . . they grew in Father Gennady's garden, you know.'

I had heard the story a hundred times, but there was

something about Eli's tales of old White Russia that captivated me every time. 'Tell me about the priest, Eli.'

Eli's attention, however, had moved to Nate, who was watching the conversation with fascination. 'Hello, young man. My name is Eli Lukich. I am pleased to make your acquaintance.' He slowly extended his hand and Nate scrambled to his feet to shake it.

'Pleased to meet you, sir. I'm Nathaniel Amie.'

Mr Lukich held Nate's hand for a second and studied his face. 'I wish you blessings, Nathaniel Amie.' His eyes returned to me. 'Now how much do I owe you, Rosie?'

'No money, Mr Lukich. I'll settle for a story from the Old Country,' I replied with a smile. This was the usual, expected answer and delight lifted every line in Eli's face.

'Then I will tell you of the time Ivan Ivanovich's cow became stuck in the river . . .'

Eli proceeded to spin his tale, painting characters as vivid as the intricate designs on a Matryoshka doll. He told us about Ivan the schoolteacher, who had bought a cow for his aged mother only to find the animal preferred the lush grass of his own garden; nevertheless he persisted in leading the stubborn bovine down the dusty road from the village to his mother's house at the forest's edge, again and again.

'Eight times Ivan led the cow to the forest house; eight times the cow appeared again in his garden. In frustration, Ivan strode across the fields to calm his temper. He crossed the river and was walking across a meadow when he heard a loud splash. Turning round, what should his eyes behold but the disobedient animal lying on its side in the fast-flowing water! Once again, the cow had followed him. Well, Ivan Ivanovich tried to move it, but it was stuck fast between some rocks. Just when he was about to give up hope, who should come over the hill but

Ivan's mother! You will never believe what happened next . . . She leaned close to the cow's ear and whispered something. Then she reached into the water and lifted the rock that imprisoned its leg. Without another word, she turned to walk home and the cow followed her. From that day on, the cow remained at the forest house. So that is the story of Ivan Ivanovich and the disobedient cow. And now, I must go. My wife is waiting for me.' He said goodbye and we watched the old man leave, happily cradling his roses. Nate's smile was wider than I'd ever seen before. 'What an awesome guy. Who are the flowers for?'

'His wife, Alyona. She's ninety-three: two years his senior. It caused a big rift in their families when they married.' Something occurred to me. 'You asked me a while back how I knew what a man in love looks like . . . well, you've just met him. Eli Lukich comes into my shop every second Thursday in the month and buys a small bunch of yellow roses for his wife. Then he takes them home and proposes to her again. He's done that every month since they married, over seventy years ago. *That's* what a man in love should look like.'

Nate blew out a long whistle. 'That's a tall order, then. You must be the ultimate romantic, Rosie Duncan, if you expect *that* from a relationship.'

It was a sideswipe I deftly avoided. 'Ah, but I don't expect it, because I don't expect a relationship at all.'

'So, real love has to be perfect like theirs?'

I shook my head. 'I don't know if love today could come close to theirs. Their love has survived the hardest tests imaginable. They were disowned by their families and then fled to the US to escape persecution. They came here with nothing and, even now, they live on practically nothing. Their four children died before any of them reached the age of five. Their love is the only valuable thing they've ever owned. They've sacrificed everything to be together. *They* are the reason love should be as strong as possible. As a tribute to them, it *has* to be all or nothing. And . . . now I'm going to get down off my soapbox because I've got carried away.'

Nate's smile was warm. 'Yes you have. But that's OK because I am learning that enjoying your deep philosophy comes with the territory.'

'So is he coming to Thanksgiving here tonight or *not*?' Celia's frustration had reached breaking point as she appeared from the kitchen.

'I don't know,' I replied, picking up a bagel and turning it over absent-mindedly.

'Aarrggh, *men*!' Celia rejoined me at the large maple table and looked out of the window to the street below. 'I think Macy's parade might get snowed on this year. There's that smell in the air.'

'No need to worry then, 'cos Santa will be there and I've heard he's OK with snow.'

'I swear you are a five-year-old trapped in a grown-up's body. So how are you and Nate getting on, then?'

That must qualify for one of the most heavily weighted questions in history, but it was delivered with such nonchalance that I had to smile. 'Just fine, thank you.' Ever the investigative journalist, Celia was not going to be defeated so easily. She wanted her story and she was going to get it. Come hell, high water or bloody-minded best friends. '*How* fine, exactly?'

I conceded defeat with a smile. 'OK, OK . . . well, he comes for coffee most weeks – usually on a Monday or a Thursday around three o'clock. And sometimes we visit places at the weekends, like the Noguchi, or the Rubin Museum of Art or talks at that Writers' Collective charity bookstore in the East Village you like so much. And we talk.'

If Celia had a pressure meter fitted, it would now be reading 'Danger'. 'I am *aware* that you *talk* . . . You have been *talking* since the summer. What on earth do you still find to discuss?'

'Well, it began with Nate wanting to work out what his "story" was and, now we know each other a bit better, we've widened our remit. It's anything and everything: whatever happens to be flowing through our minds at the moment. I can't explain it: I feel happy when we spend time together. He makes me smile and it feels good. I like the fact that he doesn't have this massive inside track on me; all he knows is the person I am now, not who I was when I first came to New York, or who I was before . . . I'd forgotten how exciting it can be to start a friendship from scratch. He likes me for who I am, not what he thinks I should be. He doesn't try to tell me how to live my life. And I like that. So, we talk, we laugh, we drink coffee – and it's *wonderful*. Of course, the conversation usually comes back to Nate and his love life – but before you ask, I have nothing further to report on that subject yet.'

Celia folded her arms irritably like a mutinous three-year-old. 'That man is so *infuriating*! Doesn't he know his sole purpose in life should be to keep us informed about his private life?'

I smiled and looked away towards the window. 'The thing is, Celia, the last conversation we had was actually about *my* private life, not his.'

If you'd told Celia she'd just won the leading role in a George Clooney movie, she couldn't have looked any more utterly shocked than she did right then. 'What? Oh, Rosie, did you tell him about what happened in Boston?'

Now it was my turn to look shocked. 'Of course not! But I

told him about Mr Kowalski and then I ended up telling him about what Dad did.'

Celia clamped a hand to her forehead melodramatically. 'I am just in my *forties* – not that anyone apart from you and my mother know this, Rosie – you shouldn't give me shocks like that! Feel my heart now – go on, feel it – I swear I have palpitations!'

'Don't worry, you'll live.'

'You cruel English florist,' she continued, taking a few deep breaths and flapping her hand in front of her face like she'd just completed the New York Marathon. 'The least you can do to make up for shocking me half to death is to tell me *exactly* how the conversation happened.'

I obediently obliged.

Nate had arrived a little late, flustered and weary from his day. This was unusual. 'Why is it that so many people in this city are pathologically incapable of waiting for anything?'

'Hmm . . . had one of those days, eh?'

The now familiar lop-sided grin reappeared. 'Oh boy, have I ever. I had three agents calling me every twenty minutes to see if I'd read their clients' work yet. *Then* my CEO calls and demands we rush through a celebrity writer's new manuscript because Fox and Miramax have optioned it for development. Whatever happened to taking your time over anything?'

'I wish you'd met Mr K. You would've got on famously.'

'Y'know, it's strange, but I feel like I already know him. I mean, you talk about him so much. It's almost like he was a kind of father figure to you.'

That took me by surprise. But I had become used to that too. Nate's perceptiveness was almost as sharp as Ed's wit. And normally the subject of my father is way off limits to anyone. But I found myself telling Nate all about Dad: how he had

186

conducted an affair in secret with a family friend for over fifteen years; how my mum had found out when a neighbour made a chance remark about 'that nice lady who comes round when you're at work'; how my family had been ripped apart by Dad's constant refusal to admit his deception was wrong and his clumsy attempts to be reconciled with Mum – even though he had no intention of leaving his mistress – not to mention the ultimate betrayal when he stopped contact altogether. Nate listened intently. He even held my hand when I confessed that Mr K was the first man I'd felt I could truly trust. I think that conversation marked a turning point in our friendship. Call it trust, respect or whatever; from that moment it was as if something deepened between us.

Celia's mouth was so wide open that it could have swallowed a Greyhound Bus. 'I can't believe you told him all that, Rosie!'

'I just trust him, Celia. That conversation's unusual, though. Most of the time we talk about anything and everything. The topic is immaterial, really. It's the company that's important.'

She smiled. 'So – you like him?'

A tiny shiver of delight wriggled free and began to dance inside me. 'Yes. I like him a lot.'

Surprisingly, Celia didn't comment before launching into another topic. 'Talking of people you like – how's Ed?'

Hmm. Difficult one. Ed was fine, really, just his usual self. Still out with a different lady each week, still effortlessly charming and dishevelled in equal measures. But behind it all, I had a small yet annoying inkling that he was hiding something. Which, admittedly, was not unusual for the 'Iceberg Known as Ed Steinmann'. But it was enough for it to solicit my attention. Since his disastrous date with The Beautiful Face of Jean St Pierre, Ed's date-life had returned to some kind of casual normality, the details of which he generously shared with Marnie and me, driving us to near distraction – so much so that Marnie said she was tempted to catch the flu again just for the respite.

'I swear, Rosie, I'm going to commit murder if I hear any more of his date stories,' she'd grimaced last week as we were loading the van with flowers for a demonstration at a trade fair.

'I know, mate,' I had sympathised, patting her shoulder. 'Maybe I should have a word with him about it.'

'A word about what?' Ed said, appearing at the back door. Marnie gave me a quick smile and retreated back inside.

'Look, mate, it's great that you're dating and it's lovely to hear about all these beautiful women you are seeing, but I think you need to go easy on the details when we're at work, OK?'

Ed's smile faded slightly. 'Oh? How come?'

'Because it's all you ever talk about at the moment. At least before it was dating and baseball, or dating and movies. Now it's just date, date, date, all the time. To be honest, it's getting boring.'

Ed shook his head and took a step away. 'Well, say what you think, Rosie. I happen to be *happy*, that's all. Are you telling me you guys don't want me to be happy now?'

I sighed and looked at the ground. 'That's not what I'm saying and you know it. Carry on having fun and date anyone you like; just don't feel you have to tell us about it all the time, OK?'

Ed shrugged and stared at me. 'Fine with me. Personally, I think you're jealous.'

'What?'

'But that's cool, really. You don't have to pretend with me, you know.'

188

'I have no idea what you're talking about.'

'Come on, Rosie, admit it: this isn't about me talking too much. The real reason you object is that every time I go out with another date it reinforces the fact that you don't have one. Like I said, you're jealous.'

Annoyed, I slammed the back doors of the van and turned to face him. 'I am not. And neither is Marnie, OK? She's just a little – how can I put this? – *sensitive* at the moment. She's fallen for someone in her theatre group and he doesn't seem to be interested. She's taken it quite hard, I think.'

Ed's expression mellowed a little. 'Man, I had no idea. Sorry.'

'It's fine. We just need to be a little careful around her right now, you know? Give her a little space.'

'Think she'd be interested in hearing how the World Series went?' he ventured.

I patted his shoulder as I walked back inside the shop. 'It's worth a try, mate.'

So, like I say, Ed had been more or less his usual self. But a part of me still sensed a discrepancy in the happiness he boasted of so vociferously and so often.

'I think you're being a little over-protective of him, Rosie,' Celia remarked. 'Ed is a big boy now. I'm sure he can handle this just fine by himself.'

'Which translates as, "butt out, Rosie", I suppose?'

Celia threw her arms around me and attempted to remove all air from my lungs in one enthusiastic embrace. 'Darling, you worry too much. Now, about the Thanksgiving guest list . . .'

'OK . . . but can we watch the parade on TV while we discuss it?'

Celia shook her head in pity. '*Sure*, sweetie. Would you like some warm milk and cookies while you watch?'

189

I smiled sheepishly. 'No thanks, Mummy. I'm fine with my bagel.'

Celia groaned as she reached for the TV remote.

Some people say it's cruel to tell kids that Santa Claus is real. And I can kind of see their point. I mean, if you grow up with parents who assure you they'll always tell you the truth and then you find out they've told you a lie, what does it do to your faith in them? I found out about Santa Claus – or Father Christmas, as he was always referred to in my home – when I was four years old, but it never shattered my faith in my parents' credibility. Plenty of other things did later on – well, about Dad, anyway. But Father Christmas remained a magical, hopeful story that this particular child always believed in. *Always*. I'm still convinced I can hear sleigh bells on Christmas Eve and, though he doesn't visit me anymore, I remain suspicious that all those grown-ups might have got it wrong after all – and, actually, he *is* real.

When I arrived at Celia's for her Thanksgiving dinner later that evening, the party was already in full swing. Nate wasn't there – much to Celia's utter disappointment – but I wasn't surprised. With Mimi and Caitlin running his life the chances of him making a decision for himself seemed decidedly slim at the best of times, so the thought of his missing Thanksgiving was preposterous in the extreme.

'Rosie!' Celia exclaimed, arriving from the kitchen with a large basket of bread rolls, which prompted the guests to join in a bizarre game of serving dish rearrangement on the table – like one of those tile games you got in your Christmas stocking when you were little where you have to move the pieces round until it makes a picture. 'Thank *heaven* you're here – I am at my *wits'* end. Half of my order didn't arrive, can you *believe* it? I have had the supplier on the phone *six* times this afternoon about it.'

I stared at her. 'This is only *half* of what you ordered?'

She nodded and punched her hands onto her hips like Doris Day in *Calamity Jane*. 'Do you think it's enough, sweetie? I'm so worried.'

'Celia, this is enough to cater for a small nation,' I laughed. 'It all looks wonderful. Here, I brought you these,' I handed her a hand-tied posy of red and white roses with tiny blue ornamental thistles in a stars-and-stripes gift-bag, 'although I have no idea where on earth you'll put them.'

After enthusing about the flowers, Celia disappeared in a blur of green silk, apron flapping as she left. I turned to meet the other guests. There were several I didn't know – who turned out to be fellow writers from her West Village Writers' Circle – together with a few familiar faces from the *New York Times*. Josh Mercer, the young reporter who had interviewed me, was there too. He asked me how Mrs Schuster was getting on, which was sweet, then introduced me to one of his colleagues in Features, Stewart Mitchell. He was tall and strikingly hand-some, with a soft Southern lilt to his voice. Originally from Iowa, he had moved to New York after gaining his Journalism degree from Harvard. It was difficult to determine exactly how old he was – tiny silver flecks in his black hair suggested he was in his thirties but his olive skin bore few signs of age. He had a shy smile and stunning green-blue eyes that seemed to be illuminated from within and his easy manner and razor-sharp wit made me like him immediately.

I ended up being seated opposite Stewart and next to Josh as we all made a brave attempt to demolish the enormous feast Celia had set before us, and the conversation flowed freely for the next few hours. This is something I love about parties at Celia's: she makes everyone feel at home. The conversation is never forced and you never feel like you have to make an effort to enjoy yourself. She has a complete gift for assembling the most interesting people, which means you end up chatting to hitherto complete strangers like you've known them for years.

One thing I noticed as the evening progressed was the way Stewart's attention kept moving to Celia. At first, I dismissed it as shyness, assuming that he was simply seeking out familiar faces in a room full of people he didn't know very well. But as time went on, I was aware of it more and more. After about the eighth course – at least, I *think* it was the eighth – when Celia started clearing away some of the many plates to make room for yet more food, Stewart and I both volunteered to help at the same time: laughing, we agreed to share the table-clearing responsibilities. I followed him into the kitchen with an armful of crockery.

'Great party,' Stewart said, carefully placing a stack of plates in the sink.

'Yes, it is,' I replied, 'but then Celia's parties always are.'

'No doubting that – here, let me help you with those.' He took the crockery from me, the shy grin flashing as he did so.

'Thank you.' I turned to leave.

'Actually, I was wondering if you could help me with something,' Stewart said suddenly, making me jump and turn back. He was looking at me like a nervous puppy, a slight blush creeping across his cheekbones.

'Erm – yes, of course.'

He leaned against the work surface, gripping its edge with his hands. 'You've known Celia a while, right?'

'Yes – just over six years.'

'And you're close to her?'

'She's my best friend,' I smiled. 'Why?'

He rubbed the back of his neck and looked to the ceiling for inspiration. 'Uh – I was just wondering what the deal is with her and Jerry.'

I wasn't entirely sure how to answer. After all, Stewart had only been working at the paper a matter of months and I didn't know how much of Celia's private life she wanted to be common knowledge. 'Stewart, I don't know if I should—'

'It's OK,' he said quickly, standing up straight. 'She told me he wasn't around any more. I just wondered if she was – uh – you know, *dating* right now?'

It was impossible to hide my surprise. 'Really?'

'*Really* really,' he nodded, the blush intensifying. 'Hey, I know there's, like, *fifteen* years between us, and I know she is probably fending guys off from every direction. I also know she's so way out of my league it's crazy to even contemplate the possibility of . . . of *us* . . . But I can't help it, Rosie. I can't get her out of my head. She *astounds* me – I mean, completely, on every level – and I can't stop thinking about her.'

'Wow . . .'

'Yeah, I know. Crazy but true.'

'Have you told her how you feel?'

A look of pure fear washed across his face. 'No! I just can't find the words, you know? I'm scared she'll take one look at me and laugh. I mean, come on – someone as beautiful and assured as her choosing a rookie like me?'

'But you want her to know?'

'Of course I do.'

This was such a surprise, yet I sensed that this might just be good for Celia. While she'd said no more about Jerry since our conversation at Bistro Découvertè at the end of summer, I knew she was lonely and something like this would give her a boost, if nothing else. So I decided to trust Stewart. 'Celia isn't dating anyone that I know of, but Jerry's definitely not coming back.'

'Do you think I have a chance?'

I grinned at him. 'Well, you won't find out unless you try.'

'But what can I do? I mean, I wanted to send flowers but I remember her saying she was very choosy about them. That was why I wanted to talk to you. You're her friend *and* her florist, right?'

'Guilty on both counts.'

'I thought about sending her flowers that reminded me of her. I was thinking those pink and white lilies . . .'

'Stargazers? Oh, no, whatever you do, don't send Celia lilies! She can't stand the smell.'

'What, then?'

'She adores orchids of any colour, but I happen to know that white ones are her absolute favourite.'

His face lit up. 'Could you send her a bouquet of them for me? I mean anonymously, of course?'

I nodded, thrilled at the surprise that lay in store for Celia. 'Absolutely.'

Chapter Thirteen

Once November begins, Kowalski's orders take on a decidedly festive theme and the workload increases. Especially so this year. Months in the planning already, the time was fast approaching for Mimi Sutton's annual charity Grand Winter Ball. A big title for an even bigger event. While still more than a touch dubious about being a Mimi Sutton Recommendation, I was pleased that we had been given such a prestigious platform.

It had been a busy day at the store and the time Ed and I had earmarked for designing Mimi's order didn't materialise. But the work needed to be done so we could order the flowers and draft in extra staff in time. So I suggested having dinner at mine so we could design in more convivial surroundings. Ed agreed.

In all the time we've worked together, I think Ed's been to my place maybe twice. He's often quipped that I'm hiding a secret there and that must be why he's rarely invited. Of course, this isn't true. It's just that, with Ed and me on opposite sides of Manhattan, when we meet up outside of work it's normally somewhere in the middle. Plus, Ed has a near pathological dislike of the Upper West Side, which he claims is the preserve of superficial shopaholics with more money than sense. But I don't see it that way at all.

It's a friendly, intelligent neighbourhood filled with fascinating people and places as varied as anywhere else in New York.

As I opened my front door and turned on the lights, Ed laughed. 'So, you finally decided to admit me to your Holy of Holies . . . Do I need to remove my shoes in reverence?'

He soon made himself at home and as I dished out the Chinese food we'd picked up he took out his sketchpad and consulted his notes. 'I went to view the venue yesterday and I think we've got a lot of scope for big displays. There's an excellent staircase leading from the lobby up to the ballroom – I see fir and bay garlands working well there.'

I sat beside him and looked at his sketches. 'Mmm, yes. Great. I was envisaging a three-colour scheme – green, white, and red for accents. We can use white gardenias and lilies along with roses for displays and table pieces. I want to avoid poinsettias, though. Way too clichéd.'

'That's fine,' Ed said between mouthfuls. 'They are *so* done already. Let's look for unusual reds then – maybe utilise red foliage, too?'

'Great.'

'I want to do some structural stuff around the pillars in the entrance lobby, too. Something bold, showy even. We need to create a sense of awe *before* people see the staircase,' Ed said, showing me the sketches he'd made.

'See, this is why I love working with you – your designs are awesome.'

'Though I say it myself, they are.'

There was a silence as we ate. Ed looked round my apartment. 'I like the style in here,' he remarked. 'Very homely.'

'Well, that would be because it's my home. And I love it.'

'Well, I love it too,' Ed replied. He put his plate on the coffee table and sank back into the sofa. He let out a sigh and turned the full force of the blue stare on me.

'Rosie, I owe you an apology.'

'You do?'

He nodded. 'Uh-huh. I've not been myself the past month. I've been frustrated with my life and I've taken it out on you. On more than one occasion. Which is unforgivable.'

'Absolutely,' I smiled. 'Except that I forgive you.'

A broad beam spread across Ed's face and his hand grasped mine. 'I'd be lost without you. But you still deserve an explanation.'

I frowned. 'I thought you just explained. You've not been yourself . . .'

'It's more than that. I've had a lot on my mind recently.'

'I know. Karin, Ellen, Mai, Susie, Elisabeth . . . did I forget anyone?' I laughed.

He looked genuinely surprised. 'Didn't realise you were keeping count.'

'I'm not.'

'You remember their names better than I do.' Shaking his head, he let out a long, heavy sigh. 'It isn't working anymore, Rosie.'

'What isn't?'

'The dating thing. At least, not the same as it did before. I don't know if it's a certain age I've gotten to or something else. I've always been more than content with dating and having fun. I never thought I needed anything more than that. But lately, I've found myself wanting to belong to somebody. Is that weird?'

I smiled but a bittersweet chill reverberated within me. 'No, mate. That's just human nature. I guess the real time to worry is when you stop wanting to belong to just any somebody and start wanting to belong to a Specific Somebody.'

'Ah, yeah. Sure. That's the time to leave town all right. *Bad sign.*' He looked away and embarked on what appeared to be an in-depth inspection of the top of his knees. 'I don't know, Rosie. Do you feel like that, ever?'

'No,' came my abrupt reply, surprising even me. 'Never.' It was a lie: I needed to change the subject; I was feeling cornered again. But the game was up when he lifted his eyes again and I saw his expression. He knew me too well. I relented. 'Sometimes, then, yes. OK, Dr Steinmann, you have an admission. But tell anyone and you die, understand?'

Ed's smile had relief written all over it.

Marnie giggled as she held out the phone to me. 'It's your *regular* admirer, Rosie!'

I glared at her and took the receiver. 'Hello?'

'Rosie! I got you a gig!' Nate's voice was all warmth and humour.

'Nate, I don't know if you realised this yet, but I'm not a musician. I'm a *florist.*'

'Ha, ha. English sarcasm is so quaint. Now listen up, I got you the commission for a big wedding – and I mean humongous . . . lavish . . . *huge* . . .'

My heart sank. 'So you're finally going through with it?'

Nate's laugh was so loud that both Marnie and Ed looked up from the other side of the shop and exchanged glances.

'What are you, nuts? It's not *my wedding,* you crazy woman. I've only promised to propose to Caitlin "sometime soon", remember? By my reckoning, that means I'm good for at least two more years. The wedding in question is for my friend. He saw that piece about you in the *Times* and, when he found out I knew you, I said I'd arrange a meeting. So can you come to my office tomorrow, about eleven?'

'I . . . um . . . don't know what to say, Nate.'

'Just say yes, woman! The wedding's spring next year . . . it's gonna be great, Rosie! I'll call him and confirm we're good to meet, shall I? Say yes.'

'Yes. But—'

'Awesome! See ya tomorrow. You won't regret this.'

I put the receiver down and jumped as Marnie and Ed appeared next to me like two wide-eyed bushbabies.

'Well?' demanded Ed.

The conversation had totally thrown me.

'I – um – Nate said he . . . There's going to be a wedding.'

Marnie squealed with delight. 'He *proposed*!'

Ed frowned and elbowed her. 'Marnie.' His blue gaze sharpened. 'He didn't, did he?'

I pulled myself together. 'No . . . He's got a friend who wants us to do his wedding. It's going to be big, apparently. So I've got to meet him at Nate's office tomorrow morning.'

Marnie's widening eyes threatened total face domination. 'A big society wedding? With movie stars?'

I laughed. 'I doubt it. But it's going to be a grand affair by the sound of it.'

'Ryan Reynolds might be there, though . . . I mean, it's possible, right?'

Ed shook his head. 'Poor, deluded child. Yeah, sure, it's possible, baby. Maybe he'll bring Keanu and Brad and Joaquin with him too.'

'Ooh, *Keanu* . . .' Marnie breathed, undeterred, as she skipped joyfully into her fantasy world. Ed and I retreated to the workroom to discuss reality, neither of us having the heart to bring her back to earth.

Sometimes, it's easier to dream than be awake.

*   *   *

I didn't sleep much that night. Once again I found myself in a dream with the face-changing embracer. Then I was running . . . running scared from an unseen adversary, skidding round dark corners, diving into side streets . . . all the time deafened by the insistent pace of a heavy beat . . . When I violently woke in the cold, dark silence of my room, I realised the beat was my own heart. I rose and paced round my apartment, switching on every light and looking in every corner, till my pulse rate eased and the fear subsided. I opened a window, closed my eyes and let the constant hum of the city soothe my soul for a long time. Then, taking a deep breath, I closed the window and extinguished the trail of lights on my weary return to bed.

Chapter Fourteen

I don't know what I expected Gray & Connelle's offices to look like, but what I saw certainly wasn't it. I think I'd pictured Nate and his colleagues working in a dusty, wood-panelled library, sitting beneath huge book skyscrapers surrounded by half-read, yet-to-be-read and discarded manuscripts from hopeful writers. The reality couldn't have been further removed from that. Instead of resembling something from an Agatha Christie novel, his office was light and contemporary: the minimum of clutter and the minimum of fuss – and not a dusty book or dog-eared manuscript in sight.

I reckon New York has an agency specifically devoted to providing über-stylish and ultra-efficient receptionists for its many swanky offices. The receptionist at Gray & Connelle seemed to be about six feet tall (most of which appeared to be legs), with effortlessly coiffed black hair and a suit so sharp you could carve roast beef with one sleeve.

'Good morning, Ms Duncan. Mr Amie will be with you shortly. In the meantime my name is Sondra and I'm able to provide you with coffee or tea while you wait?'

I wasn't sure if this was a statement or a question. 'Um . . . yes, tea would be good, thanks.'

Sondra smiled a professional smile, but I suspected her view of me was far from complimentary. 'Certainly, Ms Duncan. Take a seat, please.'

I took a good look around. Everything seemed to be white in this place – the floors, the reception desk, the flowers in the vase on the reception desk – even the modern artwork could have been titled *White with a Hint of Cream and Magnolia*. It occurred to me while I was waiting that I would be so scared to work somewhere like this. I know I would have to battle the urge to accidentally spill *very* colourful things everywhere. It was far too good a blank canvas to ignore.

A large white door opposite the white reception area swung open and Nate strolled happily out.

'Hi, Rosie. Sorry to keep you waiting so long. I just had one hell of a phone call. Come in.' He grabbed my hand and led me past efficiently smiling Sondra through the big white doors and into his office. I smiled as I looked around. He had personalised every wall with photographs – some framed, most not – friendly faces and exotic locations, autumn trees and snow-capped mountains. Above the window was a Yale pennant and a signed baseball had been granted pride of place on his large oak desk.

He saw my amusement and laughed. 'Not quite in keeping with the corporate image, huh?'

'No, no, it's not. But it's good. This whole place is *too white*.'

Nate flopped down into his comfortable-looking upholstered light oak chair. 'I know! You see, that's why I like you, Rosie. I *knew* you'd think that. You're just like me.'

We exchanged satisfied smiles.

'So – where's your friend?'

'He's due here any minute.' Nate checked his watch. 'Actually, he's late.' He pressed a button on his phone and spoke into the intercom. 'Sondra, when my eleven o'clock arrives, would you show him straight in, please?'

'Certainly, sir,' came the reply, super-efficient and stylish even when disembodied.

'So, you said it's a big wedding?'

'We're talking gigantic, my friend. And he wants only you! He said to me, "I need Rosie Duncan's flair – only her expertise will do. She's obviously a real find." A real find! His family have a fortune – we're talking *serious* money here.'

'And you think Kowalski's could handle it?' I asked, nerves beginning to flutter. I had only just got my head around the thought of Kowalski's successfully managing the Grand Winter Ball commission: the thought of orchestrating a huge society wedding was too scary for words.

'Absolutely.' Nate stood up and walked to my side of the desk. Perching on the edge of it he reached out and took both my hands. His lop-sided grin spread across his face as his dark eyes zoomed in on me. 'I believe in you. You can handle this, Rosie. You're more than able to do it. Trust me.'

For a moment silence fell and the soft, warm hands retained mine. It was as if we were the only two people in New York.

And New York was smiling like Nate.

Abruptly, the moment ended as the large white doors opened smartly. Nate let my hands go as he looked up quickly, smiling broadly to welcome his friend. 'About time, David! I said eleven, not eleven thirty. Rosie, let me introduce my tardy but very good friend – David Lithgow.'

I had already stood and started to turn when the name hit me like a boulder.

Everything went into slow motion as the world around me began to shatter. Sound and movement blurred into a swirling mass. Somewhere way in the back of my consciousness I was aware of Nate's continuing happy chatter as *that name* repeated over and over . . . *David Lithgow* . . . *David Lithgow* . . . I felt my security, my peace, my entire life dissolving as I found myself face to face with familiar grey eyes – eyes I never expected to see again. I felt sick. I needed to get out, to run away, but I couldn't move. I heard Nate's voice again as the room resumed its normal speed and I steadied myself by gripping the back of the chair.

'Rosie – I said are you OK?' Nate's voice was full of concern.

'I'm – fine, yes . . .' I stuttered weakly.

'It's so good to see you again, Rosie.' David spoke gently, but every word bruised me.

'Hello, David.' My calm reply belied the torrent of emotion shaking me to the core.

'You two know each other?' Nate asked, surprised.

'Yes,' David and I said together, his eyes still invading mine. A smile lit Nate's features. 'Well, how about that! So, let's sit and I'll have Sondra bring us some refreshment. Then we can discuss how much you're willing to pay for my friend's excellent services.' He winked at me and walked to the door, disappearing briefly outside. I sank back into my chair, eyes defiantly focused on the skyline beyond David.

He took a step towards me. 'Rosie – I—'

I froze.

'OK!' Nate reappeared and sat at his desk. 'So, David, tell me, how do you know Rosie?'

David's eyes didn't leave me. 'We go back a long way. We worked together in London for a while. It really is great to find her again – after all these years.'

I caught Nate's eyes and tried to smile. He saw through it and the corners of his grin tightened. 'Great . . .' he said slowly, his eyes surveying me as questions darted across his face. Then he turned to David. 'So, tell us about the wedding.'

David reluctantly sat down in a brown leather chair to one side of the desk. He took a breath. 'OK, well . . . it will be in March next year at my parents' place in the Hamptons. We're expecting around four hundred guests and those are likely to include dignitaries, senators, maybe some A-listers – we're not sure yet. Rachel and I want it to be a truly memorable occasion.'

I caught my breath as pain more vivid than I'd felt in a long time stabbed me inside.

Nate's eyes shot to mine. I pretended to cough. The dark eyes narrowed. 'Well, with Rosie Duncan there it's bound to be memorable.'

I coughed again, harder, as I rose quickly. 'I – I just need some water . . . if you'll excuse me . . .'

'Sondra can bring some in . . . I'll call her.' Nate offered, but I was already halfway to the door.

I tripped over my words as I fled the room. 'The designs . . . my – uh – design book is right there . . . feel free to look . . . Please excuse me . . .'

Out in the stark whiteness of the reception I paused to snatch some air. Sondra stood up. 'Ms Duncan? Are you well?'

'I'm fine . . . I need some water . . . please.'

Sondra's expression flickered and just a little compassion broke free, softening her tone. 'The restroom is just across the hall. You'll find water there. If you need me just call. I'll be right here, OK?'

I managed a smile. 'Thank you.'

In contrast to the clinical blank canvas of the offices, the restroom was filled with warm colour, soft music and comforting scent. I filled a glass with water and slowly sat down on a padded velvet couch. My whole body was shaking. Desperately, I struggled to order my rioting thoughts. *I must get away from here...NOW...it's time to leave,* said one. *Don't be ridiculous, this is my home now...I shouldn't have to leave,* scolded another. *I never thought I'd have to see him again ...* yet another thought pondered. *Yes, but you never thought he'd want to find you,* my conscience replied, *and now he's here, so what are you going to do?*

My face was hot so I went to the sink and ran my hands under cold water, patting my cheeks to cool them down. As I did so, I caught sight of myself in the elaborately framed mirror over the washbasin. My own dark eyes were full of the same fear I'd seen in Boston, just before I came to New York.

I frowned at my reflection. This was where I belonged – where I was happier than I'd ever been before – was I *really* ready to throw it all away, just because David Lithgow had reappeared in my life?

As I stood there, a change began. I don't know what happened exactly, but I felt a strong surge of anger rush through me. While a large part of me was still reeling from the shock of seeing David again, I began to take hold of my emotions. Now was not the time to run.

I grabbed a hand towel and dried my face, smoothed down my hair and straightened my jacket. With a sense of purpose that surprised me, I smiled at my reflection. This time, I wasn't going anywhere except straight back into Nate's office.

I opened the restroom door and walked quickly across the lobby past Sondra.

'How are you feeling?' she asked.

I nodded. 'I'm fine, thank you.'

This is where I belong, I told myself. *Nobody is taking that away from me.* As I reached the door to the office, I knew exactly what I had to do. I was going to take the commission. Nate and David stood up to meet me.

'Thanks for waiting for me. So, do you see anything suitable?'

David offered my design book back to me. 'They're excellent, Rosie,' he replied, with a warmth that sent icicles up my spine. 'You have such a gift for design.'

I reached out to receive it. 'Thank you.' David's hold on the book remained for a second longer than it should have done, pulling my hand a little towards him. With white-hot indignation rising inside I gave a sharp tug and he let go. I wrenched my eyes from his stare.

'David was saying you worked for an advertising agency in London?' Nate smiled, intently studying my response.

'Yes, before I decided to fulfil my mother's prophecy about me and start to design with flowers.' I smiled as naturally as I could manage.

'How is Rosemary?' David interrupted.

My smile faded instantly. 'She's well.' Tangible tension sparked round the room.

'So, David, do you want Rosie to design for your big day then?' Nate asked. 'Bearing in mind of course she's *very* sought-after in this town now, and therefore very expensive.'

David smiled. 'But worth every cent, I'm certain. I would love her to. *If* she'll take the commission, that is.'

Inside me, a battle was raging. The indignation remained, fuelling my resolve to accept the job, yet the shattered, fearful part of me screamed out in protest: *I never want to see you again!* I fought the urge to say no, even though it seemed to be winning the war of wills within me. I looked over at Nate and something in his expression filled me with a strange trust. Taking a deep breath, I agreed.

David's surprise was impossible to conceal. 'Rosie, I don't know what to say. *Thank you.* Thank you so much.' He leaned towards me and my stomach somersaulted.

'I – I really should be getting back to the shop.' I stood awkwardly, as Nate and David did the same. 'I'll see you on Thursday, Nate?'

'*Definitely.*' Nate smiled as he accompanied me to the door. Ordeal nearly over, I started to feel stronger as I stepped out of the office. Then David called to me.

'Rosie, can I call you? About the wedding? Soon?'

I felt the nausea launch a new, devastating assault on me. Scared that I was losing control, I quickly replied 'Yes, David. Call me at the shop. Nate has my card.'

Nate's arm slipped carefully round my shoulders as we neared the elevator that would grant me my freedom at last.

'Rosie, are you sure you're OK?'

His touch sent waves of relief washing over me. I stopped and, for just a moment, allowed myself to lean into the half-embrace. 'I'm good, Nate, really. It was just a shock to see him – after so long . . . I'm fine, honestly.'

Despite my reassurance, tears were threatening to reveal the truth in my eyes. And added to my tangle of emotions was a new battle: my need to leave now faced a challenge from an unfamiliar desire to remain with this reassuring dark gaze and soothing touch. As though sensing my struggle, Nate's arm turned me slowly to face him and I found myself pulled close to his scented body. His right arm enfolded me closer yet: I could feel the pulse in his neck as it gently padded against my cheek. I closed my eyes and inhaled the fragrance of his skin. He spoke: his voice deep velvet, resonating through my body.

'Rosie, what is it? Did I do the wrong thing? Have I hurt you?' His questions came in short bursts, sending a hot breeze across my hair. I reached my hand to press against his back and the muscles were firm beneath my fingers. I was in danger of losing myself in the maelstrom of conflicting senses. It was time to leave.

'No, Nate, you've done nothing wrong . . . it's OK.' I pulled away. 'But I really do have to go. I'll see you Thursday.'

Nate stood, motionless, his eyes fixed on me as the elevator doors shut him from my view. Finally alone, I slumped to the floor and sobbed as the lift began its descent.

'Sooner or later the thing you fear most will come to find you.'

When Mr Kowalski said that to me one day, not long after I'd joined him at the store, I admit I disagreed strenuously. You can *always* escape your fears, I argued, especially your worst ones. It's just a kind of game, surely? The more you understand when and where your fear will be hiding, the better you are able to choose a different route.

Mr K shook his head and I remember painful history colouring his eyes as he spoke. '*Ukochana*, the fear will hold your life in a trap – like the ones my mama used to snare rabbits. Unless you get rid of it, its grip on you will tighten as you struggle. You cannot "understand" the trap: it is real and it will kill you if you don't get free quick. Papa sends the fear, Rosie, time and again, until you are ready to get free from it at last. Sooner or later you will have to fight it to the death if you are to live.'

His words unnerved me then. And now, as they appeared to be coming true, I longed to talk to him about it. I never told Mr K about the reason I had come to New York – yet now, when I needed to share it, he was no longer there to listen.

I stumbled from Gray & Connelle's building in a numbed daze. My steps gathered speed. I knew I was heading in the wrong direction but I was unable to stop my feet from moving that way. I needed to get away, but where to? Not to Kowalski's that was for certain. Not yet. Ed would want to help, but the thought of him demanding every detail of my ordeal was unbearable. To explain why I was in such a state would mean explaining *everything* to him, and I just wasn't ready. But I couldn't go home, either: I couldn't face the thought of being alone with the raging cacophony of my emotions. I hurried on, fearing that David might be close behind, as my journey continued in its unspecific direction. Streets and sounds and smells became unfamiliar as I strayed further from what I knew. Eventually my salt-burned eyes recognised a Starbucks sign and I headed for it with relief.

The warmth of the coffee house, with its familiar smells and sounds, wrapped round my aching, trembling body like a comfort blanket. I ordered a macchiato and found a table as far away from the window as possible. It was half-hidden from view of the other customers by a large potted plant and I felt safe. My heart was still loud in my ears, its beat relentless, as I shut my eyes and tried to breathe deeply.

Images of David and Nate tore through my head, accompanied by alternate waves of revulsion and longing: an undulating waltz in the pit of my stomach. David Lithgow was here – in my city. *How dare he be here, now?* The look on his face had been pure, undiluted triumph at finding me again . . . I shook my head as the realisation hit me: I'd accepted the commission and condemned myself to months of undesired, unpleasant contact with the One Thing I Feared. I made myself take a large mouthful of hot coffee, which stabbed my throat in its fast descent. The heat dulled the effect of my nausea and my thoughts swung to Nate. And the way he'd held me. That embrace remained etched on my mind and sent a flood of tingling right through me. The scent of his body, the rapid

beating of his pulse, his strong safe arms cradling me . . .
Emotions I had packed away so carefully years before now lay
scattered around me and I was unable to shelve them again.
What was I feeling?

The sharp trill of my cell phone broke into my distress.

'Rosie? Where are you?'

A torrent of relief hit me and I sobbed back down the phone.
'Oh, Celia . . .'

'Hell, Rosie, I've been so worried. Nate's worried too. He
called me and told me about the meeting.'

Another sob sufficed as my answer.

'Sweetie – is it David?'

'Yes . . .' I moaned.

'And he's getting married?'

The pain was too much. I needed my friend. Celia swore
loudly, then regained her control and spoke with gentle firm-
ness. 'OK, Rosie, this is what we're gonna do: you're gonna get
in a cab and come here – now – and we're gonna make this
all good for you, OK?'

I had already gathered my things and was heading for the
street. 'I'm on my way.'

Chapter Fifteen

Honesty. It's a strange animal: good or bad depending on whether you're on the receiving or giving end. Why is it that people find the thing so easy to demand and yet so hard to practise? All my life, I have tried to be honest with people.

Not long after I first met her, Celia diagnosed this as part of my problem. 'You wear you heart like a Prada bag, Rosie, so everyone can see it. Sometimes it pays to be just a tad elusive.'

So I took it on board, becoming entirely elusive about my heart. I decided that nobody would be able to come close to hurting me again if my heart wasn't on show. And it worked successfully for me. Until now.

Because *now* the very person that held the key to my past had appeared in the one place I felt safest – in Nate's company. He'd *seen* my reaction in there; I couldn't avoid the process of telling him everything now. Deep down, I knew it: the time was coming when I would have to reveal all my secrets. And, though the thought sent a chord of fear chiming inside, I knew that sooner or later other friends would have to know too. Soon, I feared, the whole world would have to know. The pain of the revelations would only end once everyone knew the events of six and a half years ago: the reason why I ended up hiding in a flower shop in the best city in the world. Everyone would know – including Ed; how could I tell Ed? The thought of picking over the shards of my past with him, after so many years spent avoiding the question, sent a flood of panic from my head to my toes. But that was to come; what lay ahead right now was the distinct possibility that Nate would want to find out why seeing David had shaken me so much. Our friendship had become so important to me – no, *he* had become so important to me. Sitting in the taxicab I realised I was trapped – being pulled at speed towards the truth when all I wanted to do was run from it.

Talking about my heart had become something I feared – almost more than anything else. Because honesty meant risk; and risk meant losing people. And talking about my past . . . it meant admitting defeat again. Talking about pain that I had so purposefully hidden meant me having to *feel* it all over again – feel *him* all over again. Six and a half years ago I vowed never to feel that way ever again. About anybody. And it had worked, in a fashion. I had rebuilt my life and started to dare to believe I was happy. I could even ignore that feeling of solitary emptiness you get when you close your front door at the end of the day and find there's only ever you at home. Yes, I was lonely; but I was safe because I was in control. Control was, admittedly, a poor substitute for true happiness, but it was something I understood and felt comfortable with.

Right now, I wasn't in control and it was terrifying.

Celia met me outside her office building on 8th Avenue and walked me briskly inside the glass lobby. As we got into the elevator she gripped my hand.

'OK . . . now I need to tell you before we get up to my office, because I don't want you to get upset: Nate's here.'

Somehow, I knew he would be. My worst fears confirmed,

214

I spun round and walked purposefully back out into the atrium. Celia scuttled after me, eventually halting my escape by grabbing my shoulders and bodily blocking the way. Cornered, I scrabbled for excuses, desperate to take flight.

'Celia, let me go! You don't understand. I *need to go home* . . . I don't feel well.' It all fell on stony ground.

'*No*, Rosie. I won't let you. You're not running away. *Not* this time.'

Anger was building steadily in my gut. 'I'll do what I damn well want. Let me go!'

My shout echoed around the walls and a few passers-by turned to look at me. Celia's voice was calm and patient yet unswerving in its resolve. '*No*, Rosie.'

Something in her tone extinguished the fire within me. I blinked back stinging tears. 'Why?'

Celia released her grip. Face to face with my best friend I saw tears of compassion fill her eyes. 'Why? Because you deserve to *live*, Rosie, not be beaten by this – this *thing* anymore. Because there are good people – like Ed and Nate – who ought to know what a rough deal you've had in order to appreciate how strong and victorious you truly are. Don't look at me that way. I *know* what you've been through, remember? I've seen the struggle in you more than anyone. But, honey, you've succeeded where most people would have self-destructed. Sure, maybe you did run away; I mean no one knows what you've coped with alone. But, my darling, you're stronger than you feel! And you know it's time now: time to be honest, time to fight your past – to fight David – and prove to yourself that you can win. You know I'm right.'

I did. Despite every fibre of my being screaming otherwise, I knew it was time to face my biggest fear. Like Mr K said: this was my time to 'get free, quick'. I felt weak.

'I'll need your help.'

'And I'll be right here for you, honey, all the way.'

Holding tightly onto Celia's arm, I took a deep breath and began to walk forward. The elevator door closed. And my journey began.

Like I said, I got a job at an advertising agency in London after graduating from university. Q. J. Johnson Associates was a relatively new but highly successful company and I joined them during their boom years. Fuelled by the passion of young, aspiring designers, the company quickly transitioned from an artsy design house to a trend-setting major-league player. It was an energising, exciting place to work and I loved it from the day I arrived.

I had worked there for just over eighteen months when we landed the biggest contract in the company's history: a huge multinational company commissioned us for a transatlantic campaign.

One breezy day in early April, about a month into the job, QJ, my boss called me to ask a favour.

'Rosie, we've got some Yank designers coming to co-work with your team on this job. Damned nuisance, I know, but the client insisted we field a transatlantic team, so there's nothing I can do. Their flight arrives at Heathrow this afternoon and my car's out of action. Would you be able to do it?'

Although I was in the middle of what appeared to be the busiest day of my life, I agreed. I decided the drive would do me good and, secretly, I wanted to chat to the new designers first so as to retain artistic integrity on the project I now regarded as mine. Plus, it was the nearest thing to an afternoon off I'd had in months.

The traffic out of London was awful but weak spring

sunshine gave London that magical quality you always expect to find, but never quite do. Resigned to a long journey, I decided to enjoy it. So I cranked up the volume on the radio and sang along all the way to Terminal Four.

Once inside the terminal building. I joined the line of chauffeurs holding up ragged paper notices, over-excited long-lost friends and family members waiting at International Arrivals. Attempting to hold my pristine laminated sign with suitable nonchalance, I stood patiently as several flights-worth of passengers paraded past. Finally, after forty-five minutes of waiting, David Lithgow strolled into my life.

I remember thinking I'd never seen anyone with really grey eyes before. They were pure grey – the colour of Lake District dry-stone walls. It will seem like an old cliché but it's honestly true: from that moment I knew my life had changed irrevocably. In the days and weeks that followed I found myself working increasingly closely with him as the design work neared its completion. Friends commented on the chemistry between us – *even* QJ (a man renowned for many things but never his social perception). David and I often had lunch together and he would lean close towards me and look me straight in the eye when we spoke. It took my breath away every time. Although I didn't know it then, he later admitted he'd bribed our colleagues to leave us alone as often as possible.

A week before final completion, QJ announced that the multinational client had agreed to fund a long weekend away for the whole team. This was to have a dual purpose – to reward us for our hard work and also to iron out last-minute design issues before completion. We would work from nine till twelve each day and then relax. An entire country house hotel in Snowdonia was duly booked and we drove up on a Thursday night in late May.

217

On the Saturday evening most of the team elected to go to the local pub in the village, but I decided against it. I settled myself in the cosy drawing room with a good book and prepared for a relaxing night in. I was glad of my decision when I heard the rain begin to fall outside. Within a few minutes the windows were being bombarded with a torrent of heavy rain and hail. I was just getting engrossed in my book when, to my surprise, David appeared.

'I don't feel like warm beer and loud music tonight,' he said, flopping to the floor by the side of my chair and looking up at me. 'I'd rather stay here, with you.'

His words sent quivers of delight right through me. Feeling brave, I reached out and gently traced the contour of his cheekbone with my fingers. Then, unexpectedly, the lights went out. A power cut had hit and we were plunged into pitch darkness. Being in the middle of the countryside meant no light pollution outside and the storm blocked out any light the moon could have offered. So the darkness was complete – an inky blackness.

Still reaching out, I was aware that I could no longer feel David's face before me. My other senses raced to compensate for the lack of sight. The sweet, musky scent of his cologne grew stronger: I could hear him moving . . . then silence. For a brief moment I wasn't sure if he had left the room or not. I called his name but there was no answer, so I determined he had gone. I sat forward, straining my eyes to decipher any hint of light. As I did so, I became suddenly aware of warm breath straight in front of my face. It made me jump and I laughed nervously. 'I know you're there! Stop playing games with me: I'm at a distinct disadvantage here.'

And then his face was touching mine: brow to brow, nose to nose, his breath now hot against my lips. His hands framed my face and he spoke in a hushed, deep tone. 'I'm not playing games now, Rosie. I'm for real. Let me love you. Let me be a part of your life. I want you more than anything.'

His kiss was strong, intense and deep. It was unlike anything I had ever experienced before. Electric energy rocketed through my entire body and I *knew*. I knew that one of my Important Life Decisions had its days numbered: I was falling in love.

The elevator doors opened three flights early to admit an older male journalist and his pretty, young female companion. Celia smiled politely as the door closed again. I looked at the floor as memories, newly released after a long prison sentence, ran through my mind. I had loved David so much. The warm memory of that first kiss took me by surprise as pain-gilded emotion assumed an iron grip on my heart. I knew I loved him then; now I began to fear that the love might still be there, buried carefully beneath layers of hurt, but still very much alive. I shut my eyes.

Nobody seemed surprised that we were together. Some said they'd witnessed the signs from the moment we met. Others were delighted: they had successfully predicted how long it would take for us to pair up and were now each fifty pounds richer, thanks to an office sweepstake I was unaware of.

David revelled in their pleasure and went out of his way to proclaim his love for me as often as he could. Huge bouquets would arrive on my desk, screensavers bearing love poems would regularly appear on my Mac and one day I received a singing barbershop telegram (much to my embarrassment and my colleagues' rapturous delight). Soon, I got wind of another sweepstake – this time predicting how soon it would be before David Lithgow popped the Big Question.

It wasn't long. But it wasn't at all how I'd expected it to be when it happened. It began with a job offer.

'Darling, I just spoke to Dad. There's an opening in the Boston design house for someone to head up a new initiative. They're looking for someone who will find and develop young potential, someone with vision and passion. You're the only candidate Dad's willing to consider. We want it to be a *family* business. Come home to the States with me, Rosie.'

I laughed, confident now of his intentions. 'If that's meant to be a proposal, David Lithgow, you're going to have to make it a great deal more romantic than that. I only ever expect to be asked this question once – so make it good!'

We were walking in Battersea Park on a warm Saturday afternoon and had just reached the Pagoda. David ran up the front steps and shouted loudly.

'May I have your attention, please, ladies and gentlemen, children and – er – *dogs*.'

Passers-by stopped to gawp in bewilderment at the crazy American gesturing flamboyantly at them.

'I have an important announcement. This young lady you see before you is the most wonderfully adorable, stunningly beautiful creature in the entire world – and I wish to inform you all that I cannot imagine waking up another day on this planet without her by my side. So . . .' he paused, skipped down the steps and kneeled on one knee at my feet, '. . . so I'm asking her – I'm asking *you*, Rosie – to share the rest of my life with me – as my wife.'

The crowd of amused onlookers now broke into spontaneous applause as David's wide eyes searched mine for an answer. 'I love you more than anything. You know I do. Marry me, Rosie.'

Our audience fell silent as they held their collective breath.

'Yes, of course I'll marry you!' I replied, tears claiming my eyes, as delighted applause swelled again around us. David scooped me up into his arms and let out a whoop.

'I am going to make you the happiest woman alive. Just you wait!'

Celia handed me another Kleenex as our lift journey was halted again. The couple from the second floor departed and I began to panic.

'I want to go home. *I can't do this!*' I insisted, a heavy ball of nausea sinking to the bottom of my stomach.

'I have no idea what you're going through, Rosie, but I know one thing: your life is at a turning point right now. So you either bite the bullet and deal with this today, or spend the rest of your life hiding. It's your call.'

It didn't seem like much of a choice.

Way in the back of my mind, a light came on and a memory of Mr K's voice began resonating. 'I have learned, Rosie, there are certain times in life when you tread in the footsteps of destiny. These are moments to be treasured as they happen maybe two or three times. They are incredibly precious, *ukochana*. They are also painful. Very painful. But the pain is *necessary* for you to blossom like Papa intended. You will never plan them; you cannot guess when they may arrive. But one day you will find yourself walking in destiny – and what you choose to do will mean either life or death. When that time arrives, Rosie, *choose to live*. Choose to let Papa stretch you and make you into the work of art he planned.'

And so my choice was clear.

Mum cried when I told her I was emigrating. But she could see my mind was made up and she gave me her blessing.

David returned to Boston while I made arrangements to sell my flat and surplus belongings. A month later, I was all sold up, packed and ready to go. At Heathrow's Terminal Four I said goodbye to Mum and James, and boarded the plane that was taking me to the rest of my life. I watched England slip slowly out of view as I headed towards my destiny.

Boston was a revelation. Everything about it was new and exciting. I revelled in the culture, the new accents all round me, and the lifestyle, which managed to be both fast-paced and laid-back at the same time. Boston also meant re-establishing my friendship with Ben, with whom I'd been at university. He was working at Harvard and loving every minute of it. I swear he had become more American than the Americans – adopting a pure Bostonian accent and becoming an avid devotee of the New England Patriots, along with baseball, basketball and just about any other sport he could watch or play. We spent most Sundays watching sport or shooting hoops in his back yard.

My new job presented a real challenge, but I was in my element. I helped to create a young team and watched with breathless pleasure as fifteen recent graduates began to bloom into some of the most innovative and brilliant designers I'd ever seen. I found myself experiencing true fulfilment in my job. It felt like I had finally found who I was meant to be.

And David? David was amazing. He was everything I wanted and a constant source of surprise. I loved being with him and being known as his wife-to-be made me so happy. I knew he loved me and I was aware he needed me too. Sometimes he would just hold me all night, as if he was scared I'd disappear if he let go. I would catch him watching me intently as we worked on the white clapboard-fronted house we'd chosen to live in – and even when he knew I'd noticed him, he never looked away. Surrounded by the smell of fresh paint and coffee in the shell of my future home, I had gazed out across the large garden framed by maple trees and imagined our children playing there.

Our wedding was planned for June. Mum and James flew out to help me work through the last-minute details. The ceremony and reception were all to take place in David's parents' grand house on the outskirts of the city. Three hundred guests were invited – most of whom were friends and associates of David's father.

Mum cried when she saw me in my dress at the final fitting. She had agreed to provide the bridal party's flowers, including my bouquet, which featured white, cream, palest yellow and deep pink roses with dark green foliage in hand-tied posies. The night before the big day I sat up till the early hours with Mum, making buttonholes – just like we did all through my childhood – laughing and reminiscing together.

'Well, Rosie, this is it. Tomorrow you will be Mrs Rosie Lithgow. That sounds incredibly distinguished for my little girl.'

'Oh, Mum . . .' I groaned. 'It's who I want to be.'

Mum's smile was broad but wistful, and I wondered if she was thinking about her own wedding to Dad, so many years before. 'Just as long as you're *sure* it's what you want.'

'I'm sure.'

'Good. Now you better get to bed, young lady! You've got a life-changing day ahead of you tomorrow.'

And, as with so many other things, Mum was right.

The elevator came to an abrupt halt and the doors opened to reveal Celia's office reception. She turned to me.

'Ready?'

'I'm not sure.' It was the truth.

Celia smiled warmly and squeezed my hand. 'Hey, now's as good a time as any, baby.'

Slowly, I followed her into her office.

Nate stood by the window, hunched and agitated, staring out at Midtown Manhattan, the Empire State Building rising proudly to his right. When we entered the office he spun round and a look of utter relief washed over his face.

'Oh, thank goodness. I got so worried, Rosie! Are you OK?'

'I'm getting there . . .' Celia urged me to continue. 'Um . . . Nate, there's something you should know about me. It's something I've not talked about to many people because . . . well, just because.' And it will sound strange, but somehow his intense stare seemed to be willing strength into my body. Surprising myself, I turned to Celia. 'I think I need to talk to Nate on my own – if you don't mind.'

Celia's furrowed brow lifted a little. 'Are you *sure*?'

I smiled, ignoring the increase of my heart rate. 'Yes, I'm sure.'

'Then I'll be right outside.' Celia walked briskly out and quietly closed the door.

Now we were alone. Now was the time. Nate took a step towards me. 'Hey, Rosie, remember The Rule for me and you: I talk and you listen. You don't *have* to tell me anything.'

I smiled wearily. 'No, I know. But I think I want to. Sit down, Nate. Please.'

Chapter Sixteen

My wedding day was beautiful. Sunshine like you wouldn't believe flooded everything with gold, the early morning dew sparkling like a carpet of diamonds on the lawn in front of the grand old house. Before any of the family woke, I sneaked outside and walked barefoot in my towelling robe up the aisle, as the chair-hire guys applauded me. Part of me still couldn't quite believe this was happening. I was loved by the most fantastic man in the world and now I was going to marry him. Here, twelve hours before, we had practised our vows together alone in the early evening sun, and David had held my hands so tightly. Something about his expression had seemed far away.

'I love you with all my heart, Rosie. You know I'd never hurt you.'

'I trust you, David. I know you love me.'

His eyes closed as his fingers stroked my hands slowly. Quietly he said, 'If you love me, Rosie . . .'

'Of course I love you.'

His eyes were dark in the fading light. 'Then marry me tomorrow.'

I giggled. 'That's what I intend to do!' Then, an idea struck me. 'Turn around.'

Puzzled, he obliged. 'What exactly am I doing this for?'

'Shh,' I said, grabbing my notebook and leaning against his strong back as I wrote.

'You are a crazy woman,' he laughed.

'Mmm, but you've chosen to marry me tomorrow, so what does that make you?' I replied, tearing off the page and turning him back to face me. 'There,' I smiled, handing him the sheet.

'What's this?' he asked, a small shimmer of amusement playing across his face.

'It's your checklist,' I grinned. 'Written on this sheet of paper is everything you need to do.'

He read the note. '"One: Turn up. Two: Marry me. Three: Be happy the rest of your life." That simple, huh?'

I looked deep into the slate-grey eyes I loved so much. 'That simple.'

My husband-to-be had pulled me close and was silent. As I kissed him good night, I figured wedding jitters must be getting to him. 'It will be great tomorrow, David.'

He remained, motionless in the dusky light, watching me. 'I know.'

Standing barefoot in the dew-soaked grass, with the day I'd longed for finally here, all I could think about was being with him. Realising the time, I turned and sped back into the house. They were all waiting for me – David's mother, Phoebe, my Mum, and Lori, David's sister – already dressed and impatient to help. The room was filled with rose-scented laughter as my hair and make-up were completed, subduing to hushed awe once I was dressed. Butterflies were building in my stomach and already my face was aching from excessive smiling. Now the preparations were complete and it was *time*.

'We'll go join the guests downstairs,' said Phoebe, kissing my cheek and beaming proudly. 'You look beautiful, Rosie.

Welcome to our family.' And then I was alone. I took one last look at myself in the long mirror. *This is it, Rosie Duncan. Time to start the rest of your life. As Mrs Rosie Lithgow.*

Carefully cradling my bouquet, I left the room.

'You asked me how I know David,' I began. Nate nodded. 'He's the reason I came to live in America.'

Nate frowned. 'I'm not sure I understand.'

I took a breath. 'I fell in love with David in England when we worked together at the advertising agency. He asked me to marry him and move to Boston to work at his father's design house. So I left everything and emigrated.'

Nate blew out a long whistle. 'Whoa, Rosie, I – I had no idea . . .' He shook his head and fell silent as he took it in. He didn't look at me: I could see his broad hands moving as though physically turning the news over and over.

Fear began to gnaw at the edges of my courage. 'How long have you known David?'

'Pardon me?' The question appeared to take him by surprise. For a moment he struggled to answer, his face crowded with thoughts. 'I – uh – I knew David at Yale, then . . . I dunno, we lost touch and I met up with him . . . oh, maybe two years ago now . . . at a book launch for a friend who turned out to be a mutual acquaintance. But he never said anything about you. I would have remembered.' He looked up. 'What happened?'

I took a deep breath. I wasn't sure I wanted to say it. I wasn't certain he wanted to know. 'Nate, you're going to have to choose whether or not you want to believe me. If David is your friend then what I say may change your opinion of him – or *me* – for ever.'

Nate shook his head. 'Not possible. In such a short time you've become one of my closest, dearest friends, Rosie. Sure,

227

I like David, but I *trust* you. And the way you reacted in my office wasn't faked – it was the genuine article. Now, I'm not leaving until you tell me everything.'

I descended the impossibly grandiose Hollywood-style sweeping staircase, my beautiful raw silk gown rippling like white waves behind me. Phoebe's housekeeping staff stood at the bottom and I was thrilled to hear their gasps of delight as I approached them. Smiling ecstatically, I turned and began to walk towards the rear of the house. There, in front of me, was the garden. Guests were chatting expectantly, bathed in rich gold sunlight; a string quartet played Bach; the minister stood under a romantic, rose-bedecked arch at the end of the aisle, checking his watch.

I took a step onto the lawn . . . then jumped as David's father appeared in front of me, blocking my path.

'George? What are you doing?' I laughed.

His face was pale and stern. 'Rosie . . . we need to talk.'

'Can't it wait?' I'm kind of busy right now . . .' My laughter was a little shaky as my nerves began to tip on edge.

'No, my love. I'm afraid it can't wait. Come with me.'

'On my wedding day, just as I was about to walk down the aisle, I received a note – from David.'

Confusion drifted over Nate's face. 'A *note*?' he repeated incredulously. I nodded. 'Sorry, I don't understand.'

Neither did I. Still, after six and a half years, the recollection of that moment caused a familiar lance of pain to spear my heart. I bit my lip.

Nate shook his head, open-mouthed. 'Hell, Rosie . . . what did it say?'

* * *

228

George stepped to one side to reveal David's best man, Asher, graven-faced and holding out a crumpled piece of paper.

'What's this?' I asked carefully, panic beginning to rise within.

Asher gave me the note, pausing for a moment with his large, warm hands encompassing mine. 'Baby, this is just . . . I can't believe he'd ask me to do this.' Shaking his head, he walked away.

I looked down at the note I held, my hands trembling as I read David's familiar spidery handwriting.

'Rosie,

As you will know by now, I'm not going to be there today. I've had to go away for a while - to sort my head out. I know you won't understand but I also know that you love me and want the best for me. well, the best thing for me is not to marry you today. Or ever. I think I still love you but I don't know. Right now I need to think of me and you need to get on with your life. You'll be happy again someday and then you'll thank me for saving you from the biggest mistake you could ever make.

I know it's a mess and for that I'm sorry. But I've done the right thing and I can't apologise for it. Please explain to our guests - say I got called away, say I'm ill, say whatever.

Don't try to find me - tell my parents I love them and I'm fine.

I can't say anymore.
David

229

Slowly, I turned the paper over and saw, to my horror, my own writing on the other side:

1: Turn up.
2: Marry me.
3: Be happy the rest of your life

I sunk to the floor in a rustling silk pool as an icy numbness stole my legs from under me. Phoebe and Mum rushed to my aid but I pushed them away, my world drowning fast in a heady cocktail of shock, anger and panic. George quietly took the note from my hand, read it and slowly began to tear it into tiny pieces, letting handfuls fall to the ground like flurries of paper snow.

'Damn him . . . *damn* our son,' he growled. Phoebe let out a loud cry and rushed out of the room. George looked down at the fractured pieces of his never-to-be daughter-in-law. 'Rosie, what the hell do I say here? What the hell do I say to our guests?'

Sheer rage began to fire strength into my limbs. I struggled to my feet. 'Don't worry, that's not your problem. *I'll* tell them.'

Mum made a brave attempt to stop me. 'Rosie, you are in no fit state to say anything to anyone. We'll send James out. Stay here, my darling.'

But I wouldn't listen. Grabbing the crushed remains of my bouquet, I stormed out into the garden, with Mum and James hot on my heels. Seeing my sudden entrance the string quartet ended their piece and began to play the 'Wedding March'. Guests turned, smiling, to greet me. The smiling faces quickly tightened, transforming into grimaces as realisation hit home that all was not well.

Struggling to breathe, tears staining my face, I spoke. 'I'm sorry . . . I'm so sorry . . .'

* * *

Nate didn't move. I sat facing him, unsure what to do next. Nothing happened. I looked away, breathing hard against the encroaching pain. Way down on the street below an angry horn blared out and someone shouted an obscenity in reply. In the cold, hard silence a large wooden clock on the office wall assumed centre stage. I was aware I'd never heard it tick before – Celia's office wasn't normally quiet enough. It remained the sole voice in the office until Nate breathed out a long, heavy sigh.

'How are you still *living* after that?' His eyes, wide with indignation, rose from the floor to search my face. 'How do you ever feel hope again?'

I shrugged against the pain, my voice coolly defiant. 'It's like I said: I'm happy to watch other people's dreams come true. Just because my fairytale didn't happen it doesn't mean it doesn't *ever* happen.' My body ached. My heart was smashed. I felt drained by everything.

Rubbing my eyes, I stood up. 'I'm so tired. I need to get back to the store. Ed will be wondering where I am.'

Nate jumped to his feet and grabbed my arm. 'No, Rosie, you can't – not yet. Sit down . . . please?' Firmly he urged me back into the chair and kneeled by my side, stroking my hand with feather-soft fingers.

The office door opened and Celia appeared and screeched to a halt when she saw us. 'Oh! Are – are we good here?'

Nate looked up and smiled briefly. 'We're good. Rosie's told me everything – I think?' His eyes followed the question back to me. I shook my head, unable to speak as the lump in my throat choked my voice. Celia hastened to my rescue. She spoke, her tone authoritative, undisputable and scarily like my mother's.

'I'll tell you the rest, Nate. OK, Rosie, I've called Ed and told him what's happened. He's coming to take you home when he's closed up.' My head shot upright but Celia fielded the protest with ease. 'He insisted, Rosie. It's fine. Till then I've arranged for you to rest in our boardroom. There's a long couch in there so you can lie down. I'll come get you when Ed arrives. No buts, honey, you need to rest now.'

Nate stood. 'I'll take you.'

With tenderness he escorted me like a wounded animal from Celia's office to the boardroom on the other side of the building. Once inside he let my arm go and walked quickly to the windows, switching the blinds to block out the light. Exhausted, I lay down on the black leather couch and closed my throbbing eyes. Nate returned to my side, bending close till I could feel his breath near my face. Softly, he pushed some hair from my eyes and let his fingers rest momentarily on my cheekbone. Then, leaning closer, I felt his warm, velvet lips as they lightly brushed my brow. For a brief second I breathed in his closeness. Then, quickly, he left the room.

I'm not sure if I slept. It was impossible to distinguish dreams from the vivid freeze-frame scenes vying for supremacy in my mind. I had done so well, for so long, to ignore and contain the events of my wedding day and the following six months. *That* was the answer to Nate's question: in order to go on I simply learned to ignore my heart. It wasn't easy: for a long time it was the only thing I could think of. For the first few days afterwards, I stayed with Mum and James at their hotel, lost in a sorrow so deep that I couldn't eat, sleep or speak. I was a complete wreck – emotionally, physically and mentally.

But if you think, like I did then, I'd been through the worst of my ordeal, you would be wrong. It was about to get worse. Much worse.

A week after the fiasco of my wedding day, George called me.

'This – *situation* – with David has made your position with the company untenable. I'm sorry, Rosie. I've got to let you go.'

I was indignant. 'You can't sack me because your son jilted me. That's completely illegal!'

I heard George emit a long, weary sigh. 'Rosie, please don't make this any more difficult for my family than it already is. I'm closing your project as of today. Your team have all been reassigned within the company. I'm willing to recompense you, above what your contract requires. I've arranged for one hundred thousand dollars to be paid into your account, effective immediately.'

I listened, aghast. 'You're paying me off?'

George's tone was steady and devoid of emotion. 'No, Rosie. I'm helping you move on.'

That day, I discovered Basic Fact Number 1 about the Lithgow family: they protect their own at all costs. The Lithgows closed rank and that was the last time I heard from them.

Homeless and now unemployed, I was rescued by Ben. He insisted I go back to his apartment. I agreed and ended up staying for six months as I tried to rebuild my life.

The friendship we'd had at university years before grew stronger than I could have imagined during the next six months. Ben was awesome. He carefully picked up the shattered remains of Rosie Duncan and painstakingly pieced them back together again. He found me a job private-tutoring design students from Harvard and spent hours counselling me as the hard reality of what David had done hit me full on. He never judged, never preached at me and, through all the tears, anger and searching, never, *ever* complained. He was the first constant friend to grab a hold of my escaping life and tether it with true compassion. In Ben I found my stability, and as the hours, days and months passed I grew stronger. It was Ben who encouraged me to dream about the rest of my life, which had now returned, unexpectedly, to my own hands.

Many people in my situation would have chosen to run home; for me this was never an option. Whilst I was incapable of functioning on many levels, one thought managed to cling on stubbornly: *I can't go back.* If I went home and attempted to resurrect my old life, somehow David's betrayal of me would be even more brutal. Then and there, in the ruins of my self-esteem, I made the decision that was to become a mantra from that day to this: *I don't look back.*

This would be my single act of defiance against the man who had torn my whole world apart: *You brought me here – you brought me to America – so this is where I'm staying.*

Firmly closing the door on my past, I started to build the walls that I had only now begun to demolish, brick by brick – nearly seven years after David jilted me. Strangely enough, it took a fraction of the time to construct them than, it now seemed, was required to pull them down.

The day I arrived in New York, heart securely defended against any future attack, I began to understand the 'American Dream' – that all-encompassing, deliciously irresistible urge to believe *anything* is possible. All around me were people who had felt its attraction; like iron filings being drawn to a huge, Manhattan-shaped magnet, pulled across land and sea from the four corners of the world to this magical city of dreams. And every day since, no matter what state my life is in, I've felt the Dream calling to me – just like Mum used to do on Christmas morning when James and I were kids: 'Come on! Get up and *see* what's happening!'

*   *   *

234

A hand was gently stroking my cheek as sleep retreated and I woke. Struggling to focus, I blinked rapidly until the fog cleared in my eyes and I recognised the face before me.

'Hey there, kid. How ya doin'?'

'Hi. I feel horrible.'

Ed smiled in gentle response. 'Yeah, but you look worse.'

I managed a laugh. 'Oh, *cheers*.'

The smile left his face momentarily. 'I *know*, by the way. Celia told me everything. Don't look like that, Rosie: I know and it's OK.'

And that was it, right there. After all the years I'd refused to reveal my past to him, after all my fears about how it would affect our friendship, one simple sentence was all that was needed: *I know and it's OK.* Even though every part of me ached, knowing that Ed knew it all gave me a surprisingly immense sense of comfort.

'I'm sorry.'

'What on earth for?'

'For not telling you . . . for not sharing this with you – *first*.'

He grinned and stroked my forehead. 'No accounting for taste, obviously. I've been waiting for you to tell me this a long, long time.' He shook his head. 'Point is, I know *now*. That's all that matters, OK? You've done *so well*, Rosie. You're *doing* great. So, you ready to go home now?'

I nodded. I needed to be home.

We didn't speak much in the cab. Ed just wrapped an arm round my shoulder and remained quiet as I leaned my head against his well-loved, beaten-up brown leather jacket and shut my eyes, inhaling its familiar scent.

Once inside my apartment, he sat me on the couch and hurried round, switching on lamps, drawing blinds and coaxing my coffee maker into reluctant clanking action. My burning eyes followed him and I was instantly reminded of Ben.

During those first few weeks at his place, when just about the only thing I could do was breathe in and out, Ben looked after me completely. He was everything I needed: cook, counsellor, friend, brother, entertainer, doctor. Watching Ed busily at work now brought a rush of nostalgia and made me wonder what I had done in my life to deserve such amazingly selfless friends.

Ed returned and handed me my favourite mug filled with hot, sweet black coffee. 'Here – drink this. Then you'd better eat something.'

I shook my head. 'I'm not hungry.'

'Doesn't matter, you still need to eat. Then you need rest.'

'You don't have to do this, Ed. Go home. I'll be fine, honestly.'

The ice-blue stare searched my soul. 'Do you want me to go home, Rosie?'

I looked long and hard at this person who had done so much for me. And suddenly I realised I didn't want to be alone. 'No, I don't.'

Relief seemed to light him up from the inside out. 'Then I'm not going anywhere.' He bent forward and lightly kissed my forehead. 'I'll go fix us something to eat, OK?' He jumped up and headed for the kitchen. 'Although you may be disappointed if you were expecting a culinary masterpiece. I can't seem to find any *normal* food in here . . .' Sounds of drawers and cupboard doors being opened wafted in from the direction of my kitchen, followed by a crash and a muffled profanity, '. . . and your cupboards are booby-trapped!'

'Ed?' I called out.

He appeared like a flash at the doorway. 'Yeah?'

'Thank you.'

A huge smile spread across his face. 'You're more than welcome, Rosie.'

236

Chapter Seventeen

Next morning I awoke feeling unexpectedly stronger. In the brave light of a new day things seemed clearer. Although my body ached like I'd just done ten rounds with a herd of elephants, my soul felt lighter than I could remember. I sat up and couldn't help smiling when I saw Ed. He was fast asleep in the chair at the bottom of my bed, his dark hair all ruffled up endearingly, my patchwork quilt draped casually across his chest, with his tall body awkwardly contorted to fit the confines of his makeshift bed. Grabbing fresh clothes from my closet, I tiptoed past him to the bathroom.

About twenty minutes later, I emerged feeling refreshed from a hot shower. As quietly as possible I went into my kitchen and began to make breakfast. It was almost ready when I heard a long groan followed by a sleepy-eyed Ed as he appeared in the doorway. Only he could make dishevelled look so attractive first thing in the morning. It wasn't difficult to see why the good ladies of New York were queuing up for him.

'Morning,' he murmured, running a hand through his tousled mop of hair. 'I ache.'

'Hmm . . . I'm not surprised. Why didn't you sleep on the couch? That chair didn't look at all comfortable.'

'It wasn't. But I wanted to be there in case you woke up. You snore, by the way.'

'Oh, cheers.'

The azure-blue eyes sparkled. 'Just kidding. You OK?' He followed me to the table in the living room and eased himself into a chair as I poured the coffee.

I took a deep breath. 'Actually, I think I am. I guess it's a relief to get it all out.'

Ed took a sip from his steaming mug. 'Sure. That makes sense. Ow, *dammit* . . .' He stretched out his right arm and rotated his shoulder until it gave out a loud grating click. 'So – Celia says you're going to do David's wedding?' He was careful not to reveal an opinion through his expression, but I could guess what it was.

'Yes, I think – well, I said yes, anyway. And before you ask, I don't know why. It just seemed like the right thing to do. In for a penny, in for a pound, I suppose. Up until yesterday the biggest fear I had was seeing him again. Now I've done that so I have to face the next biggest fear: asking for answers.'

Ed's eyes remained unmoved but I caught his head shaking a little. 'You are a constant surprise, Rosie Duncan.'

'Why?'

He put his mug on the table. 'For years you've kept this secret – it ran your life and prevented you from fully trusting anyone. Then yesterday you had to face David and I saw you totally destroyed by it all over again. You know, I figured that would set you back *years* – have you scurrying back to the safety of your solitude – but today here you are: the hope is back alive in you, and now you're even daring to think of the rest of your life. I don't know how you do it.'

I didn't either. 'I'm scared to death of the situation right now, but it's like you said: I have to consider the possibility

238

that my life could move on. You were right with what you said before: there *was* a whole side of me you knew nothing about. I should have told you years ago. I'm sorry.'

Ed let out a long sigh. 'Finally, she realises the truth: Ed Steinmann is always right.' Leaning forward, he gently took my hand, his fingers slowly wrapping around mine. 'And I'm here for you, OK?'

I placed my other hand over his and felt a wave of peace washing over me.

Two days later, Kowalski's welcomed me back like a long-lost friend. Even the little silver bell on the front door sounded delighted when I entered my shop. Marnie rushed up and flung both arms round me. 'Oh, Rosie – are you OK? I've been so worried 'bout you. You didn't have to come in, you know. Are you certain you're OK to work?'

Ed laughed. 'Put her down, Marnie, she'll be fine.'

Later that morning, Marnie joined me by Old F, who was busily percolating coffee for all his worth.

'Celia told me about – you know – what happened.'

I ignored the pang of anxiety that her concerned expression evoked in me. 'I'm glad you know. I hope you understand why I didn't say something before.'

She shook her head, pink bunches swinging as she did so. 'Seriously, it's fine. You wouldn't believe Ed, though.'

'How do you mean?'

She looked round furtively, checking to ensure Ed wasn't within earshot. 'He was like a man *possessed* after we got Celia's call. I've never seen him so full of purpose. He was pretty awesome, you know. Especially when you consider who he was meant to be seeing that night.'

'He had a date?' In all the events of the past couple of days, it hadn't occurred to me what Ed had abandoned to come to my rescue.

'Only that newsreader, Teagan Montgomery – the one who made the top ten of the Manhattan's Beautiful Women poll in the *New York Post* last month?'

I stared at her. 'Are you sure?'

Marnie nodded with a conspiratorial smile. 'I'm certain of it. I offered to call her for him but he said it was "unimportant" – can you believe that?'

'He's a star. He looked after me so well after it all happened. But then he's a lovely guy.'

'Hmm. I don't think he'd have done that for just anybody, though,' she grinned, walking to the counter to serve a customer.

Being back at my shop, surrounded by familiar sights and people, I felt my hope returning. I was going to be fine.

All that day and the following week, I found myself getting back on form. Celia phoned me every day and Ed offered to come by my apartment whenever I felt I was getting scared again. But I was coping. A lot of it was an act, of course. Inside, my feelings were just as muddled and jumbled as before, yet somehow knowing other people knew about it made everything easier to handle.

One thing bothered me, though: Nate didn't visit. He called to apologise for not being there and sent me texts every day to see how I was, but I couldn't help wondering if what I'd told him had changed his opinion of me after all. This thought sat uneasily on top of the pile of emotions in my gut and remained there stubbornly, despite my best attempts to dismiss it.

Celia was quick to dispel my concerns. 'I spoke with Nate today and he was very worried about you. He's simply snowed under with work till the holidays.'

'*And* he's planning his engagement,' I chipped in.

Celia raised her eyes heavenwards. 'Or *being planned* into it, if what I hear is correct.'

'Which it's bound to be, as you are the trusty, never-fail ears of the *Times*,' I laughed.

'Absolutely. So has David called you?'

His name sent a wave of cold nausea through me. I swallowed hard. 'No. Not yet.'

Celia grinned. 'Only *I* heard Mr Lithgow has been spotted at several seasonal soirees sporting the latest desirable fashion accessory for the rat about town.'

'What do you mean?' Her sparkle was infectious and I found myself smiling with her.

'Only a *huge* humdinger of a black eye!' she announced, then leaned forward and, added, 'Now, *I wonder* why Nate hasn't been to see you recently . . .'

'Oh, no, Celia, you don't think . . . ?'

Celia shrugged but the sly smile remained. 'Who knows? I'm merely reporting facts here. It would be unethical of me to enter into conjecture. But, you've gotta admit, it's an intriguing possibility. And Nate was very, *very* angry when he left my office last week.'

I shook my head. 'I don't know, honey. Nate doesn't seem like the kind of guy who hits people. Anyway, whatever the truth is, I'm not looking forward to seeing David again.'

'Honey, you'll be *fine*! Just you wait and see.'

As it turned out, I didn't have to wait long.

It had been a crazy day at the shop as Christmas fever well and truly gripped New York. Not only were we rushing to complete garlands and decorations for our orders, but we also had to deal with a constant stream of customers through the

241

doors. Four extra staff had been taken on for the seasonal rush – Jocelyn, Heidi, Brady and Jack – all recently graduated floristry students. They worked on the orders with Ed, while Marnie and I faced the onslaught from the street.

'Hey, did I tell you I finally got a new apartment?' Marnie smiled as she wrapped a berry-red poinsettia and placed it in a Kowalski's string-handled bag for a large smiling lady.

'That's great!' I replied, accepting payment from a gruff-looking man and handing over his change.

Marnie smiled. 'It's near SoHo – a friend of my uncle's got it for me at a special price.'

'How lovely to be in your new place in time for Christmas,' the smiley lady beamed.

'Isn't it just?' Marnie smiled back, adding, 'Merry Christmas!' as the lady left. Turning to me, she continued, 'It's so cool. Mack says with the right furnishings it'll look a million dollars.'

'Mack? Ah, the guy from your theatre group . . . Marnie, I'm sorry. I completely forgot to ask you about how it went with him.'

'Uh, well, I did like you said and asked him out for a drink. And it was . . . *good*. We talked about just about everything. He's such a great guy.'

I sensed a But. 'But?'

'Totally, *completely* gay.'

'Oh, no,' I breathed in sympathy.

'No, it's totally cool though 'cos he's, like, the most *awesome* person when it comes to interior decorating. He's taking me shopping Saturday to fit out the whole place,' she giggled, and trotted merrily away to attend to a customer. I shook my head but couldn't help smiling. In the midst of all the change and pace around me it was comforting to know that a great City

242

Institution – namely, The Legend that Is Marnie Andersson's Love Live – was alive and well.

My mobile buzzed in my pocket. I didn't recognise the number. 'Hello, Rosie Duncan speaking?'

'Well, hello, Rosie Duncan,' replied a voice that made icicles stab at my spine. 'It's David.'

All of a sudden, it was harder to breathe. 'Yes – I know.'

There was a pause, then I heard him laugh. 'Good, good. I need to see you, Rosie – uh, regarding the commission order we spoke about recently. My fiancée's getting jittery about the designs – you know how it is . . .' Another, longer pause followed. I braced myself against a strong wave of pain as it crashed over me. 'Uh . . . can I meet you . . . tonight . . . ? Let's say – uh – dinner at seven thirty at Rochelle's?'

My head was spinning, but I steadied myself and answered as calmly as I could, 'I'm not sure that's a good idea.'

His tone changed for the briefest time. '*Please*, Rosie? There are things I want . . . we need to discuss.'

Though I hated it, he was right. Better to get it over with as soon as possible. 'Fine. See you then.' I ended the call before he could reply.

'You OK?' Marnie was once again behind the counter, looking concerned.

I managed a smile. 'Yes, mate. I'm just fine.'

Once, when I was about fourteen years old, I met an explorer. He had recently returned from a successful Arctic expedition and my school invited him to talk to us about it. He brought photos of snowfields and polar bears, arctic scientists muffled up against the cold in bright orange snowsuits and nightscapes illuminated by the Northern Lights.

He was asked what made him want to do what he did: his

answer was surprising. 'I was a fearful child,' he said. 'My mother was terrified of spiders and I inherited her fear. My grandmother used to hide under the stairs during thunderstorms, so I would hide there with her until I got scared of them too. I soon became scared of everything that was new and different, and anything I didn't understand. Then I began to be interested in science – especially biology and meteorology. As I studied the things I feared, I realised what I was missing out on – the wonders of this world, the intricate beauty of its varied environments. I became an explorer to make up for lost time. Anything I've previously feared I now actively pursue.'

Maybe that's what I was doing now.

I stood outside Rochelle's on West 70th Street and looked up at the entrance that rose magnificently from the tree-lined avenue. *Time to make up for lost time*, I told myself as I walked up the marble steps.

The maître d' smiled as I approached. 'Ah, Ms Duncan, how delightful to see you again.'

I smiled. 'Hello, Cecil. How's your wife?'

Cecil's bushy black moustache rose as he smiled. 'She's very well, Ms Duncan. She adored the bouquet you put together for her birthday.' He gestured towards the dining area. 'I believe Mr Lithgow is already here. Follow me, please.'

David stood as I approached the table. 'Rosie.' He offered his hand – then withdrew it quickly when I didn't accept. As we sat down, I noticed he was rubbing one thumb erratically across the knuckle of the other – a thing he always did when he was nervous. I frowned. He had appeared so confident when he'd called earlier, and I had expected him to be the same now. But to see him not in control empowered me slightly. A waiter brought menus and we ordered. Once the necessary business was complete we were left alone. As it was early, the restaurant was only a quarter full, with most of the diners seated on the other side of the room. Consequently, we were more alone than I had anticipated we would be.

David took a long sip of water and then looked at me. In the soft light I could clearly see a faint purple shadow around his right eye. It was obvious that Celia's trusty sources had triumphed once again.

He spoke at last. 'I didn't think you'd come. I didn't think you'd take the job.'

My guard in place, I answered coolly. 'I'm still not sure why I did.'

His stone-grey eyes narrowed slightly. 'I'm so glad you accepted. Honestly I am. You don't know how good it is to see you.'

His warmth threw me and I reached for my water glass to avoid his stare.

'I can't tell you what a relief it was to finally find you,' he continued, leaning towards me, his voice like velvet trade winds. 'I *needed* to find you, Rosie. I – uh – I wanted to – make things right . . .'

He was interrupted by the arrival of our wine, providing a brief respite. He straightened up to talk to the wine waiter and I grabbed the few precious seconds it provided to gather myself together. When the waiter left I seized the initiative and changed the subject.

'Nate said this was a large commission,' I began, intrigued to see David momentarily touch his wounded eye at the mention of Nate's name. He tried to reply, but I continued, 'so it's important at this meeting that we discuss numbers of pieces required so I can prepare my staff well in advance. I need to know roughly how many table pieces and large displays will be needed; which areas of the venue are to feature flowers; numbers of buttonholes required for guests and bridal party; plus, of course, requirements for the bridal bouquet.'

'Naturally,' David replied, producing an envelope from his jacket. 'I've detailed everything here for you.' He handed it over. As I reached out to take it, his hand brushed lightly against mine. The touch was softer than fine silk. I flinched, but he continued, apparently unaware, 'Would it be beneficial for your team to see the venue at any time?'

'Yes it's . . . our . . . normal procedure,' I was struggling and now he saw it. He leaned closer.

'Would you like to see it *soon*? I could arrange for you to come out before Christmas, if you wish. Maybe you could make a preliminary visit before you bring your team?'

'No.' My answer was strained. I cleared my throat and started again. 'No, that won't be necessary. Sometime in January will be fine. So, the next consideration is your specifications for colour and variety of the flowers required.'

David's gaze remained unmoved. 'That's all on the list. I thought it best not to go through it here . . . *now* . . .'

We ate our meal quickly, although I sensed David was no hungrier than I was. He explained a little more about the layout of his parents' new house in the Hamptons and I answered his questions about the type of weddings Kowalski's had catered for in the past. Throughout the meal we maintained a well-practised professional composure, much like we had assumed when we first met in London. A warm recollection eased itself slowly into my mind of the first week we worked together: our carefully constructed conversations from behind purpose-built defences. We were two people locked in a subtle game: each determined to retain the upper hand, yet both secretly fascinated with the other. Now, for the smallest moment, we were back there once more. Though guarded on both sides, tiny glimpses of that same sparkling energy fizzed through our conversation. It was devastatingly smooth warfare: utterly uncomfortable yet morbidly satisfying with its onslaught on my senses. I wondered if he felt it too.

At the end of the meal, David smiled. 'You're as adept a businesswoman as you always were, Rosie. Exactly like you were when I met you.' The vivid memory sent a diamond-edged shard of pain through my heart. His eyes flashed and the corners of his wide mouth lifted slightly. I looked away. I caught the faintest sound of a sigh and he spoke again. 'I'll get the bill.'

Once it was settled, we rose to leave and Cecil escorted us to the door. 'I hope to see you again, very soon, Ms Duncan, Mr Lithgow,' he smiled as we collected our coats and wrapped up ready for the cold outside. 'Now, you have our order for seasonal flowers?'

'It'll be with you on Christmas Eve, as arranged.'

Cecil's moustache jumped into a smile. 'Wonderful. Merry Christmas, Ms Duncan.'

'Merry Christmas, Cecil,' I replied as David and I walked outside. I turned to hail a cab, then froze when I felt David's hand on my shoulder.

'Rosie, before you go – can we walk a little?'

I slowly turned back. 'I'm not so sure that's a good idea.'

His eyes were wide as they met mine; all of a sudden, he looked lost. '*Please*?'

A thought flickered in my mind. *He might be as hurt as you.* Angrily, I dismissed it. But something in his expression struck an ancient, long-forgotten chord. 'OK. You've got ten minutes. Then I must go.'

We walked until we reached a diminutive community garden dwarfed and overshadowed by an imposing 1920s building.

Most of its former glory had faded, but it proudly retained a dustily majestic air of what it had once been. David walked a little way into the garden until he reached a small wooden bench. He sat down and looked up at me.

'Please sit with me?'

I wrapped my coat defensively around myself. 'No, thanks. I'm fine here.'

David let out a sharp breath, which rose in the frosty night air like steam from city drains. 'Look, Rosie, I know this is hard for you, but—'

Instantly I snapped back. 'Pardon me? I'm sorry, I think I misheard you, David. For a moment there I thought you said you *knew* how I felt . . .'

He opened his mouth to reply but I got there first.

'. . . Because, let me tell you, you have *no idea* how I feel. No idea at all. So don't even think you know how hard this is for me. Because you wouldn't even come *close*.'

'OK, OK, I understand. I'm sorry.' His voice softened and he held out his hand. 'Just . . . *please* . . . it would be better if you'd sit down, OK? That's all I meant. *Please?*' That lost look was all over his face again. I hesitated for a moment before relenting, sitting as far from him as I could. '*Thank you,*' he breathed. I checked my watch. He spoke again, more softly this time. 'Look at me, Rosie.'

'No, look, I'm sitting down and – and – I'm here in the first place, all right? So don't push it. Just say what you want to say and then let me go home.' My eyes kept their defiant vigil on the floor.

He swore under his breath. 'OK. Sure. On your terms it is, then.'

On my terms? my mind screamed silently. *The last six and a half years have been on your terms . . .*

With great effort, I kept my expression steady and my inner disgust hidden as David continued, 'Man, this is hard . . . OK . . . I realise I have no idea what you've been through on my account. I'm well aware that – before I start – nothing I say right now is going to sound worthy enough to compensate for what happened . . . *what I did to you* . . . I know that, Rosie. But I have to try, surely?'

I knew he was looking straight at me, in the way he used to.

'Yeah, sure, you've every right to be silent. After all, I guess I've been silent towards you for all this time. But being silent doesn't mean you have nothing to say, Rosie. Though we never spoke, I *always* had things I wanted to say to you – you have to believe that. I've often thought about you: how you were doing, where you were . . . I thought you would have gone back to England . . . And I know I never tried to contact you but I didn't know where to look . . . No, uh – no, that isn't true: I was *too scared* to look for you. I couldn't face talking to Ben, or Rosemary, both of whom I knew would be gunning for me. And then it got too late and too many things got in the way, like . . . like Rachel . . . But, hey, you don't want to hear about her. No, of course you don't. Hell, I'm making such a mess of this. I thought I'd never have to say this stuff. I thought I'd never find you, but, well, here you are . . . Here *we* are . . .'

I shifted uneasily as pain intensified in my gut.

'And now I'm struggling, because all the fine words I'd planned to say seem totally inadequate now. Nate was right: I don't deserve to receive anything from you ever again, let alone your time to hear me out.'

'Did he hit you?' I meant to keep my curiosity locked up but the question escaped.

Surprised, David laughed. 'Yeah, he totally slammed me. I didn't know he had it in him. We used to joke at Yale that he was the only guy who could win a boxing tournament with persuasive argument.' The smile left his voice. 'But I was wrong, obviously. It seems there are some subjects he'll make an exception for. Like *you*.' His words caught me offside and I was suddenly face to face with him before I had chance to think better of it. As though celebrating a goal achieved, triumph lit my opponent's eyes and broadened his smile. 'Well, *that* got you looking at me, Ms Duncan.'

Incensed, I stood. 'I'm going home. I shouldn't have come here. Good night.'

Without looking back, I stuffed my hands into my coat pockets and began to walk briskly from the garden. I heard him call my name and his footsteps quickening behind me. Shaking my head, I stepped up the pace, breaking into a half-run as I rounded the block and headed for the light of the metro station entrance a little way ahead of me. He called my name again, this time much nearer.

'Leave me alone!' I shouted back. I was almost at the subway – just a little further . . . My pursuer's steps came closer – now I could hear his heavy bursts of breath behind me. I tried increasing my speed but it was too late. My right arm jolted back as he pulled me to a halt, spinning me round to face him.

'Hit me,' he growled, between large gasps for breath.

'What?' I shot back, trying unsuccessfully to break free from his grip that imprisoned both arms now. 'Let me go.'

'*Hit me* . . .' he repeated breathlessly. 'Just damn well hit me, Rosie. Let the anger out and then we can be civil. What are you waiting for? Come on, give me your best shot!'

White-hot anger made my answer colder than ice. 'No, I won't. And how dare you trivialise everything? What, you think that's going to solve the situation between us? So I lash out to get it out of my system, is that it? That would be just great for you, wouldn't it: one confrontation and it's all over. Just like one decision solved your problem with me last time. Is that all you think it takes?'

Genuine shock painted his face. 'I – I . . .'

'I will work with you on your wedding, David, as agreed. You will receive the best service that Kowalski's can offer. Like we offer all our customers. Because that is all you are to me, OK? Just – another – client.' I paused for breath and silence fell as we faced each other. I felt the anger leave, but steel-cold defiance remain. 'I'm going home now. Please let me go.'

Still stunned, David's hands fell away. 'Can I call you?'

My eyes bore straight into his. 'Why?'

His lips moved without resulting sound, unable to offer an answer.

'Good night, David.' I turned and walked slowly away.

Chapter Eighteen

Every season in New York City has its own unique delights, but I have to admit that Christmas time is my favourite. As soon as Thanksgiving approaches and the store windows begin to feature festive themes I get a sparkly sense of excitement all through me. I've had it ever since I was a child – even though many of my childhood Christmases were tinged with sadness after Dad's betrayal of our family. Mum always managed to keep the season light for us, which I think also helped *her* to cope with the time of year. She would spend weeks preparing, baking cakes and biscuits and then, the week before Christmas, she would busy herself filling the house with roses and poinsettias, winding holly and ivy garlands around every flat surface in the house.

I remain such a fan of the season that I even enjoy the annual struggle to single-handedly lug a six-foot spruce tree up three flights of stairs to my apartment (because I refuse to pay $25 extra to get the tree delivered or choose an imitation tree instead). A real Christmas tree is something Mum always insisted on when we were growing up, and I've carried on the tradition ever since.

So this was how I came to be standing, as I had done for the past five Christmases, at Chuck's Festive Tree Yard, on an impossibly cold Saturday morning, two weeks before Christmas, wearing about twenty-seven layers to keep warm and stamping my feet to retain the circulation in my toes. Having chosen my tree – a gorgeously bushy Blue Spruce – I was now waiting for none other than Chuck himself to net up my purchase so I could drag it home.

Chuck is something of a local hero where I live. He started selling Christmas trees out of the back of his father's pickup truck in 1953, on the car lot of the old Realto Picture House, three blocks down from my street. The crumbling 1930s cinema was demolished in the late eighties and, by then, Chuck had earned enough to buy the plot. During the year, his business is a small city nursery, selling pot plants and window boxes, but every Thanksgiving he transforms the entire area into the Festive Tree Yard, packed to capacity with every imaginable variety of pine tree. Now in his early seventies, with both his son and grandson working alongside him, Chuck strolls proudly around the yard with a fat wedge of cigar stub hanging permanently out of one side of his mouth, which bobs up and down comically as he proffers his wise advice to customers.

'Nah, you don't want that one, lady. That one is for homes less classy than yours. Trust me, I know. What you need is a tree like *this*. Now, don't you go worrying about that price tag. That price is for customers I don't like, see? You, I like. So, you can have this classy tree, we'll call it a straight fifty and it's yours. What d'ya say, huh?'

The Festive Tree Yard was always busy, but this morning it appeared that everyone in a five-mile radius had decided, like me, to buy their tree today.

'I like the Norwegian Pine myself,' said a voice by my ear, making me jump. I spun around to see Ed standing there, a large cotton shopping bag from Zabar's slung casually over one shoulder and a huge grin on his face. 'Happy Holidays!'

'What are you doing here?' I smiled.

'Same thing as you. Looking at over-priced, half-dead trees,' he smirked. 'So what sorry specimen did you go for this year?'

'Blue spruce,' I replied, jutting my chin out defiantly. 'And I happen to think that a real tree is essential for Christmas.'

'Couldn't have put it better myself, lady,' grinned Chuck, appearing from the forest in front of us and handing me my tree. 'Blue spruce – a fine choice for a fine woman. Don't you agree, sir?'

'If you like that kind of thing,' Ed replied nonchalantly.

Chuck's wrinkled brow furrowed further. 'Is he referring to the tree or to you?' he asked me, clenching the cigar between his teeth as he spoke.

I smiled. 'Non-believer.'

Chuck let out a big throaty laugh. 'Aha, I see. Well, Happy Holidays, lady – and to you, sir.' And with that he disappeared back into the trees.

'So how are you getting this back home?' Ed asked. 'Hailing a cab?'

'No, walking it back.'

Ed surveyed the tree and then me, eyes wide. 'You're kidding me.'

'Nope,' I replied, picking up the end of the trunk and dragging the tree behind me, leaving a pine-needle-studded trail in the snow. 'It's all part of the magic.'

Ed wasn't convinced. 'Right . . . Here, let me help.' He scooped up the other end of the tree, cursing as the needles broke through his gloves, and hooked it under his arm. 'Onward, Duncan!'

Laughing and joking, we walked the three blocks back to

my apartment block, enjoying the snow flurries as they patted against our cheeks and landed on our clothes. The sky above us was the colour of melted marshmallows – pale pink and white – as butterscotch-hued clouds heavy with snow drifted slowly across the tops of the skyscrapers. Everyone we passed seemed to be smiling, as if the tree we carried was some kind of talisman that broke through the usual barriers of propriety and endeared us to our neighbours.

I have to say that manoeuvring the tree up to my apartment was a lot less tricky with two people – albeit with one of them moaning *incessantly* throughout. After much twisting and turning to navigate the narrow stairwells, we reached my front door and, with one final decisive effort, triumphantly delivered the spruce to its desired location. Ed let out a long whistle and collapsed on my sofa, while I made us celebratory coffee to mark the occasion.

'So,' I said, flopping down beside him, 'how come you were up here today?'

'I was just in the neighbourhood.'

'You're *never* in this neighbourhood.' I surveyed him carefully.

'Yes I am,' he protested.

'When you come to see me.'

'Yes. And also when I *just happen* to want to visit the Upper West Side.'

'You hate the Upper West Side.'

'I do not.'

I turned to face him, now highly suspicious. 'Yes, you do. You always say it's full of people with more money than brains who view shopping as some kind of vocation.'

He had to concede that point. 'One of my particularly favourite personal observations, that one.'

'Hmm. So why decide to come shopping here today?'

'I like the cheese at Zabar's.'

'You are such a liar.'

'I am not. It's a well-known fact that their cheese selection is excellent,' he replied defiantly. 'I *like* cheese.'

'Be serious.'

He held up his hands. 'OK, OK, you win, Miss Marple. I happened to be in the neighbourhood because I wanted to make sure you're all right.'

'I'm fine. I've just got my tree, so I'm happy.'

The Steinmann Stare locked on. 'That's not what I meant.'

'So what are you getting at?'

Ed sighed. 'I wanted to make sure you're all right with *me*.'

'Sorry?'

'I owe you an apology. Again. This is becoming a worryingly regular occurrence for me these days.' He rolled his eyes. 'I feel like I haven't supported you enough.'

'Yes, you have,' I disagreed. 'Anyway, the shop's been crazy, we've had the students helping out and you've been busy.'

'But you had the *David* thing.'

'All sorted. He knows where I stand and I feel better for saying it.'

Ed's voice became gentler, 'And – the *Nate* thing.'

'What Nate thing?'

'He hasn't been around lately.'

I folded my arms defensively. 'He's been busy as well.'

'What – avoiding you?'

'Ed, that's unfair.'

'You like him, Rosie. It's plain as day.'

'He's my *friend*.'

'I think he likes you too,' Ed continued.

'He's *engaged*. As in, getting married to someone else,' I

retorted. 'And you know how I feel about relationships. You are so way off on this.'

Ed held his hands up. 'I'm sorry, Rosie. It's none of my business. And it's beside the point. I wanted to say sorry for not being there for you, that's all. It's just that I've—' He broke off, running a hand nervously through his dark hair. 'I've been a little . . . *preoccupied* lately.'

'Ed, we're fine.' There was something in his expression that I couldn't place. 'What's been on your mind?'

He took a deep breath and squared himself to face me. 'Now this is hard for me because of – you know – the *iceberg* thing?'

The earnestness of his expression made me giggle involuntarily. 'I'm sorry,' I said, trying to stuff my laughter back behind a serious expression. 'Take all the melting time you need – just be sure to clear up afterwards, OK?'

The twinkle had made a welcome return to his eyes. 'Philistine. All I wanted to say was that I've had a revelation, of sorts. You remember when you said to me that the time to start worrying was when you wanted a *specific somebody*, not just anybody?'

'Erm, yes, I think so.'

'Well, start worrying.'

I couldn't believe it. 'Really?'

He nodded, a vulnerability suddenly cracking the usual steely exterior. 'Absolutely. Now is *that* time.'

I stared at him for a while and – I'm not quite sure why – I began to detect the slightest ripple of sadness deep within me. Maybe it was because someone I had always assumed would be forever single, like me, had made a leap I wasn't prepared to take. Whatever it was, I mentally pushed it away and smiled my brightest smile instead. 'Wow. That's – that's wonderful. So how did she break through the iceberg then? The sheer warmth of her love melted you, eh?'

Ed raised an eyebrow. 'You read way too many chick-lit books for your own good. It's nothing like that. It's, uh, a bit of an *afar* thing, actually. She – she has no idea.'

'Yet.'

'Sorry?'

'She has no idea *yet*. But you're going to tell her, right?'

He shook his head wildly. 'Absolutely no way, José. I am not prepared to jump that far. I've only just reached this momentous stage in my "melting". I don't want to do anything drastic.'

'That's fine, but remember Billy Whitman and his watercooler girl. Don't leave it for ever to tell her.'

He grimaced. 'I know. I will tell her – when the time is right. It's just too early for that right now.'

I smiled at him and patted his arm. 'I'm proud of you. You're doing so well.'

'Don't patronise me,' he retorted, blushing slightly.

'I'm not. I'm really pleased. So – who is she?'

'That information is classified,' he stated, military fashion.

'Right,' I said, grabbing a cushion and waving it menacingly at him. 'Then I will have to resort to other methods to get it.'

A sparkle of mischief washed over his face. 'Oh, right, attack first, ask questions later. You are *so* US military.' He snatched the cushion from behind his back and swung it at me. Skilfully, I ducked, landing a counter-blow squarely on his chest. 'Oh-ho, that's *war* now!' he yelled, pulling another cushion out and pummelling me with both at once. Giggling, I pulled my weapon back as far as I could in order to get as much swing as possible. Unfortunately for me, I lost my balance, toppled backwards and landed in an unceremonious heap on the floor.

Laughing uncontrollably, Ed reached down and helped me up, pulling me to him and wrapping his arms around me as we collapsed into breath-stealing guffaws. Gradually, our

259

laughter subsided – but the embrace remained, his chin resting on my shoulder and my cheek pressed against his neck. It felt *safe*. Instinctively, we both pulled away and sat facing each other, wide grins spreading across our faces, flushed from the laughter.

Ed checked his watch. 'Well, it's time I headed off. I want to check on the Saturday kids on my way home. And *you*,' he added, waggling a finger at me sternly, 'have a Christmas tree to decorate.'

'Yes, I have,' I smiled as we stood and went to the door. 'So, Mr Iceberg . . .'

Ed walked out into the hallway and turned back to face me. 'Yes?'

'Happy melting.'

The wide, crooked grin flashed brilliantly and he saluted me before walking down the stairs and out of sight.

Chapter Nineteen

In the last weeks before Christmas, Kowalski's was busier than I have ever seen it. Our floristry graduates' help was invaluable, not least because it meant Ed and I could focus on the last event of the year – but by far the biggest: Mimi Sutton's Grand Winter Ball. Though both of us were a little apprehensive about the job, we had meticulously prepared everything well in advance, doing as much of the structural stuff as we could before the day of the event.

Quicker than we would have liked, the big day arrived and Ed and I packed the van to take everything to the venue. It was just before 7 a.m. and the pale winter sun was barely breaking the horizon when we pulled up at the rear entrance to The Illustrian, a large hotel just off Broadway. The owners had recently renovated the ornate Victorian ballroom and this was to be the setting for Mimi Sutton's *pièce de résistance*. An enormous room on two levels, with an elaborate staircase rising magnificently from the polished marble floor, the location was breathtaking.

Our footsteps echoed conspicuously as we hurried across the ballroom carrying our boxes. It was difficult not to be over-awed by the place, and Ed sensed my trepidation at the task ahead.

'Hey, boss, it's going to be great,' he assured me.

I laughed nervously. 'I know. We're fine.'

At eight thirty, Marnie and the grads arrived, shattering the relative calm of the place with their excited exclamations over the work Ed and I had already completed. The staircase was now adorned in swathes of green garlands with white roses, carnations and tiny fairy lights woven through them. I had to admit that the overall effect was stunning and, as a centre-piece, it would take some beating. Having assigned various tasks to my team, I grabbed my camera and began to take pictures of the staircase. Twisting round to focus on Ed's structural masterpieces gracing the pillars at the entrance to the ballroom, I suddenly caught sight of a familiar figure walking casually towards me.

'Hey, Rosie.'

'Nate, long time no see, eh?' Ed replied, quickly appearing at my side. 'We had you down as Missing in Action.'

Nate rubbed the back of his neck and looked sheepish. 'Yeah, well, I was, in a way.'

Ed wasn't finished and I sensed a steely attack thinly disguised beneath his humour. 'So you thought you'd just show up and say hi, then?'

'Ed,' I cut in quickly, 'can you start the grads on the window displays, please? I'm a little concerned that Jocelyn and Brady may go a bit gung-ho with the foliage.'

He observed me carefully. 'Sure,' he replied, shooting a warning stare at Nate before he left.

Nate frowned as he watched Ed walk away. 'I take it I'm not his favourite person right now.'

I shook my head and smiled, trying to look unconcerned. 'He's fine, just a little edgy with the event and everything.'

'He's very protective of you.'

'Yes, he is. But we all look out for each other. Good team spirit, that's all. Just the Kowalski's family sticking together. Besides, I think we're going to need it today.'

Nate nodded and looked round at the room. 'It's a great space,' he smiled, 'and the perfect place to showcase Kowalski's work.'

'It is pretty special,' I agreed. 'It's—'

'I should have come to see you,' he blurted out suddenly, bringing his eyes back to mine, waiting for my reaction. 'I'm sorry, Rosie. Can we – uh – can we go somewhere? Grab a coffee, maybe?'

My heart had begun to race and I suddenly felt too warm. 'There's quite a lot to do here and – and I'm not sure the team would be too happy with my leaving them.' I glanced over at Ed, Marnie and the grads, catching Ed watching us.

Nate seemed to be thinking about something, keeping his gaze firmly fixed on me. Then, as if a silent decision had been made, he reached out and squeezed my arm, nodding at me. 'Stay there, OK?'

Taken aback, I nodded dumbly. He walked purposely over to my team and said something to Ed. Marnie caught my eye as Ed and Nate walked to one side and appeared to be deep in conversation. A big part of me didn't want to watch them, didn't want to know what they were discussing, so for a while I tried to avert my attention to the team, the other arrangements, the ceiling – *anything* rather than look at my two friends.

I was about to look back when a loud voice shattered the relative silence of the room and stole my attention. Mimi Sutton had arrived in a flurry of silk and chiffon.

'There she *is* – the woman everyone's talking about!'

I smiled weakly as she approached me. Her smile was all benevolence as she held out her immaculately manicured hand, almost as if bestowing some great honour on me by doing so.

'This is simply *perfect*,' she smoothed, casting her eye round the room too fast to actually see anything but enough to give the appearance of interest. 'I knew you could deliver.' Her eye caught sight of Nate, still locked in conversation with Ed and apparently unaware of her arrival. I saw her smile tighten and she looked back at me. 'Could I steal a few moments of your time, perhaps? There are just one or two things I need to clear up before this evening. Minor points, dear, nothing to worry about. Is that possible?'

There was something in the lightness of her voice that struck an uneasy chord inside me, but I had no reason to refuse. 'Of course. Would you like to meet my team?'

'Perhaps later. I'd like to see the staircase garlands in greater detail,' she stated, taking hold of my arm a little too firmly and propelling me at a considerable speed across the ballroom floor.

When we reached the staircase, she relinquished her grip and began to inspect the flowers and foliage adorning the banister with red-taloned fingers. 'Excellent, excellent.'

'I'm really pleased with the result,' I said, as calmly as I could, pushing the nauseating ball of concern to the pit of my stomach. 'It's by far the biggest centrepiece Kowalski's has done—'

'Why is *he* here?' Mimi snapped, her face still a picture of grace and favour and her eyes fixed on the arrangement in front of her.

'S-sorry, who?'

'Nathaniel.'

'I – um – I've no idea.'

'Don't play the innocent with me, Ms Duncan,' Mimi retorted, a scarily cold edge appearing in her voice. 'I am too busy to play games with you.'

'Mimi, I honestly don't know why he's here,' I replied, beginning to feel annoyed at her tone. 'He's only just arrived and it seems he wants to talk to my co-designer.'

'Nonsense. He came to see you and you know it. I'm not entirely sure what his relationship with you is, but I do know his relationship with *my daughter.*'

'With respect, I fail to see how my friendship with Nate is relevant—'

'It's *all* relevant, Ms Duncan. The happiness of my daughter is my greatest concern. You are threatening that.'

'Sorry?'

Mimi's eyes shot to mine, a nasty purpose igniting her glare. 'Nathaniel Amie will never make a decision on his own. He is too casual for his own good with that lackadaisical attitude to life. Caitlin cannot – and will not – wait around for him for ever. He appeared to be finally reaching a decision about their future – until *you* came along.'

My pulse was thudding at my temples and I had to fight to retain my composure. 'Nate is my friend, Mimi. Nothing more.'

'Since he met you, Ms Duncan, he has been more quarrelsome with Caitlin, less co-operative and more inclined to delay what *will be* an inevitable culmination of their courtship,' Mimi snarled through gritted teeth. 'Caitlin has forbidden him to mention your name in her presence because it causes so much conflict.'

I wasn't quite sure how to take this information. Nate's relationship with his alleged fiancée remained much of a mystery to me, even after all our conversations; but to hear that they were arguing because of me was intriguing. 'Forgive me, I don't know what you want me to say.'

'It's quite simple really. I want you to tell me you'll stay away from Nathaniel.'

'I haven't been pursuing him,' I replied, folding my arms protectively across my body, 'and I have no intention of being the cause of conflict for anyone. If Nate decides to visit my shop – which he frequently does in order to buy flowers for *your* daughter – then I can't be held responsible.'

Mimi's eyes burned as she leaned closer to me. 'Be very careful, Rosie. Do not mess with situations you cannot possibly hope to understand.'

'So, Mimi, how do you like the work here so far?' breezed Nate as he suddenly appeared beside us. Mimi's smile returned and she embraced him for three melodramatic air kisses.

'Nathaniel, what a surprise. Are you looking for me?'

'Mimi, even though being in your company is always a joy, I'm afraid I'm here on business.'

Mimi's expression clouded. 'Oh? Is it the amendments for the book, darling? Only – as you can see – my head is full of the event today.'

Nate shook his head and took a step forward, placing himself between Mimi and me. 'I wouldn't dream of discussing those with you today of all days,' he grinned. 'I'm here to see Rosie.'

Mimi's smile began to strain at the edges. 'Oh? I'm afraid Ms Duncan is incredibly busy with her own masterpiece right now. Can it not wait?'

'I'm afraid it can't. I'm here to persuade her to write a book.'

'And this conversation couldn't happen – say – *next week*?'

'Regrettably not. I, as you well know, will be visiting my parents for the holidays, so I need to clear up my commission roster before the end of the year. It'll only take thirty minutes – an hour at most. I've spoken to Mr Steinmann and he assures me the team can spare her for that time.'

I glanced over at Ed and caught his eye. He raised an eyebrow and gave a vague smile. I knew he must be dying to know what the conversation was about.

'So, Rosie, shall we?'

'I can't spare her,' Mimi blurted out, the immaculate composure momentarily broken. 'We have things to discuss.'

Nate's hand rested gently on the small of my back, turning me away from the seething Mimi. 'Then discuss them with Ed,' he replied lightly. 'See you later, Mimi.'

With that, he picked up the pace and we walked briskly out of the ballroom, through the foyer and out onto the street.

I couldn't help smiling at Nate as we walked round the corner and into a small coffee house – not least because the warmth of his hand was still present at my back. I tried to gauge his expression, but it was impossible; I couldn't tell whether the exchange had amused him, annoyed him or something else. We found a table at the back of the café and sat down. Nate grinned at me, but I noticed his chest rising and falling faster than normal. He rubbed a hand across his forehead and picked up a menu absent-mindedly.

'A *book*?' I questioned. 'What book?'

'Flowers and their importance in modern city life,' Nate replied, as quick as a flash. 'We've been in discussions about it for months – don't you remember?'

'Ah, so all those visits to my shop were just—'

'Business,' he grinned, as a young Eastern European waitress arrived to take our order. 'Just a straight Americano for me. Rosie?'

'Tall skinny decaf latte, please.'

The waitress left. A small irritable question mark lit up in one corner of my mind. *Is he just using you, Rosie Duncan?* I decided to address it straight away: the last thing I needed today was unnecessary emotional quandaries. 'I take it you *were* joking just now – about the book, I mean?'

'Hey, why the worried face?'

I looked away, suddenly embarrassed by my question. 'Nothing. Forget it.'

'You think I care about business when I can talk to you? Oh, Rosie, *of course* I was joking! Look, I needed an excuse to see you and I was pretty sure Mimi wouldn't have let you go unless I had a good reason for us to talk. Whatever else she disregards, she can't dispute the importance of business.' Nate's hand reached across the table and took mine gently. 'I just wanted the opportunity to explain.'

'You don't need to explain anything,' I began, but he wasn't finished.

'Yes, I do. I just felt so bad about the whole David thing. You have to believe me, Rosie, I didn't have a clue you guys knew each other.'

'You couldn't have known. And anyway, it doesn't matter. I've spoken with him since and made my position quite clear.'

'Yeah, so did I,' Nate admitted sheepishly.

'I know.'

His eyes widened. 'Did he tell you that I hit him?'

I nodded. 'But I knew before. My best friend is a journalist, remember.'

He laughed and shook his head. 'Ah.'

'Indeed. Don't feel bad, Nate. None of it was your fault. I just hope I haven't caused problems for you and Caitlin.'

He frowned and his hand fell away from mine. 'What do you mean?'

'Just something Mimi said.'

Instantly, I knew I shouldn't have mentioned it. Nate's eyes said it all. I quickly tried to backtrack, cracking a joke about the menu that bombed immediately. Nate's attention was elsewhere. Our coffee arrived and still he didn't say anything.

I half wondered if I should just leave him there until, finally, he spoke.

'What did she say?' he asked quietly.

I took a breath. 'That you and Caitlin have been arguing. She thinks it's because we're friends.'

Nate let out a long sigh. 'She is way off the mark.'

I wanted to reassure him. 'Look, Nate, it's fine, OK? You and Caitlin have your relationship to think of. I don't want our friendship to jeopardise that. You're getting married, and—'

'Caitlin isn't my fiancée.'

I couldn't believe what I was hearing. Had they broken up? 'Sorry?'

'At least, she shouldn't be. Hell, this is such a mess.'

Feeling my heart sinking, I wasn't sure what to say next. But looking at the vulnerability in his expression, I felt I had to say *something*. 'I don't understand, Nate. Did you propose to Caitlin or not?'

His eyes dropped to the table and he let go of my hand. 'Yes, I did. Kind of. But it was only because I was pressured into it. The moment I said the words it didn't feel right but – I don't know – I couldn't stop it. It was, you know, *out* there.'

'Nate, I . . .'

He looked up again. 'The point is, I still don't know how I feel about her, Rosie. I need more time . . . I don't feel ready to commit – well, not to Caitlin, anyhow. I don't know, Rosie. It's like I become a different person – like I'm schizophrenic or something. One minute I'm pretty sure of myself, you know, happy, content with my life, and then – then I'm with Caitlin and suddenly I don't know the man who's standing by her side. I want to be the person I am when – when I'm *here*, like this, with *you*.'

Warning bells were chiming inside my head and I began to rise involuntarily to my feet. 'Nate, I have to get back . . .'

269

'Please stay?' he urged, his eyes wild with emotion I hadn't witnessed there before. 'I need to say this now or else I'll never say it.'

Reluctantly, in spite of all my better judgement, I resumed my seat.

'Rosie, since I met you I've felt – for the first time in a long time – like I'm understanding myself. You bring out the best in me, the Nate I aspire to be all the time. And it made me realise how *unlike* me I become whenever Caitlin's around. She's an amazing woman – ambitious, independent, stunning; she's everything I *should* want to spend my life with. But there's something missing – that final magic piece that makes it all fit. I love her but I don't *love* her like I feel I should. It's probably my own failing: maybe I see marriage as another business contract. And yes, Mimi has a point in that it makes perfect sense for me to marry her. We move in the same circles, our lives are very similar, our families are good New York clans. But the truth is, you hit the nail on the head when you said I don't look like a man in love.'

'Nate, I didn't mean—'

'But you – *you*, Rosie. You're not afraid to say what you think. You've made me look hard at myself and I want to be so much better than what I've seen. You're strong and beautiful, and being your friend makes me feel – *alive* . . .'

Suddenly, I didn't want to hear any more. Whether it was the potency of his words or the mention of the term 'friend' I wasn't sure; whatever the reason, I knew I had to get out of there, fast. 'I – I have to go,' I stammered, rising to my feet for a second time. Nate stood too, grabbing my hand.

'I don't want to scare you, Rosie. I just want you to know the muddle going on in my mind. You're a precious part of my life and I won't let go of you for anyone – not Mimi, not Caitlin, not Ed. Please say you understand. *Please?*'

For a moment, all I could do was look at him, oblivious to the assembled customers, who were now all avidly watching us. I still wasn't sure exactly what Nate was telling me. Where did I fit into the picture? I didn't want to look too deeply inside my head to find out how I felt about him, afraid of what would surface. But I didn't want to lose his friendship, either.

'Listen,' I began quietly, 'I don't know what's happening with you and Caitlin – and, to be honest, I don't think I want to. I love you being my friend. I enjoy spending time with you. But I don't want to be the cause of confusion or conflict. I can't tell you what to do about your engagement: only you know how you feel. But you need to decide what you want because otherwise people are going to get hurt.'

'I couldn't bear to hurt you, Rosie.'

I could feel a blush creeping over my face. 'I don't mean *me*, Nate.'

'But I do.'

I caught my breath.

'You mean the world to me, Rosie. More than I think either of us knows yet.'

Looking straight into his eyes, I knew he was telling the truth.

'You need to talk to Caitlin,' I replied, aware that this sugges-tion carried a whole other meaning I wasn't prepared to explore right now.

'Yes,' he nodded. 'Yes I do.'

Chapter Twenty

'All hail our great returning leader!' Ed called with an elaborate salute as I approached my team. 'We're just about done here, boss. What do you reckon?'

I looked around at the venue and felt a genuine thrill at the completed design. 'Absolutely. We've surpassed ourselves with this one.'

Ed sent Marnie and the grads to clear up and turned back to me. 'Good break?'

'Yes, thanks.'

'I gather Mimi was none too impressed?'

'You could say that. Listen, I think I might skip the ball tonight. I'm just not Mimi's favourite person and I could do with a quiet night after all this. So if you could just escort Marnie . . .'

Ed hung his head. 'Rosie, I can't do tonight.'

'What? But I thought you and Marnie wanted to be here. Ryan Reynolds is going to be here. You need to keep Marnie away from him.'

'I double-booked. Yeah, I know, I suck as a best friend and I am a complete disappointment. It's just I promised someone I'd see them tonight and—'

'Wait – the Specific Someone?'

Ed's head snapped up, a look of pure horror on his face. 'What? No! My *mother*, Rosie.'

I couldn't contain my giggle – or unexpected relief – at his answer. 'Your mother?'

Ed sighed. 'Mock as you will, I promised my mother that I'd take her to dinner with my two maiden aunts. It's the fifth anniversary of my grandfather's death and it's just something we do to mark each year, OK? I didn't realise the dates clashed until an hour ago when Mom called.'

'Fine, that's no problem.'

'Hey, look, it'll be good tonight. You don't have to stay for ever and, anyway, you should be here to garner the praise for your design.'

'*Our* design.'

'Sure, but you know me. Always the shy partner in this outfit.'

I folded my arms. 'And since when have you ever been shy about anything, Ed?'

He tapped the side of his nose with his forefinger. 'More often than you realise, boss.'

Travelling back to my apartment, I found myself niggled by Ed's parting shot. What did he mean? I had just turned the key in my front door lock when my cell phone began to ring.

'Rosie? Is that you?'

'Well, this is my mobile number so it's either me or a very courteous thief,' I smiled, throwing my bag onto the sofa and walking into the kitchen to put the kettle on.

'Ah, the great British sense of humour,' Celia replied, 'so *dry*. Are you going to Mimi's ball tonight?'

'Looks like I have no choice,' I grimaced, grabbing a mug and teabag. 'Why?'

There was a long pause at the other end of the call. 'Just – just promise me you won't talk to anyone, OK?'

'Celia, honey, it's an event with hundreds of guests. What do you expect me to do, ignore everyone else?'

'Don't be crazy, Rosie. I just mean don't talk to anyone from the press.'

'Why ever not?'

'I – I can't explain yet. I'm still working out the details. Just trust me on it, OK?'

'Celia, you're scaring me. What's going on?'

'Really, honey, it's fine. Just don't talk to anyone who's likely to be a journalist. Especially if they ask about James.'

My heart sank faster than a concrete block in the Hudson River. 'What's he done? What's happening?'

'I was worried you'd act like this, James is *fine*, OK. There are some things that may or may not involve him, but they're just rumours for now – nothing for you to worry about. The press are digging for information and if they make the link between you and him they may try to ask you questions.'

'But I don't know anything about it!'

'*Exactly*. So you should be fine.'

'Are you there tonight?'

'I should be – later on, perhaps. I have to see my mother first.'

'What *is it* with my friends and their mothers today?' The question was rhetorical, but belied the frustration inside my head.

'Sorry?'

'Nothing. I'll see you later, and I promise not to talk to any nasty journalists, right?'

'Good. And try not to worry.'

'Who's worrying?'

'That's the spirit. Bye!'

Taking my mug of tea, I sat down by the window and gazed out at the frosty street outside. After a moment, my attention turned to the daunting prospect of what to wear for the ball I hadn't intended to attend.

Mr K used to find women's dressing quandaries amusing and perplexing in equal measures. When female customers would enter the store, red-faced and breathless from a good day's shopping, he would politely enquire about their purchases and would always regret asking when, twenty minutes later, their blow-by-blow accounts of the reasons behind their choices were addling his poor brain.

'Women confuse me,' he often admitted, after his customers had departed. 'They are beautiful creatures, yet they waste so much life concerned by their clothes and their appearance. And if they are not fretting about their own appearance, they gossip about other people's. Believe me, Rosie, I thank Papa every day that I was born a simple man.'

I remembered his words and they made me smile, as I stepped out of the cab in my chosen outfit – a simple long black dress with the silver velvet wrap Celia had given me for my birthday draped around my shoulders. Understated and – I hoped – sufficiently unremarkable to allow me to pass through the guests unnoticed. It was starting to rain as I moved quickly along the plush red carpet lit by rows of tiny white lights, as camera bulbs flashed from the gaggle of paparazzi crammed either side of the roped-off entrance, jostling to catch the best shot of the A-list guests. Black limousines drew slowly up in solemn procession to the end of the red carpet behind me as I ascended the stairs to enter The Illustrian, and I could hear the shouts of photographers mingling with screams of excited fans on the street. 'Cate!' 'Jennifer!' 'Over here – over here!'

Once through the grand entrance doors, I began to scan the crowd for familiar faces. After a couple of minutes, I found one: unfortunately for me, however, the face belonged to Philippe Devereau. I tried to back into the crowd, but it was too late. He strode purposefully towards me.

'Good evening, Ms Duncan. I'd like to say it's a delight, but I won't.'

I hoped my smile looked authentic enough to fool him. 'And I wouldn't expect you to say anything different, Philippe.'

His expensive veneers sneered back, but I caught the slightest glimmer of softness in his eyes. 'Actually, I came to congratulate you.'

I couldn't hide my surprise. 'You did?'

'Amazingly enough. Though I hate to admit it, the displays are excellent. You and your team have surpassed even *my* expectations.'

I wasn't entirely sure this was much of a compliment, considering how low Philippe's opinion of Kowalski's usually was. 'Well, thank you. I'm pleased with the result.'

He paused for a second and then jerkily proffered his hand. From the look of uncertainty on his face, it was clear this was something he had not attempted often. 'Truce?'

Tonight was already turning out to be a night of surprises. I shook his hand. 'Absolutely. Thank you.'

'You're welcome,' he replied. 'Besides, I have it on good authority that Mimi has had a long overdue change of heart. Apparently, Kowalski's is *so* last year. Added to that the fact that, only today, I received a commission for studio flowers on *The Letterman Show*, you and your little business are really of no concern to me any longer.' With that, he turned on his Cuban heels and disappeared into the crowd.

I had to laugh. What Mimi had planned as a devastating blow to my business had actually turned out to be the biggest relief. Kowalski's could more than hold its own in New York: we had proved that tonight.

Marnie suddenly appeared from behind one of the tall marble pillars in the lobby, nearly giving me heart failure in the process. 'Rosie! Thank *goodness* you're here! Did you see Ryan Reynolds yet?'

'No, not yet.'

'Was that Philippe? It's such as shame we have to hate him. He is one stunning specimen of manhood.'

I laughed. 'Well, he's all yours now. He's called a truce. You look lovely, by the way.'

She gave an excited twirl, the sea-green chiffon of her long strapless gown billowing out as she moved. 'You think? I got it from a vintage shop in SoHo. And this,' she indicated the small diamanté butterfly slide holding back one side of her blonde hair, 'came from the flea market Mack told me about in East Village.'

'It's gorgeous.'

'I was kind of hoping it might look good enough to get Ryan to notice me. Oh *my*, Rosie! I'm actually going to be in the *same room* as him! I'm so excited I can hardly *breathe*!' Her pale cheeks flushed and for a moment I was worried that there might just be a loud bang and Marnie would explode in a shower of sparkling stars.

'Calm down, honey! Have you had a drink?'

'No, I was too scared to take one from the waiters in case they threw me out.'

I took her arm. 'Right, well, let's go and find one to disprove your theory, eh?'

We made our way through the clamour of guests, weaving in and out of smart tuxedos and elegant designer gowns towards the centre of the ballroom. With the tiny white fairy lights twinkling from their hiding places within the garlands, the overall effect was magical. Sometimes I have to pinch myself when I see one of our finished projects, especially the large ones. This one was by far the largest event Kowalski's had attempted and it was simply stunning. I could see Marnie was thinking the same thing too; her eyes were misty and wide as she surveyed the room.

'Wow, Rosie. *We* did this!'

'Yes, we did. You should be very proud of yourself.'

A waiter approached us with a silver tray full of fine crystal glasses brimming with golden fizzing champagne. 'Champagne, ladies?'

We each reached out to take a glass as a third hand appeared by mine to claim another. Our hands bumped and I turned instinctively to apologise, inadvertently coming face to face with a familiar pair of slate-grey eyes.

'Rosie? Wow, you look – amazing.'

Marnie's grin was almost as wide as the ballroom itself. 'Doesn't she just?' She thrust out a hand and David shook it. 'I'm Marnie Andersson, Rosie's assistant.'

'David Lithgow. It's a pleasure to meet you, Marnie.'

'Oh,' Marnie replied, quickly letting go of his hand. 'Yes.'

I made the best attempt to smile that I could muster. 'I didn't expect to see you tonight.'

'Mimi invited me just this afternoon,' he smiled. 'She and my mother are great friends – Mom's on the committee for this event. When Mimi found out I knew you, she insisted I come along. I must confess it was a pleasant surprise. She didn't mention that you would be here, although I should have guessed that she'd call on your considerable talents to grace her big occasion.' His eyes left mine to look around the room. 'I must say, the displays are phenomenal. You have a true gift.'

I took a large gulp of champagne, gasping as the ice-cold bubbles hit the back of my throat. 'Thank you.'

'We should get going,' Marnie said, linking an arm protectively through mine and giving David a hard stare. 'Nice to meet you, David.'

'Look forward to seeing you in March,' David smiled as we left, 'for the wedding.'

'Not if we can help it,' Marnie muttered, propelling me through the crowds until we had reached a safe enough distance from him. 'Rosie, are you OK? I didn't realise who he was. I'm so sorry!'

'It's fine, don't worry. I just wasn't expecting him to be here. Come on, let's see if we can find Celia.'

After nearly an hour of polite pushing through the jovial maze of bodies – and finally admitting defeat – we retreated to the relative quiet of the ladies' room, only to find Celia there, holding court amongst the powdering, preening prestigious females.

'So I said to him, "Charles, I don't care if you're the *Aga Khan*, I'm not writing a feature on *that* in the *Times*." Honestly, the gall of the man! I ask you! Oh – everyone, I'd like you to meet the lady responsible for all the amazing floral displays tonight – Miss Rosie Duncan!'

All eyes turned to Marnie and me in the doorway, followed by polite murmurs of approval. Celia grabbed her purse and bustled us back out into The Illustrian's foyer.

'Girls, you look wonderful,' she gushed. 'And the displays are truly awesome. I'm so proud to know you.'

'Thank you, Ms Reighton,' Marnie beamed. 'Have you seen Ryan Reynolds yet?'

'Honey, after battling those damn photographers on the carpet, the only thing I've seen so far is the inside of the ladies' room – and I can say for certain I didn't see him there.'

Marnie turned to me. 'I think I'm going to look in the ballroom to see if he's arrived. OK, Rosie?'

'Sure, mate, I'll catch you later.'

We watched her skipping off into the crowd of people. Celia took my arm and we walked slowly towards the ballroom. 'So you haven't been asked any questions?'

'No. Apart from Marnie the only other person I've spoken to this evening is David.'

'*David?* What in the world was he doing here?' Celia demanded.

'Mimi invited him this afternoon. I think it was her way of putting me in my place.'

'Oh? How so?'

'Long story. I'll fill you in sometime. So come on, what's all this "don't talk to anyone" stuff about? What do you know?'

Celia's expression was pure concern. 'There are – *rumours* – circling right now, about your brother. Now don't look worried, honey, at present that's all they are. They came to light a while back and I got wind of it again today from our guy in Washington.'

My heart rate began to increase. 'James has been working in Washington. He's been there for over six months, on and off.'

'I know. Hey, I'm sure it's nothing. This stuff happens now and again. Rumours, idle gossip. Most of it comes to nothing.'

'But you were sufficiently concerned about it to warn me about press questions earlier.'

Celia patted my arm and smiled as we walked through the crowd, but her eyes told another story. I decided not to look further – I didn't want any more surprises tonight.

'Ooh, Rosie, I've just seen someone I need to talk to,' Celia said, her attention focused in the direction of the staircase. 'Will you be OK here?'

'Absolutely. You go ahead.'

'I won't be long,' she called over her shoulder before she was swallowed up in the crush of elegantly attired heavenly bodies.

I folded my arms and sipped the champagne as I looked around the vast space. One thing was plain to see: when Mimi Sutton threw a party it was *spectacular* in every sense. From the exquisite setting to the impossibly beautiful music coming from the chamber orchestra, everything about the Grand Winter Ball testified to the power and influence Mimi had in New York society. There was still no sign of Nate; part of me longed for his familiar smile to appear through the crowd, although I had no idea what I'd say to him after our conversation this afternoon. I looked down at my dress and caught myself wondering what he would think of me in it; instantly, I pushed the thought away. It had been a long time since a man's opinion of my outfit was important to me and the last thing I needed was yet another hang-up to add to my already considerable self-consciousness in the sea of beautiful people thronged around me. I was just beginning to feel uncomfortably conspicuous standing by myself, when I felt a touch on my arm. I looked around to see a tall, flame-haired statuesque woman immaculately dressed in a midnight-blue vintage gown, her neck adorned with white-hot diamonds, which flashed and sparkled as she spoke.

'Rosie Duncan?'

'Yes – hello.' I held out my hand but the woman didn't take it.

'It's good to meet you finally,' she said, her expression hard as polished marble. 'Although you aren't anything like I imagined.'

I wasn't sure whether this was a compliment or not, but smiled anyway. 'You'd be surprised how often I get told that.'

Humour was obviously lost on her, however, as she looked me up and down like a disapproving school ma'am. 'I must confess I was curious about why you make such a significant impression on people.'

'Really? I'm sorry, I didn't catch your name.' I offered my hand politely again and this time she accepted, shaking my hand impassively with long, cold fingers. As she did, I caught sight of her impeccably manicured nails.

'Caitlin Sutton,' she smiled – although it was more of an upturned sneer than a friendly expression. 'I believe you know Nate. My fiancé?'

I struggled to maintain my composure as the full weight of her disapproval fell on me. In her impressive presence I felt decidedly dowdy and awkward by comparison. 'It's good to finally meet you,' I managed to say, feeling my face flushing red.

Caitlin smiled again, a cruel carbon-copy of her mother's expression earlier that day. 'I was concerned that you would be – how can I put this delicately? – more of a *challenge*. But now I see that my fears were unfounded,' she said, her haughty tone instantly crushing my self-confidence. 'I can't tell you how much of a relief that is.'

'Well, it's always nice to buck someone's expectations,' I replied, feeling indignation rising within me. 'Now, if you'll excuse me, I have to—'

'I know what you're doing,' she blurted, her alabaster sheen lost for a moment. 'I know you're trying to turn Nathaniel against me.'

'Now hang on a minute—'

'It won't work. It can't work. I think you'll find that I am someone accustomed to getting what I want.'

'Of that I'm already convinced,' I replied, resisting the urge to throw half a glass of champagne over her smug face, right there. 'However, you're wrong: I have no intention of turning anyone against anyone. I don't even know you – and it's blatantly obvious that you don't know me if you think me capable of such behaviour.'

'If that's the case, Ms Duncan, then why does the very mention of your name cause so much hostility between Nate and me? You know full well what you're doing: since he's been talking to you, he's been different.'

'Then I suggest you talk to *him* about it, Ms Sutton, not me. Nate is a friend, that's all, and I'm getting tired of having to justify myself to your family.'

Caitlin's eyes flashed as she leaned closer to me. '*Stay away* from my fiancé,' she growled. 'I won't tolerate him being friends with you.'

'Tell him that yourself,' I snarled back.

'Rosie! You would *not believe* who I was just talking to—' Celia chirped, coming to an abrupt halt when she saw Caitlin. 'Oh, forgive me, Caitlin, I almost didn't recognise you – you look simply *divine* in that dress.'

'Vintage Valentino,' Caitlin replied loftily, a thin smile returning briefly to her lips. 'Celia, you never told me you had such *adorable* friends.'

'Isn't she just?' smiled Celia, clocking my expression straight away. 'And so much in *demand* these days it would seem.'

Caitlin's smile vanished. 'Quite. Please excuse me.' And with that, she was gone, the crowd parting before her like the Red Sea before the Israelites.

Celia blew out a whistle and patted my arm. '*Gracious*, sweetie, are you OK?'

I took a large swig of champagne and willed my heart to slow down, tension still prickling across my shoulder blades. 'I'm fine. That woman is something else.'

'Like mother like daughter.'

'Hmm.'

'What did she say?'

'Oh, nothing, really. She just accused me of plotting to steal Nate and causing trouble between the two of them.'

Celia snorted, shaking her head. 'She should try telling it to her *therapist*, not you.'

'Caitlin Sutton has a therapist?'

A wicked smile lit up my friend's face. 'Try *several* therapists. That young woman is a psychiatrist's wet dream. What in the world Nathaniel sees in her is beyond me.'

'Presumably what Caitlin and Mimi *tell* him to see,' I smirked, allowing myself to relax a little. But I couldn't shake off thoughts of the conversation I'd had with Nate that afternoon. While I never intended to cause friction between Caitlin and Nate, in all honesty I couldn't claim to be a wholly innocent party when it came to harbouring feelings for him. Truth was, I liked Nate – more than I would care to admit. The more time we spent together, the more I found myself contemplating what life would be like with him. Our conversation was so easy, the chemistry between us was impossible to deny – and he was the first person since David to make me feel that intensely giddy excitement of attraction. But the fact remained that he was *with* Caitlin – and I couldn't condone him breaking

285

her heart, even if it was harder than granite. If he chose to leave her – as he'd intimated earlier – it wouldn't, *couldn't* be on my account.

My train of thought was halted by a voice from the stage where the orchestra had now ceased playing. 'Ladies and gentlemen, please welcome your host of tonight's gala event: Ms Mimi Sutton!'

Loud applause echoed around the ballroom as Mimi appeared at the top of the grand staircase and descended regally, her dress a riot of crystal and sequins shimmering in the spotlights as she approached her guests. On the bottom step, she was handed a microphone and, laughing with affected embarrassment, held up her immaculately manicured hand for silence. The applause duly subsided.

'Who does she think she is – the Queen of Sheba?' Celia laughed in a low voice.

'Thank you, thank you. Welcome to our fifteenth Grand Winter Ball, here at the obscenely opulent Illustrian, which, I'm sure you'll all agree, is the very best setting for such a fabulous night. I'm thrilled to tell you that already we have raised over two million dollars for the New York hospital charities through invitations alone.'

Applause broke out across the room.

'I've had the honour of hosting one of Manhattan's premier events for all these years and yet none has given me as much pleasure as tonight's celebrations,' Mimi continued. 'Because here, this very evening, I have an announcement to make that has thrilled me and, I know, will thrill you all too.'

'Prepare yourself,' I whispered to Celia. 'You may need to write this down.'

'I'm on it,' Celia whispered back with a mischievous grin.

'This Christmas the Sutton household will be welcoming a

new member – officially. My daughter, Caitlin, has accepted the hand of the very charming Nathaniel Amie of Gray & Connelle publishers.'

The guests applauded enthusiastically as a spotlight swung into the crowd to illuminate Nate and Caitlin, smiling and waving shyly to those around them. *They look incredibly relaxed for a couple with relationship problems*, a little voice ventured inside my head. I caught my breath and pushed the aggravating thought away.

'And, as if that weren't enough for this poor old heart of mine to bear, I now have pleasure in announcing that they have finally set a date! Caitlin and Nathaniel will become Mr and Mrs Amie on May the twenty-fourth next year!'

As the crowd demonstrated their joy and surprise at this news, camera flashes caught the happy couple's identical expressions. I kept my eyes firmly fixed on Nate, who was laughing and smiling with his fiancée by his side. There was certainly no hint of panic in his face, as there had been hours before in the coffee shop; nothing but the unadulterated happiness of a man in love. Celia patted my back as if sensing my thoughts. Suddenly, the room was too hot; it was difficult to breathe. I had to get out of there as fast as possible. Turning to Celia, I made my bravest attempt at a smile.

'Well, I think I've had enough excitement for one day. I'm going home.'

Celia's eyes were full of concern as she smiled at me. 'I completely understand, sweetie. You call me tomorrow, OK?'

Leaving her in the middle of the excited gaggle of guests, I pushed my way through the bodies until I reached the icy fresh air at the entrance. Descending the steps, the red carpet now dirty brown and damp from the rain-soaked feet that had tramped up it earlier, I emerged onto the sodden sidewalk and held my arm out to hail a cab. Several yellow taxis, their back seats already full, passed me by and I pulled my silver wrap tighter around my shoulders to keep the bitter December night air at bay.

Several minutes later – with no cabs in sight – I decided to walk to the next corner, more in an attempt to stay warm than in the hope I'd find a taxi on a Saturday night. I was just walking from the bright lights of The Illustrian's grand entrance, when I heard a familiar voice behind me.

'Rosie! Wait up!'

I turned to see David sprinting down the red carpeted steps and heading towards me. At a loss for anything better to do, I stopped and waited for him to reach me.

'No cabs, huh?' he observed, breathless from the run.

'No. Not the best time to try to find one, either.'

'You look frozen to death. Here – take my coat.'

Suddenly vulnerable, I shook my head. 'No, thanks.'

His laugh was more of a defence mechanism than amusement. 'Be serious.'

'I am serious. I'm fine. Taxi!' The yellow cab ignored me and sped past.

'Rosie, come on. I'm offering you my coat, not trying to attack you.'

I turned to him, willing my face to unfreeze and the goosebumps now covering my arms to disappear. 'I'm *fine*. Thank you for your concern.'

David shook his head, his expression a mix of humour and frustration. 'Hell, Rosie, you know how to beat a guy up, don't you?'

I stared at him blankly and then looked defiantly back at the road. My hands were going numb and my feet had already succumbed to the sub-zero December night.

'OK. Take that attitude if you want. But I won't be responsible for standing by while a lady freezes to death on the sidewalk. So I'm doing this for your own good.' Taking off his long, dark grey overcoat, he draped it firmly across my shoulders. By now, I was too cold to argue so I didn't protest, thankful for the warmth it afforded me. And that's when it happened: all the fire left me and I was suddenly struck by the absurdity of the whole situation. Maybe it was the cold, or maybe it was just that I'd done my fighting for tonight: whatever it was, I began to giggle uncontrollably, my breath turning into rapid puffs of steam rising into the freezing night sky. I turned to face David, wrapping his coat tighter round my shivering body and stamping my feet in a bid to coax the circulation back to my toes. His face was a picture. 'OK, now you're scaring me. Do you need a doctor?'

His concern only served to increase my mirth. 'No – no, I'm quite in control, don't worry. It's just been a really long night, that's all. Thank you – for the coat, I mean. It's lovely and warm.'

'Tough night then, huh?'

'You could say that, yes.'

He stuffed his hands into his dinner jacket pockets and looked up the street. 'So where are you headed?'

'Um, I'm – I'm not sure. I just needed to leave the Mimi Sutton Experience in there.'

David's smile was as warm and welcome as the coat I now wore. 'Right with you on that one. I don't know how Nate can bear her company, let alone consider her as a future mother-in-law.' His eyes narrowed. 'I saw you talking to Caitlin Sutton.'

The memory made my shoulders tense. 'Being *talked to* would be more accurate. I don't think I'm top of the Sutton family Christmas card list this year.'

'Because of Nate, right?'

That was a step too far and I felt the old defences building again. But I was enjoying David's coat too much to start another argument, so I opted for diplomacy and changed the subject. 'It's just been a terrifically busy day for me, you know? I wasn't really in the mood for a party after all the work we had to do today. I'd have been happier with a hot chocolate and an early night.'

David clapped his hands together. 'Excellent idea.'

'I hope you don't mean the early night?'

'No, you crazy woman! I meant the hot chocolate. Or coffee, anyway. There's a diner just around the corner from here. How about we grab a drink and maybe something to eat – seeing as both of us elected to leave before the banquet this evening?'

I paused for a moment – after all, this was the man whose betrayal I'd been running from for the past six-and-a-half years. But then it suddenly occurred to me: he was no longer a threat. My biggest fear had been seeing him again. Now I had done that and survived more or less unscathed by the experience. After all, I'd agreed to work on his wedding. There's only so long you can maintain a position of being wronged: the best way I could show my strength in the situation now was to move on – and be seen to be moving on. I couldn't do anything about the situation with Nate – that had been made clear to me this evening – and, while I was still on my guard with David, I found that I felt stronger than I had in a long, long time. It gave me an immense thrill to feel myself finally ready to move forward.

'Sure,' I smiled, taking him by surprise, 'why not? Lead the way.'

Joe Junior's Diner was the kind of Manhattan icon that you see whenever a film calls for a diner scene. A large chrome bar stretched the length of the room, with a whole assortment of

New Yorkers sitting on tall stools huddled over hamburgers and enormous sandwiches, while other customers were seated on red leather bench seats. On every table were bowls of huge pickled gherkins, Heinz Tomato Ketchup bottles and stainless-steel sugar pourers. Dean Martin crooned through the crackly speakers and everyone spoke much louder than they needed to, raucous laughter breaking through the general din of the restaurant, while several cross-room conversations batted back and forth over the customers' heads.

At our table mid-way down the diner, David and I grasped hot coffee mugs and gazed out through misted windows at the black, asphalt-grey and neon cityscape beyond. David had ordered two large pieces of apple pie, which the waitress told us was 'da specialty of da boss', and as the scent of cinnamon, hot apple and warm pastry filled my nostrils, I discovered that I was actually hungry.

'So, what was the real reason you were leaving?' David asked, mid-mouthful. 'It wasn't on my account, I hope?'

'Don't flatter yourself,' I replied, smiling to reassure him I wasn't touting for a fight. 'No, like I said, tough day. Ed and I were up at five this morning to pack the van.'

'Ed? He's your . . . ?'

'Co-designer.'

'Oh.'

David's eyes fell from mine and he stabbed at his apple pie self-consciously. 'I just wondered . . .'

'Ed's my co-designer – and my best friend. I love him to bits and he looks out for me. It's a good working relationship.' When I put it that way, I couldn't escape the nagging feeling that I hadn't said enough; that, somehow, this succinct description didn't do Ed justice. But it was all I could say: there were no words readily available to describe the rest.

291

'I see. So,' he raised his head again. 'Is there – anyone?'

'In my life? No. I'm quite happy as I am.'

'I can see that.' His eyes drifted to the window again and he was silent for a while.

Unsure what to do, I took another bite of apple pie and looked around the diner at the people crammed into every available space. Everyone was talking at once; whole conversations conducted simultaneously that, amazingly, everyone at the tables heard, digested and responded to. Ed often says the reason New York diners are like this is that nobody in the city has enough time to actually listen to a conversation because everyone is way too busy to do anything save draw breath – and even that has to have a schedule. Thinking of Ed caused me to catch my breath, which made David look back at me.

'You OK?'

I pointed at my plate. 'Hot pie,' I lied, pretending to have burned my mouth.

David's smile vanished as fast as it appeared. 'Rosie, I have to know. Has there been anyone since . . . since I last saw you?'

His question hurt but I felt obliged to answer. 'No,' I replied, careful to keep my tone light and matter-of-fact. 'But that was my decision.'

David blinked and shook his head. 'Was it because of me – because of what I did?'

I looked down at my pie and didn't answer.

It was enough of a reply for him. 'I see.'

'Did you order pastrami on rye?' A middle-aged waitress wearing a uniform several sizes smaller than she needed appeared at our table, her singsong Bronx accent cutting into our conversation. 'Or I have house cherry pie here?'

The interruption provided a moment for me to gather my

thoughts and I took a slow sip of coffee as David confirmed that neither was our order.

'OK, my mistake. You people have enough coffee?'

David looked at me and I held my hand up to refuse.

'OK,' the waitress replied, chewing gum and blessing us with the briefest flash of her nicotine-stained teeth. 'That's fine. En-joy.'

David leaned forward confidentially. 'I should have lied. That cherry pie looked amazing.'

'You always did have a sweet tooth.' It had escaped my lips before I realised it. I looked away again.

'Still have, I'm afraid.'

I smiled despite the stab of pain inside. 'You'll have to watch that if you want to fit into your tuxedo.'

'I will.' His hand reached uncertainly across the table and touched the back of mine with the lightest contact.

'I'm so sorry, Rosie. You deserved much more than I gave you.'

Feeling braver, I looked straight into his eyes. 'Yes, I did.'

He smiled. 'Well, at least we agree on something.'

'Finally, a breakthrough!' We laughed and a small shard of mortar dislodged itself from the invisible wall between us.

'Listen, are you still sure about Kowalski's handling my – the wedding?'

'We're fine about it. My team are more than ready for the challenge, as I think we proved with the Ball tonight.'

'I meant *you*, Rosie.'

Slowly, I withdrew my hand from underneath his fingers and cupped it around my coffee mug. 'Yes, I'm fine. How are all the other preparations going?'

He gave me a rueful smile. 'It's like a military operation, what with my mother and Rachel's mother—' He broke off, concerned that he'd entered dangerous territory once more.

I decided to put his mind at ease, finding a vestige of comfort in the sense of progress it gave me. 'So – tell me about Rachel.'

David blew out a whistle and rubbed his chin, betraying his nerves as he did so. 'Rachel? Well, she's – are you *sure* you want to hear about her?'

'I wouldn't have asked if I didn't.'

He stared at me for a moment, confusion passing across his eyes. 'OK. Well, she's a History professor at Yale – the youngest in her department – and I met her when my company was asked to develop a promotional campaign to attract new students. I hadn't worked with educators before, so Rachel was brought on board as a consultant. We just kinda hit it off, I guess, and then things progressed from there. We've been together a little over eighteen months and it's – it's good.'

I smiled, picturing Rachel as a compliant, studious professor who no doubt followed David's every whim without the least whiff of resistance. No wonder things were good for him. 'It sounds like you've found something worth keeping, then.'

'Yes. Yes, it feels that way, at least. I don't know – I'm older, wiser, I guess. The whole "settling down" thing doesn't scare me like it used to . . . Sorry.'

'No – no, it's fine.' I stopped for a moment, unsure whether to continue.

'You're going to ask me if that's what it was with us, aren't you?' he asked.

'Yes. I suppose I've always wondered what the reason was.'

David sighed and reached across the table to gently take my hand again. 'I was an idiot, Rosie. I freaked and didn't have the guts to tell you. I'd gotten so carried away with the whole romance of the thing: the overblown proposal, the wedding plans, everything. The *idea* of it was so beguiling, so beautiful, that I just ran with it. Then the day before our wedding, when I could see it all finally happening for real, I was terrified. I couldn't deal with the *reality* of for ever. That's not to say I didn't love you; I did, in my own way. But looking back I think I was more in love with the *idea* of marriage than I was with the actual deal. Even if I'd gone through with it, I don't think I'd have stayed long – and that's no indictment on you, Rosie, believe me, that's just where I was. I felt like I was at the helm of a runaway railroad car, powerless to stop it. My only option was – to *jump*.'

I stared back at the man who had – as he put it – jumped out of my life, six and a half years ago, and now it made sense. Maybe I should have looked closer at the one-man-express train moving our wedding plans forward with such momentum. Maybe then I would have seen the fear in his eyes as I did now. 'You should have told me, David. We could have worked it out or – or at least prevented that débâcle on the wedding day.'

'My father said you were amazing,' he ventured, letting go of my hand. 'He said you were so strong and fearless. Dealing with all the fallout of my mistake, handling all the mess – he said you put me to shame.'

'Your father took my job and paid me off,' I replied, staring straight into his eyes. I may have been finally ready to understand David, but it would take a long time to forget his father's actions. 'I never heard anything from your family ever again. It was like they were punishing me in your place.'

'I know, I know and, believe me, I have discussed this at length with my father. He reacted badly; he saw his family compromised by one of its own and panicked. He knows he was wrong. In fact, it was he who pointed out the article in the *New York Times* about your store. That's how I knew you were here. Can you ever forgive me, Rosie?'

I let out a sigh and smiled at him 'You know, I think I already have.'

Chapter Twenty-One

With the excitement of the Grand Winter Ball over, I was finally free to plan and prepare for my own Christmas. I have to say that, despite being relatively organised in everything else, when it comes to Christmas shopping, I actually *like* being disorganised. Running Kowalski's demands a lot of my time, especially during the approach to the festive season, so it makes sense for me to do my Christmas shopping nearer the big day. And somehow leaving the gift-hunting until just before Christmas makes the whole thing more magical, if a little hectic. Consequently, I can nearly always be found dashing around shops on the morning of Christmas Eve, snapping up last-minute bargains for my friends and family. Sometimes it means that people receive quite random gifts for Christmas, but most of the time it means I have to think that little bit harder about what to buy and end up finding something really unusual.

This year was no exception. I spent the morning rushing round the small shops, boutiques and specialist book stores on the Upper West Side, selecting gifts, cards and brightly patterned wrapping paper, then visited Zabar's for a few treats and essentials, before hauling my heavy bags thankfully into a waiting cab for the short journey to my apartment. While my aged coffee machine grumbled into life, I cleared the table, grabbed my scissors and sticky tape and started to wrap my purchases. I love this part of Christmas preparations: the 'production line' process of selecting gifts, wrapping them and writing tags, where you begin with countless bulging bags and end up with a pile of gorgeously inviting presents. This year, I'd made gift tags from glossy green holly leaves, writing the recipients' names on each one with a gold pen and attaching them with brown parcel string. After an hour of frenzied cutting, wrapping and sticking, I sat back to admire my handiwork.

I had a quick lunch of tomato soup and rosemary focaccia, then I carefully repacked my bags with the heap of presents, headed downstairs and hailed a cab.

'Present round, is it, lady?' asked the tanned Italian-American cab driver, smiling a grin that the Cheshire Cat himself would be envious of.

'Yes, it is,' I replied. 'And I can pay you for a whole after-noon, if that's OK?'

'Is it OK? *Is it OK?* Sure it's OK, lady. You're my Christmas come early – my wife will be thrilled. She's had her eye on a hat in Bloomingdale's for a month and she's been like, "Tony, you get me that hat for Christmas or I'm leaving you for your cousin Marco." But she won't leave me, I know. Marco is an idiot and I cook a better lasagne than she'll find this side of Napoli. Plus, my aunt Maria looks like a *moose*. My wife don't want *that* moose for a mother-in-law, trust me. There's no contest. So where we headed first, huh?'

It seemed that my penchant for finding and giving last-minute presents had rubbed off on my friends this year: Celia was out visiting family, so I left her gift with her next-door neighbour, Mrs Andrews, who promised to deliver it the moment Celia arrived home; Marnie and her sister were braving the crowds at Macy's, so I posted her present through her letterbox, thanking my lucky stars that I'd bought her something small and unbreakable; and when I called Ed he said he had some errands to run but suggested he come round later to collect his gift. My other presents distributed, Tony drove me back to my apartment.

'Happy Christmas,' I said, handing over the fare, plus a generous tip. 'I hope your wife likes her hat.'

'She'd better,' Tony grinned, 'or else I'm leaving her for her cousin Margarita. Happy Holidays, lady!'

I have to admit that I probably love Christmas Eve even more than Christmas Day. It's been this way since I was a child. Perhaps it's the remnants of stardust from my Father Christmas-filled childhood dreams, or maybe it's because Christmas Day always seems to be somewhat of an anti-climax when it actually arrives. Whatever the reason, the night before Christmas always offers a sense of wonder: a heady mixture of expectation, memories and truly indulgent warm fuzzy feelings.

I always boil a ham joint studded with cloves and cooked with bayleaves, which I then stuff inside the turkey on Christmas morning. It's something I first did when I lived in London – a friend gave me the recipe – and its mouth-watering aroma adds to the Christmassy feel of my home. Mince pies and cookies are a Christmas Eve tradition for me as well: I love the floury, spicy endeavour of creating little pies and biscuits, the smell of their baking and the joy of seeing stacks of the finished product on cooling racks and plates.

Once the ham was on the hob and the pies and cookies cooling in the kitchen, I wandered back into my living room and admired the decorations. James used to call me a 'tinsel-holic' when we were younger, saying I was the only person he knew who could use enough tinsel to service an entire house for just one room. I'd toned down my festive adornments since then, opting for a mixture of classic floral garlands and poinsettias with unabashed kitsch baubles and twinkling lights. My favourite Christmas CD, purchased from a pound shop in England years ago, was playing away merrily – Bing Crosby and Frank Sinatra crooning seductively through a selection of seasonal tunes. With the scents of cooking ham, cinnamon, allspice, nutmeg and coffee combining with the sounds of classic crooners and the sight of my magnificent tree, the overall effect was wonderfully evocative and homely.

About eight o'clock, a knock summoned me to my front door – and there was Ed, trademark leather jacket pulled up around his cold rosy face and thick woollen scarf tied round his neck. His jeans were tucked into walking socks and his boots bore the merest hint of snow on their soles.

'Come in, come in,' I said, ushering him into the warmth of my apartment.

'Wow,' he breathed, 'you really do the whole Christmas thing, huh?'

'I do,' I smiled happily. 'Can I get you a coffee?'

'No, I can't stay long, sorry,' he replied, shrugging his shoulders apologetically. 'I have the dubious honour of attending a Steinmann family Christmas gathering, so I'm headed there when I leave here.'

'Sounds like fun,' I smirked, walking into the kitchen to check on the ham.

Ed followed me into the living room, pausing to look at the tree by the window. 'Oh, sure, three whole days of celebration with a family of psychiatrists. The after-dinner conversation

300

is so analytical it's like sitting in a perpetual rerun of *Ally McBeal*. So, I thought, who better to offer me the last bit of sanity I'm likely to witness this side of New Year than Rosie Duncan, New York's finest florist?'

I joined him in the living room, handing him a hot mince pie from the stack in my kitchen. 'How kind. Here, wrap your chops round this.'

'You have such a delicate turn of phrase,' Ed grinned, popping the whole pie into his mouth in one go, then puffing and blowing as the heat of the filling hit his tongue. '*Mmwonderful*,' he mumbled, brushing crumbs from his lips. 'These are good, Rosie. Wow. You are the epitome of the Christmas spirit, aren't you?'

'I am indeed. Welcome to Rosie Duncan's Tinseltown,' I grinned, sitting on the arm of my sofa as Ed sunk into the armchair opposite. 'It's great to see you, anyhow.'

'Well, you know, I had to come see what the famous tree looked like once you'd wreaked your artistic talents on it. After all, I'm partly the reason it's here in the first place.'

'Yes, you are,' I grinned. 'I hope you feel suitably proud?'

Ed placed a hand on his heart and faked an emotional response. 'It's – it's – more magical than I could've ever *dreamed*,' he gushed, a thoroughly wicked glint in his eyes. 'So what about your family then? Do you miss them?'

I nodded. 'A little. Mum will be visiting family – my cousin still lives nearby, so they tend to do Christmas Dinner together. Gran, who's just turned ninety-three, will be celebrating with the other residents of her sheltered housing place up in Newcastle, probably consuming far too much sherry for her own good. And as for my brother, as far as I know he's spending the holidays in Washington this year. To be honest, I actually like having a quiet Christmas by myself in my little apartment.'

He grinned. 'Trade you anyday.' Reaching into an inner

pocket of his jacket, he produced a small, exquisitely wrapped box and handed it to me. 'Here. Merry Christmas.'

'Oh, mate – thank you. It looks fabulous.'

'Yeah, well, I didn't wrap it. I just sweet-talked the lady in the shop and she did it for me,' he admitted. 'But hey, she did a great job.'

I retrieved his present from underneath the tree and gave it to him. 'Merry Christmas right back.'

'Wow, Rosie, you didn't have to . . . Who am I kidding? *Of course* you did. I am, after all, your bestest bud in the whole wide world, not to mention your über-talented co-designer. Listen, don't open yours till tomorrow, OK? Kind of a tradition thing with us Steinmanns.'

'All right. Well, the same goes for you, then. Wouldn't want you breaking with tradition on my behalf.'

'Good. That's settled. Presents tomorrow and not before.'

A question that had been buzzing around my mind all day chose the next moment to present itself again. 'So, have you given your Specific Someone a gift this year?'

Ed stared at me, suddenly a little unsure. 'Yes,' he answered finally, 'yes I have.'

I ignored the thud of disappointment in the pit of my stomach. 'Ed, that's wonderful! Well done. Does she know how you feel about her yet?'

He laughed. 'Nope. She has no idea.'

'Well, maybe you should tell her.'

He wasn't convinced by this suggestion. 'You think?'

'Absolutely. Make it a New Year's Resolution to let her know you like her. Or else how are you ever going to know if she feels the same?'

His eyes narrowed. 'I'm pretty sure she doesn't. I think I would have gotten the vibe by now.'

'Mate, some people are very good at hiding their hearts.'

'Like *you*, you mean?'

His question knocked me sideways a little. 'Yes, I suppose. Oh, come on, you know me. I spent six and a half years of my life hiding the truth about what happened in Boston and it took the man who jilted me turning up unannounced to make me open up about it.'

'So you reckon I have to be a low-life guy with no common sense and a fear of commitment who sneaks up on her in order to get the truth out?'

'No, that's not what I meant, you nut. But you can't expect her to know you like her if you don't tell her. You might be surprised at her response.'

A wry smile made itself at home on Ed's lips. 'Maybe I'll try that, boss.' He checked his watch and stood up. 'Now I have to go or else my family will be calling the hospitals to trace my surely broken little body. Come here.' He wrapped his arms around me and pulled me tight against the spicy-scented warmth of his battered jacket. 'Promise me you'll always be *you*, Rosie Duncan. Don't feel you have to hide from me again, ever.' His breath was comfortingly warm as he kissed the crown of my head.

'I won't, I promise,' I murmured into his jacket, allowing myself to revel in the feeling of security his arms around me provided, listening to the sound of his beating heart.

Breaking the hug he looked at me for a moment, then turned to leave. 'Merry Christmas, Rosie,' he called over his shoulder as I watched him walk down the hall.

During the holidays I make and receive a lot of phone calls: Mum, Gran, James, Celia (although I receive many, *many* times more calls back from her when her family are driving her to distraction, which is pretty much most of the Christmas break) and my friends from school, who I'm still in touch with. But the person I look forward to speaking to the most is Ben. Although we tend to email each other throughout the year, together with countless weekend phone calls, our indulgent hour-long Christmas Eve conversations are the ones I covet most. We normally spend the majority of the call talking about him: what's happening in Boston, how Harvard is faring with the latest intake of students, what new weird and wonderful extreme sport he's discovered and what relationships he's had, is in, or is planning to enter. This year, however, I had a lot to tell him. Once he'd recovered from the shock revelation of David's reappearance, his questions came thick and fast.

'How many times have you seen him?'

'Three times. The last time we went for coffee and it was good.'

'Did he explain himself at all? Was he apologetic? Or the old, arrogant Lithgow we all know and hate?'

'He was very apologetic. He explained what had happened and he kept saying sorry for it all. He was most unlike the old David: older, more thoughtful.'

'Heck, Rosie, what did you say to him?'

'I told him exactly how I felt. I didn't let him off lightly.'

'But you went for *coffee* with the man! What were you thinking?'

'Ben, relax! It was unexpected but it turned out well. We were able to have a really frank conversation about everything and I think we laid a lot of ghosts to rest.'

'You're falling for him again, aren't you?'

I couldn't believe he could even consider that as a possibility after all this time. 'No! Absolutely not! If anything, it's made me realise I don't feel that way about him any more.

Besides, I'm working on his wedding – I'd hardly be doing that if I still had feelings for him, would I?'

'I suppose not. Oh, Rosie, be careful with that man. I know you've cleared the air between you and, believe me, nobody could be happier about that than me. But I don't believe he's all changed now. People just don't.'

'People make *mistakes*, Ben. I have to believe what he told me, otherwise how can I ever move on?'

A long sigh travelled all the way to my ear from Boston. 'I don't want you to ever have to go through what I saw you go through again, OK?'

'I know, mate. Thanks.'

'So how's Ed doing?'

It seemed like an odd question. Ben had met Ed a couple of times when he'd visited New York and I was aware they had instantly found a lot in common, particularly baseball. 'Erm, he's fine.'

'It's just that in your last email you mentioned him a lot.'

'Did I?'

Ben's laugh was warm. 'Only about *fifteen* times. Something happen with you guys?'

'No, of course not. Stop teasing me.'

'I'm not. I am merely stating a fact: you talked about him a lot.'

I shook my head, even though Ben couldn't see it. 'Well, I wasn't aware of it. We've been working together a lot this month, so I guess that's why.'

'Whatever. Now, tell me more about this *Nate* bloke.'

There wasn't much to tell. Since the Grand Winter Ball, he'd more or less kept himself to himself – and, to be honest, that suited me fine. Later that evening, Mum called. She reeled off the usual details of what she was doing, who she'd seen, what

305

her plans were over the Christmas break and so on – but there was something different about the tone of her voice that made me feel uneasy.

When she'd finished speaking, I had to ask what was troubling her.

'Oh, it's nothing, dear,' she replied, completely unconvincingly.

'Mum – come on. I know there's something on your mind.'

There was a pause. 'I think James is in trouble.'

My Christmas Eve cheer dissolved instantly. 'Why? What's he said?'

'He hasn't *said* anything, Rosie, it's just that when I spoke to him this morning he was very . . . evasive.'

'In what way?'

'Well, I asked him what he was planning for Christmas and his answer was incredibly vague. You know your brother, darling, he's usually in a hurry to tell me every detail of all the fabulous parties he's been invited to and all the beautiful women he's dating. But he wasn't like that today. It was – and I know I'm going to sound completely paranoid when I say this – but it was almost like he was annoyed that I'd asked him about it. Then he made some preposterous excuse about having to dash off for a meeting – on Christmas Eve, I ask you – and disappeared. Do you know anything? Did he say anything to you when he visited a while ago?'

I decided not to mention the phone conversation I'd overheard, nor the scant details I had received from Celia. 'No, he didn't tell me anything. Look, I'm sure it's fine, Mum. He's probably just got himself into another mess with a girl and he doesn't want to talk about it yet.'

'I do hope you're right, darling,' Mum replied. 'Promise me you'll keep an eye on him? Washington is so very far away from Stone Langley and I feel awful that I can't take care of my lovely boy.'

I promised I would and said goodbye. Slumping back into my armchair, I rubbed my eyes. I didn't want to deal with the questions dangling dangerously in my head. What with David's re-emergence, the strange situation with Ed, and Christmas on the way, I felt neither prepared nor inclined to tackle any of it this year. All I wanted was a nice, quiet Christmas, enjoying it in my own way and resting before the bustle of the New Year began.

Christmas morning was bright and sparkly, a sharp frost the night before giving the snow outside a coating of glitter in the pale December sunlight. I woke early – even though I was spending the day alone, I wanted to enjoy every last minute of it – and pulled on my super-thick white towelling robe, which is several sizes too big for me so it's excessively snuggly. Padding through to the living room in my slippers, I switched on the tree lights and paused to admire the sight and scent of my tree. Then I grabbed the pile of unopened Christmas cards from the mantelpiece and shuffled through to the kitchen to coax Hissy into something resembling activity. Coffee mug in hand, I picked a couple of mince pies from the pile on the cooling rack and made my way back to the living-room table.

Remembering Ed's gift from last night, I retrieved it from under my tree and sat down to carefully unwrap it. Inside was a small, square, red velvet box that creaked as I opened it. Lying on a padded bed of black velvet was an antique brooch in the shape of a rose – rose quartz and emerald-green paste stones forming its petals, stem and leaves. I suddenly remembered that, on one of our trips to Greenwich Village a few months back, we had visited a tiny antiquities store and Ed had taken great pleasure in mocking me about the reaction I'd had to so many sparkly jewellery pieces in one place.

'You're such a girl,' he'd grinned.

'Guilty as charged,' I had smiled back. 'I love this stuff. My gran always says that they don't make jewellery like they used to and I agree with her. Costume jewellery like this, it's – well, it's *magical*. You can pretend to be a princess when you're wearing one of these.'

Looking at the brooch I now held in my hands, I felt the same childlike thrill shimmering through me as I had in that store. This was by far the most unusual present Ed had ever given me and the surprise of it, coupled with the depth of feeling bestowed by his choice, moved me to tears. Wiping my eyes and laughing at my utter girliness, I picked up the stack of Christmas cards.

I was halfway through opening them when I heard a knock at my front door. Opening the door, I was surprised to see no one standing there. Reasoning it must be someone's kids in the building playing Christmas pranks, I was about to close the door when I noticed a small brown woven basket with the most amazing arrangement of winter white and Christmas red roses, complemented by dark green palm leaves curled and pinned to make a bouquet effect. Bending down to pick it up, I saw a card nestling amid the blooms. Opening the envelope, I walked back into my apartment as I read the typed note:

**May your days be merry and bright,
For you deserve the happiest of all Christmases.**

xx

I heard the door at the entrance to my apartment block slam and hurried to the window, just in time to see a yellow cab pulling slowly away along the snow-edged street. Turning the card over I saw a company name from Lower Manhattan – Turner's – one I wasn't familiar with. Sitting back at my table, I placed the basket in front of me and turned it slowly, inspecting every inch of its composition. The style wasn't one I could identify, either. Mum often says that each florist signs their work – not physically like an artist would, but in the composition and arrangement of the flowers. Working in New York during the past six years, I have come to recognise most of the major florists' styles. But this particular arrangement threw me completely. Mentally I compiled a list of possible senders. I discounted James (too thoughtful a gesture to come from him), Celia (she wouldn't send something anonymously as she prefers to bask in the glory of her generosity), David (not something he'd do, and he didn't know my address anyway), Marnie (she'd be more likely to send me a magazine subscription or kooky handmade jewellery than flowers) and Ed (as he'd never send flowers he hadn't designed himself). The only remaining possibility was Nate; yet I couldn't understand why he would choose Christmas Day to send me flowers when the most contact we'd had since Mimi's event were three text messages. Unless he was trying to say sorry, perhaps? Or maybe attempting to let me know that his loved-up performance at the Grand Winter Ball was just that – an elaborate pantomime for the crowds?

Thinking about everything was too much, especially on Christmas Day. So I pushed the quandary away, switched on my TV, found a channel showing *White Christmas* and snuggled down for a wonderfully quiet day.

Chapter Twenty-Two

No matter what situation I find myself in, I always expect the start of a New Year to be positive. Somehow, with the old year packed away and a fresh one laid out before you like clean linen, it's possible to believe that anything could happen during the next twelve months.

I have kept a diary ever since I was a little girl. My diaries help me to make sense of life. They demonstrate my ability to cope with problems and remind me of my dreams and aspirations. And they make me laugh when I read them with age-educated eyes, years from when the first tear-stained words were scribbled on the pages. As a personal ritual, every New Year's Day I always revisit the January 1st entry in the preceding year's diary, partly to remind myself where I've come from but also to see which of my hopes for that year actually came to fruition. It never ceases to amaze me how much I've achieved, or how many of my dreams remain unfulfilled. Some would argue that I never learn; I would say I never stop believing the best is yet to come.

After all the unexpected events of the past couple of months, this ritual now took on a greater significance than before for me. But I wasn't prepared for the difference between last year's page and my latest New Year's entry. Gone was the timid optimist, hopeful for the future yet too hurt by the past to really grasp the year ahead; in her place was someone I barely recognised: confident, happy to discuss her feelings, looking at the year ahead as one big possibility. Even though I knew that finally facing David had laid ghosts to rest for me, I was still shocked by the change I saw in my own expansive hand-writing. A deepening closeness with Ed, my conflicted feelings for Nate and my reaction to meeting David again were all documented – where previously I would have shied away even from committing my feelings to these private pages.

Buoyed by this, I embarked on January's tasks with a sense of renewed purpose and vigour. Our order book was the health-iest it had been for several years, with three large weddings between January and David's nuptials in March – and now that the prospect of the Lithgow ceremony no longer filled me with such dread, the future looked promising.

I mentioned to Ed and Marnie about my mysterious Christmas Day delivery, but both of them claimed to know nothing about it. Celia was over the moon that such a deli-cious conundrum should happen to me – and instantly assumed that Nate was the secret sender. I still wasn't sure: as the weeks passed and January neared its end, I received nothing but polite text messages – so the idea of him sending the flowers as a covert message seemed ludicrous. Eventually, I gave up, as other more pressing things vied for my attention. Kowalski's remained as busy as it had been before Christmas – something neither I nor my staff had witnessed before. With increased sales, we were able to take on two of the grads permanently, the extra pairs of hands invaluable as the wedding orders were completed.

Ed said no more about his Specific Somebody, but he was different somehow – more reserved, more contemplative than usual. The Steinmann Wit still remained gloriously present, so I reasoned that he was working things out and would seek my advice when he needed it. Despite my genuine pleasure for him, a part of me felt slightly removed from him all of a sudden, as if he were imperceptibly moving away from me, like a fractured ice sheet in spring. With the David situation put to rest in my mind, I began to notice an unfamiliar pull in my heart – a need to consider the future and where it might take me. In my braver moments, I even found myself contemplating the possibility of loving someone again – although this was quickly shelved the moment my insecurities kicked in. Watching Ed pursuing – albeit at a snail's pace – the woman he longed for, caused an oddly heady mix of sadness and hope to wash over my soul. Maybe, if the great Iceberg himself could let someone in, there was hope for me yet.

On the last day of January, news about my brother broke.

It began with a series of phone calls to Kowalski's from journalists, demanding to speak to me (Ed fended off every attempt), followed by several hacks coming into my shop on the pretence of placing orders, trying to score an exclusive interview. I hid in the workroom, being brought cups of Old F's finest decaf whilst Ed, Marnie and Jack insisted I wasn't in. Not even able to go home – as I was reliably informed by a neighbour that the press had set up camp outside my apartment building – Celia arranged for a car to pick me up at the rear of the shop and bring me to her office. By the time I arrived, CNN and ABC had both picked up on the story, with the BBC not far behind them.

Even when I was safely ensconced in Celia's office, I still remained ignorant of the situation James was in. After twenty minutes of reassuring my best friend – who blamed herself

313

entirely for not telling me the full extent of the rumours – I managed to calm her down sufficiently to find out the details of the crisis now unfolding across Washington and New York.

'James has been accused of being in cahoots with Mrs Elizabeth Darnek, wife of well-respected Senator John Darnek. They're saying James was her lover.'

I groaned but Celia held up a hand.

'There's more?'

'There's much more, I'm afraid.'

I folded my arms and prepared myself for the gory details.

'Senator Darnek was one of only three senior congressmen trusted to advise the President on possible lucrative building contracts in the Middle East. It was felt that certain Arab states would be agreeable to the US placing significant sums of money into mutually beneficial developments, in return for open talks to resolve conflicts in the area. These politicians were hand-picked by the President to suggest developments that matched the criteria, giving them unprecedented power of attorney over the process.'

'I don't understand what this has to do with James.'

'FRS Construction, one of the companies James represents, is a multimillion-dollar building corporation, which has recently faced scrutiny for alleged arms deals in return for exclusive building contracts across Africa and Asia. This has yet to be proved, of course, but in politics suggestion is often more persuasive than the truth. His affair with Mrs Darnek has been common knowledge amongst the hacks on Capitol Hill for several months – never reported, but understood within the journalistic fraternity as gospel. So when the President's Development and Progress Committee suddenly identified FRS Construction as the best contractor to undertake the chosen Arab-US development, reporters in Washington smelled a rat.

The long and short of it is that someone alerted a senator opposed to the initiative; he lodged a complaint with Congress and the story broke at around 9 a.m. today.'

The news hit me like a thunderbolt, throwing my mind into chaos as I tried to make sense of what I'd just heard. I was angry that James could be so stupid; frustrated that, true to form, he had created a mess he couldn't get out of alone; incensed that I didn't pick up on the signs . . . Then I remembered his whispered phone conversation in my apartment, months ago – and suddenly everything made sense.

'I think he tried to stop it,' I said, as the memory returned in full colour.

'What? How?'

'When he came to visit, in the autumn. I overheard a call he was making, saying he wanted out of whatever situation he was referring to.'

'Well, I hope for his sake that he manages to express that publicly,' Celia replied, her face grave and anxious, 'because he's about to be thrown to the lions here.'

'What about the woman?'

She grimaced. 'Elizabeth Darnek has been a politician's wife for too many years to let this bring her down. She's already issued a statement unreservedly apologising to Congress and her husband, blaming James entirely. She claims he sought an affair with her purely for the influence she could assert over her husband. Add to that Washington's desire to draw attention away from the Senator's misdemeanours, plus the clichéd image of the evil Englishman, and James is ripe for vilification.'

'I need to call him.'

'I would imagine his cell is well and truly unobtainable by now, honey.'

'Then I'll try his personal number. Maybe the press won't have found it yet.'

Celia walked to the door. 'Then I'll leave you in peace. Coffee?'

'Yes, please – and thanks for everything.'

'You are entirely welcome. Make the call.'

Taking a few deep breaths to calm myself down, I quickly found James's number. After five rings, a muffled voice answered.

'Yes?'

'James – is that you? It's Rosie.'

There was a pause on the line. 'Rosie? How great to hear you. It's Hugh. Hugh Jefferson-Jones – do you remember me?'

I smiled despite the growing nervous nausea in my stomach. Knowing James was not alone – and with the infamous *Huge* Jefferson-Jones, of all people – lifted my spirits considerably. 'Of course I remember you, Hugh. Hello again.'

'Great bit in the *NYT* about you, by the way,' Huge's booming voice sounded almost jovial in stark contrast to the severity of the current situation.

'Thanks. Is James with you?'

'Yes – yes he is. I'm trying to work things out my end. With the Consulate, I mean.'

'Could he be indicted?'

I heard a long sigh as Huge picked his words with extreme care. 'It's possible. But we have to hope that, once the initial media frenzy dissipates, the situation can be considered rationally and objectively.'

'And until then? I've seen scandals like this, Hugh. They can go on for months.'

'Quite true. But we must hope this one fades sooner. For now, however, James will stay with me, as a guest of Her

Majesty's Consulate-General. I am pushing for political asylum, with the offer of him facing trial back in the UK, should it be necessary.'

'Be honest with me, Hugh. Is James likely to go to prison for this?'

'The indicators at this stage are that it's possible a civil suit could be brought against him. As he isn't a US citizen, it's unlikely he'll face a gaol term. For now, I'm advising him to lie low whilst I negotiate.'

'Can I do anything?'

'Just sit tight, Rosie. And pray it doesn't come to prosecution.'

Right on cue as I ended the call, Celia appeared with coffee. I explained to her what Hugh had told me, watching her expression for any suggestion of her own opinion.

'I think your brother's saving grace is that no contracts were awarded – the FRS recommendation was merely theoretical at the time it was revealed. Had it been signed and sealed, James would be facing a far more serious situation than he is right now.'

'How did the media make the connection between me and James?'

'It wasn't me, I swear. But I'd hazard a guess that someone you know alerted them to your association.'

'Mimi?'

'Possibly. Or maybe even Philippe?'

That didn't seem likely, especially given as he was now restored to 'flavour of the month' with Mimi. Perhaps I was wrong, but despite his obvious abhorrence of me, I couldn't quite believe that he'd alert the national press to my association with James. I didn't even think he knew I had a brother, let alone that said brother was an adulterous, scheming idiot.

I rubbed a weary hand over my aching eyes. 'I don't know, Celia, every time I think life is going well it seems to jump up and bite me again.'

Celia offered a sympathetic smile and patted my hand. 'That's just life, honey. You should be used to crushing disappointment by now.'

Knowing the paparazzi were camped outside my apartment building, I couldn't go home, which was frustrating. Celia gave me the keys to her apartment and I headed over there as soon as I could. Later that afternoon, Marnie called me.

'Rosie, how are you? We've been so worried about you.'

'I'm fine, honestly, just frustrated I can't get home.'

'How long do you think this is going to last?'

I looked out of the window to the street below. 'I've no idea. This is so ridiculous, Marnie. I need to be at Kowalski's, not holed up in my best friend's apartment.'

'I'll stop by after work and bring you some stuff if you like?'

I couldn't help but smile. My assistant sounded so grown-up all of a sudden. 'That would be wonderful, thank you.'

I spent the next couple of hours trying to keep busy, but it was no use. My mind wouldn't settle. Flicking through magazines, watching random shopping channels on TV and listening to music all did nothing to help me. I was just contemplating whether to try baking something when I heard a commotion outside. Walking to the window, I saw to my horror a large CBS van parked and a swarm of photographers jostling for prime position on the side-walk. My mobile started to ring, making me jump.

'Hello?'

'Ms. Duncan, this is Dan Donnelly, CBS News. Can you confirm the whereabouts of your brother?'

'No, I can't. Leave me alone, please.'

'Is James Duncan's behaviour something you condone?'

318

'What? No, of course not, I . . .'

'Then would it be correct to assume that both you and your family are shocked and disgusted by your brother's actions?'

Anger was rising steadily within me as I answered. 'Look, I've asked you to leave me alone. Please go away.' Hands shaking, I snapped my phone shut and stood frozen to the spot. Celia's door phone began buzzing and someone on the street yelled, 'There she is! Up there!' as the crowd below looked up at me and their cameras began flashing wildly. Sinking to the floor by the window, panic gripped every fibre of my being. I was trapped – hemmed in by the waiting mob downstairs. My mobile rang again and I answered it angrily.

'Just leave me alone! Go away and . . .'

'Rosie, honey, it's me, don't hang up,' Celia interjected quickly. 'I think someone here's told the press where you are.'

'They're already here. I can't get out.'

'OK, listen to me. I've just spoken to Marnie and we're going to get you over to her apartment, OK?'

'Won't they follow me there?'

'Trust me, honey, journalists are essentially lazy. They're not going to bother trying to track down the home addresses of all Kowalski's staff – it's too much work and they're all on short deadlines with this story. I was an easy tip for them. So we'll get you to Marnie's and then you can relax a little. Meanwhile, I'm going to find the jerk who ratted on me here and kick his sorry ass all the way to Tennessee.'

Despite feeling scared, I couldn't help but smile at this. The poor informer's days were severely numbered with Celia gunning for him. The clamour of voices was growing louder outside. 'But how am I going to get there without them following me?'

'Don't panic, Rosie. This is what we're going to do . . .'

* * *

An hour later, I was sitting in Marnie's apartment while my assistant dashed around, making sure I was comfortable, making me spiced chai tea and generally fussing over me.

'I know I shouldn't say this, but that was *so* exciting!' she beamed as she flopped down onto the orange corduroy sofa beside me. 'It was like something out of a movie.'

I took a sip of exotically-spiced tea and smiled back. 'Yes, I have to admit it was a little thrilling.'

Celia's elaborate plan for sneaking me out of her apartment under the noses of the hacks was worthy of the silver screen. Heaven only knows how she managed to find three sets of workman's overalls, hard hats and a construction company van at such short notice (with Celia, it's always better not to ask). Marnie arrived with Sergei, the apartment building's manager half an hour after Celia's phone call and both of us changed into the overalls, giggling when we donned the bright yellow hard hats. Then, checking the coast was clear, Sergei led us down a service staircase to the back door, where Chad, one of Celia's colleagues, was waiting in the van. Emerging onto Celia's street, we sped past the backs of the waiting journalists whose eyes and lenses were still trained on Celia's apartment window.

The sense of joy at eluding the press pack was immense – Marnie and I even high-fived in the back of the van as it headed downtown to Marnie's SoHo home.

Marnie's apartment was just like her – bright, kooky and kitsch. Flowers were placed in a motley crew of containers, from old cookie tins to flea market glass vases and even an old green Wellington boot in the kitchen window. Rainbow-dyed cushions were scattered across the sofa, chairs and stripped wood floor and cosy blankets were stacked in a large white wicker basket underneath an old upright piano by the living room window. Nothing matched, yet all the furniture, picture frames and furnishings seemed to fit perfectly together. Most of all, it was welcoming, something I found incredibly re-assuring given the crazy day I was having.

'I'll grab some clothes and things for you from your apartment on my way home,' she said, plonking a stack of magazines on my lap. 'In the meantime, just make yourself at home and feel free to go out if you want to. Celia says nobody will expect you to be in SoHo, so it's OK for you to be walking round here.'

After she left to return to the shop, I decided to venture out, borrowing one of Marnie's impressive collection of colourful felt hats from the old mahogany hat stand by the door just to make me feel safer. Stepping out onto the street, I breathed in the sharp January air and revelled in my freedom.

I spent an hour browsing a second-hand bookstore just down the street, buying a well-worn blue leather bound edition of the Victorian language of flowers and a couple of poetry books, then headed a couple of blocks down to Oscar's, a small coffee shop in the ground floor of what had once been an old bakery.

The television was on in the corner at one end of the counter as I entered. I chose a table opposite and sat with my back to the screen, reading one of my bookstore purchases whilst listening to the newscaster talking over my shoulder. Unsurprisingly, a discussion about James was in full flow and a representative from the Consulate-General was giving a dispassionate response to questions about the affair.

'All we will say at this time is that Mr Duncan is in a safe place while we liaise with the federal authorities on his behalf. He is fully co-operating with the investigators and has agreed to remain in New York until such a time as the situation can be satisfactorily resolved.'

'What can I get ya?' asked a rotund, balding man who had appeared by my table.

'Coffee and something to eat – what would you recommend?'

He smiled broadly and leaned against the chair next to mine. 'Well, let's see, lady. You want something sweet or savoury? No – wait – don't tell me. Let me guess.' He studied my face, one hand on his chin. 'Now you look to me like you haven't eaten much today, am I right? Good. So, that means you've come to the right place, 'cos we only do large here. Trust me, I own this place.' He offered me his hand. 'Oscar Arrighi.'

'Rosie – pleased to meet you.'

'Likewise. So, now we've been introduced, we're family, which means I can share with you my Mama's secret weapon for combating a bad day. Which, I assume, you've had today, am I right?'

I shook my head. 'You can tell all that just from looking at me?'

Oscar dismissed this with a wave of his hand. 'It's all part of the job, Rosie. That and the fact I just saw your picture on TV.'

Panicked, I rose quickly, but Oscar's large hand rested on my shoulder. 'Now don't you go worrying, lady. I won't tell anyone and none of the dumb schmucks in here will have noticed.' He indicated the other customers who were all hunched over newspapers or engaged in conversation oblivious to everything else. 'And I ain't gonna call the TV station either, so relax, OK? Between you and me, I hate journalists. My cousin Luca got in a little trouble last year and the lousy hacks sat outside my Aunt Isabella's for three whole weeks. They gave her a hernia what with all the stress they caused. So you're safe here. What you need is my Mama's meatball calzone. Trust me, you'll lose your worries after the first bite. Sound good?'

I smiled up at him. 'Oscar, that sounds fantastic.'

By the time Marnie arrived home that night, every network was crawling with commentators on my brother's stupidity. Celia was right, almost every news programme cast James as the evil Englishman, taking advantage of a trusting senator's wife in order to steal upright American taxpayers' hard-earned cash. Daily chat shows quickly followed suit and even Letterman joked about it on his *Late Show*.

'Y'know, when the President encouraged the Senate to forge closer relationships with the Brits, this wasn't *quite* what he had in mind . . .'

One strange consequence of all the media attention was a sudden upsurge in visitors to Kowalski's. Ed called me a couple of days after I'd arrived at Marnie's to report busier trading than we'd ever seen at the shop.

'I tell you, Rosie, the store's gone crazy. I mean, forget the Mimi Sutton Effect, this is so much bigger! We did forty percent higher business this week than we did the same time last year.'

I couldn't believe it. 'Seriously? I thought all the news stuff and cameras outside the store would put people off.'

'Are you kidding? This is the Upper West Side, Rosie! You put thirty photographers outside a store and anyone who's anyone turns up. We had *Joan Rivers* come in here this morning – Marnie was in bits!'

'That's completely barmy!'

'I know! The best thing is, Rosie, the whole neighbourhood has turned up to support you. Mrs Katzinger was the first one in here when the news broke, worried how you were, and Delores Schuster came by this afternoon. She went outside and gave the photographers a piece of her mind – you should've seen it!'

'That's so good of her, though.'

'She did it because you mean a lot to her, Rosie, they all did. I'm pretty sure the hacks will get bored and leave soon. There were less of them this morning and they're not sticking around as long as they were. Still, while ever you're on their hit-list, it's great for Kowalski's. Notoriety sells in this town, baby!'

I stayed at Marnie's, safe from the media spotlight, for the next two weeks. While I was frustrated at not being able to go to Kowalski's, I actually found myself enjoying my enforced holiday. I pottered around the vintage boutiques and arty shops near Marnie's apartment, caught up on some reading and went to the cinema – something I hadn't had the time to do for a couple of years. I also spent hours dreaming up new designs, which I shared with Ed on his frequent visits to check on me.

'You know, I think all of this has actually done you good,' he said one evening, as he sat at the 1960s purple vinyl-covered dining table eating Vietnamese food with Marnie and me. 'It's given you the chance to really concentrate on your design work. And with the added business at Kowalski's, I reckon the future couldn't be brighter for us.'

He was right. I looked at my team and felt an overwhelming sense of hope rushing through me. This issue was my brother's problem, not mine. I had done nothing wrong and my customers had proved that they believed in Kowalski's and me. In an odd way, it felt good to know that, even in adversity, my business could flourish.

After a while, the media's attention switched to Washington, where some senators were beginning to voice suspicions over

324

the Darneks' credibility. Dismissed as publicity-seekers by the more respected correspondents, nevertheless the press junket indulged them, lapping up every new revelation as it broke. With enough juicy gossip now emerging from Washington to satisfy their bloodlust, the press corps quickly abandoned their camp in my street, which meant I could finally return home and, more importantly to Kowalski's – and some semblance of normality returned to my life. Mum called frequently, upset that even her beloved BBC had 'stooped to the level of lesser broadcasters' to cover the unfolding saga. I heard nothing from James, but this was maybe just as well, given the fact that he was supposed to be in splendid isolation, courtesy of the British Consulate-General. Ed and I discussed the whole sorry affair at length, yet even this faded with the passing days, as really there were no resolutions to the whirligig of unanswerable questions.

Celia continued to apologise, fussing over me like a neurotic nanny, despite my assurances that I didn't blame her for James's predicament. She sent fruit baskets, arranged for grocery deliveries and phoned at least five times a day, checking to make sure I was still coping and not dangling from the nearest high rafter. She really needn't have worried: I wasn't scared or suicidal; I was just incredibly angry at my brother's complete lack of thought for anyone other than himself. It was his utter selfishness that had got him into this situation – and countless other lamentable scrapes beforehand – and now he was expecting the whole world to stop and bail him out.

In the event, his help was to come from a most unexpected source.

The media attention had switched to possible legal consequences of the scandal and had started to speculate that James might be subpoenaed to appear before the Grand Jury. For a time, this reignited the attraction for the press, with several journalists from not-so-quality publications sneaking into Kowalski's posing as customers but seeking dirt on the situation. Ed suggested I take a few days off until the next wave of interest washed the hacks in another direction.

I was holed up in my apartment with the phone unplugged, when the door intercom buzzed smartly.

'Hello?'

A familiar voice came from the tinny speaker. 'Rosie, it's me. I have bagels. Can I come up?'

I smiled and pressed the button. 'If you have bagels you are more than welcome.'

Celia appeared at my front door, breathless and carrying several Zabar's bags. 'The traffic is so bad you wouldn't *believe*,' she gasped, bustling into my kitchen and wrestling the packed bags onto the work surface. 'I had to *walk*, for heaven's sake!' It sounded like the worst possible hardship in the world, but as far as Celia was concerned, it was.

I giggled as I watched her fling open the fridge and produce item after item from the bags. It reminded me of Mary Poppins and her carpet bag: I half-expected to see a birdcage and a standard lamp emerging from the carriers. 'Did you buy the entire store?'

'Stop mocking me, Rosie Duncan,' Celia retorted, grabbing a plate and emptying bagels onto it from a crumpled M&H Bakers paper bag. 'I just brought you some essentials, that's all.'

'Celia, your idea of "essentials" is most people's idea of a banquet.'

'Well, you deserve a banquet, sweetie. So get the coffee on because . . .' she paused for dramatic effect, '. . . we are *celebrating*!'

'Celebrating what?'

Celia's eyes sparkled as she passed me on her way into the living room, plate of bagels held aloft. 'So bring the coffee through and I'll tell you already.'

She took a deep breath and placed the bagels on the coffee table. 'OK. I had a breakthrough.'

'With what?'

'With your brother.'

'Sorry?'

She reached forward and clasped my hand. 'Sweetie, I heard those rumours way back before Christmas and I didn't tell you. I thought it was the usual Washington baloney we hear all the time and I didn't want to worry you. Besides, as you well know, James and I haven't been the best of buddies, so I didn't think you'd believe me anyhow. But I've just felt so *awful* about this whole mess and I wanted to help.'

'You have been helping, hon. I mean, all the shopping and the phone calls, not to mention busting me out of your apartment in a Hollywood-style a fortnight ago. *That* was impressive. You've been really kind.'

'But it's not *enough*, Rosie. At least, it wasn't enough for *me*. I couldn't bear for you to have to endure the worst that my profession can do to people. It's a side of journalism that I don't much care for – the way that we hunt people down just to get an exclusive. We forget the person behind the story and all we can think of is getting our hands on the scoop before anyone else.'

'I don't really understand where this is all leading, Celia.'

She squeezed my hand again. 'James is off the hook.'

I couldn't believe my ears. 'What? How?'

'I had a breakthrough yesterday – I would have told you straight away but I had to make sure the right people heard

327

it first. I got the call an hour ago and I headed straight to Kowalski's, but Ed told me you were here. So I picked up some groceries on the way and here I am!'

My heart was thumping fast. 'What's happened?'

'I'd like to claim it was my brilliant journalistic instinct, but in truth it was just the most *glorious* coincidence,' Celia rushed on, on the edge of tears as she spoke. 'After all, so much of journalism is down to chance and being in the right place at the right time. But whatever – the thing is that I've been interviewing our Arts Editor's daughter for a piece I'm planning on New York kids moving to other cities to pursue careers. Sandi is an intern on Capitol Hill in Washington and she hopes to make it to presidential staff one day. I've been emailing her for a couple of weeks, finding out about her current responsibilities, aspirations for the future and so on. She's worked in several offices but most recently was assigned to one Senator John Darnek.'

'Oh my life . . .'

'Yes, *I know*! Two days ago, she called me. She was inconsolable and said she needed my advice. It turns out that a few days ago Senator Darnek's secretary was taken ill, so Sandi was drafted in to cover. Elizabeth Darnek called to speak to her husband and, by all accounts, was incredibly rude to the poor girl. So Sandi panicked and accidentally hit the memo function on the intercom when she was transferring the call. Turns out she inadvertently recorded a *crucial* conversation between the Darneks.'

'Why crucial?'

'Elizabeth Darnek talked about James – about how *she* had ensnared *him* – and it was clear from the conversation that John Darnek was well aware of the situation. Even more than that, they talked at some length about their intention to use the affair to bribe both James and his company, insisting significant funds were surrendered in return for the Darneks' silence. Well, Sandi was terrified when she realised her error, but she didn't know what to do.'

My head was abuzz with the news. 'How does this help James, though?'

Celia smiled. 'I'm getting to that. You see, it's fortuitous that Sandi chose to call me: I mean, I've known her since she was a little girl, but there are countless others she could've chosen. It just so happens that I know Thom Michaels, Head of Internal Comms at the Senate Office. I knew that the recorded memo would still be on the secretary's phone – the code to access the memo messages is only held by Darnek's secretary and *one other person . . .*'

A light was dawning in my mind. 'Thom Michaels?'

'Exactly! So, I called him.'

'But couldn't you have got in trouble for having that information?'

Celia threw her head back and laughed. 'Probably, had it been anyone else. But Thom and I . . . well, we go *way* back. And I happened to know that there is *no* love lost between Thom Michaels and John Darnek. He was *most* interested to hear of the – um – *intercom malfunction*, shall we say?'

'So what's happened since?'

'Thom called me this morning to say that he'd handed it to the Senior Prosecutor, who's very kindly made the contents of the call public. *Very* public.'

Celia wasn't kidding. Within hours of her visit, the story was everywhere, the news channels dominated by increasingly lurid details of previously hidden misdemeanours by the Senator and his wife. Such was the backlash against them that James's involvement paled into relative obscurity, as the full force of the media spotlight fell squarely on the Darneks.

James returned to London, where he was quietly 'released' from his contract with FRS – together with a sizeable sum to help ease the transition. Proving my theory that he has more lives than a very lucky cat, James quickly found a new line of business – providing media advice to high-profile people, of all things – and, predictably, regained his prosperity soon after.

I told James that it was Celia who had been responsible for saving his sorry hide. He couldn't believe it, especially given their track record of mutual dislike, but nevertheless he was a changed man by the experience. Celia received a typically ostentatious and ridiculously expensive bouquet of flowers (not from my store, of course – I have a suspicion that a certain Mr Devereau's establishment may have had the dubious honour of my brother's patronage), but I had the distinct feeling that this uneasy truce wouldn't last long between them.

Chapter Twenty-Three

As February ended, preparations for the Lithgow wedding began in earnest. It was agreed that the whole team would work to complete the larger items for delivery the day before the wedding, with Ed and I booking rooms in a nearby hotel so we could complete the bridal bouquets, buttonholes and last few small arrangements overnight, to ensure their freshness on the day.

A week before the event, Ed and I travelled up to The Hamptons to visit David's parents' home – the venue for his forthcoming wedding. I wasn't relishing the prospect of seeing George and Phoebe again, so I was more than a little relieved when I discovered that only David and his fiancée, Rachel, would be available to meet us. Despite my history with David, I have to say that I was intrigued to meet the woman who'd tempted him to contemplate marriage again.

Rachel Moray was nothing like I'd expected. Far from the small, compliant beauty I had pictured her as, happy to follow David's every whim with wide-eyed admiration, she was a shade under six feet tall, of athletic build and strong character. I instantly liked her, unlike Ed, who had decided to pity her from the very beginning and was unwilling to be parted from his preconceptions so readily. As we left the car and crunched

331

our way across thickly spread, pale yellow gravel to the front door, Rachel appeared from the garden, ruddy-cheeked and breathless, a large bunch of basil in her hand.

'Hello, you must be Rosie. David's told me so much about you – your amazing floristry and what a good friend you were to him back in London. It's a pleasure to meet you both.'

'This is Ed Steinmann, my co-designer,' I smiled as Ed reluctantly shook her hand and mumbled something cordially unintelligible.

'Great, well, David's waiting in the orangery, so if you'd like to follow me?'

As we stepped through the doorway into an elaborate marble atrium, Ed pulled my sleeve and whispered, 'Bet he hasn't told her *everything* about you.'

'Shh! She'll hear you. Just *behave*, Steinmann.'

'*Yes, ma'am!*' Ed saluted me with mock respect. 'Just don't expect me to like the guy, OK?'

We hurried to catch up with Rachel, who was striding effortlessly ahead at a surprising pace. After passing through several equally lavish sitting rooms, we walked into the orangery – a two-storey-high, glass-domed Victorian conservatory looking out onto perfectly clipped lawns that were sweepingly impressive, even in the drab March light. David was seated at a cast-iron table, plans and papers spread out before him and a vivid memory of him sitting at his desk in London flashed into my mind. It never failed to amaze me how someone so disciplined and driven in his work could have such a messy desk. At first, it had bugged me intensely, until I realised that what I saw as disorder was actually a complex planning system known only to him. Feeling a shiver travel down my spine, I shook the image from my mind.

'Rosie – hi! Welcome to the latest Lithgow family acquisition.

Nice, huh?' he grinned, standing as we approached. 'And you must be the famous Ed. I gather you and Rosie are great buddies.'

'The *best*,' replied Ed, a little too defensively, as he shook David's hand. 'Someone has to look after her, you know.'

David's smile tightened. 'I'm sure Rosie can look after herself.'

'OK,' I blurted quickly, 'we don't have much time, so I need to hurry this along, if I may.'

'Certainly,' smiled Rachel, giving David's arm a playful cuff as we sat down. 'Honestly, Rosie, the way he's so relaxed about our wedding, you'd think he wasn't planning to attend!'

I kicked Ed sharply on his shin under the table before he had a chance to speak.

'You didn't have to kick me *quite* so hard,' Ed moaned as we drove home, later that day.

'Yes, I did. You were likely to say something that would have embarrassed everyone – not least Rachel.'

Ed turned to face me with a strange smile on his face. 'I can't believe you care what Rachel feels, given she's "the competition" in all this.'

'Competition? Don't be so overdramatic. You are so way off the mark.'

'I mean it, Rosie. The guy dumps you like a rock at the altar, screws your life up and disappears for six years. Then he suddenly shows up, throws all the past in your face again, asks you to work at his *wedding*, of all things, then introduces you to the woman he's decided is worthy of his affections – where, presumably, you weren't – and expects you to *like* her?'

'Well, thank you for that glowing assessment of my situation,' I shot back, thinly veiling the deep hurt his remark had caused. 'The fact is, whatever David did in the past is exactly that: *in the past*. It's not Rachel's fault, so there's no reason

I should bear her any ill will whatsoever. I don't want David: she's welcome to him. It might just be that he's met his match after all these years.'

'Well, it sucks big style.'

'Mate, I know you're just trying to protect me and, believe me, it's great to know you're fighting my corner. But all I need to do is to get this wedding done and out of the way, so at least I can have some closure on this. OK?'

Reluctantly, Ed agreed. 'Well, all right. But I have every right to hate it.'

'You're truly a man of conviction, Ed.'

'That's what Nate says.'

The mention of Nate's name made my heart jump. 'How do you mean?'

'Uh, I wasn't going to tell you . . .'

'So tell me now.'

He sighed and looked out of the passenger window. 'It's nothing. We've just been meeting up, now and again. Turns out we have more in common than our taste in baseball teams.'

'So how long has this been happening?'

'Since just before the Grand Winter Ball. We caught a ball game, grabbed a pizza and ended up at Joe's drinking bourbon till the early hours of the morning.'

'But he's hardly contacted me since . . . since the announcement of his wedding. Why would he see you and not me?' I could feel tears welling up and I swallowed hard.

'Hey, Rosie, give the guy a break. He was embarrassed before Mimi did the whole public reveal thing – he didn't know what to say to you. Especially after the conversation you guys had that afternoon.'

I struggled to contain my composure at this bombshell. 'He told you about *that*?'

'Yeah, he did. Don't be angry, Rosie. The guy needed someone to talk to about it all. He needed advice from a guy's perspective. We all need it, sometimes – a guy who understands.'

'And that was you?'

'And that *is* me.'

I couldn't hide the pain in my voice any longer. 'Then why hasn't he talked to me? And what right does he have telling you about our conversation? It was private, not something to broadcast to all and sundry.'

'Well, thank you for the vote of confidence, Rosie.'

'I didn't mean – oh, Ed, I'm sorry. I just really need to talk to him about everything. I – *miss* him.'

Ed was silent for a long time, the only sound the hum of the car engine and the whoosh of passing cars on the freeway, as the lights of Manhattan loomed ahead. I tried to catch a glimpse of his face, but the driver in front was braking erratically, forcing me to keep my eyes ahead.

When he eventually spoke, his tone was low, empty even. 'Then I'll ask him to meet you.'

'Really?'

'Yes. You two obviously have stuff to discuss.'

Ed didn't say another word as we drove through New York to his street, giving me only the briefest of smiles as he left the car and ran quickly up the steps to disappear into his building. I sat motionless in the car outside for some time, engine still running, my mind buzzing with activity yet frustratingly blank, before finally pulling away to head home.

Chapter Twenty-Four

For the rest of the week, Ed and I carried on our work as normal, but there was a definite change in the air. We laughed and joked as much as we ever had, but it was as though an invisible barrier now sat stubbornly between us. Marnie noticed it the day after our venue visit and, after two days, finally plucked up enough courage to ask me about it.

I was working on one of the larger garlands for the entrance to the orangery when Marnie came into the workroom, closing the door quietly behind her.

'So what's happening?'

I looked up from my work. 'About what?'

Marnie folded her arms and adopted a serious stance, which with her babylike features only served to make her look like a five year-old about to scold a teddy. 'About you and Ed. Something's different with you guys.'

I looked back down to the garland, trying to avert her stare. 'We're fine, honey. You're imagining things.'

Marnie was not going to be placated so easily. She squared up for a fight. 'I am *not* imagining this, Rosie. You've been keeping each other at arm's length. I'm not blind, you know – or as dumb as you think I am.'

'Oh, Marnie, I don't think you're dumb.'

'Well, you both act like I am. Anyway, that's beside the point. What happened in The Hamptons? Was it because of your ex?'

'No, it was nothing to do with him.'

'Then *what*? Come on, Rosie, you know I can tell something's up here. I asked Ed about it and he said I'd have to ask you.'

Nice deflection, Steinmann. 'Ed and I are fine. I think perhaps the fact that we're doing David's wedding is playing on his mind a little. He's very protective of me and it means he sometimes gets angry on my behalf. But I've already told him he doesn't need to be concerned. I'm fine, honestly.'

'I don't believe you. Just promise me you guys will work things out? It's *weird* working here at the moment.'

I watched her leave and tried to ignore the growing sense of frustration within me. The truth was I had no idea what was wrong with Ed. I'd gone over and over it in my mind since Friday and I still couldn't work out what had happened between us on the drive home. The barrier was unavoidably real; the problem was how to determine what it was and then find a way to break it down.

Nate called me that afternoon and asked if he could visit Kowalski's. 'I've a hankering for Old F decaf – and I think the couch misses me too.'

When I went to find Ed to tell him, he was nowhere to be found. He'd obviously decided to make himself scarce, leading me to conclude that Nate had probably talked with him about visiting me before he called. It bugged me beyond words that Ed and Nate now confided in each other. It's crazy, I know, but I couldn't help feeling as if I'd been written out of the friendship. Not that I would have wanted to sit in a bar drinking bourbon with them and discussing the Mets season, of course.

It would just have been nice to have been included in whatever they were talking about.

Nate arrived at three o'clock and the little bell swinging happily upon his entrance into Kowalski's might just as well have been a triumphant fanfare for the way my heart skipped when I saw him. In the two months since we'd last met, he had changed considerably – surprisingly so, in fact. Not only was his hair longer but his countenance seemed altered – subdued, maybe. The lop-sided grin and cheeky sense of humour remained, however, and within a few minutes we were laughing like we always had done.

'So, how was your time as a national media target?' Nate smiled as I handed him his coffee.

'Um, *interesting*. Let's just say I'm in no hurry to repeat the experience. Mind you, Kowalski's seemed to benefit from it all – our orders are up this year.'

'Ah, not all bad news then, hey?'

'I think we made the best of a bad situation, yes. So, how was Christmas?'

Nate groaned and slapped his hand to his forehead. 'You wouldn't believe how dire the whole thing was, Rosie! First we had to endure the ridiculously elaborate show that is a Sutton family Christmas. You would have *died*. I thought I'd stepped onto the set of *Dynasty* by mistake. I swear even the Christmas tree had shoulder pads. The entrance lobby looked like an explosion in a sequin factory. Every available surface was stuffed with gaudy baubles and enough greenery to start a forest fire, and as for the food – well, it made Celia's parties look like a picnic in Central Park!'

'Sounds delightful.'

'Mimi even had choristers "singing in" the turkey.'

'You're kidding?'

'Seriously – there were three choirboys standing in the dining room entrance, singing "O Holy Night" as the waiters brought the turkey in.'

'Wonderful.'

'And then Caitlin had to endure the true horror of an Amie family New Year. Most of my brothers riotously drunk, my mother and father pretending they weren't having an argument and my two grandmothers shouting merrily in conversation – even though each is as deaf as the other and had no idea what the other one was saying. Complete nightmare from start to finish. How about you?'

'Me? Well, I had a quiet one, for a change. Although I did receive a mystery delivery on Christmas morning.'

His expression remained steady, even though I was looking hard for any flicker of acknowledgement. 'Really?'

I told him about the floral basket and the intriguing note – and still he displayed no outward signs of recognition. If anything, his eyes looked a little sad. 'It's a cool gesture. It must've made your day.'

'It did, I guess.' Confused by his reaction, I changed the subject. 'And the wedding preparations? How are they going?'

He gazed out of the window. 'Good, all good. Although I half wonder if Caitlin might have planned a better guy to turn up in my place on the day. It seems I'm surplus to requirements when it comes to planning. That's fine by me: I'll just sit back and watch the Mimi-Caitlin juggernaut steamroller through town.'

'But you're happy about it?'

His eyes met mine blankly. 'Yes. Of course.'

'Then, forgive me, I don't understand . . .'

'Why I said what I did before the big announcement? I have no idea, Rosie. Sometimes it's like I completely know

340

what I want and then . . . I don't know. Maybe I'll never feel totally happy with the situation. Maybe I'll always be one of those guys who complain incessantly about their wives, yet stay in long marriages with them. It's just easier not to fight stuff, you know?'

'So, everything you said was . . . ?'

He placed a hand lightly on my shoulder, his thumb moving in slow, gentle circles as he spoke. 'True, Rosie. At the time. No, still true now. I won't have Caitlin or anybody dictate who I spend time with – that hasn't changed.'

'But your feelings for Caitlin have?' I mentally kicked myself for asking; it was supposed to be an internal question. Nate's expression changed, his eyes meeting mine.

'I don't know what I want, Rosie. But I want you in my life.'

'You're planning your *wedding* . . .'

'I'm aware of that. But I can't help thinking there could be another way.'

'What are you saying?'

He leaned towards me, his voice an urgent whisper. 'I don't know, OK. I just *need* you in my life.'

'Nate, I already am. We're friends, remember?'

He placed a hand on my knee. 'As a friend, then. Only a friend – if you want?'

This was too much for my brain to handle. Irritated, I stood up and was about to answer when the little silver bell above the shop door jingled loudly as a thick-set man in a long grey overcoat rushed into the store.

'Rosie Duncan?'

'Yes, that's me.'

He shook my hand hurriedly. 'John Meenaghan. I'm a neighbour of Eli Lukich – the old Russian guy who comes in here?'

'Yes, I know Eli. What's the matter?'

'I really didn't know who else to contact, Ms Duncan. It was only because he had your card on his refrigerator door that I'm here.'

'What's happened?'

John took a deep breath and placed a sheepskin-gloved hand on my arm. 'I'm sorry to have to tell you this. We found Mr Lukich in his apartment this morning – with his wife.'

Panic gripped my heart. 'Is he . . . ? Are they . . . ?'

The tears in his eyes confirmed my worst fears. 'Alyona died some time ago, we think. The stench in his apartment was overwhelming. The police think he refused to believe she was dead. She was lying on their bed with her head on a pillow, dressed in a white lace gown and surrounded by bunches of dried yellow roses. The officer who discovered them believes Eli just gave up trying to live. There was no food in the apartment and the electricity had been cut off. I'm so sorry, Ms Duncan.'

The thought of Eli's silent, deathly vigil at the bedside of the woman he loved so passionately was too awful to comprehend.

'So when he was visiting Kowalski's to collect his yellow roses his wife was already dead?' Nate asked, appearing at my side and placing a steadying arm at my back.

John nodded. 'There's a simple memorial planned for them at St Agatha's cemetery tomorrow morning at ten o'clock. Can you come?'

'Absolutely. Can I do anything?'

'Could you provide a couple of wreaths? I'm willing to cover the cost.'

I shook my head. 'No need. It will be my gift to them.'

When John left, I sank slowly into the couch and buried my head in my hands, sobbing. Nate sat by me, his arm tentatively draped around my shoulders as if he was scared to intrude on my grief. The awful reality of the Lukichs' lives and deaths seemed so unfair, in a world where people treated love as a commodity, using it and discarding it seemingly at will. Eli's world had ended when Alyona died; his only remaining purpose a hopeless vigil maintained in her honour. The yellow roses I gave him each month were his only connection to the woman he had endured so much for. And yet I had no idea that, after the stories and laughter and mock bartering which accompanied each of his visits to Kowalski's, he returned to the stark reality of what little life he still possessed. I remembered what I had said to Nate, months before, about Eli Lukich being the epitome of what a man in love should be; now, in the light of his death, he had proven my theory, taking his life-long devotion to its ultimate conclusion.

Ed, Marnie and Nate joined me at St Agatha's the next morning for Eli and Alyona's funeral. John had organised a whip-round in his apartment block and one of his neighbours arranged for their cousin – an undertaker – to provide caskets. Ten people huddled together in the little cemetery church as the minister recounted the sparse details of the Lukichs' lives – a short eulogy that did their epic life struggle no justice whatsoever. Following the brief service, I was grateful of Ed's arm around my shoulders as we slowly processed to the freshly dug grave and watched the caskets being lowered together, two wreaths of white and yellow roses and lilies adorning the coffins. Then, one by one, each mourner stepped forward to say goodbye and drop a single yellow rose into the grave. Ed and Marnie hugged me before retreating respectfully.

As people walked away from the graveside, I noticed Nate wiping tears from his eyes.

'Are you OK?'

'I want what they had, Rosie.'

'I don't know if that kind of love is possible today, Nate.'

'What if I *want* it to be?'

Looking deep into his eyes, I squeezed his hand. 'Sometimes wanting isn't enough. You need to find something that will make you happy enough not to care about anything else.'

He shook his head. 'What if I've already found it and it's not mine?'

I couldn't answer him. Slowly, he bent his head and kissed my cheek, the warmth of his face making my skin tingle. Then he turned and strode away down the hill to where Marnie and Ed were waiting.

Heart pounding, I turned back to face the grave. 'Eli Lukich, you look after that beautiful wife of yours,' I whispered. 'I'll never forget you.'

Work on the Lithgow wedding had to continue after the funeral, despite the fact that none of us was in any mood to work. Jocelyn and Jack held the fort out front whilst Marnie, Ed and I worked on the large displays. When Marnie left the work-room to fetch coffee, Ed appeared at my side.

'Rosie, I'm an idiot.'

'So tell me something I don't know.'

'I got mad when we drove back from seeing David – over nothing. Going to the funeral today put everything into perspective. I'm sorry.'

'It's fine, hon. I just want us to be *us*, you know?'

'Yeah. Me too. And hey, it looks like old Nateyboy is back on the scene?'

I pulled a face. 'Hmm, well you could say that, although I don't think I'll ever work him out.'

'Whoever said guys are simple, huh?' he smirked. 'I think he likes you.'

'You've said this before and you're still wrong. I think he's confused. And engaged. *And* planning his wedding.'

'And battling his feelings for you.'

'Not this *again*, Ed . . .'

'No – hear me out, Rosie. I think he likes you and – and I think the feeling's mutual.'

I could feel a traitorous blush creeping over my cheeks and looked away. 'You don't know what you're talking about.'

His voice was low and feather-soft. 'I think I do.'

I turned to face him and, the moment my eyes met the steely-blue Steinmann stare, I felt my heart rate quicken. 'I don't know what I feel,' I answered, with more truth than I'd intended. 'There's so much – *stuff* – whizzing about in my head and I honestly can't make sense of any of it. I've kept my emotions under lock and key for so long that it's like I've forgotten how to use them. Be warned – this is an inevitable side effect of the melting process. It's scary and it's perplexing and it's something so out of your control that you just get swept along with it all.'

'Is it David?'

'No – well, yes partly. I spent so long being happy to cast him as the dastardly villain that it doesn't compute now I've made peace with him. But it's more than that: it's everything – David, Nate—' I broke off as I realised what should have come next: *and you* . . . Struggling to grasp the reins of this runaway steed, I changed tack and forced a laugh. 'But I'll be fine. Honestly. Once this wedding is done and we can just go back to being "the Kowalski's family" it'll all be clearer, I'm sure of it.'

A welcome smile assumed centre stage on Ed's face. 'Come here, Duncan,' he grinned, wrapping his arms around me and holding me close. I hugged him back, thankful for the sense of reassurance I found there.

Chapter Twenty-Five

The day before David's wedding, Ed and I packed the delivery van and drove up to The Hamptons. I was keen to get as many of the larger pieces as possible in place by evening and had taken the unusual step of closing the store for the day, so that my whole team could pitch in.

As weddings go, the Lithgow nuptials were some of the most lavish we had ever been asked to provide for. Compared to the last time George and Phoebe had organised a wedding for their only son, this was an epic event in every sense of the word. What the Lithgows were saving on venue costs they were more than making up for in every other detail: caterers from a top Manhattan restaurant, ten white peacocks to roam the lawns, an entire service team brought in from George's favourite hotel in Boston and a twenty-piece orchestra were just a few of the wildly expensive elements of the day. In terms of the floral displays, David and Rachel wanted lilies, peonies and gardenias lining the route for the guests and bridal party – from the footpaths leading up to the house, through each room towards the orangery itself, where the largest, most detailed displays would be. This meant long garlands made of the theme flowers with length upon length of dark green and white ivy, intertwined with

347

tiny white fairy lights for the footpaths, countless table pieces, four arches to surround the doorways leading to the orangery and eight huge feature displays around the area where the guests would sit for the ceremony. It was a lot of work – even with five pairs of hands.

When we arrived at the house, it was already a hive of activity. Ed and I left Marnie and the grads with the van as we dodged delivery men, security staff and members of the wedding planning team on our way to the front door.

As we passed through rooms jammed with workers, Ed let out a whistle. 'This is crazy! I can't believe anyone would want this much stuff at their wedding. Whatever happened to the notion of a wedding being about two people in love?'

I gave him a playful nudge as we ducked under a drooping banner being hung by two ladies on step ladders at either side of the door. 'You old romantic, you.'

'No, I mean it. The whole wedding industry is built on people being persuaded to pay ridiculous sums of money for things they don't need.'

'What, like we do?'

Ed stopped to let a delivery guy – who was pushing an enormous stack of chairs on a trolley – go in front of us. 'Shame on you, Rosie! What *we* do is to respond to our customers' needs, not sell them unnecessary rubbish. And may I remind you that you can *never* have too many flowers at a wedding?'

'I think this wedding may disprove the theory,' I grinned, despite my stomach flipping at the prospect of the task ahead. I checked my watch. 'Right, we need to find David or Rachel to OK the schedule as soon as we can. We have a lot to do and I'd like to be able to let the team get away by six this evening. What time are we booked in at the hotel?'

Ed checked his clipboard. 'Any time from five thirty. Dinner's at eight, if we want it.'

'And they're cool with us working on the bridal party flowers?'

He nodded. 'I spoke to the manager yesterday. He's cleared their second dining room for us *and* is providing a coffee machine too.'

'Nice. I definitely think we'll need the coffee.'

'Did someone say coffee?' smiled David, appearing from the orangery, notebook in hand. 'I'm sending out for Starbucks. How many in your team?'

'Five, including Rosie and me,' Ed replied, shaking David's hand.

'Before you go, can you sign this off please?' I handed him our time schedule, detailing where we would be working through the day. As I did so, my mind flashed back to us working together in Boston prior to our own, ill-fated nuptials. There was always such electricity between us, even when we were engaged in mundane tasks. It was still there; only today, with so much now resolved, it felt good again. I'm finally moving on, I thought, smiling at him. Everything's going to be OK now.

'That seems fine. If you need a room cleared for your team, just talk to Jean-Claude, our wedding planner.'

Jean-Claude was a consummate professional: flamboyant and gushingly enthusiastic in front of clients; steel-willed and regimented towards everyone else. Like an omnipotent ringmaster he assumed centre stage wherever he stood, barking orders like a Gallic sergeant-major, whilst his team and countless workers scurried, jumped and ran about with his every command. As we approached, he was in the middle of a scathing attack on three delivery men, who were gawping helplessly at him, a large pallet of tables half-emptied before them.

'*Non*, leave zese tables zere for now. You! What are you doing wiz *zese*, uh? You are meant to be arranging zem at five fifteen precisely! You have a watch, uh? Zen use it, *imbecile!*' Turning to see Ed and me, his countenance made a lightning switch to one of zealous benevolence. 'Ah, Mademoiselle Duncan, how wonderful to see you! Ah trust zat everything is to your satisfaction?'

'Yes, thank you. We'd like to start with the orangery, if we may?'

Jean-Claude consulted his file – which was bigger and grander than anyone else's for a reason. 'Good, good. Ah will make sure you are not disturbed.' He spun round to address the table guys again. 'You 'ear zat, *non*? Nobody eez to disturb ze florists!'

Ed and I suppressed our giggles until we were outside.

'What's so funny?' Marnie asked as we reached the van.

'Oh, you'll find out,' Ed replied, lifting the van's roller doors and swinging himself inside. 'OK, people, let's get to work.'

In the years since Mr Kowalski left us, I often wonder what he would make of the larger jobs Kowalski's now handles. His philosophy was always that smaller was invariably better; the mainstay of Kowalski's business being made-to-order bouquets and arrangements. When I first met him, he had just taken on the shop's first large-scale commission – and it scared him half to death.

'When you are running this store, *ukochana*, you may have more courage to venture into this kind of thing. For me, this is too heavy on my nerves. I am old already, but this task has formed more lines on my face than all my sixty years put together.'

350

As for the Lithgow wedding, I think it may well have given Mr K heart failure. Even with all my team working flat out, we reached 5 p.m. with the footpath garlands still to assemble. Working in the wide entrance hall, I could see Marnie and the grads – balanced at precarious angles on chairs and ladders – surreptitiously checking their watches when they thought nobody was looking. I took Ed to one side.

'We're not going to finish before seven at this rate. These guys need to get back.'

Ed rubbed his forehead and sighed. 'I agree. Why don't we see if the great Jean-Claude can spare a few bodies to help us fit the footpath flowers?'

'Good idea.' As he disappeared to seek an audience with the man himself, I called Marnie, Jocelyn and Jack over. 'Right. As soon as these staircase features are set, you can head back.'

'But what about the garlands?' Jocelyn asked.

'We'll sort those. It's only a short walk to our hotel, so Ed and I won't be chasing the clock. Good work, everyone.'

I watched my team make their final adjustments, say their goodbyes and leave. Their commitment and work ethic filled me with an immense sense of pleasure – and it showed in the completed project. While Ed organised our impromptu 'garland squad', I took the opportunity to walk slowly through the house, checking the placing of each arrangement, meticulous in my attention to detail. It's something I make an effort to do for each project Kowalski's undertakes.

I was just inspecting the arch over the orangery doorway when I felt someone step behind me.

'You've surpassed yourself,' David breathed, his voice deep and close to my ear. 'Everything looks amazing.'

I turned my head and met his graphite gaze. 'Thank you,'

I replied, feeling incredibly vulnerable all of a sudden. 'My team has worked so hard.'

'But it's your design, your direction.'

'Mine and Ed's.'

'But *you're* the boss, Rosie.'

'We both are – in most things, anyway.' I looked back at the arch and replaced one of the peonies whose petals were showing signs of age. 'But I agree, the design's worked well.'

'Do you have time for a drink? Before you leave?'

'I'm not sure. Ed and I have work to do tonight.'

David held his hands out in an honest plea. 'Come on – one drink? Surely that won't take long?'

'We're done here,' Ed reported, arriving at my side. 'Ready to go?'

'I – I still have some checks to make,' I answered, making a split-second decision as David smiled. 'You go; I'll be done in about half an hour.'

He looked at David, then back at me, concern barely concealed by his expression. 'You sure? You should get some rest before the work starts again.'

'I'll get some, I promise. You know me. I just want to do my final checks.'

Ed shot a look at David. 'Ever the perfectionist. Can you make sure she actually leaves here within the hour?'

David grinned. 'I'll guarantee it.'

'Only when she puts her mind to something, she can lose track of time,' Ed continued, seemingly reluctant to leave. I noticed David's left foot tapping gently, a sign of irritation I remembered from our days in the London agency.

'Stop worrying, mate. I won't be long.'

Glancing at David once more, Ed nodded at me and walked out.

I followed David through a maze of doors to a large library at the rear of the house. He opened an aged wooden globe drinks cabinet filled with bottles of all shapes and sizes. Working quickly, he poured two drinks and handed one to me.

'Southern Comfort with a splash of water,' he said with a wry smile. 'Just the way you like it, right?'

Butterflies had begun to dance inside me. I couldn't believe he would have remembered something like that after seven years.

'Let's head to the orangery,' he smiled. 'Then we can talk as you check.'

The setting for tomorrow's ceremony was undeniably breathtaking. With all the displays, gold chairs and cast-iron wedding gazebo now in place, it was a perfect, if thoroughly ostentatious, venue for an ultra-romantic wedding. I moved around continuing my inspection, constantly aware of him watching me. The scrutiny was so disconcerting that I felt the need to make polite conversation as I worked.

'So has Rachel seen all this yet?'

'No. She wants it to be a surprise tomorrow.'

'And your parents? Have they been banished from their own home?'

'Staying with friends.'

This was hard work. I tried a different approach. 'So how are you feeling?'

He didn't answer, his eyes still burning into my back.

'Nervous? Confident? Blasé?'

I felt him move closer. 'I'm just thinking.'

'Thinking what?'

He was at my side, his face serious when I looked at him. 'I was walking around here today, with all that activity, all that endeavour on my behalf – and it made me think what I missed before . . .'

His words cut through my softened defences. 'David . . .'

He reached his hand to lightly rest on my arm. 'I don't mean what you think. I mean, there was so much about our wedding that I missed because I was too wrapped up in the logistics of it to enjoy the emotional stuff. I'm sorry.'

I relaxed a little. 'No, I'm sorry. I spent so long casting you as the ultimate villain that it's difficult to break the habit now.'

'No need to apologise, Rosie. I more than gave you enough reason to think ill of me. So where next?'

'Over there and then I'm done.'

We walked over to the gazebo and I began fiddling with the strands of fairy lights woven in and out of the exquisite iron-work.

'This looks wonderful. My father found it after a mammoth search. Would you believe there's a company in Maine that supplies gazebos for weddings all over the world?'

I laughed. 'Actually, I would. There are more businesses founded on the crazy whims of brides than you realise.'

'And most of them are being employed here,' David admitted, rubbing the back of his neck.

'Hmm, I noticed,' I grinned, feeling the spark reignite between us. 'I mean, *peacocks*?'

'Jean-Claude's idea.' His eyes were alive with mischief as he adopted a French accent in a perfect mimic of his charis-matic wedding planner. '"You *must* 'ave peacocks, Monsieur Leethgow! Ze peacocks weel be somesing *nobody* could expect. Ah would not be doing my job if you did not 'ave ze peacocks!" And Rachel was all, "Darling, the peacocks are a definite!" So four hundred dollars later, we 'ave ze peacocks.'

'You always were a brilliant impressionist.'

'Yeah, but my disappearing act sucked.'

'Yes, it did.' It occurred to me as I answered him that only a few months ago his joke would have crushed me. It felt good to be able to laugh about it.

He looked at me for a while, a strange smile on his face. 'We're really OK, aren't we?'

'I think we are.'

'Can I say something?'

'Sure, go ahead.'

He took a deep breath, his eyes fixed on me. 'Meeting you again – after all this time – it's been a revelation. I always knew you were special but now – well – you're different . . . Stronger, I guess. And I was a stupid fool not to see it.' He reached out and I found myself taking his hand as my heartbeat thundered in my ears. 'I'm so incredibly sorry for breaking your heart. I let you down and I can never undo my stupidity.'

Squeezing his hand, I shook my head. 'David, enough. It's done and in the past. Let's keep it there and move on. I forgive you. And I'm sorry for hating you. I was hurt, but letting the memory hurt me over and over again was wrong.'

'You shouldn't apologise.'

'I think I want to.'

'You're amazing. Hell, Rosie . . .'

His hands were stroking my face as we stood under the wedding gazebo, his body moving closer, his breath hot and immediate as his kiss fell urgently on my lips. And the worst thing was I *let him* kiss me. For the briefest of moments, I gave in to a desire long-suppressed and hidden deep within the shadows of my past, as memories of our life together flooded my mind and my senses.

Then, the reality of the situation brought me crashing back to the present and revulsion powered through my body as I wrenched my lips from his, pushing him away. 'What the hell do you think you're doing?'

Shocked, David stepped towards me, desperation gripping his features. 'I-I thought that's what you wanted . . .'

'No. *No!* It's the day before your wedding! What were you thinking?'

'Rosie, hear me out. I'm in love with you. I've been falling in love with you again since we met in Nate's office. I was a fool before. I never realised what I had. But now you're here – *we're* here. And we have time.'

'Time? We have no "time" – and there's no "we", either.'

Grabbing my shoulders, David pleaded with me, his eyes filled with frustrated tears. 'Rosie, I love you. Run away with me. Tonight. We can have everything we should have had before. I will be everything I should have been for you. I will spend every waking moment making amends for the love you've been denied so long. Let me love you, Rosie. We still have time.'

Sickened by every word, I backed away from him, grabbing my workbag and moving swiftly towards the door. 'Look around you, David. Everything here is waiting for you to marry Rachel tomorrow. You should be thinking of *her*, not me.'

'What if all I can think about is you?'

'Don't be ridiculous.'

'I'm not, Rosie. I can't get you out of my head. I haven't been able to think of anyone else.'

'Stop it – stop saying that . . . You – you don't know what you're saying . . .'

He ran a hand through his hair. 'I've never been more certain of anything in my life. You haunt my dreams, Rosie Duncan. I can't bear to think you could be anyone else's but mine. You *were* mine, once: you could so easily be mine again. I *felt* it when we kissed – and *you* felt it too, didn't you?'

'No – I—'

'*Didn't* you? You can't deny it, Rosie. You kissed me back. Deep down, it was what you wanted! Come on, if nothing else then admit that to yourself. Nothing's changed between us. The old magic's still there. And this,' he indicated all the pristine wedding flowers surrounding us, 'this is just something that will all be gone in two days. It's meaningless to me. You're all I want now. You could be mine tonight and this could all be gone tomorrow.'

I stared at him as a terrible, gut-churning thought screamed out in my head. 'This is what happened last time, isn't it?'

He opened his mouth, but there were no words there.

'I'm *right*, aren't I?'

'It – it was nothing, Rosie.'

I could feel anger burning through my core, sending quivers of energy through me. 'Who was she?'

'Rosie, I—'

'*Who was she?*'

'No one. Nobody that mattered.'

'Well, presumably someone who mattered enough to make you miss your own wedding?'

David groaned and put his head in his hands. 'Oh, back here again. So much for the big "I forgive you" speech. Can't we move on from this?'

'Evidently you can't.'

'Look, Rosie, I made a mistake, OK? I panicked. After I left you that night I went out to a bar, met a woman – heck, I didn't even know her name – and woke up at four in the morning in her bed with a hangover from hell. I freaked. I knew I couldn't come back to you after – after what I'd done. So I drove to a twenty-four-hour diner on the outskirts of the city and called Asher to meet me there. While I waited in the car lot for him to arrive, I wrote you a note on the only piece of paper I had. And yes, I *know* it was your note to me but what else could I do? Asher begged me to reconsider but I refused and drove off before he could stop me. I was hoping he'd be his honourable self and deliver the message anyway. I spent the next three months just driving. I was a *mess*. I only called my father when I ran out of cash. He told me to come home and I did. I found out he'd settled things with you and that was that. But you have to believe me, I left because you didn't deserve a man like me in your life.'

'And what about Rachel? What about what she deserves? If you wake up tomorrow morning in *my* bed, how much of a mistake will you have made then?'

He slumped down onto a chair and stared blankly at me, the fire extinguished from within him, and I saw the frightened child inside the man. Nobody would have blamed me for dealing a fatal verbal blow then and there, but, instead of white-hot anger I now found a well of compassion inside. I walked back into the room and sat beside him.

'Look at us, eh? One too scared of commitment, the other too scarred by it.'

He nodded but he was a broken man and his voice belied the fragility of his state. 'I'm sorry, Rosie.'

'Do you love Rachel?'

'Yes – yes I do.'

'Then marry her tomorrow.' How strange that the same words were relevant on the eve of a different wedding.

He hung his head. 'How do I know it's the right thing?'

I gently patted his knee, smiling as realisation dawned on me. 'Because of this.' I gestured to the opulent surroundings of the orangery.

He lifted his eyes to follow the sweep of my hand. 'I don't understand.'

'Because, even after the débâcle of our wedding – all the pain, all the mess – you care enough about Rachel to walk the road again, with her. You said it yourself: you were a wreck after what happened before. So it would have to take someone incredibly special to make you want to risk it again. Don't throw away what you have just because you're scared. If you love her enough, you'll be here tomorrow, waiting for your bride. Don't let her arrive to find you gone. Nobody deserves that.'

Without another word, I rose and walked slowly out.

Chapter Twenty-Six

I didn't tell Ed about what happened with David; he didn't need to know and I didn't need to relive it. Despite my apparent cool composure during the latter part of our conversation, when I left the house it was a different matter: I shook uncontrollably during the whole of the ten-minute walk to the hotel. While I wasn't entirely sure what had just happened, of one thing I was convinced: it was something I had to experience. Something cathartic had invaded my soul when I fought David off; maybe I needed to prove to myself that I no longer harboured feelings for him, or perhaps I just needed to find out what I *didn't* want in order to bring me closer to discovering what I really needed.

When I arrived back at the hotel, Ed seemed relieved to see me but didn't press for further details, which I was immensely grateful for. We worked till gone midnight creating bouquets for Rachel and her seven attendants, plus twenty buttonholes and two corsages for David's mother, Phoebe, and Rachel's mother, Eunice. A few hours of snatched sleep later, we were up again, taking breakfast at six before heading over to the house for last-minute touches. Eunice met us in the entrance lobby, all feathers and fluster, fawning over the bridal bouquets with loud cries of admiration.

'How's Rachel?' I asked, once she'd sufficiently regained her faculties to hold a civil conversation.

'Beautiful. Amazing. Very nervous, but then isn't that the bride's prerogative?'

Walking into the orangery, I saw David, already seated in his chair. I caught his eye and he smiled: nothing more needed to be said. Ed and I made our final checks, sprayed the arrangements with water to give them a dewy freshness and retreated quietly as the groomsmen arrived, filling the glasshouse with their raucous laughter.

I didn't see Phoebe or George – something I was glad of. I would see them later, of course, at the evening reception to which all my team had been cordially invited, but at least then I would have supportive people round me. As Ed and I walked back to the hotel once more, the guests were beginning to arrive, the street filling up with cars.

Ed's hand brushed lightly against mine. 'Was it like this . . . ?'

'At my wedding? No – nowhere near as epic as this. I wouldn't have had peacocks, that's for certain.'

'No kidding,' he smiled. 'Does it feel weird, seeing it all happening again?'

I thought for a moment. 'No, actually. Not at all.' I was telling the truth. It felt right. Seven years ago, I thought that my wedding held the key to my future happiness, and spent all the succeeding years thinking I'd lost it for ever; now, conversely, another wedding was where I found it at last.

Later that evening, I stood with my team in the large drawing room of the house, watching with pleasure as they celebrated another successful Kowalski's design.

Marnie – a vision in a yellow satin prom dress with jade green sash and matching shoes – gave me a hug.

'Well, boss, that's the wedding of the year over, huh?'

362

'Yes, thank goodness!'

She lowered her voice. 'And you're OK with it all?'

I patted her arm. 'Absolutely.'

'Good. It makes you think, though, doesn't it?' She let out a long sigh and looked around her at the wedding guests.

'What does?'

'I mean, who's going to be crazy enough to want to marry me?'

'Plenty of people, mate, I'm sure.'

Marnie wasn't convinced. 'Name one.'

'That waiter from Ellen's.'

From the way she screwed up her face, I could tell her opinion of that suggestion. 'I told you before, he's too needy. I mean it, Rosie. Name one person – who I haven't dated already – who would want me to be his wife.'

'Zac,' Ed interjected.

Marnie's cheeks turned the merest shade pinker. 'Zac who?'

'The Fit Guy from Patrick's.'

She laughed but her eyes remained on Ed and me. 'He wouldn't be interested in me.'

Ed groaned. 'For the love of all things sacred, Marnie, can you not tell when somebody likes you?'

'Well, I—'

'*Every* time that poor guy comes into the store you pretend like you can't see him,' he continued. 'Yet he *still* follows you around like a sick puppy and pines for you when you aren't there. You know you like him.'

'I do, but he . . . but I . . .' She folded her arms and stared at Ed. 'Are you telling me that all this time I've been calling him "Zac the Fit Guy" and thinking he doesn't like me, he's felt the same way?'

He turned to me with a helpless shrug. 'She's a genius, Rosie, who knew?'

'I need alcohol.' Shaking her head incredulously, Marnie headed in the direction of the bar.

Ed nudged me and pointed over at the door, where Nate was standing. He appeared to be looking for someone. I raised my hand and he approached us.

'Hey guys, what can I say? This place looks astounding!'

'Why, thank you, sir,' Ed grinned, leaning over and whispering something to Nate, who nodded. 'Hey, Jocelyn, Jack – let's go get some food.'

As they left, Nate slipped an arm round my shoulders. 'So, how are you?'

'I'm good. You?'

'Avoiding my fiancée. And her mother.'

'They're here?'

'Uh-huh. But, look, I want to talk to you, OK?'

'Of course.'

He looked around him. 'Not here. Take a walk with me.'

I followed him through the guest-filled rooms, past the orchestra and out to the front lawns, where the tiny lights hidden within the garlands lining the footpath gave the whole area a magical glow. We stepped carefully across the damp lawn and round to the rear of the house, following a small, marble gravel pathway to a darkened summerhouse. Nate stopped and thrust his hands in his pockets.

'Rosie, there's something I need to talk to you about.'

I crossed my arms protectively. 'Nate, I'm not sure we should be—'

'It's about the flowers,' he blurted out.

My nerves began to tingle. 'What flowers?'

'On Christmas Day.'

'Oh?'

'You see, I—'

'Nathaniel? Are you out there?' Mimi's voice cut sharply through the evening air.

Nate uttered a profanity under his breath. 'I'll be there in a minute, Mimi.'

'We need you *now.*'

He shook his head and gripped my arm. 'Look, I have to go. I'll arrange something, OK?'

'What do you mean?'

He had already started moving away. 'A time to talk. I'll be in touch, soon.'

'But—'

'Soon, I promise.'

Alone in the dusky garden, my head was awhir with questions, unresolved emotion and weariness from a severe lack of sleep.

'Rosie? What are you doing out here?' Ed appeared in the doorway of the orangery. 'We're going back now – you coming?'

I shivered and began to pick my way towards the house.

'First David, now Nate: every time I turn my back you're off with another guy,' he quipped as I reached him. 'I'll try not to be offended.'

I slipped an arm through his and smiled up at him, pushing my questions to the back of my mind. 'Ah yes, but *you're* the one I'm going home with tonight.'

Ed rolled his eyes as we walked back into the house. 'Together with Marnie, Jack and Jocelyn, I know.'

Chapter Twenty-Seven

A week after David's wedding, I met up early with my team to receive the delivery from Patrick's. As we carried the boxes into the store, I couldn't help noticing the shy smiles and playful banter being shared by Marnie and Zac.

Ed caught my eye as we passed each other going in and out of the shop. 'Hey, have you noticed . . . ?' He nodded in the direction of Marnie and Zac, arms laden with boxes.

'Hmm, I know. Bit of a turn up for the books, isn't it?'

'A *what*?'

I pulled a face at him. 'Ah, excuse me. I forgot you don't speak English. I mean it's a bit of a change for her. With Zac the Fit Guy?'

The penny dropped. 'Oh, I *see*. Absolutely.'

'Seems like your brotherly advice at David's wedding may have been heeded, after all.'

'Go figure. And there was I thinking nobody else appreciated my wisdom,' he winked.

When all the boxes were inside and Zac's delivery chit was signed, he and Marnie wandered back outside to his van. The sky had been leaden grey overhead all morning and now it began to rain, lashes of water pelting down the shop windows and splashing onto the grey sidewalk. When it rains like this in New York it somehow makes every colour brighter and shinier: the yellow cabs and red brake lights of the traffic reflect in the glassy sidewalks and roads that have been transformed by the rain into strips of charcoal-grey that look like polished granite. Everywhere you look in the city you can imagine a film scene being set – and now, as if by magic, Marnie and Zac became the stars of their very own silent movie, right outside Kowalski's windows.

Ed and I had been goofing around as usual, but now our laughter subsided and a strange silence descended over the shop's interior as we watched the scene unfolding outside.

Zac had removed his jacket and given it to Marnie, who stood holding it over her head like an awning. By now the rain was falling at full pelt, soaking through Zac's shirt and flattening his usually spiky blonde hair against his face – yet to look at the expression he wore, you would think he was basking in the brightest, warmest summer sunshine. Arms folded across his body, he gazed at Marnie as if his every dream were embodied in her: at once surprised, delighted and elated by their conversation. As they laughed and joked, we noticed them moving closer – almost imperceptibly at first, their body language switching between brave and shy in equal measures.

For Ed and I, watching the very beginning of a relationship was a strange experience indeed. Not altogether unpleasant, I sensed both of us caught by its uncertain charms: joy at seeing Marnie's obvious delight, wistfulness at the startling simplicity of the event, maybe even some regret . . . As ever, Ed's expression remained steady, but I was innately aware of a range of other emotions sparring away beneath his carefully constructed exterior. Was he thinking about his Specific Someone, I wondered. Was he drawing comparisons between Marnie and Zac's conversation and those he was undoubtedly having with her, or making notes as he prepared to reveal his feelings? It was impossible to tell – and I was in no hurry to explore the possibilities further in my mind. As for me, well, I have to be honest: as happy as I was for one of the Kowalski's family to be finding love, I couldn't shake the boulder-heavy feeling that Marnie, like Ed, was moving on, becoming yet another newly paid-up member of the Getting On With My Life Club – a society whose exclusive membership I feared I would never join.

The scene on the corner of West 68th and Columbus continued in its silent splendour as all around them people hurried past, eyes blinded to the magnificent love scene right under their noses.

Finally, Zac reached into the van and produced a single, vivid orange gerbera, which he presented to Marnie. Then, he leant forward to plant a kiss on her forehead – and Ed and I both instinctively looked away, unwilling to intrude on this most tender of moments. When we looked back, the van was leaving as Marnie waved from the sidewalk. The little silver bell tinkled happily as she walked back into the store, twirling the flower – the very bloom that she most resembles – in her fingers with a faraway smile. She passed Ed and me without a word and disappeared into the workroom.

Ed shook his head, a sly smile easing across his features. 'Wow. Our little Marnie is all grown up and dating Zac the Fit Guy.'

'I know,' I smiled, 'I feel quite emotional.'

I was only half-joking. *Would I ever feel that again?*

I turned to say something to Ed, but he had disappeared, leaving me alone in my empty shop, a million questions buzzing around my head.

* * *

369

Later that day, Celia dashed in on her way to the office. 'I just wanted to make sure you were still coming to my dinner Thursday night, sweetie.'

'I'm not sure, hon. We're still recovering from the wedding and I don't know how busy we're going to get here.'

My best friend folded her linen-jacketed arms and surveyed me sternly. 'Rosie Duncan, I *need* you at this dinner! I have people coming that are – uh – that could be important.'

'Meaning what?'

'Nothing. I'll explain later.' Was it my imagination, or was the great *New York Times* columnist – famed for her wit and vivacity – struggling for words all of a sudden?

'You're blushing!'

'I am *not*. There have just been – uh – developments recently that may – or may not – portend well for the future.'

I feigned shock, revelling in my friend's uncharacteristic coyness. 'Celia Reighton, are you talking about a *man*?'

'Well, I would hardly be talking about a *woman*, would I?'

'Who is he?'

'I can't go into this now, Rosie. I've a million and one places to be this morning and I'm already late. So are you coming Thursday or not?'

'Not unless I get a name,' I grinned.

'*Rosie . . .*'

'Celia. You know it makes sense. And you know I won't give in.'

'OK, OK. Stewart Mitchell.'

'The guy from the Thanksgiving Dinner last year?'

Celia looked at her watch impatiently. 'Yes.'

'The one who sent you flowers?'

'From *your store* – yes, I know, Rosie, so don't do that shocked *schlock* with me, OK? He confessed everything last week so

370

we're – well, I'm just seeing what happens. The dinner is our first – you know – official couple event.'

I grinned. 'Well, I think it's positively lovely.'

'So you're coming now you've thoroughly embarrassed me?'

'Of course. What time?'

Celia was already heading for the door, finally reprieved from my teasing. 'Seven thirty. And bring something for the table – anything you like. Just not lilies.'

Marnie appeared at my side as Celia left. 'Did I hear right? Has she got a man?'

'You heard right,' I smiled.

Marnie clapped her hands. 'Ooh, this is so exciting! It seems like everyone in New York is falling in love this week. Celia, me, Ed . . .'

My head snapped to attention. 'Ed?'

Marnie giggled. 'Yes, Ed. His Specific Someone, I mean. I'm not totally wrapped up in my own life not to notice, you know.'

My heart sank to my toes as I picked up the order book. 'Of course. Ed's Specific Someone.'

The little bell above the door chimed happily as a young couple entered. They were the happiest two people I'd seen in a long time – even Marnie and Zac paled into insignificance beside them – giggling and so completely engrossed in each other that they appeared to be oblivious to everything else.

'Can I help you?' asked Marnie, stepping from behind the counter to meet them.

'Roses,' laughed the girl, never once taking her eyes from his. 'We need roses.'

'O-K,' Marnie smiled, shooting me a rolled-eyed look. 'So how many would you like?'

'*Armfuls*,' breathed the girl.

'Bucketfuls,' giggled the man.

'And what colour were you thinking?'

For a moment, the spell between them was broken as both turned to look at Marnie. It was clear they hadn't considered this. 'What would you recommend?' the girl asked.

'Well – what's the occasion?'

The man slipped an arm protectively around the girl's waist. 'We're getting married.'

'Congratulations! When's the Big Day?'

'Today. In about three hours to be precise – at City Hall,' the girl answered, reaching up to brush a strand of hair from her fiancé's forehead.

'Whoa – that's amazing!' Marnie squeaked, completely forgetting her professional demeanour – much to the delight of the young couple, who both began talking animatedly at once.

'We met last month . . .'

'*Last month*, would you believe it?'

'. . . and I just *knew*, you know?'

'We both *totally* knew . . .'

'. . . so we just said, "What the heck!" . . .'

'What the heck – let's just get *married*!'

'So – here we are!'

Verbal confetti thus expelled, the couple stood there in the middle of the floor, his'n'hers grins proudly displayed for all to see.

'OK,' said Marnie, gathering herself together. 'Let's think this through. What are you wearing for the ceremony?'

'Cream jacket and shift dress,' the girl replied.

'Dark blue suit,' said the man, 'with a cream silk tie that my grandma gave me.'

'She's the only one who knows,' confided the girl, suddenly self-conscious.

'Wait – none of your family know you're getting married today?'

The girl shook her head.

'They don't get it – any of them,' explained the man. 'Only Grandma Evie. For years she's been saying to me, "When you gonna get married, Jimmy? I'll be dead soon and I want to see my grandson married before I go."' The girl smiled at Jimmy. 'So when I met Anya, I just knew right away that she was the one. Grandma Evie would be there if she could, but she's too frail. So she gave me this tie and her blessing.'

'And your parents don't approve?' ventured Marnie.

'They don't *care*,' Anya answered, her young face betraying the pain the situation must hold for them.

Jimmy patted her hand. 'Both our parents are busy people with busy lives,' he said. 'Like everyone in this city – and *then* some. They have little time to worry about their kids.' He shrugged. 'It happens. My folks are lawyers, Anya's are professors at Columbia University. They're successful and highly respected in their chosen fields.'

'And you don't think they'd want to know that you're getting married?'

'My parents never married,' Anya replied, reaching out to gently stroke the petals of a sugar-pink rose nearby. 'According to them, marriage is an "outdated institution perpetuated by conservative Neanderthals in a bid to suppress the masses." Conformity to traditions like marriage only disappoints them.'

'And my folks spend so much time dealing with the fall-out of broken marriages that they've forgotten to see the magic in it,' Jimmy added, 'even with each other.'

'So you could call us traditional radicals, I guess. It's up to us to prove them all wrong,' Anya smiled – her eyes still tellingly sad. 'Though they're going to go crazy when they find out.'

Jimmy smiled. 'So seeing as we're unavoidably destined to disappoint our folks, we might as well do it in style.'

'So what colour roses would you suggest?' Anya asked.

Marnie turned to me, a sudden look of panic on her face. I smiled back encouragingly, but she shook her head. 'Rosie, what do you think?'

Stepping from behind the counter, I took a long look at the couple. 'Your wedding is a celebration,' I began, selecting blooms from the flower buckets as I spoke, 'of how much you love each other.' I looked at Anya's strawberry-blonde shoulder-length bob and Jimmy's blue-black closely cropped hair.

'Yes, it is,' said Jimmy, watching me with curiosity.

'And love comes in many colours,' I continued, gathering more flowers whilst resisting the urge to giggle at the sound of myself – all I needed was a croaky Polish accent and a pair of ancient half-moon spectacles balanced on the end of my nose, and my transformation into Mr K would be complete. 'So how about this?'

I held up the handful of roses I had just selected – a pastel confection of sugar-sweet hues, like the retro cupcakes that M&H Bakers were famous for across the Upper West Side: sugar pink, primrose yellow, marzipan gold, pale lilac and clotted cream, all nestled up to one another. 'Add some magic,' I pulled some stems of gypsophila (Mum calls it 'baby's breath', which somehow makes the tiny white, star-like blooms even more enchanting) and arranged them around the roses. '*Et voilà!*'

'Wow,' Anya breathed. 'It looks like a candy shop with stars!'

'And finally, we just finish it off with some deep mystery,' I smiled, choosing several glossy dark green banana leaves and curling them carefully around the rose stems. Holding the completed bouquet in my hand, I held it out to Anya, who squealed with sheer delight.

'It's perfect – isn't it, Jimmy?'

Jimmy's eyes were sparkling as he smiled at his bride-to-be. '*You're* perfect.' He turned to me. 'Thank you so much for this.'

'And you'll need this,' Marnie appeared by my side and pinned a buttonhole rose to Jimmy's lapel.

'This is awesome, guys. Thank you. How much do we owe you?'

Marnie looked at me, a curious smile playing on her lips. 'It's a *blessing*, right?'

It was absolutely the right thing to say. A shiver of delight raced through me from head to toe as I recalled the very few occasions where Mr K had chosen a young couple to 'bless'. In the six years since I'd taken over Kowalski's, I had never done a 'blessing' – but now, looking at this young couple, so in love yet so alone, they seemed to be the perfect candidates for my very first act of professional kindness. 'It's on the house,' I smiled.

Anya and Jimmy looked at me aghast. 'No way – seriously, how much do you need? I mean, there must be sixty dollars of roses here, at least,' Jimmy protested.

I handed the bouquet to Marnie, who hurried off to trim and bind it. 'We have an old tradition here at Kowalski's,' I explained, Mr K's words ringing in my head and tugging on my heart as I spoke. 'When we come across a story that touches our hearts, we offer a blessing. It's your wedding day and you should be sharing your love with the whole world. Seeing as your families won't be there to bless you, we will step into the breach. Consider these flowers a wedding present from Kowalski's.'

Anya's blue eyes filled with tears, which began to spill freely over her pale pink cheeks. 'There must be something we can do to repay your kindness?'

Marnie arrived back at my side and presented Anya with the bouquet.

'Just be happy,' I replied, feeling a thick lump of emotion building in my throat, 'and tell people that you know a great florist.'

'Absolutely. Do you have some cards?' Jimmy took a handful from Marnie. 'Well – thank you, thank you both so much!'

Marnie and I watched Jimmy and Anya leave, ridiculous smiles spreading across our faces.

'How *adorable* were they?' Marnie sighed. 'And how happy?'

'Mmm, I know,' I replied, shocked to feel a sudden wave of sadness washing over me.

'One day, Rosie, that will be me and you.'

'What, getting married at City Hall? Sorry, hon, you're not my type.'

Marnie gave my arm a playful punch. 'That's not what I meant and you know it.'

'Well, maybe for you and Zac the Fit Guy, eh?' I smiled, desperate to deflect attention from me. It didn't work, of course: even Marnie in her newly loved-up state, could see what I was doing.

'For *both* of us, Rosie. We *have* to believe that kind of love is possible.'

'We do?'

'Absolutely. Or else, what is there to hope for?'

For once, I had no clever answer for that.

Life at Kowalski's quickly returned to normal, albeit with Marnie decidedly happier than I'd ever seen her and Ed increasingly tight-lipped about his Specific Someone.

Much to Celia's relief, I attended her much-publicised 'coming out' dinner to officially witness the unveiling of her new relationship. She needn't have worried, of course: *everyone* at the paper knew exactly what was going on – an occupational hazard of working with journalists, I guess. Stewart was as strikingly good-looking and utterly besotted with Celia as the last time I'd seen him, while Celia was surprisingly restrained – *peaceful* even. It was good, if a little disconcerting, to see my best friend so in love.

The following week, with almost a whole month until the next wedding on our books, I allowed myself a rare opportunity to relax, taking a day off midweek – an occurrence akin to the passing of Halley's Comet as far as my astounded team was concerned – in order to catch up on some much-needed rest. After indulging in the sheer unadulterated luxury of a Wednesday morning lie-in, I met Celia for lunch at her favourite restaurant on the sixteenth floor of a building directly overlooking Central Park.

'So, how's the toyboy?' I joked, giggling as Celia squirmed in her chair.

'Stewart is just *fine*, thank you very much,' she replied, blushing slightly behind her foundation. Her coyness didn't last long, however: less than twenty seconds later her careful composure disintegrated and she clamped a hand to her heart like a lovesick sixteen-year-old. 'Oh Rosie, I'm telling you, that man is just the *sweetest* thing! Did you know he's taking me to the Orchid Show at the New York Botanical Gardens next weekend? I've read about it every year since they started it but I've never got round to going. So he's taking me. He said he wanted to "surround the most beautiful woman in New York with her favourite flower", would you *believe* it?'

'It's so good to see you excited about him,' I smiled, pushing away the sliver of jealousy that was surreptitiously snaking itself around my heart. 'He's a lovely young man.'

'I know! I worry that he's too young, sometimes.'

'Celia, don't be ridiculous! He *adores* you and it's clear that you're very fond of him.'

'It's more than that, sweetie, I . . . Oh, what the *heck* – I'm *in love* with the guy! I'm like a kid again with it. After Jerry I didn't think there'd be anyone else, so I'm stunned by the whole thing. I guess I'll just have to get used to being the older woman, that's all – although I have absolutely no intention of becoming the responsible one in our relationship. But then Stewart is a bit of an old head on young shoulders, so I guess it all evens out.'

I lifted my wineglass. 'Here's to toyboys and growing old disgracefully!'

'I'll drink to that!' Celia clinked my glass and took a large sip of wine as the Queen of the Subject Change geared up for another handbrake turn. 'So, your conversation with Nate at David's wedding: what *exactly* did he say about those flowers?'

'That's just it: he didn't get the chance to say anything. Mimi interrupted him just as he was about to tell me.'

Celia's eyes rolled heavenwards. 'That *woman*,' she growled, thumping her hand on the table, startling the neighbouring diners, 'she manages to get in the way of everything!'

I sighed and looked out at the spring green of the Park below. 'I don't know, mate. After all the stuff with David the night before, I don't think I could have coped with any more revelations.'

'But you *like* Nate, don't you?'

'Yes, of course I do. But he's engaged to someone else and, despite his occasional protestations to the contrary, I think he may actually be in love with Caitlin after all.'

Celia pulled a face and took a long, thoughtful sip of her white wine. 'If he likes you, he should deal with that situation once and for all. I've never met anyone so laid-back in my life.

One day, Nate is going to wake up and realise his whole life has happened already. It's about time he took control. So,' she stared seriously at me, 'supposing he *did* let Caitlin go, and *supposing* he was free . . . Would you want to be with him?'

'I – it's complicated.'

Celia let out a cry of frustration. 'It's *always* complicated, Rosie! Welcome to life in general. You just put that to one side and career headlong into the abyss.'

'Oh, well, when you put it like *that* . . .' I laughed.

'Rosie Duncan, you are a cruel, cruel woman.'

'OK, OK, I'm sorry. This whole situation with Nate has been blowing hot and cold for months. Most of that time, I didn't really think about it because I was so against the thought of someone else in my life.'

Her eyes twinkled conspiratorially. 'And now?'

'Now I'm not sure. Nate is wonderful and I like him a lot. It's just . . . I don't know if I need someone a little more decisive, you know? And then there's Ed.'

I could tell my friend was confused. 'What about Ed?'

'He's just been different the past few months. More elusive than usual.'

'The Iceberg Man is *more* elusive?'

'I don't know, he says he's met someone.'

Her eyebrow made a bid for the skies. 'And that's a bad thing?'

'I'm not sure. No, no, of course it's not a bad thing. It's just that – I guess I feel like he's leaving me behind. And Marnie, too.'

Celia shook her head. 'Marnie's leaving?'

'No, not leaving. Moving on – she's going out with Zac.'

'Wait,' Celia's eyes were sparkling. 'Tell me it's not true: she finally hooked up with Zac the Fit Guy?'

I grinned. 'The very same.'

'When?'

'About a month ago. Ed and I witnessed the whole thing.'

'That is so good. He'll be good for her.'

I nodded, twisting the stem of my wineglass absent-mindedly.

Celia caught the hesitation immediately. 'So what's the problem?'

'There's no problem, honestly. It's just . . .' I sighed and looked at my friend. 'Everyone's moving on apart from me. Or at least that's what it feels like.'

Celia's concerned smile was one hundred per cent genuine. 'Sweetie, that's *life*. We move on, we find love – sometimes we lose love and have to find it again. It's all part of life's rich tapestry. But as for you, you have to decide what you want, Rosie. Not what Ed wants, or Nate, or David – but *you*. You've hidden your heart so carefully for such a long time; it's only natural that it's a little rusty. But you'll get the hang of it. You just need a little faith and a huge dose of that hope you're so famous for. So tell me again: what did Nate say?'

'He said he'd be in touch.'

Celia shrugged. 'Then you must wait until he does.'

I didn't have to wait long.

When I arrived home, something was waiting for me by my front door. Stooping down, I picked up a small woven basket of flowers and took it into my apartment. Nestled amidst the yellow roses was a card:

Meet me for coffee at Kowalski's, 8 p.m. xx

Turning the card over, I saw the shop stamp – Turner's – and my heart began turning cartwheels inside me: it was the same florists that had created my Christmas arrangement. *It had to be Nate.* This was his way of arranging a time for us to meet – and where better than my beloved shop, scene of so many of our meetings during the past year? Ed must be opening the shop for him: maybe this was what they'd been discussing when they had met up: how Nate felt about me . . . After all, I reasoned, who knew me better than Ed? Despite my reluctance to admit it most of the time, Ed knew me in ways other people could only aspire to. He understood me: sometimes challenging but mostly accepting who I was; always there, always ready to talk. Even during the past few months, when I'd sensed him drifting slightly, he'd been as supportive of me as ever, and I loved that we had that kind of friendship. My mum often says that finding a true friend – one who knows who you are and loves you anyway – is more valuable than all the gold in all the banks in the world. And she is right. Ed had endured every rollercoaster twist and turn of my life along with me in recent months. And now he was still fighting my corner: making it possible for Nate to move closer to me. Amazing. I only hoped that, when he finally mustered up the courage to talk to his Specific Someone, she would realise what a special guy he was.

I can't remember getting ready that evening. My thoughts were everywhere and nowhere at once; vying for attention as I looked on, helpless to stop the tumult inside me. Nate had seemed so certain that staying with Caitlin was the right thing before – and I had reconciled myself to the fact that we were just two people who could have been together if circumstances were different. Everyone has their 'What If' relationships, where you know someone could be The One if only life had dealt you a different hand. I'd just assumed that Nate was mine: we would always remain friends and that undeniable chemistry would always be there; and maybe, in the quiet,

381

secret moments of our lives, we would muse over how things could have been different, wondering how life would have been had we met each other at the right time.

Even as I left my apartment and walked quickly through the streets of New York, I felt a pull inside me; terror and hope holding hands to sprint into the bright unknown of my future. So much had changed recently that I simply stopped trying to understand it and, for the very first time in my life, gave in to my circumstances and just went with the flow. I was turning in circles no longer: gone was the perpetual cycle of memories and hurt. Now, the city smiled at me as I trod quickly on its sidewalks, heading for uncertainty with hope fuelling each step. Mr Kowalski's words rang out in my head as I walked: '. . . *when that day arrives, Rosie, choose to* live.'

I reached Kowalski's at eight exactly, pausing by the door to calm my thundering heart. *This is it, Rosie Duncan*, I told myself. *Beyond this point lies the future.* Hope coursing like quicksilver through my veins, I opened the door.

As the silver bell heralded my arrival, I caught my breath. The interior of the store had been transformed by hundreds of tiny white lights, framing the galvanised steel flower buckets, windows, couch and ceiling. It was as if a myriad of stars had fallen from the heavens and made their home at Kowalski's. Even Old F, bubbling happily and warming the entire space with the aroma of his finest coffee, was resplendent in fairy lights.

'Hello?' I called out, my voice shaking with sheer breathless emotion.

The workroom door opened and a figure stepped in front of the counter, his features thrown into shadow by the blanket of stars behind him.

'Welcome to Kowalski's.'

Chapter Twenty-Eight

Ed took a step forward, light from the streetlamp outside illuminating his features. 'Hi Rosie.'

I froze. 'Ed? What are you doing here?'

'Waiting for you.'

'Did Nate send you?'

'In a way, yes.'

'Where is he?'

Ed frowned. 'I have no idea.'

I struggled for words. 'But – the flowers?'

He shrugged self-consciously. 'Yeah, I'm sorry about that. I couldn't create something myself – you'd have rumbled me straight away – so I chose Turner's. They're new, so I was pretty certain you wouldn't have heard of them. At Christmas it was a kind of a spur-of-the-moment thing, you know? I wanted to give you something but I didn't know whether I was ready for you to know – uh – what was going on.'

'But – but I thought they were—'

'From Nate? Yeah, I realised that the moment you told Marnie and me about it. That's why he made a reference to them at the wedding – he was going to explain who sent them. You have him to thank for my being here, actually. You're all we talked about when we met up. He told me he had feelings for you, but he said he knew your heart belonged to someone else. So, we planned all this and he set the wheels in motion when he spoke to you.'

'You did this – to deceive me?' I could feel my defences building.

Ed's face fell. 'No, Rosie, never to deceive you.'

Tears stung my eyes. How *dare* Ed play games with me, after everything he'd seen me go through? The last thing I needed was to be yet another name on his never-ending list of dates – another fleeting past-time to divert his attention. Incensed, I turned on my heels and made for the door. 'Goodbye.'

'I love you!'

I didn't move. I couldn't. So there I stood, my hand still gripping the door handle, my heart in my mouth and my breath coming in short, sharp bursts as I fought back tears.

'I love you, Rosie Duncan.' His voice was soft and low, barely more than a whisper. 'I've loved you from the first moment we met and I haven't stopped loving you every day since. For so long I hid it – pretty well, it would seem – and I thought it would always be that way. But then – then I woke up one morning and I realised: I *love you* more than I've ever loved anyone before. And it's hard for me to admit it, because it means I'm not the cool, in-control guy I like to think I am. It means I must finally concede defeat in the self-sufficiency stakes. It means I have to bare my own heart, and risk it being thrown back in my face. But there's one thing I'm certain of: I love you, Rosie, with a love that sets me on fire each day and keeps me awake at night. So here I am: a melting iceberg in the middle of Kowalski's.'

Tentatively, I let go of the door handle and faced him. He was breathing heavily, his chest rising and falling quickly in the streetlamp spotlight. Moving closer I could see the battle within him painting his face.

'Ed, I had no idea . . .'

'No, well, you wouldn't. I am the master of clever side-steps, remember?' A tear glistened in the glow of the fairy lights as it travelled smoothly over the contours of his face, leaving a silver streak marking his cheek. He brushed it away with an irritated swipe of his hand. 'I'm sorry. Whoever thought the great Ed Steinmann was such a sap?'

'So why did you decide to tell me now?'

Sadness coloured his eyes as he smiled. 'Believe it or not, I was following the advice of a good friend.'

'Nate?'

'You.'

'Me?'

'You said it, Rosie: unless I tell her, I'll never find out if she feels the same way.'

'Then *I'm* the Specific Someone?'

'Yes, you are.'

And there it was. Such a simple sentence, yet the brevity of it hit me with hurricane force. For months Ed's mention of his Specific Someone had rankled with me inexplicably; I'd dismissed it as envy at a friend moving on. But the truth was, I was *jealous* – not of Ed falling in love, but of the woman who had stolen his heart. When he appeared to be drifting from me, the reason it hurt so much was that it seemed to confirm how much he didn't want me. And even walking here tonight, when I thought I was thinking about Nate, Ed was the one who, in fact, claimed most of my thoughts. It was *his* opinion of me I cared most for; *his* support and time I valued more than anyone's; *his* friendship I most covetously guarded.

It was time to face the truth.

Stepping forward bravely, I reached out my hand and, with trembling fingers, stroked the tears from his cheek. I felt his arms around me, pulling me closer, felt his breath brushing my face like a warm summer breeze.

'I want to love you, Rosie. I want to show you how love *should* be and let you melt me completely. And every hurt, every wound your heart has suffered over the years, I want to heal with my kisses, every day, for ever.'

'Oh, Ed . . .'

New York froze around us as his lips met mine – a hundred million questions answered in a single heartbeat. At that moment, Ed became everything: hands and lips, bodies and breath, hearts and souls. I lost myself in his embrace, the warmth of his love enveloping me like a blanket. And I *knew*. I knew I was home.

When we finally broke apart, I gazed into his eyes and I saw Ed Steinmann for the very first time.

I saw a man who looked like he was in love . . .

This city is not mine by birthright: yet New York chose to make me belong. It has soothed my pain, reignited my dreams and resurrected my hope. Deep within its vibrant heart, I found my own. And this is where my heart will stay for ever.

Read on for an exclusive extract from Miranda's next novel *Welcome To My World* coming in 2010.

How It All Began . . .

Right at the start, there are two things you should know about Harri: one, she doesn't usually make a habit of locking herself in toilet cubicles during parties; and two, she is normally one of the most sane, placid individuals you could ever meet.

But tonight is an exception.

Because this evening – at exactly 11.37 pm – the world Harri knew ended in one huge, catastrophic event. In the space of three and a half minutes, everyone she loved collided in an Armageddon of words, leaving mass carnage in its wake – sobbing women, shouting men and squashed *vol-au-vents* as far as the eye could see. Powerless to stop the devastation, she resorted to the only sensible option left available to her – seeking refuge in the greying green vinyl haven that *is* the middle cubicle in the Ladies' loo at Stone Langley Village Hall.

So here she is. Sat on the wobbly toilet, black plastic lid down, head in hands, life Officially Over. And she has no idea what to do next.

It was Viv's idea in the first place. Harri should have said no straight away but, being Harri, decided to give her first Sunday school teacher the benefit of the doubt.

'You know how useless Alex is at finding suitable girlfriends,'

Viv said, lifting a steaming apple pie from the Aga and inadvertently resembling a serene tableau from *Country Life* as she did so. 'He's hopeless! I mean, twelve girlfriends in the last year and not two brain cells to rub together between them. Danielle, Chelsea, Georgia, Saffron, two Marys, three Kirstys, an *India* for heaven's sake – and the last two I can't even remember . . .'

Harri smiled into her mug of tea. 'Lucy the weathergirl and Sadie the boomerang.'

Viv looked up from her flour-covered *Good Housekeeping* recipe book. 'The *boomerang*?'

'Yeah – you know – The one who keeps coming back when you chuck her,' Harri grinned.

'Harriet Langton, you are awfully sharp for someone so generally nice.'

Harri gave a bow. 'Thank you, Viv.'

'So, anyway, about Alex . . .' Viv smiled – and then presented Her Big Idea. It was so seemingly innocuous, so subtle in its introduction, that nobody could have predicted the ferocity of the disaster it was about to cause. It began with a nib feature in Viv's favourite women's glossy magazine. In between articles on the latest handbag that Hollywood starlets were scrapping over and scarily titled features such as 'Over 50's and the Big-O' was a small column, entitled *Free to a Good Home*.

'People write in,' Viv explained, 'and nominate a man they know, to be recycled.'

'Recycled?' Harri repeated incredulously, 'Into *what*? That sounds horrific.'

'It's not like going to the bottle bank, Harri, for crying out loud. It's presenting a man who's been unlucky in love – you know, divorced, recently separated or just plain rubbish at finding the right girl on his own – to a whole new audience.'

'I can't believe that works,' Harri giggled. 'I mean, who writes in to a magazine to ask out a guy they've never met who, by the sound of it, has a very good reason to be single in the first place?'

Viv shot her a Hard Paddington Stare. '*Plenty* of people, apparently. You would be amazed at how many responses this column gets. Listen to this . . . "*Our February Free to a Good Home candidate, Joshua, received over two thousand letters from women across the UK, all keen to prove to him that true love is still very much alive and well. Josh thanks all of you who replied and is currently whittling the responses down to his top 10, whom he will contact shortly to arrange dates. Good luck, ladies!*" . . . Well? How about that? What does that tell you, Harri?'

Harri wrinkled her nose. 'It tells me that there are too many desperate women out there. Two thousand sad, lonely and deluded individuals letting their dreams get abused in the name of journalism.'

Viv's enthusiasm was unabated. 'No it doesn't. It means that concerned friends and mothers – like, well, *me* for example – can have the opportunity to find someone truly worthy for the men they care about. After all, we mothers know our sons better than anyone else, so who better to pick the perfect girl-friend for them than us?'

'You aren't thinking about nominating Alex, are you?' Harri's eyebrows were raised so high you could almost see them above her head like a crazed cartoon character. 'No way, Viv! How would he feel if he knew his own mother had put him up for auction in a meat market like this?'

'I'm not suggesting *I* nominate him, sweetheart,' Viv said with a reproachful motherly smile.

'I'm glad to hear it.'

'I'm suggesting *you* nominate him, dear.'

The suggestion hung in the air between them, sparkling in

389

its audacity, unleashed at last on an unsuspecting world. Harri needed a few moments to take it in.

'*Sorry?*'

'Well, I mean, you know better than most how woefully inept my son is at forming meaningful relationships. You've had the pleasure of living through each disaster with him. I know he confides in you and values your opinion. He is a lovely, honest, good-looking young man and he will be a fantastic catch for the right young woman. And you're always saying his problem is that he goes for the wrong sort of girls . . . Well, this is the perfect opportunity to find the *right sort of girl* for him. Don't you think?'

Viv had definitely missed her true calling, Harri mused. She would have made a great Prime Minister, or UN Negotiator, or crazed terrorist . . .

She should have refused, point blank. She should have laughed it off, changed the subject or just grabbed her coat to leave. But everything Viv said was true. Alex was her best friend: a real gentleman and undeniably attractive but, in truth, possessed a near legendary bad taste in women. Harri had shared many a late night heart-to-heart with him about his latest flame and had helped to pick up the pieces every time the fire died. And it was true that she believed he deliberately pursued women he had no intention of settling down with. Viv was right about it all and in the light of this Harri couldn't fault the reasoning behind the Big Idea.

So Harri said yes. And that's when the trouble started.